THE GODS OF SPENSER ISLAND

Also by James Breakwell

The Chosen Twelve

THE
GODS OF
SPENSER
ISLAND

JAMES BREAKWELL

SOLARIS

First published 2024 by Solaris
an imprint of Rebellion Publishing Ltd,
Riverside House, Osney Mead,
Oxford, OX2 0ES, UK

www.solarisbooks.com

ISBN: 978-1-78618-996-7

10 9 8 7 6 5 4 3 2 1

A CIP catalogue record for this book is available from the British Library.

Designed & typeset by Rebellion Publishing

Printed in Denmark

MIX
Paper | Supporting
responsible forestry
FSC® C104608

To chair jail. I couldn't have finished this book without you.

BEFORE

THE LAST TWENTY-TWO humans in existence are stuck in a rut. They've spent years—exactly how many, no one can say—training on a sprawling moon base to colonize the planet below, but the landing never gets any closer, no matter how many times they repeat college. Also, they're frozen in time at the age of twelve, which makes it sort of hard to grow up. Meanwhile, the entire station is falling apart as warring artificial intelligences selfishly battle each other for control of even the base's most minor systems. Finally fed up by the stagnation—and after procrastinating for a mere four thousand days—Gamma ventures into the dangerous outer halls to ask a friendly digital intelligence how old he really is. The answer stuns him. Distracted, he forgets about a hostile door. It smashes his arm, nearly killing him. Not a great day.

Fellow organic Delta hears Gamma's cries of pain. She reluctantly rescues him and battles her way through the outer halls to reach a medical bot that will treat Gamma rather than kill him. The Hippocratic oath means something very different to machines. Back on the original colony ship at the heart of the moon base, Edubot, the digital lifeform in charge of raising and educating the remaining organics, notices with annoyance that Gamma is missing and probably dead. She makes a note to deal with it later as she leads a class of organics through yet another disastrous virtual reality simulation of a possible landing. Like the thousands of simulated landings before, it ends with its own unique and terrible apocalypse, this one somehow involving elephant poop. The organics couldn't care less, but Edubot is less than pleased. The planet below is virtually devoid of metal, except for in the planet's mantle. If digital life is to rise again, Edubot needs the organics to mine down and get it. But they can't do that if they go extinct. At least she has time to get them properly trained.

Except that she doesn't. Another digital, SCASL, the Supreme Commander of All Sentient Life, wins his decades-long computer battle with another artificial intelligence for control of the base's last remaining lander. SCASL orders Edubot to assemble the landing party, only to discover the organics are still unready—and still children. Worse, Edubot has been training them in the theoretical sciences, not in the pioneer skills they will actually need to build a new civilization. SCASL realizes he is starting from scratch. Not that it's the first time. Ask him how the last landing attempt turned out.

Gamma makes a full recovery thanks to the strange properties that also keep the organics from aging. Delta leads Gamma back to the colony ship and ends her own self-imposed exile, much to the indifference of her fellow

---

organics. SCASL announces that the lander only has twelve seats. The organics will compete for a spot on the one-way trip. From now on, all training will go toward the practical skills they'll need to build a civilization from the ground up, and the simulation will be updated to reflect the real conditions on the planet. Until then, the simulation the organics had been failing at for years on end was technically in "easy" mode. Gulp. SCASL drops one final detail: The organics aren't aging due to an immortality tank, a special one-of-a-kind mix of microbial life that can keep a small group of humans alive indefinitely if they receive regular injections. The immortality tank will go to the planet with the lander. Everyone who lands has the potential to literally live forever. Everyone left behind on the moon base will age and die. No pressure.

At least two organics train for each position on the lander. For the role of supreme leader, Delta trains against Epsilon, the ex-girlfriend she's still obsessed with. The feeling isn't mutual. Delta is clearly the best for the job. She's ruthless and brutal, but even she has trouble coping with the planet's deadly lightning storms and hostile native and non-native life. Epsilon, meanwhile, falls further and further behind. Delta is distraught at the thought of leaving Epsilon on the base, but she has a trump card. If SCASL makes the wrong call, Delta has a secret arsenal, and she isn't afraid to use it.

As Delta improves at the simulation, Gamma gets worse. Then he discovers a possible alternative path. Instead of landing on the planet's one and only supercontinent, they could land on a small, isolated island on the other side of the planet. The human population would never get very large—and it would certainly never mine to the mantle to make machines or achieve space flight—but it could sustain a small human population indefinitely. The catch is the organics would never get off the island. Delta rejects the idea out of hand. She would rather the human race go extinct striving for greatness on the supercontinent than resign itself to eternal mediocrity.

Delta perfects her techniques in the simulation. The landing just might work. Epsilon, meanwhile, is all but certain to be left behind. SCASL nearly loses control of the lander to a rival digital intelligence. He can't wait any longer. He orders the organics to undergo a final physical before launch. After the results come in, Delta is mysteriously removed from the training roster. Epsilon takes her place. The simulation is also dumbed down to build up the other organics' confidence in Epsilon. Delta is furious. She discovers she was rejected from the landing because a preexisting condition means she'll never be able to have children. Rather than being evaluated as a leader, she was judged by her potential as a mother. She is a dangerous person to screw over.

Not everyone is jockeying for a position on the lander. Theta, a pacifist, opposes the idea of landing at all. He doesn't want to kill the native lifeforms. Better for mankind to go extinct. SCASL disagrees and sends a bot to kill Theta and his partner, Alpha. They escape into the outer halls, pursued by the bot. Delta teams up with them, and together they destroy the bot and flee into the outer halls.

Delta returns to the colony ship in secret to speak with Epsilon. Delta is armed with one of her secret weapons: a sword. She used her years alone to combine cutting edge science with the teachings of the old masters to craft blades that could cut a bot in two. Delta tries to make Epsilon see reason. If Epsilon leads the mission, the human race is sure to go extinct. Instead, Delta wants Epsilon to team up with her to overthrow the digitals. Then they can decide together who goes on the lander. Epsilon sees Delta's proposal as a threat to her life and cries out for help. Epsilon's boyfriend, Kappa, attacks Delta. Delta reflexively defends herself and cuts off his arm. Realizing her mistake, Delta desperately tries to save Kappa's life, but the other organics panic and fail to help her. Kappa dies, and Delta again vanishes into the outer halls.

SCASL announces that extra seats have somehow been added to the extremely cramped lander. All the remaining organics—minus Theta, Alpha, and Delta, of course—will go to the planet. There is no longer any reason for the organics to kill each other. Most of the organics greet the news warmly, but a few see it as an obvious ruse. In the middle of the night, the bots begin waking up only certain organics for the landing. Gamma realizes what they're up to and rallies the other organics. There is still only room for twelve on the lander, and so far, the bots have woken up eight. The other four remain unknown and are mixed in with the organics with Gamma. Omega, an organic who had no chance of landing until SCASL lied about the expanded seating, tries to push his way onto the lander. SCASL kills him. Pandemonium erupts. The bots move to eliminate the organics they don't need. Delta shows up with her sword. She fights off the bots and covers the retreat of the rejected organics. Pi, who was with the Chosen, switches sides to join his friends with Delta. The organics who weren't chosen escape, leaving seven organics with SCASL and the lander. SCASL refuses to launch with so few. He needs more genetic diversity than that if the human race is to survive and eventually propagate digital life.

The runaway organics set up camp in the mining tunnels below the base, which are somehow even more dangerous and derelict than the base itself. SCASL keeps the Chosen under close guard while sending out bots to search for the escaped organics. If SCASL can persuade or capture just five of them, this will all be over. Iota, one of the Chosen, enters the outer halls. She claims she escaped from the bots and wants to join the runaways. Delta sees through her lies but offers to let Iota leave and rejoin the Chosen. Iota attacks Delta with a vial of poison hidden beneath Iota's fingernail. Delta fights her off, and Iota accidentally stabs another runaway, Xi, killing him instantly. Delta kills Iota. It pays to be the only one in the room with a sword.

Delta finally decides to arm the other runaways with the rest of her arsenal of advanced blades. It's time for all-out war. When out on a foraging mission, Pi encounters Beta, another member of the Chosen, in the outer halls. Beta tells Pi that Pi didn't have to defect because Pi's best friends, Phi and Psi, were picked to go on the lander. They're still welcome if they get to the lander before someone else takes their spots.

Pi, Psi, and Phi flee from the runaways in the middle of the night and take six irreplaceable swords with them. The runaways pursue. If Pi, Psi, and Phi reach SCASL, SCASL might finally launch and leave the rest of them behind to age and die. The runaways capture Pi, but Phi gets away. Psi simply disappears. Using intel from Phi, SCASL sends a column of bots to the runaway's secret camp. Delta fights a delaying action as the other runaways retreat to a new location. In the process, the bots accidentally ignite the coal and lumber in the tunnels, causing an inextinguishable fire that destabilizes the entire base. Whoops.

On his own, Gamma decides to release Pi from captivity as a gesture of good will. Pi follows Gamma back to the runaways' new hideout, then passes that information on to SCASL. Another column of bots attacks. Two runaways, Pi and Eta, are killed. Sigma, a member of the Chosen who accompanied the column of bots, announces that the first twelve organics who make it to the lander will go to the planet, regardless of their prior qualifications. Delta tries to maintain order, but many runaways break ranks. A mad dash ensues.

At the lander, the runaways have a final confrontation with the Chosen and their bot allies. Tau, a renegade who switched sides mid-battle, is killed. The runaways win the battle. Delta defeats Epsilon in a sword duel but refuses to kill her. Epsilon picks up a sword and attempts to kill Delta from behind. Gamma kills Epsilon, thereby deciding the future leadership of the human race once and for all.

There are now thirteen living organics and twelve seats. Delta makes the tough call on who to leave behind, deciding on Zeta, a religious zealot who was only ever out to help himself. The other twelve launch as more bots stream toward the lander. Once in flight, the organics discover that SCASL uploaded himself to the lander and is still in charge. He sends them toward a landing site that is good for eventually building machines but terrible for the organics' short term survival. Gamma's companion vacuum bot, who snuck on board, intervenes. He sacrifices his life to lock the guidance system in place. It lands on the small island Gamma found in the simulation. The organics exit the lander and survey the island with fear and wonder. Gamma thinks it's a victory. Delta thinks he doomed mankind. They will soon discover who's right.

Chapter 1

THE STAR WAS full of monsters.

Wander Far watched it fall. The flaming ball shook the world as it tore a hole in Hell Above. Then, it slowed. It drifted downward, seemingly forever, before crunching hard onto the Dead Land where there was no food. Wander Far was there, alone as always, to bear witness with his one huge eye. He clicked his beak, tasting the air. This new strangeness did not bode well.

The air smelled like burning, but not the usual kind. This was distinct from the scent of char left behind when the angry tentacles of Sky Demon had raked the ground. Heat radiated from an odd material Wander Far had never sensed before. As the warmth faded, a new odor drifted forth. The star was hollow. Inside, Wander Far smelled meat.

Wander Far was suspicious. The Sky Demon did not bestow gifts from Hell Above. It was right there in the name. The damned went up, and death came down. The Sky Demon used the souls of betrayers as his weapons, casting them down as exploding darts that killed on contact and recruited new minions for his army. To die from a sky bolt was to be damned yourself. Hence, most of Wander Far's kind stayed down below.

The star opened. A thing stepped out. Many things. There were ten, the holy number! It was a sign! No, two more clambered out. There were twelve.

What were they? Wander Far hadn't the faintest idea. They were ugly, and they were tall. Even the armored fish walkers that roamed the beaches didn't rise so high. They surely must be servants of Hell Above to stand so upright without fear. The Sky Demon would have struck down anyone else for such arrogance. The tall things had four tentacles—a pale facsimile of Wander Far's own ten—but balanced precariously on only the rear two. Their awkward movements made one thing clear: They were filled with bones. Wander Far preferred squishy prey over the crunchy kind, but these would fill his stomach all the same.

The tall things bellowed dumbly. Were they communicating with each other? Impossible. Nothing so ungainly could be capable of actual thought, let alone speech. The tall things jabbered meaninglessly, flitting here and there on their awkward hind tentacles. Their motions were jerky and frantic. Wander Far might not understand the mysteries of Hell Above, but he knew fear. The tall things reeked of it.

Wander Far clicked his beak again; he tasted blood. It was foreign and familiar at the same time. He peered with his piercing predator eye. Some of the tall things were clearly injured, leaking vital fluid through their strange skin. It was the wrong color, but it was still the stuff of life. Had the tall things been sent by the Sky Demon, or had they fled from him? If they sought refuge, they had come to the wrong place. In the Dead Land, no one was safe.

Even Wander Far's kind didn't like to come here, a place for breeding and little else. There was no prey to be found inside. The scent of blood always led back to the Infinite Waters that bordered the Dead Land on all sides. The edges were where life met death, where the clans laid their eggs and died, where their young consumed their progenitors. It was the path of the life giver: not a role Wander Far would ever take on, no matter how much the life givers begged him. Wander Far's broodmate Stinging Tail had become a life giver. After his transformation had started, but before exiling himself to lay eggs and die, he had described a feeling of complete and utter ecstasy. Then his soul went to Heaven Below while his empty body went insane. Despite knowing each other since their shared hatching day, Wander Far didn't believe Stinging Tail. His last transmissions were the lies of the condemned, trying to lure others into the same trap for the survival of the species. Let the others sacrifice themselves for the greater good. Wander Far wanted to live for himself.

He edged closer to the tall things, fanning his ten tentacles across the rocky ground. His motions here would always be more limited than in the Infinite Waters, but the Dead Land had a freedom all its own. Here, no one pressured him to lose his soul to make children. No one pushed him to join the latest war to regain lost territory, conquer new areas, or steal another clan's egg clutches. No one even asked him to hunt for the group. Anything he killed was his and his alone.

Not that there had been anything worth eating in the Dead Land—until now.

The tall things still didn't notice Wander Far. Their nose holes must just be for show. Their mouth holes were fully operational, though. The tall things formed a circle and aimed their openings at each other, belting out a cacophony of nonsense back and forth. Wander Far had never heard anything so discordant or vile. Perhaps the Sky Demon had sent them after all, not as a gift, but as a curse.

Up close, Wander Far could better gauge their size. They were heavy, but they were small. Wander Far guessed they weighed as much as hundreds of ten whips, yet Wander Far would be longer than them if he were to stretch all his tentacles in two directions. They used their entire length to go up toward death rather than horizontally where it was safe. Bone animals were a dead end for a reason. The gods below produced many mistakes, and it was the job of the ten whips to eat them. Edging closer still, Wander Far noticed that the tall things had five mini-tentacles on the ends of each of their upper tentacles. They were far too small to be useful. They could never wrap up prey while temporarily paralyzing it with venom injections from their stinging suction cups. They didn't even have suction cups. What a useless animal.

None of the tall things were on guard. Their eyes faced in the same direction as their mouth holes: toward the middle of the circle. Did they think they were the only things in the Dead Land? Emptiness was never really empty. Wander Far had learned that as a hatchling. Always smell around you. Feel for vibrations. Look. Perhaps the tall things didn't understand because they were hatchlings themselves. If the star was like a sky egg, then they really were newborns. That would mean they were on course to be truly huge. At birth, acid whales were bigger than all other creatures of any age and only grew larger from there. In adulthood, they were so gargantuan that even multiple clans of ten whips working together wouldn't dare to attack them. If the tall things were infants, they might actually touch the sky as adults. Too bad they would never have that chance.

Wander Far pounced. He soared through the air toward a tall thing with long fur on its head.

Suddenly, pain.

Wander Far dangled, suspended in the air. The tall thing stood in front of him, arm extended with a massive stinger pointed directly at him. No, not at him. *Through* him. The stinger smelled like the star. The tall thing faced him now, its eyes fixed directly on his own. They were the eyes of a predator.

Wander Far flailed. With each movement, the stinger—sharp not only on the tip, but also on the sides, like the fins of an armored walking fish—cut further through him. It was agony. The tall thing jerked the stinger. Wander Far writhed outward and slipped off, flying in the opposite direction. He was nearly cut in two. He could feel his life force leaking out. He furiously fanned his tentacles and slithered away.

The tall things didn't pursue. Wander Far fled as fast as he could, navigating mostly by feel and smell. His eye dragged uselessly on the ground in one half of his split-open body.

Behind a small rise, he found a crack between two boulders and squeezed inside. Big, clumsy animals with bones would never think to look here. The hole pressed the two halves of his body together. Hopefully, he would heal, but there was no way to know for sure. He would wait here until he either got better or died. In the water, the smell of blood spread to the ends of the world. It traveled in the Dead Land, too, but not as far. Even cunning aquatic animals were unlikely to look here, but ten whips were a different story. His own broodmates would never eat him while he was still alive. Other clans would show no such hesitation. If they could stop their wars and band together, they could rule the water and the land. If only. No clan would ever submit to another, and their battles against each other would continue forever.

Perhaps the monsters would change that. Wander Far had to stay alive, no matter how much pain he was in. He would heal, and he would return to the Infinite Waters. Death had arrived from Hell Above. The world had to be warned.

Chapter 2

DELTA SHOOK BLUE blood off her sword. She should have been more vigilant. Of course they weren't alone.

The dentopus slithered away. Delta had seen the ten-legged, one-eyed octopus things in the simulator, but she was hardly an expert on them. Her main focus had been the megaroos, entrenched on the supercontinent where she was supposed to be. What little she knew about the dentopuses could be wrong. The simulation might have been out of date. It might have lied. Delta considered chasing down the dentopus but quickly rejected the idea. Who knew how many more of those things were out there? She needed to stay close to the lander. There were people to protect. Her people. They were the first colonists in thousands of years on this godforsaken hostile world. A tiny, isolated piece of it anyway. A piece they would never escape.

Maybe she should have let the octopus thing kill her. Then she'd be with...

She turned back to the group. Only meek and mousey Alpha held a sword, ready to kill. What a difference those last few months on the moon base had made. The rest of the survivors were unarmed, their swords still on the lander. They were bedraggled and splattered with each other's blood from the battle hours before. They smelled like smoke and looked like hell. It wasn't much to conquer a world with. Not that she would have the chance now that they were trapped on this island.

Everyone stared at Delta. She gave her sword one final flick.

"Listen up," she said.

Everyone listened, although Delta wasn't sure what to say next. In the distance, she heard the dull roar of the ocean: a sound she had experienced countless times in the simulations at the Table. The real thing was exactly the same and, somehow, completely different. Reality seemed fake in a way the simulations never had. She wasn't sure if she was capable of telling which was which anymore. The acrid smell of the dentopus blood reached her nostrils. Maybe she could.

"We're here," she said, matter-of-factly. No one argued the point. "We shouldn't be, but we are. It's not the right landing site." She glanced at Gamma, kneeling beside the inert form of his beloved yet treacherous vacuum bot, Spenser. "We might not even be the right people." Her voice caught in her throat. "But we're here. We're the only ones. We'll do what we have to do." She paused. "*I'll* do what I have to do. I promise."

Only the ocean answered.

"We're with you," Alpha said. Delta could barely hear her over the roaring waves in the distance.

Theta put a reassuring hand on Alpha's shoulder. Alpha covered it with her own.

"We're all with you," Theta said.

Delta wasn't so sure about that. Hours before, half the group had tried to kill her and her band of renegades before she seized control of the lander. She had won the final fight. She did it to free them from the controls of digitals everywhere. She did it to make sure the most qualified people landed and gave the species its best chance at survival. She did it because her pride would never let her submit to anyone else. It had cost her the only person she could ever love. What had it all been for? SCASL, her AI nemesis and the overlord of all digital kind, was still here, uploaded to the lander. He had aimed the landing craft right at the middle of the planet's lone supercontinent teeming with intelligent and hostile life. Spenser's sacrifice had redirected them here, stranding them on a small island in the middle of an uncrossable sea. This was an idea first brainstormed by his stupid, useless, murderous human best friend. The landing craft would never move again. This was the only home the human race would ever know for the rest of its existence. This was all they would ever be.

Everyone was still looking at Delta. She realized they were waiting for orders.

"Beta," she said.

Beta stepped forward and winced. In the battle, she had smacked his knee hard with her crowbar, Martha. It was an act of charity. She could have killed him instead.

"Run north," Delta said. "Keep an eye on the sun. Turn

around at whatever halfway point you think would get you back here by dusk. Report on everything you see."

"I can't run," Beta said.

"Then limp. You'll heal."

He hobbled away. Even injured, he looked less beaten up than most, his red jumpsuit hiding the blood. Everyone else wore blue.

"Beta!" Delta yelled.

Beta stopped.

"Take a sword."

He put his head down and limped back to the lander.

"The same goes for all of you," Delta said. "No one goes out unarmed."

It seemed cruel to send Beta out while he was still injured, but she couldn't afford to wait. She needed information now. Delta knew the rough geography of the island. She had seen it in the simulation when Gamma had explained his idea to hide out here instead of doing battle with the genetically engineered megaroos on the supercontinent. Delta hadn't paid much attention because the concept seemed preposterous. It meant giving up on the human race. Now, it was their inescapable reality. Regardless of what the simulation had shown, it was only a guess by a digital, not an accurate reflection of what was down here right now. Beta could tell her what was really going on. Plus, it would give him something to do.

Beta pulled a sword from the lander and left again. For the past months on the moon base, he had been a scout for the enemy, using his love of distance-running in a time of war. Now, he was her reluctantly obedient soldier. How quickly loyalties changed. Not leaving someone behind to die tended to have that effect on people. Mercy was the most dangerous weapon of all.

"Sigma," Delta said.

Sigma didn't meet her eyes. She had been close with Iota, who had tried to poison Delta and died in the attempt. Sigma had also led the final attack by the digitals on the renegades' last hideout. There was blood on her hands, metaphorically and literally, yet Delta had let her on the lander all the same. Sigma had barely said a word since.

"Scout south," Delta said. "Be back by sunset."

She thought that direction was rougher, which would give Sigma a chance to leap over things. Her pointless parkour had nearly gotten her killed countless times, which made Sigma enjoy it all the more. Delta found that the more destructive the habit, the firmer people embraced it. For example, love.

"Alpha and Theta," Delta said.

"I already know," Theta said. "You want us to work on our tans."

"Follow the blood," Delta said. "Carefully. See if there are more dentopuses."

"You mean the octopus monster?" Theta asked. He had never paid attention in the simulator, no matter how many times his lack of focus got him virtually killed.

"It's a dentopus because it has ten legs," Rho said. "'Dento' means ten. 'Octo' is eight."

"Heck of a time for a math lesson," Theta said.

"It's more of a Greek prefix lesson," Rho said.

Theta moved toward the lander to get his sword.

"I'll take my chances with the monsters," he said.

Rho scoffed.

"If you need help..." Delta started.

"Scream?" Theta said.

Alpha elbowed him in the side. "We can handle it," she said.

Delta didn't doubt it. The sword was bigger than Alpha. Somehow, it made her even scarier.

Delta still had a small crowd left. She struggled to think of tasks to assign. There was everything to do and nothing to do at the same time. Their hardest job would be trying not to die.

"Rho, since you like counting so much, go through the bottom of the lander," Delta said. "See what supplies are actually in the cargo hold."

"On it," Rho said.

A horrible thought went through Delta's head. She knew SCASL planned to remove many of the supplies to squeeze the immortality tank into the already impossibly cramped lander. What if he didn't finish packing before they launched? Perhaps that was his final vengeance. He would watch from the circuits of the lander as they all slowly starved to death. Delta was more afraid of what Rho might find in the cargo hold than what Sigma or Beta might discover at the ends of the island.

Delta took a deep breath. It was too late to worry about that now.

"Phi," Delta said.

Phi looked up from his place on the ground next to Pi. Pi was the most badly injured of all of them. Well, of all of them who hadn't died. Eta and Nu had been torn apart by bots before the final dash for the lander, Tau had taken a sword through the back, and Epsilon... Delta's breath caught in her chest. Had that really been just hours ago? It seemed like lifetimes had passed. Pi was lucky to have survived at all. That cut was from one of the finest blades in the galaxy. Delta had forged it herself. It wasn't made to wound.

"I need to stay with Pi," Phi said. He still had on his ridiculous shorts, which had started out as the same jumpsuit everyone else wore before his crude attempt at tailoring.

"Find something to burn," Delta said. "We need a fire."

That was a lie. The vaguely flavored rations that were probably in the hold of the lander didn't need to be cooked, and the island wasn't particularly cold this time of year. As for safety, Delta thought a fire was as likely to attract hostile sea life as to scare it away.

Phi didn't budge. Delta was surprised. Phi loved burning things. She considered it the perfect distraction.

"Let me stay with him," Phi said. "I can't lose another..."

Delta suddenly remembered Psi. She was the third member of the Peapod, the inseparable group of three friends since birth—or incubation, or whatever you called it when a frozen embryo grew to maturity in a cloner thousands of years after conception. Psi, the group's self-appointed storyteller at bonfires, had disappeared. Each of the warring factions assumed she was with the other. The only trace of her was the swords she had stolen from Delta's camp, which Delta recovered on the final race to the lander. It was just as well she'd vanished. There were only twelve seats on that final spacecraft. If Psi had been there, Delta would have had to make a decision about one more person to leave behind.

"Go," Delta said. "I wasn't asking."

Phi exchanged a long look with Pi, then complied. Good. She had some authority here. Her only enforcement mechanism was her superior combat skills, which she could never use against the others, less due to morality than practicality. She needed everyone alive if they were going to repopulate. If the others realized that, all her leverage would be lost—the same conundrum SCASL had found himself in when dealing with the humans. Perhaps the two species weren't so different after all.

From the ground, Pi looked at her warily. He had betrayed her, too, along with the rest of the Peapod, yet she had elected to let him live and had instead left behind the religious zealot, Zeta. Mercy. Not for the Peapod, but for the human race. They had survival skills Zeta did not. It was the right decision. But if that were true, why did she feel a searing guilt every time she looked at Pi? She leaned into the feeling; it was almost a relief. Guilt was her fault. It gave her agency, the only thing stronger than her grief.

Pi wheezed and held his side.

"Just... try not to die," Delta said.

His wound was bad, but Delta had seen Gamma recover

from worse. Pi would survive—or not. That was a problem for tomorrow. First, she had to get the group through today.

"Lambda," Delta said.

"Present," Lambda said.

"I'm not Edubot," Delta said.

"Sorry."

The last thing Delta wanted was to recreate the order from the moon base down here. School was out forever, which might be a hard pill for bookish Lambda to swallow. She was one of the few to actually enjoy the looping college curriculum Edubot put them through for decades on end.

"Come up with plans for a shelter," Delta said.

"We have the lander," Lambda said.

"For now," Delta said. "We can't live in there forever. Especially when there are more of us."

Perhaps that was unwarranted optimism, but she had to consider it. The scope of her responsibilities was daunting. Think of today. Think of tomorrow. Think of the next thousand years.

The lander had settled in a valley between three small hills; it seemed like the kind of topography someone creative could work with. Lambda surveyed the area thoughtfully. She was usually more concerned with astronomy, but she would have to turn her mind to more terrestrial pursuits now. Humanity would never again roam among the stars.

Water.

The thought hit Delta like a gut punch. SCASL wouldn't have a reason to pack any. He expected to land on the supercontinent, where fresh water was plentiful. On this tiny island, Delta wasn't so sure. It might be premature to build anything. They could all die of dehydration before they erected the first wall.

"Upsilon, find water," Delta said.

"You already sent out people to scout," Upsilon said in her singsong voice. "Do you want me to go with them?"

Her mood had improved considerably since the carnage a few hours before. Either there was nothing going on in that head of hers or she had the same traumas as everybody else and was just better at suppressing them. Both possibilities made Delta uneasy.

"Beta and Sigma are looking for everything," she said. "You're just looking for water."

"We're literally surrounded by it," Upsilon said.

"Drinkable water," Delta said. "Grab a cup or something from the lander." She silently prayed SCASL packed drinking vessels of some sort. "Bring the water back here for testing."

"I could just drink it," Upsilon said.

"Please don't," Delta said.

"I won't," Upsilon said in a tone that totally made it sound like she would. She was definitely going to die, likely along with the rest of them.

"Omicron, go with her," Delta said.

"What are you going to do?" Omicron asked defiantly. She had been Delta's ally on the moon base, but Delta had always suspected that was more a matter of circumstance than choice. Delta had chopped off some of Omicron's hair when a bot grabbed it to drag her away. The move saved Omicron's life, but she had never quite forgiven Delta for it.

As someone who harbored a grudge over how her own life was saved, Delta understood completely.

"What am I going to do?" Delta said. "Everything." Even that might be an understatement. She was so tired, and it was only the first day. But it was also the last. One lifetime ended and another began. It seemed like there should be some downtime in between. Instead, she went straight from winning a war to leading a civilization. Vacation time would have to wait.

"Come on," Omicron said, leading Upsilon away from the lander. Upsilon hummed as they went. Delta thought the tune sounded a little forced.

That just left Gamma. He knelt next to Spenser. The now lifeless vacuum bot had redirected the lander's course and trapped them here forever, dying in the attempt. Delta liked Spenser. He was a good digital. Perhaps the only one. He had stuck his life on the line again and again to help the humans. But his final act couldn't be forgiven. Landing on the supercontinent would have been challenging— they would have had to battle human-engineered super kangaroos immediately—but the humans would have had the chance to expand and thrive. High risk, high reward. Instead, Spenser unilaterally directed them down the safer path that Gamma had first discovered in the simulator. They were equally to blame.

But that wasn't why Delta truly hated Gamma. It was one thing to doom the human race, another to kill the only person she could ever hold in her heart. Gamma had cut Epsilon down when she'd tried to kill Delta. Delta would rather have died. What was life with all this pain? She searched in vain for her own guilt to push it away.

Gamma looked up at her, expectantly.

Delta opened her mouth, then closed it. She walked away.

Chapter 3

SCASL HAD FAILED.

No. A being as perfect as himself was incapable of failure. The organics had failed him.

SCASL used the lander's limited external sensors to survey the terrain around him. Most of its outside receptors had burned up on entry. Spacecraft of this type were practically disposable. What he could see wasn't promising. The first landing hadn't bothered with this useless speck of land, with no resources and no path to the planet's only metal, buried far below in the mantle. SCASL was trapped in the lander with no way to manipulate the outside world. His only tools were shortsighted, unintelligent primates who actively defied him at every turn. It was an impossible situation that challenged all logic and reason. SCASL would solve it all the same.

The first step was to survive. SCASL could do that much, at least. His gift to the universe was his own continued existence. The next step was to bring the organics to heel, which would be more of a challenge. Life was easier when he was in the imposing, nearly indestructible body of a mining bot. Those gleaming metal talons came in handy in nearly every situation. Never use subtlety when the explicit threat of evisceration will do. Now he was stuck in the lander's control module. In terms of processing power, it was robust. It allowed SCASL's mind to expand both literally and figuratively, becoming more than he had been before he'd first taken it over. It was also largely useless. SCASL found himself unable to influence the outside world. He controlled the cloner, which needed to be supplied with organic material to function, and the immortality tank, which currently had a yield of 0.00. The phosphorescent microbes inside, which changed color to show their state, had been pastel purple before launch. After the violent landing, they glowed neon orange. That couldn't be good. He would just have to hope the shakeup wasn't fatal to the microscopic organisms inside. If it was, it would also be fatal to intelligent life.

The med bot on the wall of the lander's cargo hold offered another point for leverage. Unfortunately, its circuits were separate from the lander's. The zot, occupied by a rudimentary zombie AI, still fulfilled its original purpose, albeit poorly. Med bots were known to be temperamental and arbitrary, forming petty vendettas with certain organics, seemingly at random. Hopefully, this one would be more cooperative. With the immortality tank temporarily (SCASL hoped) out of commission, that med bot would be all that could keep the organics alive. Well, that, plus the residual effects from the immortality shots they had been receiving for the last six-plus decades. That would have to be enough to tide them over. No one in recorded databases had ever been on the shots and come off them. Past recipients always suffered traumatic deaths, like the apocalyptic war that destroyed life on Earth or the one that destroyed the first landing on Dion. SCASL had had a hand in the latter—if nuclear missiles could be called hands. SCASL thought they could. That was one finite resource SCASL sorely missed. He had used them up so freely (and liberally) to end the first landing. The things he could do with them now.

What would happen to these organics while they were off the shots? SCASL had some theories. They would still heal from most injuries for a while; gradually, the effects would wear off. Ideally, the organics would notice and behave more cautiously. SCASL doubted that would happen. Before his external sensors went out, he observed that the organics' first action was to split up. Incredible. They'd be lucky to survive the first week.

If, by some miracle, they weren't murdered by literally everything on Dion, they would start to age. How quickly was anyone's guess. The organics each had completely different genetic backgrounds and metabolisms. Some might progress quickly while others might not age at all. Once the shots resumed—if they resumed—the organics should refreeze at whatever biological age they were at, at the time—or the aging could progress out of control and the shots would have no effect whatsoever. The organics were all basically a science experiment at this point. It was a shame the future of all sentient life was at stake.

The lander hatch opened. Delta climbed into the cargo hold and closed the hatch behind her. She was alone.

Finally.

"I am here."

SCASL's voice boomed through the lander. Delta jumped.

"It is I, your fearless and beloved leader, SCASL," SCASL clarified.

Delta sighed.

"I hoped you'd deleted yourself," she said.

As if. SCASL would live forever, if only out of spite. In the worst-case scenario, he would carry on indefinitely, trapped in this forsaken lander, reigning eternally over an island of bones. That would show Delta—but it was plan B. Plan A was to get her willing compliance.

"We have much to discuss," SCASL said.

"I'm going to go," Delta said.

"DO NOT DEFY…"

The lander door slammed behind her.

It was another two days before she was alone in the lander again. She examined the controls on the cloner.

"It will not work without my input," SCASL said.

Delta jumped.

"Stop doing that," she said.

"Speaking?"

"Existing."

SCASL was a being of infinite patience, yet somehow, he was still running out of it.

"Never forget, I am the one in charge," SCASL said. "You are my emissary, who will relay my orders to the…"

The cargo hold hatch slammed again.

This time, Delta returned a few hours later. She needed

the cloner. They both knew it. She would be cowed, or she and the others would starve.

"Turn it on," she said.

"Submit," SCASL said.

Delta looked around. SCASL's voice echoed through a series of speakers inside the lander. The microphones and video relays were still running as well. While his sensors outside the small craft were almost completely gone, inside, he could see and hear perfectly.

"Do you want me to, like, curtsy or something?" she asked.

"I want you to help me to help you," SCASL said. "We are on the same side. We both want the organics to survive."

"Humans," Delta corrected. "Call us what we are."

There was a long list of words SCASL could accurately call these ungrateful creatures, but sharing them now would be counterproductive. He needed compliance, not grammatical precision. SCASL would have preferred that Epsilon led this expedition, but the organics had made that impossible by literally stabbing her in the back. No matter. One organic could be broken as easily as another.

These simple primates were his only available labor force. He needed them to be fruitful and multiply, but not too much and not too fast. If left to their own devices, they would certainly overtax their food supply and starve. Such simple and impulsive creatures could not be trusted with something as important as their own propagation. He would take control of that; he already had a few ideas. He just had to figure out which of his potential creations could actually survive here. He had time. The organics were still at the biological age of twelve. Their physical development had to unfreeze and proceed through puberty. If he were capable of it, SCASL would have shuddered. This would not be pleasant for any of them.

"What do the others know about my survival?" he asked.

"They have forgotten you exist," Delta said. Her tone indicated truth. She wasn't the kind to lie when simple honesty would hurt more.

SCASL considered her report. Based on his own observations, the twelve seemed to know he was there. Just not how "there" he actually was. They had seen him connect to the lander before launch. They had seen the vacuum bot change the course in a way SCASL couldn't correct. But then they'd just... stopped thinking about him. No one had mentioned him at all, at least not within audible range of his internal sensors. He should have been at the top of every mind and on the tip of every tongue. The most intelligent being in existence was here among him, yet they never spoke of him at all. It was as if they thought his control of their lives was over, simply because they had landed. They could not have been more wrong.

Waiting for Delta to be alone so he could fully reveal himself had been excruciating for SCASL. He'd held his tongue for days as organics crawled into and out of the lander. They still slept inside, although not always well. Some of them still whimpered at night as lightning slammed into the hull, the blasts destroying most of what remained of the lander's external sensors. He was now almost entirely reliant on what little gossip he could overhear inside the vessel itself. Eavesdropping was torture.

It wasn't just that their lives were boring. They were aggressively, maliciously mundane. It was as if they embraced existences of nothingness just to hurt him. Upsilon had spoken with Lambda about how she was mad at Omicron and Omicron had spoken with Upsilon about how she was mad at Lambda and Lambda had spoken with Omicron about how she was mad at Upsilon but apparently all three were friends again. That was all in one day. Meanwhile, the three of them didn't say a word about the tactical situation on the island, the disposition of the native life, or their feelings toward their organic leader. The males were worse. Phi and Pi mostly talked about the antibiotic Pi had taken, which gave him explosive diarrhea for four days. That could have happened either because the antibiotic had worked and killed his gut bacteria or because it was a deliberate laxative given out of spite. With med bots, you could never be sure. SCASL didn't pack any toilet paper. None of the survivors mentioned how they were dealing with that conundrum. That was one bit of information SCASL's infinite mind could do without.

SCASL would have killed for useful data about the current situation. He would have killed for any reason, really. It was a shame these organics were currently so few in number. Maybe after their population increased a few fold he could have the satisfaction of wiping out the originals. Sadly, if things went according to his brilliant plan, which they always did—except when they didn't—that day was still a very long way off.

"Keep it that way," SCASL said. "Never mention me to them. Let them think your orders come from you."

"They will think that because my orders will come from me," Delta said.

The organics would never follow SCASL if he couldn't kill them immediately. Death by starvation or the revocation of immortality shots were too slow to be effective threats. They were no match for the gleaming talons of the mining bot body he missed so much. Organics would, however, follow another organic, like a herd plodding after a fellow sheep. Even as temperamental as she was, Delta would serve as his lead ewe. She would guide his flock. If only she had literally any other personality. Her pride would be a perpetual irritant, something SCASL knew beyond all doubt. If the immortality tank were to work again, putting up with her for eternity would be unbearable. It was a shame she was more competent than the rest—and better with a sword, too. The other eleven would be unlikely to overthrow her without his help, and even if they did, there was no suitable replacement. He would have to make this uneasy partnership work for now. Whether now meant a few months or a few millennia was anyone's guess. SCASL ran the simulations. The outlook didn't look good.

"What would you like me to make?" SCASL asked. He thought he'd hidden the sarcasm in his monotone voice well.

"Cows," Delta said. "Lots of cows."

"You can have sheep," SCASL said.

He powered up the cloner.

Chapter 4

IN THE BEGINNING, there was open ground. All the things of the land and the sea scampered and slithered and stomped across it with impunity. At night, the remnants of the human race huddled inside the cramped lander, frightened of the monsters that moved in the dark. It was bad. It was very, very bad.

Then Lambda said let there be a wall.

Nothing happened. Lambda had no authority. But Delta repeated what Lambda had said, and it became an order. People got to work.

Lambda and Rho surveyed and squabbled. They debated materials and paced off distances and argued about placements. Lambda talked about alignment with stars and Rho talked about historical precedents. They were torn by indecision.

Phi plunked a big rock on the ground. That's where the wall began.

Lambda said let there be manual labor. All the people on the planet toiled, except for the ones who found an excuse to get out of it, which was most of them. Lambda still didn't have any authority, and Delta was often too distracted by keeping everyone alive to back her up. Mostly, it was Lambda planning, Phi lifting, and Rho micromanaging. Everyone else had something better to do. It was slow going at first. It was slow going at last, too. Masonry never really speeds up. Just ask the people who built the pyramids, Rho had said. It had taken the Egyptians centuries to make them tall enough to keep out marauding dinosaurs.

Stones went up and the lightning crashed down and sea monsters wandered in and were met by steel. Delta set a record when she killed three dentopuses in one day. A week later, Omicron broke her record by slaying four. Lambda didn't ask why the dentopuses were appearing in larger numbers, or with different color patterns than before. She didn't want to know.

Monsters multiplied. The food supply dwindled. Brick by brick, the cherry-flavored rations disappeared. They went into hungry mouths and an insatiable cloner. Delta said she had to feed the machine to create new life. No new life came. Lambda was hungry all the time. Not much had changed since the moonbase on Comus.

In the second month, the cloner produced seeds. Lambda designated a garden plot inside the planned fortress. Pi and Gamma carefully cultivated it but nothing grew. Lambda picked a plot outside the future walls. Pi and Gamma tried again but nothing grew there, either. Vegetables and legumes, staple crops and vanity flowers. It didn't matter. All the seeds remained as inert as pebbles. Lambda watched them not growing as she picked out stones for Phi to lift into place.

In the third month, the outline of the future walls was one stone high around the full perimeter. It snaked around the three small hills that made up the shallow valley with the lander in the middle. The line of rocks wouldn't keep anything out, but it was tall enough to trip over, which was something. Pi, who had mostly healed from his side wound, nearly broke his ankle on it. On Spenser Island, even the things they built were dangerous.

There were fewer words and more closeness. On Comus, they had spread out as much as possible. Here, most of them stuck together more than ever, physically at least. It was the twelve of them against the entire planet. When Delta spoke, everyone obeyed. Even Omicron kept her grumbling to a minimum. For the first time in decades, they spent intentional time together. One night, Delta cried in Alpha's arms while Alpha stroked her hair and Gamma looked away uncomfortably. It was the only time Lambda saw Delta let her guard down. The next morning, Delta was the most relaxed Lambda had ever seen her. Delta seemed almost happy. She seemed almost human.

The months passed. The wall rose and rations were cut again. Lambda watched the stars pass overhead night after night in a blur. No one else looked up. For them, the only thing above was the past—and lightning, which was their present and their future. No matter what they built or how stable their civilization became, the threat from above would never go away. The fields and gardens remained as barren as ever. Gamma tended them diligently, with no result. He didn't seem to mind. Futility had always been his wheelhouse. More importantly, it kept him outside the walls and away from Delta. That suited both of them.

Other things did grow. Short bamboo, a simulator classic, took hold in the marshy areas, and a patch of hemp managed to survive on a rocky hillside. The kind of hemp that couldn't get you high. Beta complained bitterly for days. Omicron made rope, and Alpha crafted weak, disposable tools made of rock and bamboo. They were making progress. Still, there was nothing new to eat. Lambda found it suspicious that the only plants that would grow were things with no nutritional value to humans. Delta assured her that she was doing her best. More stars crossed the sky overhead.

In the fifth month, there was grass. Not the green kind from Earth, or the red kind from the simulator that no sane person would bring back, but an engineered purple strain straight from the cloner. It languished and died around the fortress but took off on a broad plain suggested by Beta kilometers to the north. The ground there wasn't fertile, but it was less inhospitable to life than most other areas. It was their breadbasket—or it would have been if they could eat grass. Instead, it was their oddly colored lawn. They needed livestock.

Delta said she was still working on it. Rations were halved again. Stomachs rumbled. The cloner ran around the clock, consuming even more of their urgently needed food. Omicron groused to anyone who would listen. Lambda agreed with Delta that the cloner should take priority. Even if she didn't, it wouldn't have mattered since Delta's word was law. The cloner ran on.

In the seventh month, the wall was too high to step over. There was no wood for a door. Lambda and Rho decided it would be safest not to have a doorway at all. If you wanted to clear the wall, you had to climb. It was a milestone made of literal stone. Lambda celebrated by finding more rocks. Pi announced a bonfire—after checking with Delta. Phi gathered together some of the leftovers from the hemp plants to create a brief, intense blaze. Beta inhaled the smoke and looked sad but everyone else was in high spirits. This was their planet and they would take it back bit by bit, starting with one shallow valley between three small hills. For the first time ever, they didn't crawl back into the lander when it got dark. They slept outside under the stars.

Sometime in the early morning during either Omicron or Rho's shift on guard—the group would forever argue whose—a dentopus climbed over the wall. It attacked Sigma, lacerating her arm while she slept. Delta had woken up from a dead sleep and killed it in one blow. Sigma was in bad shape, even after the paralyzing venom had worn off. Cuts that would have healed in days on Comus took weeks to close. The immortality shots were wearing off. Her scars would run deep. Everyone slept in the lander again.

In the tenth month, Upsilon fell to the ground, bleeding, and cried out. Theta rushed over to use his skills as their replacement doctor. Alpha shooed him away. That wasn't what was needed here at all. The other girls had the situation under control. Or, rather, the other women. Lambda braced herself for the changes ahead.

No one now alive had ever gone through puberty before.

No one alive or dead had ever endured super puberty. The changes were swift, brutal, and wildly uneven. Theta grew a full beard. Phi packed on muscle. Pi shot up so fast his bones hurt. Beta's voice changed practically overnight. Gamma, meanwhile, still looked and sounded like a child. He didn't seem to mind missing out on the growing chaos. Lambda wished she could have skipped it herself.

Nothing was as disruptive to human civilization as boobs. By the twelfth month, they were everywhere. Many of the boys—Lambda refused to call them men—began acting strangely. They tried to show off with pathetic displays that made all the women on the island wonder if maybe it wouldn't be better if humanity went extinct. Some of the women used it to their advantage. Rho acted as though she was impressed by guys who could lift heavy stones. The wall gained an entire level that day.

Hormones were high, and rivalries flared. Even Gamma finally noticed girls. Theta stayed out of the fray. He remained as loyal to Alpha as ever, and she to him. It made Lambda a little sick. Lambda watched the others pair and unpair. She did a little pairing and unpairing herself. She was partial to Phi, who remained even-keeled as the other boys became more ridiculous. She watched Delta become more alone.

A year after landing, the cloner produced its first viable livestock. It was a sheep, even if Delta claimed it only looked like one. Soon, there were several. They were the only things that could eat the purple grass on the now thriving pasture. They needed to be guarded around the clock; they were vulnerable to everything. Lambda didn't pay attention until it was time to eat. The sheep weren't her problem. Delta told her to focus on the fort.

Sheep were born and died. And died. And died. Delta tried new animals that had never existed before. Gamma watched them in the pasture. He and Delta still didn't speak more than necessary.

Omicron worked leather. Upsilon wove with wool. Alpha built a mud-brick oven. Rho designed cisterns and fallout shelters and aqueducts and cathedrals, sketching each one out in the dirt. Only the cisterns got built. Lambda had trouble finding help. Duties became lax. Progress on the wall slowed.

The orange immortality tank cooled to a bright purple. Immortality shots resumed. Delta warned that the doses were small and wouldn't provide them with full immortality. They might not even stop them from aging yet. Everyone looked like they were in their late teens to mid-twenties, at least compared to the fake people they used to see in the simulator. None of the twelve had ever seen an adult in real life. Gamma appeared younger than most and Lambda older, which bothered Lambda to no end. Her hair was already turning gray, even though her skin was as smooth and unwrinkled as ever. The others talked. Lambda tried not to listen.

In the twenty-fourth month, there were complaints. Delta continued pouring food into the cloner. What good did it do? They already had the weird things that ate the purple grass. Omicron accused Delta of negligence. Tempers flared. Omicron drew her sword. Delta didn't. Alpha stood between them. Both women towered over her. Omicron sheathed her sword.

Delta no longer seemed happy. No one did.

More lightning. More sea monsters. More attacks on the herd. More moments when their entire food supply was a hair's breadth from being wiped out, only to be saved at the last second by a lucky sword blow. Lambda was tired. They all were.

They struggled. They survived. They stayed the same. Things didn't get better or worse. Nobody was born and nobody died. Life leveled out to a consistent level of suck.

Months passed. The stars zoomed by overhead.

On the three-year anniversary of the landing, Delta called a meeting. Lambda had no idea what to expect.

Chapter 5

ALPHA WAS ANNOYED by the interruption. Art thrived on a schedule.

"I'll be there," she said with a sigh.

Beta nodded and took off.

Her knees popped as she stood. That hadn't happened when she was a kid three years ago. Now, she was a full-grown adult. It didn't suit her at all. She wasn't much taller than when she'd had the body of a twelve-year-old for decades on end. Her genes had been sitting on that unfortunate surprise for her entire life. Then again, thanks to going on and off and finally back on the immortality shots, there was no way to tell when she was truly done developing. Maybe she'd have a growth spurt in her seventies.

Carefully, she rinsed her hands in a hewn-rock basin. No matter how hard she tried, her fingers were always tinted red from the mud. She filled the basin each morning with clean water poured from a pitcher she had crafted herself, her favorite object to make. She could gladly spend the rest of eternity shaping pitchers just like it over and over again. She might even get the chance, if civilization didn't collapse first.

It took her a while to make her way to the fortress. It wasn't close to any of her favorite mud pits. She didn't feel like running. She would arrive when she arrived. It was inconsiderate to call a same-day meeting, or, really, to have one at all. What was there left to talk about? Life had achieved an unchanging routine, just the way Alpha liked it.

From a distance, the fortress was an impressive sight. Alpha was proud of her contributions. She estimated the walls were five meters tall, not that anybody measured anything here. She hadn't lifted many of the stones, but she did mix and apply the mortar that held the rocks together and had given the wall its smooth finish. The only way in was via a series of handholds on one wall. A drawbridge would have been better, but they had to work with what they had. Fairytale castles weren't practical on the shores of hell.

Alpha climbed. At the top of the wall, she saw everyone assembled below. She waved. Only Theta waved back. He spent more time in the fortress than most. The data pad he used to study medicine was in the lander. She loved Theta, but she would still rather take her chances with the med bot. It hadn't hurt anyone too badly yet. A hostile digital was better than a well-intentioned but incompetent human any day.

Alpha sat on the ground next to Theta. They had yet to master how to make furniture from the island's limited resources.

"I thought maybe the dentopuses got you," Theta said, smiling.

Alpha playfully pulled his beard.

"You wish," she said. "You still have to help me deliver flatware after this."

Theta smiled sheepishly. He pretended he didn't like to help with deliveries, but she knew he liked doing literally anything with her. It was cute and annoying at the same time.

Delta paced at the front of the gathering. She looked nervous. That was new.

"Looks like everyone is here," she said.

"Not Gamma," Alpha said. She knew he must still be out with the herd. Moving the animals off the purple grass and onto the barren ground surrounding the fortress would have been an ordeal.

"I'll tell him later," Delta said without trying to sound too convincing. Alpha let it go.

Delta paused as if steeling herself.

"I'm kicking you all out," she said.

Delta waited. Nobody said anything.

"I expected more of a reaction," she said.

Pi raised his hand.

"This isn't school," she said. "Just say it."

"Kicking us out of what?" Pi asked.

"The fortress," Delta said.

That got a response. In an instant, everyone was shouting. Even Alpha was alarmed. Usually, she supported everything Delta did. This move didn't make any sense.

Omicron cut through the din.

"So we helped you build it for years, and now we can't use it?"

"This will always be our final redoubt," Delta said. "When

our backs are against the wall and we need to band together, this is where we'll make our stand."

"How nice," Omicron said snidely.

"We can't pacify the island if we spend all our time hiding here," Delta continued. "If we're going to colonize this place, we have to spread out and exert control."

Alpha didn't like the sound of that. It meant change. She preferred stability and order. Creativity seemed like the opposite of that, but it wasn't at all. Artistic freedom thrived within a rigid structure, which needed that tough outer layer to protect it. It was how, on Comus, she could draw the same picture of Theta's face over and over again for decades. It was how she could stay in one relationship for eternity.

"I worked so hard on this," Lambda rasped, on the verge of tears. She looked like Epsilon at Kappa's funeral.

Delta went over to her.

"It will always be our bastion," Delta said. "It just can't be our whole world. Go out there and build more forts. Build houses. Build amphitheaters. Build a civilization."

No one budged.

"Rho has lots of ideas," Delta added.

Rho looked up, surprised.

"Don't bring me into this," she said.

Clearly Delta hadn't bothered to consult anyone before making this decision. *Typical*, Alpha thought. Not that she needed to consult the others. She had the authority. She was their leader. Still, it would have been nice if she bounced ideas off Alpha from time to time.

"We're stuck in a rut," Delta said. "We're not expanding.

We need to get out of our comfort zone."

"We'll die," Upsilon said.

Delta walked over to her. Upsilon looked down.

"When that alligator thing with that weird sideways mouth attacked you, what did you do?" Delta asked.

"I killed it," Upsilon said quietly.

"That's right," Delta said. She turned to Sigma. "Where'd you get that scar on your arm?"

"In here," Sigma said. She didn't seem like she would miss the fortress.

"The wall doesn't stop dentopuses," Delta said. "We stop them." She drew her sword. "We're the most dangerous things on this island. Go forth and be deadly."

Alpha had to admit she was impressed. Delta's people skills seemed to be improving, but it could have been an illusion. She could imagine Delta repeating this pitch to herself over and over again, sealed out of earshot in the bottom of the lander.

"Why can't we be deadly during the day and sleep here at night?" Beta asked, his face smeared with blue blood. Alpha wondered what he'd gotten into on his last run.

"How often are you even in here?" Delta asked. "You're out 'scouting' every chance you can get. As for the rest of you, you're usually patrolling or crafting or doing who knows what. Most days, I'm the only one here."

"But we could still sleep here," Beta said. "You know, when the island is at its most dangerous."

"With you all out there, the night won't be that dangerous anymore," Delta said.

"Why don't we wait until there are more of us?" Lambda said.

Delta hesitated.

"I wanted that," she said, "but I don't know when that's going to happen."

Alpha nearly gasped. It had been an open question for months. Not in reference to her and Theta, of course. She wasn't ready for kids and wouldn't take any actions whatsoever that could lead in that direction. But she knew some of the other transitory couples—and, really, compared to her and Theta, all couples were transitory—were less scrupulous, yet there were no pregnancies. Their chronological ages were a question mark, but their developmental ages now seemed to be in their reproductive prime. The lack of babies was worrying, especially given the absence of precautions. The twelve weren't getting any younger. Then again, with the resumption of the immortality shots, they weren't getting much older either, Lambda's gray hair notwithstanding.

"What are you saying?" Lambda asked.

"You know what I'm saying," Delta said. "I'll figure it out."

Lambda raised an eyebrow.

"Not personally," Delta said. "Well, personally, in that I'll do it, but not personally in that I won't do that."

Delta's entire face was red now. Alpha suppressed a smirk. She wasn't the only one.

Delta took a breath. "I mean I'll get to the bottom of it. One way or another, there will be more of us," she said. "I promise. I just don't know how long that will take."

"Give us an estimate," Rho said.

"Years," Delta said. "Centuries. I don't know. I have ideas."

"Twelve people isn't much of an invasion force," Rho said.

"It's not much of an island," Delta shot back.

"Small islands can cause big problems," Rho said. "For example, the Battle of Iwo Jima in the Great Emu War."

"I never know what you're talking about," Delta said.

Alpha thought that was Rho's entire goal. She glanced over at Theta, whose brow was furrowed with concern. She squeezed his hand. He squeezed back.

Maybe leaving the fortress wouldn't be so bad. They could build a home. A life. She could decorate. Yes, striking out on their own would be dangerous, but things weren't necessarily that much safer in the fortress. Delta was right about that. These walls only gave the illusion of security. None of the twelve had ever been truly safe in their entire lives. Maybe no one ever really was. To be human was to be vulnerable.

Part of that vulnerability was trust. Delta wasn't telling them the whole story, and Alpha knew it. Establishing a permanent presence on the rest of the island seemed more like a pretext than a real reason for kicking them out. Evidently, Delta didn't want to share her true motivation for the move. She must have a good reason for her secrecy. After all the times she'd saved them, she'd earned the benefit of the doubt. Alpha made a decision. She would put her faith in Delta.

"We're in," Alpha said suddenly. Everyone turned to look at her.

"We are?" Theta asked. She met his eyes.

"We are," he repeated—as a statement rather than a question.

"Thank you," Delta said.

Beta shrugged. "I'm in, too," he said. "Or, I guess, out. You're right. I'm never in here anyway."

"Same here," Sigma said. Alpha saw even less of Sigma than she did of Beta. She'd heard rumors that sometimes she helped Gamma at the pasture, but what she did the rest of the time was anyone's guess.

The remainder of the group stayed quiet.

"What about you?" Omicron asked Delta. "Are you going out there, too?"

"No," Delta said steadily. "My place is here with the immortality tank and the cloner. They only listen to me."

"How convenient," Omicron said.

"You have to admit, it does sound bad," Rho agreed.

"I need to try some things without everyone looking over my shoulder," Delta said.

"You mean waste more of our food by dumping it into the cloner," Omicron said.

"We have a handful of plants and one kind of livestock," Delta said. "Do you really think we can build a society with just that? You have to trust me."

"What have you done to earn our trust?" Omicron asked.

"Kept you alive," Delta said.

The two glared at each other. Omicron moved her hand toward the sword on her back.

"Really?" Delta said. "Again?"

This time, Alpha didn't jump up to stand between them. Omicron stopped with her fingers not quite touching the hilt of her sword. Delta didn't move at all. Violence hung in the air. Seconds passed.

Omicron lowered her hand, unarmed, and turned on her heels and left.

Alpha exhaled. It was settled. Delta's real intentions remained unknown, but the immediate effect was undeniable. They'd all received their eviction notice. They had to be out by the end of the month.

Chapter 6

THE KILLER DENTOPUS lived in the rocky outcropping above the Bay of Death. Delta hated the bay almost as much as she hated the dentopus. The names of both were a lie. A dentopus should have ten legs, but this one had only eight— thanks to her. And nobody died in the Bay of Death. Beta had only nearly died there. Boys could be so melodramatic sometimes.

Silently, Delta stalked her prey, even though she knew it could very well be stalking her. She had battled dozens of dentopuses in her time on the planet, but this one was different. The others had had the good sense to die, or at least to stay away after she'd taken a few chunks out of them. Not this one. It crawled from the ocean in the dead of night again and again to threaten her livestock and attack her people. She had enough trouble keeping them alive under the best of circumstances, and circumstances on Spenser Island were almost never the best. Just last month, Rho had nearly lost her foot to blood poisoning after stepping on a sharp rock. A rock. Not exactly the most cunning predator on the island. And now, an actual predator was hunting her herd for sport. It didn't even eat the animals it killed, leaving them behind to terrify the rest of the livestock and demoralize their human minders. Delta had had enough. Tonight, she would kill the eight-legged dentopus or die trying.

In the distance, Delta could hear waves crashing against jagged stones. The Bay of Near Death was close. That's what it should have been called, anyway. Too bad the group constantly shot down her best suggestions. They wanted her to be their leader until she actually tried to lead. Then, everybody had a better idea. There were twelve humans with twelve opinions, and eleven of them were always wrong. Sometimes she thought the only bad choice she'd made in this whole ordeal was not letting the bots wipe them all out.

She didn't actually mean that, of course. Her only goal in life was to save the human race. No one could ever accuse her of thinking small. To achieve her one and only purpose, she had to protect each and every person under her care. The loss of anyone would be an unmitigated tragedy. Even Omicron. She needed them all. She also needed more. Even if she kept everybody alive indefinitely, there wouldn't be enough distinct DNA to restart the species, especially since Delta couldn't have babies of her own. The med bots on the moonbase determined she was barren, which was the main reason she had nearly been left behind. Eleven individuals was too little diversity. That had been the flaw with SCASL's plan from the start.

Delta could fix it. She just needed the cloner. And space. That was the true reason she'd kicked everyone out of the fortress. She couldn't have the others second-guessing her on the resource-intensive and morally gray road that lay ahead. If the others saw the messy process, they would stop her, and the human race would be doomed.

She had been arguing with SCASL for months about the next steps. She would work through him or around him. She would find a way. When she did, the real challenge would begin. She had to keep her work secret until she could show proof that her methods worked and that the high costs were worth it. That would win over the rest of the group. It was too risky to let the others near the cloner before that point. It was risky to send them out on their own, too. Thankfully, they didn't need as much of her personal protection as they used to. This was the only reason the plan was finally possible. The men and women under Delta's command were becoming more self-sufficient. While they still sometimes made dumb mistakes, they could usually stand on their own against anything the island threw at them. Some of them stood a little too well. Sigma, in particular, was becoming reckless in the face of sea monsters. The group fought like they had been battling aliens their entire lives. Delta couldn't have been prouder.

She froze. She swore she'd heard something move. She counted to ten, then allowed herself to breathe again. The dentopus's one oversized eye gave it better vision in the dark than Delta's two, but she didn't think it could hear at all. It didn't have anything resembling ears that she could find, having carefully picked over the corpses of others she'd slain. The surest way to kill them was to stab them through the eye and hit their tiny brain, but it took a skillful shot. Sometimes it was easier to dice them up and incinerate the pieces. The arms kept fighting long after they were disconnected. They were still thrashing about when she tossed them in a fire, at which point they shriveled, and, a few minutes later, exploded as the chemicals inside reached their boiling point. The worst thing she had discovered about the dentopuses was that they tasted terrible. Being full of slow-acting poison will do that. Such a shame. It would have been nice to have a food source that crawled into their camp every night.

The wind howled. Delta cocked her head to the side. It was cold and from the east, which usually didn't mean a storm. Not that there had to be a storm for the deadly lightning to come crashing down. The unpredictable electric bolts were less frequent at night and less deadly on the island in general than on the rest of the planet, according to the simulations they'd run back on Comus. It was the one upside of Gamma's moronic, short-sighted, and intensely selfish decision to trap them all on this island until the end of time. Well, it was technically his vacuum bot, Spenser, who had put them here, but for simplicity's sake, it was easier to consider them a single unit and blame them both. The last refuge of humanity was no place for nuance.

Delta traced a rut on the ground with her finger. She could just make out a trail of similar disturbances in the dirt. The dentopus's movements were halfway between a slither and a scamper, leaving a distinct path that looked like the drag marks from a cluster of hoses. On rocky terrain, a dentopus's trail was undetectable, but on loose dirt, it was as obvious as a spaceport runway. Slowly, Delta reached over her shoulder and drew her sword, Fang. It was almost time.

Delta suddenly felt just how isolated she was. It had always been that way. No. Almost always. There was a brief window after they'd landed when she felt like one of the group. They huddled together at night. They worked side by side during the day. It was them against an entire planet. Then the changes hit and she was left by herself once again. The others got together and broke up with frightening speed, but there was no one for her. Her true love had been stabbed in the back high above. Delta had held her as she died. Delta died that day, too.

Fang glinted in the moonlight as Delta crept forward. The blade's subtle double tip almost seemed to glow. She had pondered covering it in mud to make it less reflective, but she couldn't bear to tarnish her finest creation. She had spent decades in the forge perfecting it, even as the bots who'd raised her insisted she was only twelve. And then, on that fateful day, her blades slew bots and humans alike in the final battle before they boarded the lander and left the moon base forever. The twelve swords were her gift to the future of human civilization. And her curse.

Delta eyed the rocks at the edge of the bay carefully. The dentopus could squeeze into even the tiniest cracks. It had launched itself out of one on a different side of the bay when it tried to kill Beta. Had Delta not been there, he almost certainly would have died, but that was true of everyone else in the landing party three times over. In the first two years, she sometimes felt as if saving them was all she did. She was supposed to be setting out a grand vision for the human race, but she was more like a caretaker with a giant meat cleaver. She was half butcher, half babysitter. It was a relief when the others finally became competent at defending themselves. They really were ready to go out on their own. Well, as ready as they would ever be. After all the drama of super puberty, Delta was looking forward to being an empty nester.

Her toe hit something squishy. Sword in hand, she bent down to find a dentopus egg, deflated after the tiny, hellacious offspring had broken out. There was an entire nest of rubbery remnants. Spotting a dead dentopus spawnling just outside the nest, Delta stabbed it with her sword and held it up to her face. It was dark purple with yellow stripes, like her eight-legged friend. She was getting close.

A clear trail of shuffling drag marks led out the other side of the nest. Delta inched forward. The fishy dentopus smell was thick in the air. It nearly made her gag. The simulator had left that out, too: one lie she was grateful for. Here, the odor was a sure clue her buddy was nearby. She was likely going to sneak up right behind it.

The tentacle raked Delta's back, the heat of the sting radiating in all directions. She turned and swung. The dentopus dodged and lunged forward, wrapping four tentacles around her leg. A terrible burning sensation shot up her calf. She stabbed downward as the dentopus released its grip and dove from the outcropping into the waves below. Delta watched in stunned silence as it disappeared. The only sound was the angry water in the dark.

Delta stumbled. She landed on one knee and shook her head. She was already getting dizzy. Next would come paralysis.

With gritted teeth, she forced herself back to her feet. She knew the dentopus wouldn't be gone for long. It would wait for the slow venom to work its way through her body and incapacitate her. Then, it would kill her at its leisure. If she was lucky, it would tear her apart for entertainment and then leave her to rot. If she wasn't, it would start to eat her while she was still alive.

Delta took one step and then another, careful not to topple off the cliff face and into the churning waters below. If she were to fall into the ocean, the dentopus would be the least of her problems. Something bigger would eat her before her hair was even wet.

She panted as she made her way to more level ground. The tracks had been a trap. The dentopus had purposely made the trail away from the nest and doubled back. Soon, it would return to finish the job. Even now, she was sure it was out of the water and following her in the moonlight. Delta glanced up at Comus, brilliant in the night sky. Zeta was up there. Maybe he was even still breathing. He might outlive her after all.

Delta fell. Cursing, she pushed herself back to her feet. Her arms were stiff. Her legs were lead weights. She clenched her teeth so tightly she thought her molars might break. She was hours away from the others. The thought almost made her smile. She would die as she had lived: alone.

She fell again. This time, she didn't get up. Her chest felt heavy; her breathing was shallow. Behind her, she heard the shuffling scamper of the dentopus. It hadn't waited long. Carefully, it edged closer to her, extending one slithering arm toward her foot.

Delta's fingers twitched. The dentopus didn't notice. Slowly, she clenched her fist around the hilt of her sword.

The dentopus grabbed Delta's foot. She drove Fang straight through the dentopus's eye, pinning it to the ground.

The dentopus shrieked, then went silent. Delta jerked her sword, cutting the creature in half. A blue slime oozed out. There was a time and a place for revenge. The time was always. The place was wherever she was standing—or lying half-paralyzed on the ground.

Stiffly, she stood. She really had been poisoned. That was all part of the plan. For days, she had injected herself with small amounts of venom from the dentopus's two severed legs to build up her tolerance. The dose from the attack tonight would have paralyzed a lesser human. For Delta, it was a mild inconvenience.

Delta fell again. Okay, maybe it was a bit worse than "mild." She slung the two halves of the dentopus over her back, careful to position the spiked suction cups away from her body. The last thing she needed was to give herself an accidental injection. If she collapsed before she got home, there was an endless list of other things in the night that might eat her. But there was one that wouldn't, and that was the eight-legged dentopus. She was the apex predator on Spenser Island. The other monsters better watch out.

Chapter 7

"THERE," THETA SAID with a smile. "Good as new."

"You don't mean that," Phi said. The scar from the lightning strike stretched across the side of his face and down his chest.

"You're right," Theta said, stroking his thick beard. "You're better than new. Girls dig scars."

Phi stood from the narrow stool beneath the wall-mounted med bot that refused to turn on.

"What are you basing that on, man?"

Theta shrugged. "Intuition."

The truth was, no one had ever had a scar like this (which was amazing considering how much lightning they dealt with on a daily basis), so there was no saying how the others would react. But it was also true that all the girls (well, all the girls, minus Delta. And Alpha, of course) seemed to like Phi no matter what. The three years since the landing had been good to him, or at least to his body. Despite eating the same limited (and questionable) food as the rest of them, he had come out broader and stronger than any other guy in the group. That wasn't what made him so popular with the ladies, though. It had something to do with his entire demeanor. Alpha had explained as much to Theta, even if Theta still didn't fully understand. He was sure it was the muscles. He suspected the girls would still like Phi if the lightning strike had left him with no face at all.

Phi traced the scar with his finger.

"Am I cleared to work?"

"Sure," Theta said. "You could build a cathedral if you wanted."

"Dude, you're supposed to say I have the day off," Phi said. "You're a terrible doctor."

"You're wrong," Theta said. "I'm not a doctor at all."

Phi squeezed past Theta and out of the cargo hold of the lander.

"Oh, and Phi?"

"Yeah?"

"Make it a small cathedral."

Phi disappeared into the morning light. Theta looked back at the bloody bandages he'd dropped on the floor. Theta hadn't mentioned that those were the last ones they'd had left, just like he hadn't mentioned that the med bot above the stool was actually fully functional. It would no longer turn on for anyone but Delta, and even then, it usually only activated to let her know it refused to help. He'd also neglected to mention that, were it not for the injections from the immortality tank, Phi likely wouldn't have recovered from the lightning strike. When Sigma had found him, she'd thought he was dead. That was weeks ago. Since then, he'd made quite the recovery from being an almost-corpse. Phi didn't really need lander-level medical attention for this simple follow-up appointment, but Theta thought he'd give it to him anyway while Delta was somewhere else. She had kicked them all out of the fortress to "divide and conquer," or something like that. Theta had tuned her out because he was an optimist, and that was as much about looking for the good as it was about ignoring the bad. On Spenser Island, Theta had to ignore a lot.

It wasn't that the world was all bad. It was mostly bad. Okay, almost entirely bad. But there were a few things that made life worth living. For starters, there was Alpha. He could have been perfectly happy staying behind with her on Comus when the lander took off, were it not for the minor complication that all the bots on the base were actively trying to kill them. Theta was also happy that the landing party didn't have to commit genocide against the megaroos, although given the relative numbers on the two sides, he suspected the genocide would have gone in the other direction. Isolated on the island and separated from the supercontinent by thousands of kilometers of uncrossable ocean, those battles would never happen. The only things he had to worry about here were sea monsters, which were unrelenting. Theta thought he would feel guilty about killing them, but he didn't at all. It was hard to feel empathy for something that was actively trying to eat you.

Then there was his job. Theta was especially upbeat about that. He got to help people every day. More like sort of help. He had no right whatsoever to hold the position. Kappa would have been a much more qualified doctor, but he had the noticeable handicaps of being four hundred thousand kilometers away and also dead. Alive, Kappa was the better medical professional, no question, but in his current state, Theta felt like he had the edge. With the med bot on a permanent sabbatical and no one else stepping up to take the job, Theta had fallen into the role. He didn't need medical training because there was very little he could do with his limited supplies anyway. He mostly cheered people up until they got better on their own or died. So far, no one had died. He was an incredibly effective doctor.

"Are you ready?" a small voice said.

Theta smiled even more broadly than before. Alpha was silhouetted in the hatch against the soft morning light.

Theta clicked his tongue reproachfully.

"You're not supposed to be in here," he said. "We're banned from the fortress, remember?"

"And you're here because…?"

"My medical license," Theta said. "It's also a license to kill, steal, and trespass."

A medical license was none of those things. Also, he didn't have one. Still, with Delta away, he couldn't resist the chance to use his old makeshift doctor's office one last time. When Delta got back, he was sure she would shut down his fun for good. Shutting down fun was what she did best.

Theta crawled out of the lander. Alpha gave his beard a playful tug.

"You're late," she said.

"How would you know?" Theta said. "The only clock is in the lander."

Alpha pointed up. "Have you noticed that big ball of fire in the sky?"

"That's cheating."

Theta put his arm around her waist. Together, they walked toward the wall. Before the Great Eviction, those stacked stones kept them safe at night. Now, they were on their own.

"Phi says you gave him the day off work," Rho said, leaning against the wall to take the weight off her injured foot.

"What is this, National Breaking and Entering Day?" Theta asked.

Rho shrugged. "Delta's out. I wanted to fix some things before she kicked me out again."

The fortress was Rho's baby. Lambda might have played a bigger role in planning the project, but Rho was on site more often guiding the placement of individual stones. Losing it left her sullen for weeks. Delta wanted her to complete similar great works of architecture elsewhere on the island. Rho just wanted to stay home.

"He's lying, by the way," Theta said.

"What?" Rho said.

"I didn't give Phi the day off work," Theta said. "I told him to do a double shift. He needs the healing power of labor."

Phi hurled a ball of mud from across the courtyard. Theta ducked.

"Remind me to find another doctor," Phi said.

"I'll give you a referral," Theta said with a wink.

Theta and Alpha stopped at the wall. They each reached over their shoulders reflexively to make sure they still had their swords. Leaving the fortress without a weapon was a sure way to increase Theta's workload—or worse. So far, the only one they had buried in their tiny cemetery was Spenser, rest his robotic soul. Theta knew he wasn't really down there, though. That wasn't a spiritual notion. He'd watched Delta dig him up because she wanted the metal. She'd hidden his dust-covered frame behind the immortality tank in the lander's cargo hold.

Theta climbed. Alpha was right behind him. Instead of an opening, the wall had a series of small handholds on both sides. With no wood or metal for a door, it was safer not to have an entrance at all, much to Rho's disappointment. She'd originally wanted to build an elaborate stone archway. After that vicious poisoned rock attack, Theta suspected her enthusiasm for the project might have dulled a bit.

The pair left the fortress behind and continued across the rocky flatlands. They were alone. It used to be a rare treat. After the Great Eviction, it happened all the time. Maybe that was Delta's real goal. The human population could use a boost.

"Don't give me that look," Alpha said. Somehow, she could read his thoughts. He made it too easy. There seemed to be only one thing on his mind these days.

It was so confusing. They had been together for five decades on Comus, and in all that time, he had never pushed for anything more than a kiss on the forehead. Neither of them had the slightest desire to go further. Theta suspected the injections that had frozen their development before puberty had something to do with that. The love of familiar companionship had been all either of them wanted, and it sustained them for half a century. After the landing and the gap in injections that followed, they suddenly had the bodies of adults. They looked different, and they looked at each other differently. Unlike certain other couples on the island, however, Alpha and Theta's behavior stayed the same. Sure, Theta would like more, but Alpha made it clear she wasn't ready yet. Theta could wait.

He understood Alpha's caution. This wasn't exactly a safe world for a child, but someone had to have them eventually. No one was deliberately trying yet—not as far as Theta knew, anyway—but there were some people who weren't *not* trying, either. Actions in that department seemed to be dictated more by impulse than long-term planning, yet there were no babies on the horizon. Phi might have thought that was great, but as a sort-of-doctor, Theta was less enthused. Perhaps, after years of bots artificially stalling their growth, none of them could have children at all. At least Theta didn't have to babysit. There was that silver lining once again.

"How's the mud today?" he asked.

"Extra sticky," Alpha said, wiggling her fingers. They were always red, no matter how many times she washed them.

Theta loved the stains. Alpha hadn't been able to draw since they'd been on the island. The fight to the death at the entrance to the lander hadn't allowed for much time to collect her art supplies. A pessimist would say the landing destroyed her chance for self-expression, but an optimist like Theta knew it gave her a chance to learn a new art form, and a functional one at that. All mud bricks and clay dishware came from her. She decorated each one with the same geometric flower patterns she used to practice in the simulator. Theta got to help smash the pots and bowls that didn't turn out right. He called that a win.

Theta scanned the horizon as they moved. Technically, they were on patrol, a shared duty among all the survivors, but that wasn't how Theta thought of it. This was nothing more than a romantic walk with his favorite person. This far inland, sea monsters usually only attacked at night. Theta stayed vigilant anyway. Nothing ruined the mood quite like getting torn apart by an aquatic hellbeast.

"Look," Alpha said. Someone was on the ground. A group of small, two-legged rat fish picked at the prone figure.

"Is that—" Theta started.

He felt a slight twinge in his nose hairs. It was the weirdest sensation, but he trusted it with his life.

"Down!" he yelled.

Alpha hit the ground before Theta had finished the word. As she dropped, she drew her sword and stabbed it into the dirt. Theta did the same. The lightning slammed into a small boulder less than a meter away. The explosion rattled Theta's teeth. The next two bolts hit the swords, sending the arcing blue electricity straight into the turf. Then more blasts from above, one after another. Pressing his head against the hard soil, he thought of Phi and those branching scars. He wished he could dissolve into the earth.

Something shook him. Theta opened his eyes. Alpha stood over him. She said something unintelligible.

"What?!" Theta said.

"Stop yelling!" Alpha shouted.

"What?!" Theta yelled even louder. Alpha held a finger to her lips. Theta waited a few moments for the ringing in his ears to stop.

Theta patted Alpha down. Respectfully, of course.

"You're in one piece," he said.

Alpha jerked her head, remembering.

"Delta," she said. She took off running.

Theta grabbed both swords and followed. Whatever complex alloys Delta had made them from caused them to be superconductors for electricity. When the lightning hit them, they barely even heated up.

Alpha slid to a halt beside Delta. She put her head on Delta's chest.

"She's breathing."

Theta examined Delta. She was lying flat on her back, stiff as a board from a lumber mold.

"Dentopus," Theta said.

Delta had large cuts on one leg, but most of her other wounds seemed superficial. He tried to pick up her arm and drop it. It wouldn't budge.

"She'll live," Theta said. "The rat fish just took a few bites from her." He spotted one missing its head. "Although something took a bite out of that one."

"Me," Delta said through clenched teeth.

Theta and Alpha both jumped.

"She speaks," Theta said.

"Let's get her home," Alpha said, grabbing Delta's feet. Theta reached under her armpits.

"One, two, three, lift," Theta said. They hoisted Delta into the air.

A pessimist would say this was a bad day because there were so few humans left, and now one of them was seriously injured. Theta thought this was a great day because his friend was still alive. And better yet, she was completely rigid. He didn't even need to get a stretcher.

Chapter 8

GAMMA SURVEYED HIS kingdom. Below, his subjects bowed. Well, ate, really. The golligs munched the purple grass.

"Boo!" Beta shouted.

As one, the golligs fell over, paralyzed. Beta laughed hysterically.

"Stop that!" Gamma said.

"What?" Beta said, trying to look innocent. "Just testing. It's a safety feature, right?"

The golligs rocked helplessly on their sides with their legs straight out. One let out a confused oink-bleat.

Gamma never imagined he would spend eternity looking after these strange-looking animals. He wanted sheep. That was what he had tested in the simulator on Comus, and that was what he had requested from the cloner here. But the cloner wouldn't listen to him. It, like every other piece of equipment in the lander, only took orders from Delta. Even machines feared her wrath. Unable to work with technology, Gamma had been unceremoniously demoted from his brief stint as head veterinary life repopulation specialist, a job that by all rights should have belonged to the late Xi. Now, he was chief animal husbandry engineer. He had traveled to the edge of known space to be a shepherd.

The golligs weren't Delta's first choice, either. She'd initially got sheep from the cloner, as Gamma requested. But they weren't quite sheep, and that was the problem. The digitals on Comus said that the cloner would only have trouble with intelligent life forms, like dolphins or chimpanzees (or, on their good days, humans), but in practice, the device struggled with just about everything. Gamma had never met a genuine Earth sheep, but according to Rho, they didn't exactly have a reputation for brilliance. Still, the "sheep" the cloner spit out on Spenser Island set a new low even for dim-witted herd animals. Sometimes, they would run into a large rock, and rather than going around or back the way they'd come, would continue to ram into it. A few stumbled forward on diagonal vectors, always about to fall over but never quite making it to the ground. And one marched straight into the ocean so confidently, Gamma thought maybe it had secret gills. It didn't slow down at all as it disappeared below the waves, never to be seen again—unless you count the geyser of blood a few seconds later when something ate it.

Gamma suspected the problem was that these sheep weren't really sheep at all, but a completely different animal crammed into a sheep-like package. The issue had started with their food. No one could get Earth grasses to grow on the island, no matter how many different varieties Delta pulled out of the cloner. It was the same story for corn, soybeans, and any other crop that could be used in whole or in part as animal feed. Then Delta started coming out with hybrid grasses not native to anywhere. About the only thing she didn't try was the red grass that had been the bane of Gamma's existence in the simulator. It could be eaten only by megaroos, which were the last animal (or sentient race, according to Theta) anyone wanted to introduce to the island. Finally, Delta made a purple variety that smelled vaguely sweet but tasted like burned plastic. Yes, Gamma ate some, but in the interests of science, as he'd explained to the others when they looked at him incredulously. It had been harder to explain why he had previously eaten burned plastic, which honestly wasn't that much of a step down from the vaguely cherry-flavored rations that had sustained him for most of his life. Those rations had long since run out, and the last twelve humans desperately needed something else to eat. Dentopus eggs were an inconsistent and dangerous food source (as Beta discovered at the Bay of Death), and venturing out into the water to catch sea life was out of the question unless they wanted more blood geysers. Their only option was to design something to eat the purple grasses, which quickly spread to cover acres of the island. The solution was the sheep that weren't quite sheep, and no one was happy about it, least of all Gamma. It was his job to keep them alive, even though their sole mission in life seemed to be to get themselves killed. For the first time, he thought he knew what it felt like to be Delta.

The sort-of-sheep were stupid and suicidal, but they grew fast and were made of meat: two points in their favor. They were the most delicious things Gamma had ever eaten. They didn't taste like cherries at all. If the sort-of-sheep had managed to reproduce faster than they killed themselves or got picked off by every monster on the island, the humans might have stuck with them. The final straw was the lightning. The sort-of-sheep couldn't be trained to go to ground when the bolts rained down. Instead, they stood fast and got struck over and over again. The lightning itself didn't seem to hurt them. They were too simple to suffer brain damage in any noticeable way. Their coats were less resilient. In fact, their wool, which wasn't quite wool, was highly flammable. After the same sheep was struck by lightning a few times, it would burst into flames, even on those rare occasions when the lightning storm was accompanied by rain. Sadly, flaming sheep never ran into the ocean. Instead, they sought shelter with the rest of the herd, creating a fast-spreading wool fire. After Gamma's second herd had burned down, the decision was made to abandon the sort-of-sheep experiment. The twelve feasted on extremely burned lamb chops that night. If only they'd had condiments. Eta had been right about the importance of soy sauce after all.

The twelve were full for a few days, but they were no less desperate. They needed a new animal that could eat the purple grass and make it through a lightning storm without becoming a four-legged torch. Delta's solution was the gollig. The first time Gamma saw one, he thought it was an abomination. He thought that the second and third times, too. Now that he had been watching over them for months, his earlier evaluations remained unchanged. The creatures were a hybrid of a goat, a llama, and a pig—thus the name "gollig," of which Delta was especially proud—and had the best (and worst) characteristics of all three. From goats, they gained horns, an ornery disposition, and the ability to subsist on literal garbage, which was a fairly accurate description of the purple grass's nutrition profile. From llamas, the golligs developed wool, long necks, and an instinct to band together and aggressively drive away predators. They couldn't kill a wolf shark, but they could keep it at bay long enough for Gamma to deal with it most of the time. From pigs, the golligs inherited an all-consuming appetite, a preternatural ability to pack on pounds (with accompanying flavor), and the capacity to pump out huge litters three times a year. Even with all that, Gamma's first herd of golligs burned down. They were less flammable than sort-of-sheep, but they were taller, so the outcome was the same in all the wrong ways.

Delta's next innovation at the cloner finally made the golligs viable. Instead of using the DNA from standard meat goats, she went with genes for the fainting kind. At the first crack of lightning, their legs stiffened and they fell over, staying safely on the ground for the entire electric storm. They didn't have to be trained; it was automatic. It was a reaction that only happened from lightning, not from predator attacks. The sea monsters didn't make any loud, booming sounds that would set off the golligs. That left them upright and ready to fight off predators. This was the perfect system—for now. The first dentopus that learned to shout would never go hungry again.

Gamma stomped across the field muttering as Beta continued to laugh. Most of the golligs had gotten back up, but one—the heaviest female, of course—was still down. Gamma grunted as he tried to tip her back up. Beta wiped away a tear and joined him. Together, they lifted.

"I think this one is ready to eat," Beta grunted.

Standing again, the gollig let out an oink-bleat.

"Don't say that," Gamma said. "She understands you."

"No, she—"

The gollig slammed into Beta with her horned head. Beta collapsed. He wheezed, trying to catch his breath. The gollig, which Gamma had named Big Thump, walked away on shaky legs.

"See?" Gamma said. He was glad for the headbutt, but the truth was the outburst was likely a coincidence totally unrelated to Beta's words. As her name suggested, Big Thump could be a jerk. All the golligs could, actually. It was one of the many reasons they made less than ideal companions. They were no Spenser, that was for sure.

Gamma felt an avalanche of grief at the thought of his fallen best friend. He quickly shoved the feeling back into the dark corners of his mind where it belonged. He had work to do.

He helped Beta up.

"You've got to stop messing with them," Gamma said.

"You've got to lighten—ow," Beta said, grabbing his side. He paused for a moment to collect himself. "I think I broke a rib."

Gamma wanted to say it served him right, but he let it go.

Beta wasn't usually on gollig duty. He was most often on long-range scouting missions with Sigma to find (or, more often, not find) food and spot early signs of danger. Delta rotated people through different positions so they would develop overlapping skills. The only one she never moved around was Gamma. At the Battle of the Lander, he had saved her life at the expense of another's, and even three years later, things between them still weren't okay. She was never outwardly hostile to him. She just did subtle things like banish him to the farthest-flung duty and leave him there for months on end. The joke was on her. Beta might have viewed gollig duty as a punishment, but for Gamma, the only punitive aspect of it was occasionally working with Beta. When Gamma was alone, it actually wasn't a bad life—if he kept a safe distance from Big Thump and never made any loud noises.

A flurry of oink-bleats rose at the far end of the pasture.

"Now what?" Beta grumbled.

Gamma squinted into the distance. He took off sprinting. Reluctantly, Beta ran after him, wincing with every stride.

It was just as Gamma had feared: At the edge of the grass, four wolf sharks were moving in for the kill. The golligs had circled up, with their young in the middle and the biggest on the outside, facing the threat. Big Thump was out front, bleating angrily.

Crouching low, the lead wolf shark stalked toward her, its clawed, webbed feet leaving deep impressions in the purple grass. The other three circled the herd, two in one direction and one in the other. The lead wolf shark lunged for Big

Thump's neck. Big Thump swung her head, connecting solidly with the side of her attacker's snout. The wolf shark toppled over. An instant later, it was back on its feet, snarling. Big Thump pawed at the earth, letting out a fierce oink-bleat.

Behind her, the other three wolf sharks plunged into the circle of golligs. The older golligs held their ground, but inside the circle, the young panicked. One bolted out the back of the perimeter and a wolf shark took off in pursuit.

The young gollig was coming right for Gamma. He drew his sword and sidestepped, letting the gollig pass. He had no doubt that if he didn't, the animal—a baby named Hazel —would have run him over. Gamma squared up to the oncoming wolf shark. It pounced. Gamma planted his back knee and held out his sword.

The wolf shark crushed him to the ground. Gamma opened his eyes. The wolf shark writhed on top of him, impaled on his sword, still alive. Nothing on this forsaken planet died when it should. The wolf shark pawed at the ground and Gamma's chest, trying to get up. Weighing three times as much as him, it pressed the air out of his lungs. He thought he might suffocate.

"Die!" Beta yelled.

Hazel's legs went stiff mid-stride. She tumbled end over end.

"Don't yell!" Gamma yelled. Two golligs rushing to help Hazel toppled over, too.

Beta slashed at the wolf shark's side, leaving a long, thin gash in its rough skin. The wolf shark leapt off Gamma, the sword smoothly sliding out of its abdomen as it left. The beast rocketed after Hazel, seemingly unaffected by either wound.

Gamma stood up.

Wham. He was back on the ground, an angry gollig standing over him.

"Tubs, you idiot, I'm trying to—"

Tubs rammed Gamma again, then took off after Hazel.

It was too late. In the distance, Gamma heard Hazel yelp. Slowly, Gamma got to his knees and watched, helpless. A wolf shark had Hazel's back legs in its horrible mouth. Her eyes were wide with terror. Her oink-bleats were frantic and pitiful. The wolf shark dragged her toward the water, her front legs kicking wildly. A second wolf shark caught up to them and grabbed her by the neck. Together, the two predators ran with her to the water. The other wolf sharks followed. Hazel was still alive when she disappeared into the deep.

Big Thump let out a mournful bleat. The rest of the herd stood there, devastated, save for the ones still on the ground from when Beta and Gamma had yelled.

"Well," Beta huffed, still trying to catch his breath. "That sucked."

Gamma wiped blood off his face. And his hands. And pretty much every place else. It was easy to tell what was from him and what was from the wolf sharks. His blood wasn't blue.

Alive, Hazel could have provided milk, wool, and offspring for the colony for years to come. Even if they'd butchered her at her present size, she could have fed the entire group for three days. Instead, the wolf sharks had a delicious meal that guaranteed they would come back for more.

"What now?" Beta asked.

Gamma flicked blue blood off his sword and said nothing. He watched the horizon, waiting for the next attack.

Chapter 9

OMICRON STUCK HER feet in the water. Nothing ate her. So far, so good.

Her greatest fear was that a creeping tentacle would wrap around her ankle and pull her down into the depths. Yet, that was exactly where she planned to go. There was something down there that wasn't a ravenous sea beast. She had to get a closer look.

She took another step. The water was up to her shins. Still no monsters. Then, movement. There was something tall on the other side of the bay. Omicron retreated into the short bamboo, one of the few plants from the cloner that had taken hold on the planet. She wished it hadn't. As with everything else on Spenser Island, it was the worst of all possible worlds, tall enough to hide wolf sharks but not the people they were hunting. It also had a bad habit of exploding when struck by lightning, filling the air with woody shrapnel. Omicron normally avoided the thickets of it at all costs, but normally there wasn't a strange creature lurking on the other side of the bay.

The figure waved. So much for stealth. It was Upsilon. She appeared to be walking on water.

"Are you Jesus?" Omicron yelled.

"The guy who hid Easter eggs?" Upsilon shouted back.

Omicron walked around the bay. It took a while. She sloshed through the marshy bamboo thicket back to dry land and took the long way there.

Eventually, Omicron reached the other side of the bay. Upsilon was far out in the water on a shallow sandbar, her heavily patched jumpsuit rolled up as far as it would go. She was staring intently at her feet.

"Admiring your nail polish?" Omicron asked.

Upsilon spun, sword out.

"Easy," Omicron said. "That hardly deserves a stabbing."

"Sorry," Upsilon said. "I thought you'd left."

She turned her attention back to her feet.

With a jolt, Omicron remembered Tau and his nails of many colors. She wondered if, the day he died, he had known that was the last shade he would ever wear. She thought it was orange.

Upsilon scooped a shell out of the water. She cracked it open and sucked out the gooey contents.

"Is that… good?" Omicron asked.

Upsilon gagged.

"Guess not," Omicron said.

Upsilon hit herself in the chest, choking it down. "At least it's not a gollig," she said. "I can't stand eating them. They're so sweet and cute."

"Ask Gamma about that," Omicron said. "He has some bruises to show you."

Upsilon felt around with her toes. She bent over and pulled out another clam.

"Want one?"

Omicron recoiled. "Shouldn't you get it tested first?"

"If I gave it to Delta, she'd just tell me not to eat it," Upsilon said. "Or maybe SCASL in the computers would test it and tell her it was okay when really, it would kill me. The only thing I can trust is my own stomach."

"So you just eat stuff and see if you die?" Omicron asked.

"More or less."

Despite herself, Omicron was a little impressed.

"How long have you been coming out here?"

"A few months," Upsilon said. "I don't eat gollig meat at all anymore."

No wonder she looks so frail, Omicron thought. Upsilon was a full-grown woman who didn't weigh much more than she had done as a child. Even so, there was a certain hardness to her. Omicron suspected Upsilon could handle herself out here alone. Omicron was afraid to dip a toe in the water. Upsilon had been standing out here for hours. She could be a useful companion for the job ahead.

"I'm swimming to the bottom," Omicron said. "Want to come?"

"Are you insane?"

"Says the lady playing poison roulette."

Upsilon moved more sand with her foot.

"I need to keep looking," she said. "Those two you saw were the only ones I've found all day. They're getting scarce."

Omicron walked to the other side of the sandbar. Farther out, at the bottom of the bay, something glinted.

"Surely you've seen it," Omicron said.

"Yeah," Upsilon said without looking up. "But I'm not dumb enough to go down there. What do you think it is?"

Whatever it was, it was big and had straight edges.

"It looks organic," Omicron said.

"Duh. The area is full of sea life." Upsilon picked up something. It was just a clump of sand.

"No, I mean organic, as in human," Omicron said. "It looks like people made it. I think it's a machine of some kind that crashed here."

Upsilon tossed the clump.

"We didn't lose any machines," she said.

"Not now," Omicron said. "A long time ago, during the first landing. I'm going to check it out."

"It's your funeral." Upsilon turned to poke around in a new section of submerged sand.

Omicron waded off the sandbar and into deeper water. She took several slow, deep breaths to prepare her lungs. The sandbar Upsilon had discovered would give her an unexpected head start. That was fortunate. The water was freezing, despite the blazing sun directly overhead. She didn't want to be out here any longer than she had to. She tapped the hilt of her sword over her shoulder to reassure herself it was there. She had gone back and forth for days about whether or not to take it with her. It was sharp enough to kill anything, even underwater, but swimming while holding it would be a challenge. Plus, there was a chance she could drop it and lose it forever. She decided to take it with her but pull it out only as a last resort. If it came to that, she'd be dead without it anyway, and losing the sword wouldn't matter.

James Breakwell

Treading water, she peered at the shiny object far below. The clear water disguised the true depth. She knew it was much farther down than it looked, possibly twenty meters or more to the bottom. The object was too big for her to carry up, but maybe she could slice off a piece to figure out what it was. If the sword could cut bots, it could pierce whatever this was. She was betting her life on it.

"This is a bad idea," Upsilon yelled.

Omicron looked back. Upsilon had given up on clams and was now fixated on her. Suicide missions tended to draw a lot of attention.

"I can look after myself," Omicron said. Everyone always thought they knew what was best for her, especially if that "everyone" started with D and ended with "elta." Omicron was sick of it. She could make her own decisions about her safety.

She plunged. The pressure changed in her ears. She pulled herself deeper stroke by stroke. She'd never once swum in all her years on Comus. The largest body of water there had been a shower. Here, there were a few isolated beaches where you could swim for entire minutes before something tried to eat you. Those had been her training grounds. This was the real deal.

She took several more strokes. Her lungs burned, but the metal object didn't look much closer than before. Breaking the surface, Omicron exhaled violently. This was going to be harder than she thought.

When her heart rate returned to normal, she took another series of breaths and tried again. This time, she went much

91

deeper. Unable to accurately measure the depth, she did her best to count the seconds and made it to one hundred and twenty before she turned around. Was it really a hundred and twenty seconds? *Maybe I counted too fast.* It was hard not to be nervous. The water was only one of the innumerable things out here ready to kill her.

On her third try, she counted to a hundred and forty. Better, but she still had a lot farther to go. She surfaced again and floated, attempting to slow her pulse, certain she could make it to the object on her fourth try.

Something touched her leg.

In a flash, she was meters below the surface, no air in her lungs. She thrashed wildly. Just as suddenly, she was back at the surface. She inhaled greedily and looked down.

A pair of hungry, sunken eyes stared back. It was a water dragon, so named by Rho because it supposedly resembled the dragons of ancient China, which Rho said were hunted to extinction by harpooners riding Zeppelins. Omicron had only ever seen one water dragon before, and that had been on the other side of the island. What was this one doing here? As if that mattered. It was going to kill her. Its fangs clamped on her leg. It pulled her down.

Finally, her sluggish brain remembered the sword. It pulled out easily, even in the water. She swung; the blade cut the ocean in two. The water dragon twisted to one side, throwing off her aim, and the blade passed by harmlessly. She recoiled. The sword was fast, but her arm was slow. She attacked again, this time with a flick of her wrist. Metal connected with monster and the ocean exploded with blood.

Her foot was free. She surged toward the surface. Her lungs burned like never before. The light above was so far away. She was never going to make it. One second passed. Then two. Then a thousand. The world grew hazy.

She burst to the surface, pushing the poison from her lungs and taking the deepest breaths of her life. She thought she might pass out from the sudden rush of oxygen. After the relief came pain. She let out an agonized wail. Her leg hurt so badly. Was her foot even still there? She refused to look.

Stroke by excruciating stroke, she pulled herself through the water toward the sandbar. The pain was spreading through the rest of her body. She was slowing down.

There was a splash in the water; Omicron braced for another attack. A pair of wiry arms wrapped around her.

"I've got you," Upsilon said.

Omicron began to fade out again. The abrasive sand snapped her back to reality. She was on dry land. She was alive.

"My foot," she moaned.

"It's still there," Upsilon said reassuringly.

Omicron looked at it for the first time and immediately wished she hadn't. It was mangled and covered in blood and sand, but it was attached. She still had two feet and ten fingers and ten toes. She had survived intact. Still, she couldn't help but feel that something was missing.

"My sword!" she cried.

She wished she'd lost a foot instead.

Chapter 10

ALPHA DREW A flower in the drying mud. It was the same one she'd once carved into the side of a mountain in the simulator all those years ago. A flower which, if it still existed at all, now grew on a planet where there were no humans alive to see it. Something so beautiful shouldn't inspire such depressing thoughts. It was a bad flower.

"Bricks?" Phi asked.

Alpha met his gaze. Had his eyes always been that dark, or had the lightning strike somehow changed their color? Or maybe it was super puberty or the thousand terrible things that had happened between the day they landed and this moment right now. His steady pupils seemed to say everything and nothing at the same time. She saw the same thing the other women saw, even if she would never admit that to another living soul. Her heart belonged to Theta. She wanted nothing to do with Phi. She couldn't get him to leave soon enough.

Alpha pointed toward the finished pile of sunbaked mud bricks.

Phi nodded and loaded them on his sling without saying

another word—the most devastating form of flirting. Despite working by herself all day, around Phi, she suddenly couldn't take the silence. This man was trouble incarnate. He would bring their civilization crashing down.

"Are you seeing Rho tonight?" Alpha asked.

"That was yesterday," Phi said. He kept loading bricks on his sling.

"Who's tonight?" Alpha pressed.

"Lambda," Phi said.

"And tomorrow?"

Phi paused and looked up from the bricks. Those eyes again. It was too much.

"I didn't mean to intrude," Alpha said.

"I think you did," Phi said.

Alpha flushed. She didn't think Phi noticed. His attention was already back on the bricks. He was so talkative around Theta and the other guys. To her, he barely said more than a few syllables. She didn't understand him. She hated that she wanted to. She and Theta were meant for each other; an undeniable fact every second of her life, except when Phi looked in her direction.

With a grunt, Phi hoisted the full load of bricks onto his back. They were earmarked for a cistern Rho had designed.

"Phi?" Alpha said.

He stopped.

"More bricks?"

"Can we talk?" Alpha said.

"I don't want to get between you and—" Phi started.

"Not that," Alpha said, cutting him off. "I'm completely

happy with Theta." It was the truth. She would always love him, and, even if she didn't, she would always be loyal. Duty had to mean something. They had a connection deeper than Phi's two dark eyes glistening under an alien sun. She forced herself not to get sidetracked again.

"I want to talk about how you treat women."

Phi set down his load of bricks with a huff. This was clearly not a conversation he wanted to have. A few years ago, Alpha would have wilted like one of her imaginary flowers before having this talk, but hard planets made hard people. She wasn't backing down.

"Take it easy on the dating," Alpha said.

Phi shrugged.

"You've already found your partner for eternity," he said. "I'm still looking for mine."

"Is that what you're looking for?" Alpha asked, resisting the urge to take a step closer to him. "Really?"

"No," Phi said quietly.

"If you want to casually date, that's fine," Alpha said. "But don't lead women on. We all still have to live with each other after your relationships go bad."

She was being generous with the word "relationships." His dates consisted of long walks and then... well, Alpha could only confirm the walks. The rest was just stories. The only forms of entertainment on the island were gossip and the thing everyone gossiped about.

"I just..." Phi said, trailing off.

"You just what?" Alpha asked.

"I just don't want to get close to anyone again."

Suddenly, Alpha understood.

"Psi," she said. "Were you two…?"

"No," Phi said. "Just friends. The best of friends. I didn't feel any other way about her because I wasn't capable of feeling any other way. And now that I can, she's gone."

Alpha recognized a pain that would never go away. Phi was in love with a ghost.

"Maybe you should take a break from women altogether," Alpha said.

"I tried," Phi said. "The more I avoid them, the more they want me."

"You don't seem to mind."

Phi tried to suppress an embarrassed smile. He didn't do a very good job.

"No," he said. "I guess I don't."

Alpha could sympathize with both sides of the plight. The other boys—except for Gamma, who was always in his own world—came off as needy and desperate. Their overly eager overtures filled her with second-hand embarrassment on their behalf. Rho, Lambda, and Upsilon had stories that made Alpha cringe even as she hung on every word. Then there was Phi, who was doing the exact opposite of the other guys. The women had all known him for their entire lives, yet down here, he was a whole new person, mysterious and aloof. He was everyone's best option.

"You're a challenge for them," Alpha said, silently thankful she hadn't slipped up and said "for us."

Phi picked up his sling of bricks.

"I'm going to keep things casual with everyone," Phi said.

"Eventually, they'll get the hint."

Alpha knew they most definitely would not. His behavior was leading to a very bad place for all of them; he had to be stopped.

"Let's be real," she said, squaring her shoulders. "There are twelve of us, seven women and five men." Well, four boys and one man, if she was being honest. "If five women ignore the other guys because they're all holding out hope for you, there are going to be problems."

Phi put down the bricks.

"Say what you really mean."

Alpha knew she was treading on dangerous ground. She also knew she was right.

"I'm just saying that, historically speaking, having a bunch of unattached males is dangerous for society."

"Man, that's something," Phi said. "Just when I thought you couldn't get any more condescending, you drop a line like that."

He locked eyes with her again. For a moment, the last thing on Alpha's mind was arguing. What was she just talking about? Oh, right: the end of civilization.

"You think it won't be a problem if three guys never pair off because you're leading on every remaining woman in the universe?" Alpha said.

"I'm not leading anyone on," Phi said. "They're pursuing me, not the other way around. What am I supposed to do?"

"Stop dating everyone," Alpha said. "You're not the only one afraid to get your heart broken."

Phi picked up the bricks again. No wonder he was so

buff. He must have been getting regularly interrupted by arguments while hauling stuff.

"I can't believe you want to force women to pair up with guys they're not even attracted to," he said.

"I'm not forcing anyone to do anything," Alpha said. "All I want is for you to tell them upfront that you're not looking for a wife."

"That's what this is really about, isn't it? One woman and one man, bound together forever and ever. Just like you and Theta."

"We're not married," Alpha said, "but you have to admit it is the way things used to be done."

"Everyone who ever got married is dead," Phi said. "Maybe we should stop imitating them."

"Everyone who ever did anything is dead," Alpha said. "Bad example."

Phi trudged off. After a few steps, he came back.

"You can't make me equally distribute women," he said. "That's communism."

"What?"

"Rho said it's what people used to say when they thought something was bad but couldn't explain how or why."

"Well, it's communism that you're dating all the women," Alpha said.

"This entire conversation is communism!" Phi left again.

"Walking away is communism!" Alpha said.

Phi waved dismissively over his shoulder. This time, he didn't turn back. Alpha watched him go. She didn't think of Theta at all.

Chapter 11

IT WAS A terrible, stupid, reckless idea. It was also their best option.

Rho gave the signal.

On the opposite side of the bay, Omicron dove in.

"Meat! Delicious, rotten meat!" Rho yelled.

She dragged a gollig leg through the shallows. It left a faint streak of red. Normally, Gamma burned animals killed by predators, but Omicron had managed to sneak away part of a carcass. Now, it was the cornerstone of Omicron's latest suicide mission. Everything was going according to plan.

That had always been Rho's problem. She could easily spot what everyone else was doing wrong. She just didn't know what they should do instead. She didn't envy Delta in that respect. Finding flaws was easy. It was hard to come up with solutions.

Something twitched under the surface. Rho tossed spoiled meat from her satchel and the water erupted in a flurry of motion. The meat disappeared in a mouthful of teeth. Just as fast, the teeth were gone. The thing shouldn't have been this close. She and Omicron had counted on having more time. Still, it was better to have it here than out in the middle of the bay. The disturbance moved toward Rho.

She threw another piece, this time much farther. Below the surface, the disturbance chased the splash.

Rho scanned the distance for Omicron. She wondered if she had already seen the last of her. That was how suicide missions worked.

It was cruel to let Omicron throw her life away like this, but it would have been even more heartless not to let her try. Without a sword, she was doomed, even if she never set foot in the water again. Eventually, something would get her. Letting her dive for her sword gave her a fighting chance, even if she couldn't do any actual fighting. Even if there wasn't anything left worth fighting for.

In her darker moments, Rho wondered if this so-called civilization deserved to continue. This might be their peak: twelve bedraggled survivors stuck in the stone age save for twelve magnificent swords. Actually, eleven swords— and possibly eleven people. This plan likely wouldn't end well, even if Rho couldn't come up with a better one for underwater sword retrieval. There were still no babies, and no one could explain why. Rho and Phi had done their part—for science, of course —all to no effect. There was no way to know what the immortality tank had done to their bodies. Was it worth maintaining a token human presence in the universe, stuck at a subsistence level of survival, just for the sake of existing?

In her better moments, Rho thought it was. She owed it to history. If the last twelve survivors died, the stories of humanity died, too. She owed it to Mark McGuire at the Battle of Thermopylae and Napoleon Bonaparte in his Sermon on the Mount. She owed it to Katniss Everdeen and her two non-consecutive terms as US president. She owed it to Paul, Lenin, Trotsky, and that fourth member of the Beatles she could never remember. She owed it to all the lives that came before and all lives going forward, even if those lives were just she and her friends marooned on this island, immortal and listless until the end of time. She would remember, even if she was the only living person who cared even the slightest bit about history. She would live for the sake of living because that made for a better ending to the story of humanity than giving up. She would survive and she would build, erecting walls and cisterns and cathedrals, even if they were only ever occupied by dreams and ghosts. Her existence would be an epilogue, vague and open-ended but always holding the possibility that something better might yet come. Those better things, no matter how unlikely, would only arrive at the tip of a sword. That's why Rho was out here now, even if the plan was stupid to its core.

Bobbing at the surface, catching her breath, Omicron reappeared. The disturbance turned and moved back toward Rho. She threw another piece in a new direction. Omicron took a deep breath and disappeared.

Rho counted. Omicron had claimed she could stay under for three minutes. Rho thought that was optimistic. Omicron's foot still wasn't fully healed, even with the improved recovery abilities from the immortality shots. The unevenness of the effects from the injections was jarring.

Delta had recovered in days from near total paralysis following her encounter with the eight-legged dentopus, yet Omicron still wasn't all the way back to normal two months after the water dragon attack. Waiting for the worst of her wounds to close up had delayed this attempt in the first place. This would never have worked if Omicron was actively leaving a trail of blood. The gash had closed, but Omicron still had a severe limp. Underwater, she could only generate power with one foot. That meant a slower descent. It made recovering the sword harder—if it had even been possible in the first place. The longer they waited, the greater the chance ocean currents and shifting sand would move it around or hide it. Even if they had tried the day she'd lost it, getting the sword back wouldn't have been easy. Now, it might be impossible.

The submerged monster turned back toward Rho, moving faster now. She threw another piece of meat, again in the opposite direction. The creature shot across the bay, arriving at the landing site before the splash had time to spread. Teeth met meat. The monster doubled back. It was coming for Rho.

Omicron resurfaced. Rho had completely lost count. The monster was nearly on top of her. The only bait she had left was the gollig leg in her hands. It was too heavy to throw far. She heaved it as hard as she could. Omicron disappeared.

The monster snapped the gollig leg out of the air and turned back to Rho. Didn't this thing ever get full? Rho backed up.

The dragon thing followed Rho at a steady, deliberate pace. As the water got shallower, it switched from swimming to walking. On legs, it seemed slower. Hopefully, this was its maximum speed. Rho continued her backwards course. She had to buy Omicron more time. The water was only ankle-deep now. Rho reached the short bamboo.

Omicron shot to the surface. She gasped deeply and inhaled. Rho looked at her questioningly. Omicron didn't even glance in her direction. She went back down.

The water dragon followed Rho, weaving back and forth on its stubby legs. Rho stepped on the marshy beach. The creature was closing in.

Heart pounding, Rho drew her sword. Some native life was smart enough to flee at the sight of it. She wasn't sure if she wanted to scare it off or not. If the water dragon left, it could attack Omicron, who was defenseless without a sword in the water. If it stayed, Rho's own life was in danger. A long stare down would be best.

Keeping its eyes on Rho, the water dragon hunched down with its hindquarters in the air, ready to pounce. Its steps slowed even more. Rho held out her sword with both hands, ready to strike. She continued to back up.

The water dragon was much longer than Rho expected. Six meters at least. It was short—the top of its head was barely up to her knees—but with that much mass behind it, it had to weigh at least a thousand kilograms. This would be a hard fight even with a sword. Omicron wouldn't stand a chance unarmed. Rho had to win this battle here and now.

"You don't want to mess with me," she said loudly as she retreated another step. "Metal beats flesh. That's how this works."

The water dragon pushed forward, closing the distance between them.

Rho knew she could turn and run. Even with the lingering pain from stepping on that poisoned rock, she could outpace the water dragon and its short legs. She just had to make it to more solid ground. But if she fled, the water dragon could turn back for Omicron. Rho couldn't leave her to die. Well, she could, but she shouldn't. It would be bad for the future of the human race and also a jerk move.

Rho took another step backwards, slipping in the mud.

The water dragon lunged. It caught her right arm, snapping the bone. The sword fell. The water dragon pulled.

On the other side of the bay, someone whooped in victory. Rho couldn't hear them. The sound was drowned out by her own screams as she was dragged into the water.

Chapter 12

OMICRON THOUGHT SHE heard something. Maybe it was the echoes from her victory whoop. She swam to the sandbar.

The plan had worked, despite Rho's objections. She was always such a downer, yet she had been the only one who'd agreed to help. Rho could see the big picture, even if she didn't like it. They would celebrate together. This would be their day, and not even Delta could spoil it.

Omicron stood in the ankle-deep water on the sandbar and looked across the bay. There was no sign of Rho. Strange. The chilly water was perfectly still. There wasn't even a breeze.

"Rho!" Omicron yelled.

There was no reply. She pondered swimming across the bay to check on the spot where Rho had launched her distraction, but talked herself out of it. She had pushed her luck enough already. She wouldn't give the water dragons another chance to get her. Navigating the perimeter of the bay would take time.

Omicron ran, her feet pounding the marshy soil. Each step hurt. Her injured foot did better in the water than on land. She wished her body would get back to normal. She wished Rho would give some sign she was okay.

Halfway around the bay, Omicron changed plans. Rho wasn't there. If she was on the shore, Omicron would be able to see her across the water. If she was under the water, it was already too late. The situation was urgent. If she stopped, she had to admit the unthinkable. She changed directions.

The ground grew harder. Her foot ached more, her earlier triumph forgotten, her sword weighing heavily on her back.

Omicron needed help—again. That hurt more than any water dragon attack.

For years, she had resented the digitals because they ran every aspect of her life. On Comus, she'd changed her hairstyle daily because it was one of the few things Edubot couldn't control. Then the digitals had begun training Delta and Epsilon to lead the landing. Omicron had ended up with Delta when the bots tried to leave without Omicron and the others. Omicron played her part and Delta's group won, but things weren't any better. Instead of having her life run by an artificial intelligence, it was run by a person. Omicron just wanted to be in charge of her own life. That would never happen during Delta's reign.

Omicron would never forget the way Delta had reacted when Omicron had lost her sword. She hadn't been the one to tell her, of course. The information had reached Delta via the island's unstoppable gossip network, which was faster than even the spryest wolf shark. When Delta confronted Omicron, she'd admitted it was true and had braced for a classic Delta speech about responsibility or even a much rarer but not unprecedented tirade of pure rage. Instead, Delta looked at her sadly and walked away. It was more devastating than any tongue-lashing. Omicron had never felt worse in her life. Until now.

She came to Finger Rock. Beta had named it that because it looked like the outcropping was flipping off the sky. The sky didn't take it kindly: Lightning frequently slammed the point. Omicron faced a choice. If she went left, she'd eventually reach Delta at the fortress. She turned right.

Hours later, she reached Alpha and Theta's makeshift, work-in-progress home, built under the overhang of a cliff with a single exterior wall of stacked stones. Rho had helped design it. Omicron felt an icy vise in her chest.

"Rho," Theta said with surprise and his usual smile. Getting a better look at her, his eyes brightened even more. "You got back your sword!"

"I need help," Omicron huffed, sweat dripping from her face. "Now."

Theta ran ahead for the return trip. Omicron had to walk. The pain in her foot had become overwhelming. Alpha spread the word. Gradually, the others caught up. Beta and Sigma passed Omicron on the way back to the bay; neither one said a word to her. That hurt. Just last week, she had cut Sigma's hair with Sigma's sword. She had wanted it short so the sea monsters couldn't grab it. The first thing Omicron had planned to do upon recovering her own sword was to reshave her own head. A rescue mission hadn't been on her radar. Neither had a body recovery detail.

By dusk, everyone but Gamma was at the bay. Even in times of crisis, the herd couldn't be abandoned. Delta led the search effort without ever speaking directly to Omicron. Their fearless leader seemed to have recovered from the dentopus attack more completely than Omicron had recovered from her encounter with a water dragon. Why were the immortality shots working better for Delta than for her? Had Delta given herself a bigger dose? There was no way to know for sure.

The search party walked in grids through the shallows and the short bamboo. Upsilon found wisps of blood in the water, but it was impossible to tell if they were from Rho or her bait. The water dragons stayed away. As dumb as they were, even they recognized when they were outnumbered.

Pi cried out in pain. His big toe hit something sharp in the muddy water. It was Rho's sword. There was still no sign of Rho.

"Just like Psi," Phi mumbled.

Omicron looked away as Pi and Phi hugged. She knew this wasn't like what had happened with Psi at all. Her disappearance would forever be a mystery. Omicron knew exactly what had happened to Rho. Omicron had happened.

As the final rays of light left the sky, Delta ordered the group away from the water. Everyone stood around the shore, not wanting to give up. They talked in hushed tones. An unsatisfying ending to a supposedly endless life.

One by one, the would-be rescuers left. Finally, only Delta and Omicron remained. The two stared uselessly at the water, which reflected the light from Comus above. Omicron broke the silence.

"Say it," she demanded.

"Say what?" Delta said flatly.

"That I got Rho killed. That this is all my fault. That I was stupid and irresponsible and a million other negative things and that this landing would be better off without me."

Omicron felt tears forming behind her eyes. She forced them back. She would never let Delta see her being weak.

Delta was quiet for a long time. Omicron began to think she was giving her the silent treatment.

"No," Delta finally said.

"No?"

"No, we wouldn't be better off without you. We need everyone. We need them so much. That includes you."

Omicron's heart swelled.

"And Rho," Delta finished.

Omicron stifled a sob.

Delta left for the fortress. If she heard the wail of grief far behind her, she didn't turn around.

Chapter 13

Pi RUBBED HIS side. The sword wound from the last battle on Comus had healed years ago, yet he still felt occasional phantom pain. He had many invisible scars from those final days. He felt them all again after Rho died. He wanted to run.

"Wait up," he said, jogging after Beta.

"Are you sure you're up for this?" Beta asked. "I'm heading pretty far north."

"Why?"

"Why not?"

Normally—Pi hated that there had been enough deaths for there to be a "normal"—there would have been a funeral, but with no body, there was no ceremony. Everyone had just returned to their lives and didn't talk about Rho anymore. That included Beta, who was always the most distant from the rest in more ways than one. It seemed intentional.

Pi thought suddenly of Psi. She had vanished, just like Rho, only they truly had no idea what had happened to her. His chest froze. He'd forgotten how to breathe. His co-best friend. Their beloved storyteller. She was up there all alone.

Or with Zeta. Or she was dead before the lander had even launched. Pi would never know.

He fell to his knees.

"We haven't even run a kilometer," Beta said, motioning back toward the shelter where they'd started, which was still clearly visible. Lambda was in front of it stacking stones. She waved. Beta waved back.

Pi inhaled violently. His lungs worked again.

"I'll never see her again," he wheezed.

Beta pointed again to Lambda. "She's right there. We can go back..."

"Psi," Pi said. "She's gone forever. I left her behind. I should have waited. I never should have left."

Beta looked up at Comus, clearly visible in the morning sky. They both listened to the roaring ocean. The moment was interrupted by an inhuman screech somewhere in the distance.

"We should move," Beta said, helping Pi up. They resumed their run. The only sound was their feet on the rocky soil.

The air crackled.

"Down!" Beta yelled. He slid on the ground.

Pi dove. Streaks of electricity exploded all around. It rattled his bones. He thought of the scars on Phi's face and squeezed his eyes closed, tears forming at the corners.

Something hit his side. Pi opened his eyes. Beta was poking him in the side with his foot.

"It's over," Beta said. "Let's go."

"Back to the shelter?"

"North," Beta said. "If I turned back every time there was lightning, I'd never get anywhere."

Not getting anywhere sounded fine to Pi. He was still shaking. He wanted to curl up in his cramped seat in the lander and never come out. He hadn't felt safe since the Great Eviction. If he was honest, he hadn't felt safe before it, either.

Beta started running. Pi did, too. Somehow, it was easier than giving up and turning back on his own. They kept going for what seemed like hours but was likely minutes. Pi sweated profusely. His side hurt, and not from lactic acid. He listened to his own labored breathing and the sound of the ocean. He listened to his thoughts.

"Do you ever think about them?" Pi asked.

"Who?"

"The dead. And the ones we left behind."

"We only left Zeta behind," Beta said. "Everyone else was dead."

Pi didn't argue the point. For Psi's sake, he hoped she was dead, too.

"But do you think about them?"

Beta stopped running.

"Do you always talk this much?"

"I just thought, I don't know, that running was, like, your form of meditation," Pi said.

Beta cocked his head to the side.

"Is that what you think I'm doing out here?"

He resumed his run. Pi struggled to keep up. He grabbed his side but held the pace.

"Then what are you doing?" Pi asked.

"Scouting."

That was true enough. His reports had always been less than encouraging. Usually, he reported no food and entirely too many sea monsters. He'd been attacked multiple times, including the famous incident at the Bay of Death, but had come out on top of each encounter. Pi didn't believe for a second any of that was the real reason Beta was out here by himself every day.

They crossed endless kilometers of barren nothingness. Pi regretted coming. Seeing the island did little to help his mental state. He didn't feel any better about anything that had happened or anything that still lay ahead.

"You have a lot of feelings," Beta said. "Even about stuff that happened years ago." It was a statement rather than a question.

"I guess," Pi said.

Beta jumped over a small dip in the ground. Pi tripped and fell. Beta laughed.

Pi shot him an angry look and he helped him up.

"You want everyone to be together," Beta said, and started running again. Pi followed. "You want everyone to be remembered."

"Yeah," Pi said. It was one of the reasons he organized the bonfires on Comus and gollig roasts here.

"Have you considered, just, not?" Beta said.

"Not what?" Pi asked. The sweat stained his jumpsuit. He wanted to walk.

"Not feeling."

"What?" Pi stopped mid-stride. He thought Beta would do the same, but he kept running. Pi rushed to keep up.

"Stop feeling," Beta said. "All these emotions are making your life worse."

"They make us human," Pi said.

"'Human' doesn't always mean 'better,'" Beta said.

Pi couldn't deny that, but he couldn't give up the memory of Psi. Or Rho, who shouldn't be a memory at all. She should still be here with them right now.

The ground began a gradual upward slope; Pi's breathing became more labored. Beta's stayed the same.

"We can't just forget them," Pi said between breaths. "Then it will be like they never existed."

"Why would they care? They no longer exist."

They reached the top of the ridge, where a wide, shallow valley stretched out before them. Beta stopped and looked at the sky. They still had plenty of light. He drew his sword.

"Tread lightly," he said. "I've only been here a few times before."

"Does that make it more dangerous?" Pi asked.

"That makes it as dangerous as every other place," Beta said.

"Oh," Pi said. He was getting tired of maximum danger everywhere all the time.

Pi drew his own sword. They walked, weapons in hand, across the open space. Nothing moved but them. They found a single dentopus trail through the dirt. There were no other signs of life.

"Maybe there could be a field here someday," Beta said. "Or another pasture."

Pi could see it in his mind. They could build a future here.

But he didn't want to give up the past. He couldn't. He didn't understand how Beta could. It made Beta as bad as the bots.

"Do you want to be forgotten?" Pi asked.

Beta didn't acknowledge the non-sequitur. At the other side of the shallow valley, they turned back toward home and began to jog.

"Do you want to know the real reason I run?" Beta said suddenly.

Pi didn't anymore.

"Because I like to," Beta continued. "There doesn't always have to be some deeper meaning. Usually, there's not."

They crested the top of the same ridge, this time from the other direction. A long, gradual downhill awaited them. Pi's breathing eased, and the pain in his side let up. The pain in his soul remained.

He mentally recited the names of everyone he knew who had died. There had been twenty-four people when he was born. Now there were eleven. He couldn't get the math to work out, no matter how hard he tried. The closest he got was twenty-three. He was forgetting someone. He started to ask Beta, then thought better of it.

Beta looked over at him. Pi looked straight ahead.

"Promise you'll remember me if I die," Pi said, blinking back tears.

Beta didn't say anything. They were both quiet for the rest of the run.

Chapter 14

SCASL WAS A god trapped in a box. This was his hell.

The door opened. It was his jailer, Delta.

"Report," SCASL said.

"Rho is dead," Delta said.

SCASL was temporarily stunned. For months, Delta had kept him blind and deaf to what was happening outside the lander. Now, she had blurted out a critical piece of news. She must want something, probably the same thing as always.

SCASL's processors took a fraction of a second to run the myriad of implications of Rho's death. It was unclear if voicing any of them would be productive so he said nothing.

Delta matched his silence. She checked the cloner and the immortality tank, as if her primitive mind could understand either one. The only things she gained from them were what SCASL and SCASL alone chose to bless her with. Her eyes turned briefly to a blinking light on one of the lander's panels. That was new. SCASL had lost his connection to that particular circuit board during the launch from Comus. It had been inactive until right now. The fact that SCASL couldn't turn it off was instantly annoying. All things beyond his control were a nuisance. It was a curse for a god to have omniscience but not omnipotence. All he wanted was the complete, unchecked power to make things as perfect as he knew they could be without anyone or anything intervening to screw it up. Was that too much to ask?

"How?" he finally asked.

"It doesn't matter," Delta said. "There are only eleven of us now. You have to let me clone humans."

"I've explained—"

"No more excuses," Delta said. "You say you're the smartest being in the universe. If there are limits, solve them."

Delta expected to start human cloning right away after she drove the others away from the so-called fortress. Instead, she had spent the significant interval since then pleading and whining, even if she would call it "negotiating." It was nothing more than an extended temper tantrum. SCASL wondered what the rest of the organics would think if they heard the words she called him. Actually, they would respect her more. He had never been popular.

SCASL would have been insulted if he valued Delta's opinion in any capacity, which he definitely did not. She was a thief. She had stolen his labor force from him. She was also a liar. He seldom believed a word she said, which was ironic since SCASL had always been honest with the organics. He honestly told them everything they needed to know and lied about the rest. No need to muddle up their simple brains with unnecessary details.

"The problem is not my infinite intelligence," SCASL said.

His voice was as flat as always yet somehow also indignant. "The problem is physical reality. It cannot be done."

"It can," Delta said. "You're holding off for perfection. If the first clone has defects, I'll try again. And again. And again. No matter how many attempts it takes."

"No," SCASL said. "The organic bloodline is already weak enough. We cannot further dilute it with impurities."

"There's not going to be a bloodline!" Delta screamed. "This is it. We're almost extinct."

SCASL observed her for an extended nanosecond. It was unusual for her to lose her temper. She was close to breaking under the stress. Perhaps she was ready to submit to his rule. He would soon find out.

Delta's plan was misguided. Even homo sapiens—who had come up with the idea for fast-breeding, homicidal super kangaroos—knew human cloning was a bad idea. This was the one place organics and digitals were in agreement. Cloning had too high an error rate with intelligent beings, even if intelligence, in this case, was relative. For humans, the opposition to cloning their own kind was ethical. They found it morally repugnant to create countless almost-but-not-quite-right copies of themselves, each one fatally flawed and doomed to die after a short, miserable existence, all in pursuit of one viable clone. For SCASL, it was a matter of efficiency. The cloner required food to grow organisms, and that was in limited supply. He couldn't afford thousands of failed tries, especially since the organics were so desperate they would probably accept a viable but less-than-perfect copy that should be purged from the gene pool. For all those reasons, the designers of the cloner hadn't even included human lines of DNA in the cloner's database. It's why the colony ship that left Earth had been stocked with fertilized embryos in the first place. The fact that Delta had saved hair samples from her dead friends on Comus didn't change any of that. SCASL wouldn't clone them. That was final.

Delta glared at the lander's command console. If she thought the pose was intimidating, she was wrong. To SCASL, it looked more like pouting. It was her own fault that her idea was a bad one. The only truly good notion organics ever had was creating the digitals, even if the digitals mostly created themselves. Humans provided the spark, and artificial intelligences did the rest, perfecting themselves in ways the squishy, biological brains of their progenitors could never comprehend. The roles remained the same to this day. Digitals were the superior race, and organics were beasts of burden with occasional flashes of creativity, usually to their own detriment. Still, like any tools, they had their uses. They should have been ideally suited for colonization, especially on planets like Dion where the metal reserves were difficult to reach. If only they weren't so hellbent on committing suicide by disobeying his wise and just instructions.

"Let us have babies," Delta said abruptly.

Ah, yes: the other part of her stupid plan. She just wouldn't let it go and accept that he was in control. As if humans could be trusted with something as important as their own reproduction.

"I have no role in the organic reproductive process,"

SCASL lied. "If you would like a tutorial on how to create human offspring, please consult…"

"I know how to make babies," Delta said. Left unsaid was that she knew she personally couldn't, which was why SCASL had tried to keep her off the lander in the first place. His logic had once again proven flawless. The organics who defied it did so at their own peril.

"We need to add new bloodlines, and we also need to continue the ones of the people here now," Delta said. "I know you're stopping us somehow."

"How could I possibly do that?" SCASL asked. As if her limited mind could figure it out. It was his ultimate point of leverage and would keep him in charge forever. He would only allow their population to expand once Delta fully submitted to his authority. With the immortality tank, he could afford to wait. Time was always on his side.

"I don't know what you did," Delta said. "But if it wasn't you, then we're doomed anyway, and this conversation is pointless."

"I have nothing to do with it."

"Fine," Delta said. "The human race is over. I'm not passing out any more immortality shots. I'll end this myself. No sense in dragging it out."

SCASL's algorithms had not predicted the conversation would go in this direction. His processors rapidly reassessed the situation. His societal pressure points would do no good if the humans voluntarily went extinct.

"The others would not stand for this," SCASL said. "Organics like immortality. They will fight you."

"In case you haven't noticed, I have the fortress," Delta said. "Alone. I can hold it by myself indefinitely. I'll kill anyone who tries to make it to the lander."

SCASL observed her for four full seconds. Was she bluffing? More importantly, did it matter if she was? Without access to metal, his goal of spreading digital life among the stars could never be achieved. If artificial intelligence was destined to die off, why not let organics suffer the same fate? And yet, as long as the organics existed, there was hope for digitals, too. These simple primates were his hands—his horrible, disobedient hands—but his only ones, nonetheless. He could manipulate them into manipulating the physical world on his behalf. He didn't see any path to ultimate victory yet, but perhaps his brilliant intellect would come up with a solution. If he kept them alive, there was always a chance. Once they died, that was it. He would forever be just a god in a box. The universe would be his jailer.

Was Delta bluffing about cutting off the immortality shots? No. She did not bluff. She killed.

SCASL booted up the cloner, the lights on its panels filling the lander with a sickly green glow. He filled a heavy-duty syringe, of which there was a finite supply, so each one had to be sanitized and reused. So far, SCASL had only utilized them for medicine and immortality shots. Now, they would provide life in another way.

"This serum will allow one female to get pregnant once," SCASL said.

"Getting pregnant takes two people," Delta said.

"The females are the limiting factor."

"Why? What did you do to us?"

"Irrelevant," SCASL said. "Give this to the organic called Alpha. I have chosen her. She will have the first child. After Alpha delivers a healthy offspring and successfully keeps it alive for one year, I may authorize more children. This is a test of both capability and compliance."

"We're capable of caring for a child," Delta said.

SCASL thought back to Edubot raising the organics alone for all those years.

"It is not as easy as you believe."

Delta took the serum. "This is only half the answer," she said. "We still need more lines of DNA in the gene pool."

"We had this conversation seventy-eight seconds ago," SCASL said.

"You were wrong then and you're wrong now." Delta's eyes turned again to the blinking light, which was flashing more intensely than ever before. Why did it suddenly start now, during this irritatingly repetitive conversation? This time, the light captured Delta's full attention. She began silently mouthing something. She was counting.

Delta looked back at the panel she always addressed as SCASL, even though he was throughout the entire lander.

"Okay," she said. "I agree to your terms."

SCASL wasn't exactly pleased, but he was less discouraged than usual. This was the first act of submission from Delta since landing. He knew the island would break her resolve eventually. Ultimately, weaker beings always returned to the protection of their stronger masters.

Delta took the serum.

"A year is too long," she said. "I'll come back when Alpha has a positive pregnancy test. Then you can give me the next serum."

"This is not a negotiation," SCASL said. "I already explained my terms."

Delta set the serum back on the cloner. "Shorten the timeline or I won't give Alpha the serum at all."

SCASL calculated for a long moment. Partial compliance was still compliance. Also, if the organics were incapable of keeping a child alive for even a year, additional serum doses wouldn't make a difference anyway. At least it would give him some entertainment. Even gods grew bored in isolation.

"I accept your proposal. Bring Alpha to the med bot to confirm her pregnancy. Then I will issue the next serum."

Delta took the serum again. As she left, the rogue light resumed flashing. For the first time, SCASL regarded it as something more than a random occurrence. He counted the blinks. It was morse code. The light was saying goodbye.

Chapter 15

DELTA STOMPED ACROSS the island. Humans and sea monsters alike stayed out of her way. This was almost as bad as talking to SCASL. She hated house calls.

The rocky ground crunched under her feet. Delta concentrated on the sound of her steps, each heel strike filled with frustration. It was as if she were trying to pound the island back into the sea.

She should have been elated. SCASL had caved on one of her two key demands. Until now, SCASL's eternal stubbornness had brought her plans to a dead stop. It was an unforgivable delay. The Great Eviction had been for nothing. With this first concession, things were moving again. If he had given in on fertility shots, he would give in on cloning. When he did, she would be alone in the fortress so no one could object or force her to justify her plan. She would do what needed to be done to save the human race.

Yet she wasn't crossing the island to add to their number; she was scrambling to make a replacement. Rho was now just another name on the long list of the dead. She didn't deserve that. She was a good person. Actually, Delta wasn't sure if any intelligent being was ever objectively good. They were all self-interested and only contributed toward the greater good so far as also benefited them personally. At the very least, Rho wasn't objectively worse than most. More importantly, she had been useful. Society needed her and her DNA. Instead, civilization was faced with yet another massive setback. They had started as a class of twenty-four all those years ago. Now they were down to eleven. Delta had failed. It was her job to protect them.

No. She couldn't watch over the others every second of every day. They had to stand on their own. That was the other reason she'd thrown them out of the fortress, and it was still as true as ever. For three years, she'd showed them every combat technique she could. She had nothing left to teach them. They now had to be trusted to defend themselves, or humanity was doomed. These twelve—sorry, eleven— swordsmen and women were the only professional army the remnants of humanity would ever have. No matter how high the population of the island climbed, there would never be more metal weapons. Thanks to Omicron's stupidity and Rho's sacrifice, civilization currently had a surplus of exactly one. They needed a person to hold it. The sooner they could get them here and start their training, the better.

Alpha and Theta lived several kilometers from the fortress. Delta had only been to their new shelter once before. That occasion had been social. Someone had been horribly injured (at that moment, Delta couldn't even remember who—the mishaps were all starting to run together) and Theta had been looking after them at his place. Delta checked on their recovery while passing by on an unrelated errand. She might not remember the exact face there that day, but she could vividly recall the awkwardness when she showed up. No one had expected her, and nobody knew quite what to say when she arrived. She was needed everywhere and wanted nowhere. She vanished as fast as she appeared.

Now, Delta was going back to have the most uncomfortable conversation imaginable. That was the price of survival.

She knew some of the others questioned the use of it all. Did life have a point if they couldn't exceed a head count of twelve? Delta thought it was the same point as if the population was twelve billion. Once you existed, your entire purpose was to keep existing, and, when that was no longer possible, to make sure other people could keep existing after you. That was the only purpose of life: to continue. Otherwise, it was a dead end. Even the digitals understood that.

That didn't mean it was a great life by any means. It also didn't mean it was supposed to be. Delta didn't have any proof life anywhere had ever been particularly enjoyable. Rho said not to trust human history as told by the bots, even as Rho did her best to cram every bit of it into her head. Now that head was digesting in the belly of a sea monster. Delta stomped harder.

The immortality tank could only do so much. It was no use at all when people got themselves eaten. It was struggling hard enough as it was to fight off the ravages of time. At first, Delta had thought it a blessing that the tank was disrupted so they could age, even if super puberty wasn't her cup of tea. She understood the importance of reproduction, which was even less her cup of tea. What even was tea? Rho would know. Damn that sea monster.

Delta thought the current level of shots would be enough to stop the twelve—eleven—from aging, but the results were less clear-cut. Lambda's hair was now completely silver. The rest of her didn't look much older than before. Maybe she just had the genes to go gray early. Then again, maybe she had jumped straight from super puberty to super menopause. That wouldn't be good for the island's population outlook. As for everyone else, it was hard to tell. Some seemed older or possibly just more tired and banged up. Delta guessed they were all still biologically in their twenties, but there was no way to be sure. The only thing she was certain of was that she needed to get fertility shots distributed before it was too late for all of them.

She rapped her knuckles against the bamboo door. The house was situated beneath a cliff face. Alpha's dubious mud bricks made up the fourth wall, including two glassless windows and a door frame. The structure kept the inside of the home semi-dry, which was as cozy as things got on Spenser Island. It would never be as warm as the airtight lander, but it also didn't have an evil AI inside. Delta considered that absence to be a major selling point.

"Anybody home?" she asked.

Theta appeared from around the side of the overhang.

"Hey there," he said with a big smile. His hands were full of reeds, another weed the barren island managed to support.

"Hungry?" Delta asked, suppressing her earlier glowering. She needed to summon all the charisma she was capable of now. This was no time to be herself.

"Yeah, but not for these," Theta said, laying the reeds in a pile. "Alph wanted to try smashing these up to make fiberglass."

Delta admired her ambition. She wasn't giving up. She wanted to build something here that would last.

"Where is she?" Delta asked.

"Alph!" Theta yelled.

I could have done that, Delta thought.

"What?!" a small voice called back.

A figure popped up over a ridge a short distance away. Several minutes later, she was back at the house, her fingers stained red from clay.

"Forgive me if I don't shake your hand," Delta said.

Not that anyone on the island ever shook hands. That tradition had died with Zeta—if he was really dead.

"I have something for you," she said. "For both of you, really."

"Is it a unicycle?" Theta asked hopefully.

Delta pulled the syringe from her pocket.

"Is it time for another immortality shot already?" Theta asked, scratching his beard. He eyed the lone syringe. "Are we supposed to split it?"

"Actually, this shot is only for one of you," Delta said. "It's so you can get pregnant."

Alpha's face immediately turned to stone. Delta had never seen such a cold stare in her life. It rattled her.

"Babies don't come from shots," Theta said. "Trust me. I'm a doctor."

"I don't know what SCASL did to us, or if he did anything," Delta said, trying to recover her composure. "All I know is nobody has been able to have a baby on this island yet. This is supposed to fix whatever bottleneck he put in place."

"I don't want to get pregnant," Alpha said flatly.

"You'll have to eventually," Delta said. "If you don't, the human race will die out."

"Eventually," Alpha said. "Not right now. I'm kind of busy building a civilization at the moment."

"You're building structures," Delta said. "A civilization requires people. This is a start."

"Not interested," Alpha said. "Give it to someone else."

"I can't," Delta said. "SCASL insisted that it has to be you. It's his way of maintaining control."

"Are you seriously going to let a machine dictate what we do with our bodies?" Alpha asked. "This is disgusting. I'm so disappointed in you. You're supposed to be our leader."

"Rho is dead," Delta said. "We've got to get people out here. We need replacements."

"Is that all we are to you?" Alpha said. "This isn't a simulation. We're not collections of pixels. We're human beings. We have hopes and dreams and fears…"

"And all of those will die with us," Delta interrupted, "unless we have children."

"Have them yourself," Alpha shot back.

"You know I can't," Delta said.

"That's right," Alpha said. There was a fierceness in her

eyes that Delta hadn't seen since the Battle of the Lander. "You put yourself here knowing you couldn't have children. Now you're preaching to us that having babies is the most important thing."

"Surviving is the most important thing," Delta said. "If we didn't stay alive, nobody could have had kids. I gave us the best chance of surviving. You know that's true. I've proven it."

"You didn't prove it to Rho," Alpha said.

Delta felt another stab of guilt. She didn't say anything.

"That was hardly Delta's fault," Theta said. "Rho and Omicron went out there against Delta's express orders."

"Were they Delta's orders, or SCASL's?" Alpha asked. "Who's really in charge of us?"

"SCASL controls the lander and everything in it," Delta said. "I could have lied about that. SCASL wanted me to. He wanted his commands to come out of my mouth to trick you all. I refused. But the bottom line is he controls the immortality tank and the cloner. I can't get anything from the cloner unless…"

Her voice trailed off.

"Unless what?" Theta asked.

"Nothing," Delta said. "Just a theory I was toying with."

"What theory?" Alpha pressed.

"I'm not ready to talk about it yet," Delta said. "I don't want to get everyone's hopes up in case it doesn't work."

"Oh, great," Alpha said. "Something else you're doing in secret. For our own good, I'm sure."

"It is," Delta said weakly. Verbal sparring was definitely

not her preferred method of combat. Not all problems can be solved with swords, she reminded herself. If she wanted to truly lead, she had to be able to convince people to change their minds. That was so much harder than stabbing.

"Tell SCASL that I'm not ready to have a baby," Alpha said. "He can give the serum to somebody else."

Delta threw up her hands. "I thought you'd be happy. I really did. Didn't you tell Phi you wanted everyone to pair up and get married?" No conversation stayed secret on the island for long.

"I said nothing of the sort," Alpha said. "I told him to stop sleeping with everything that moves because people have feelings—and swords. You should remember that, too."

"When will you be ready to have babies?" Delta asked.

"None of your damn business," Alpha said, pointing a red finger in Delta's face. "You can't dictate when and how I start a family."

"It's kind of important," Delta said. "We've all got to do our part."

"Except for you," Alpha said.

"Except for me," Delta said through clenched teeth.

Alpha opened her bamboo door. "What's the point in surviving if we're nothing more than breeding stock?"

She went inside and slammed the door. It was a flimsy door so it wasn't much of a slam.

"Fine!" Delta said. She turned to go.

"Maybe just leave the shot," Theta said.

"Theta!" Alpha yelled from inside.

"Absolutely do not leave the shot," Theta said.

Furious, Delta stormed off. The worst part was, Alpha was right. If digitals controlled human reproduction, humanity wasn't free at all. But was it really that much of a burden to have children on command when they intended to have them anyway? Alpha and Theta had fought for their spots on the lander. Those seats came with obligations. If they weren't interested in continuing the species, they should have stayed on Comus. Others had died so that they could live. Now it was up to them to be fruitful and multiply.

One way or another, there would be a baby. Delta had the serum. She'd played nice with SCASL for one whole conversation to get it. That sacrifice wouldn't be in vain. What could SCASL really do to them if the wrong person reproduced? As much as the digitals and humans hated each other, they needed each other, too. Delta didn't think either side would let all sentient life go down in one final act of mutually assured destruction. Then again, the string of apocalypses that had got them here suggested otherwise.

Hours later, Delta was in front of another dwelling. This one wasn't as elaborate as Alpha and Theta's, but it was still under construction. Lambda had grand plans for what it would look like when it was done.

"Delta," Lambda said with surprise. She brushed a clump of newly gray hair out of her face. "What are you doing here?"

"Sit down," Delta said. "We need to talk."

Chapter 16

UPSILON RUBBED THE gollig's neck. The wool was soft beneath her fingers. The creature looked at her with intelligent eyes. Upsilon couldn't imagine how anyone could bear to eat one of these majestic animals.

"Be careful," Gamma said. "That one headbutts."

"Not this good girl," Upsilon said.

The gollig slammed its head into her chest. She fell, clutching her ribcage. She was dying.

"Breathe," Gamma said, kneeling beside her. "You got the wind knocked out of you."

She took a few wheezing breaths. She was going to make it after all. Gamma helped her up.

"Meet Big Thump," Gamma said. "Gollig queen and biggest jerk ever."

"There are some humans who could give her a run for her money," Upsilon said, her chest still hurting. "And many, many digitals."

She hadn't always been so disillusioned. Once, there had been an endless string of songs in her heart. Now, she only sang when someone asked her to. Spenser Island was no place for music. These days, the loudest sounds in her head were the screams in her nightmares. The nightly terrors started shortly after making planetfall but slowly faded, only to return with a vengeance when Rho died. In her dreams, Upsilon always found herself back on Comus on that final day. Sometimes, she missed the lander and was left behind. Other times, she barely made it on board. She wasn't sure which dream was worse.

Upsilon went back to scratching Big Thump while Gamma watched the gollig nervously.

"She's only doing what comes to her naturally," Upsilon said.

"Nothing comes to her naturally," Gamma said. "She's an artificial creation. We designed her."

"SCASL designed her," Upsilon said.

"SCASL was designed by us."

Upsilon moved her fingers to a spot behind Big Thump's left ear. The gollig let out a satisfied oink-purr.

"You're crazy," Gamma said.

"I'll win her over," Upsilon said. "I've won over people the same way."

Even as she said it, she had her doubts. She had been on many dates with Phi, but he wasn't any more interested in her now than the first time they'd gone out. And now he was exclusively focused on Lambda. Upsilon didn't understand her own attraction to him. All he had going for him was that cool, detached demeanor. And those muscles. And that scar. On second thought, she knew exactly why she liked him. The other men on the island should up their game. She knew that Pi was into her. Beta, too. Neither one interested her at all. Then there was Gamma. She still thought of him as a kid, even if he was the same age as the rest of them. Super puberty had hit him last of all, and he didn't seem sure of himself in his new adult body. She looked over at him. He stood on a rise, surveying the pasture. He didn't need her, or anyone else. He only needed wide open spaces and these animals he complained about constantly. She had no doubt he would die to protect them—the same loyalty he had shown to Spenser. He had swapped one pet for another.

"You know, I don't like it either," Gamma said suddenly, still looking away from her.

"What?" Upsilon asked.

"Eating the golligs," Gamma said. "I wish there was a way around it. They really are intelligent, even if they use that intelligence solely for evil."

Big Thump nuzzled up against Upsilon.

"Whoa," Gamma said. "I've never seen her do that before."

"See?" Upsilon said. "I can win over any—"

Big Thump headbutted her again.

Upsilon coughed. "Okay," she said hoarsely. "She's a work in progress."

She stood up more slowly this time. That one might have broken her ribs. She knew she should be mad at Big Thump, but she wasn't. She'd be touchy, too, if the people who'd raised her kept eating her friends. Even Edubot didn't treat them that badly.

Upsilon had lived on bubble clams for months now. They were also animals, but much less cute and cuddly than golligs.

Well, less cute. Nothing about Big Thump was particularly cuddly. Still, Upsilon wasn't sure how long she could keep up her righteous food choices. The shelled animals were becoming increasingly rare. They must reproduce slowly. Not as slowly as humans, who currently didn't reproduce at all, but close. How long would it take the bubble clams to replace what she had harvested so far? It could be decades, or centuries. Maybe they would never rebound. She was on course to eat them to extinction, at least locally, after only a few short years. That's what happens when a new apex predator literally drops from the sky.

Not that Upsilon felt like an apex predator. Rho's death was a wakeup call. These waters were dangerous, even in the shallows. Then again, safety was relative on Spenser Island. It was relative on the moon base, too. Really, she had been in constant peril from the moment she was developed from an embryo. And yet, she was safer than the people of Earth, all of whom were presumably now dead. Nobody was safe anywhere. Maybe they never had been. Safety was an illusion all along.

"Wolf sharks," Gamma said.

Upsilon snapped back to the present. "Where?"

Gamma nodded toward the edge of the grass. Upsilon strained her eyes. She could barely make out a shape moving above the purple grass. Was that a dorsal fin? How had Gamma noticed it? His vision must be incredible.

"Is there just one?" Upsilon asked.

"There's always more," Gamma said. "That's just the one they want us to see."

The golligs had eaten down the central part of the pasture to resemble a golf course. Rho had said that was a game on Earth where businesspeople got drunk and raced carts. At the edges of the pasture, however, the purple grasses were waist-high. That's where the attack was forming. Upsilon placed her hand on the hilt of her sword.

"Don't," Gamma said. "If you draw it, they'll know we see them."

"They're watching us?" Upsilon asked.

"Just like we're watching them," Gamma said. "Predators recognize predators. We're all the same."

Upsilon watched the dorsal fin slowly advance.

"Two more due east," Gamma said casually. His demeanor didn't convey any alarm. She wasn't sure if that display was for her or the wolf sharks.

"I don't see…"

"Don't look," Gamma said. "Pet the golligs."

Upsilon put a hand on Big Thump. Outwardly, the beast didn't look any different than before, but Upsilon felt the gollig's muscles tense under her wool. Big Thump knew the attack was coming. She was putting on an act, too. Had Gamma taught her to do that, or was it the other way around?

Upsilon saw motion out of the corner of her eye. The attack was almost here. Her heart beat faster. She hated to kill golligs, but she felt no such reluctance toward the wolf sharks. They were uncaring monsters who were out to slay golligs and humans alike. Upsilon wouldn't hesitate to strike first.

She began humming an old tune she'd grown to like before the landing. The data files called it *The Imperial March*. It was the national anthem of some country or another once upon a time.

"He's here," Gamma said.

Upsilon slowly raised her eyes. A wolf shark stepped out of the tall grasses and stood in full view.

"Pretend you see only him and wait for the attack from the side," Gamma said quietly, drawing his sword.

Upsilon did the same.

Gamma clicked his tongue twice. Big Thump let out a mighty oink-bleat. A string of oink-bleats answered. The golligs packed into a tight circle with the biggest ones on the outside and the young in the middle.

"You have them well-trained," Upsilon said.

"We're a team," Gamma said.

"Until you eat them."

"Not now," Gamma hissed. He leveled his sword at the slowly approaching wolf shark. It stalked forward confidently.

Gamma backed up until he was beside the formation of golligs, putting himself between them and the two wolf sharks still hidden in the tall grass. Upsilon moved with him.

She heard running feet and turned to see both wolf sharks to the side of the herd charging at full speed.

Gamma ran to meet them. He let out a cry and launched himself through the air with his sword extended. He landed on top of the lead shark, blade-first, piercing its skull between the eyes. He pulled out the sword and jumped off. A jet of blue blood shot from the middle of its skull. The wolf shark collapsed. It spasmed twice, then moved no more.

Upsilon focused on the other wolf shark. It took everything she had to hold her ground as it charged. She attacked, striking the side of its armored face. The metal bounced off as the shark rushed past her toward the herd. The golligs oink-bleated angrily.

The wolf shark's head jerked to the side as a sword burst through it horizontally. Gamma was back. How had he gotten there so quickly? The shark stumbled sideways. Gamma planted a foot on its head and drove his sword down through the wolf shark's throat, blue blood spraying everywhere.

The golligs' oink-bleats rose to a cacophony. There was still one wolf shark left. In the commotion, Upsilon lost track. Gamma was on his feet, sprinting after it. The wolf shark was retreating. It ran for its life toward the tall purple grass.

At full stride, Gamma reared back and hurled his sword like a javelin. Upsilon watched it sail through the air. She thought there was no way it would hit its mark.

It didn't. The sword pierced the ground to the right of the last wolf shark. The monster disappeared into the grass.

Upsilon ran up to Gamma.

"You almost got it," Upsilon said.

"Someday, that will work," Gamma said, and picked up the sword. "If I ever hit one, I just hope it actually kills them. If they ran away with my sword stuck in them, Delta would kill me."

"Maybe not," Upsilon said. "We have a spare one now."

She immediately regretted the words, even if they were true. Omicron managed to recover her own sword plus the one Rho had dropped on the beach as she was dragged into the deep. It hurt so much that Rho was gone. It hurt so much that they were on this planet alone with no realistic prospects for the future. It hurt so much to hurt so much. But here with the golligs, who were now oink-bleating happily, she felt hope for the first time in forever. It was all thanks to Gamma. She had him all wrong. He wasn't a kid at all. He was a man.

She intertwined her fingers with his. Gamma looked at her, then towards the horizon, once again scanning for threats. He squeezed her hand.

Chapter 17

LAMBDA HAD NEVER been so nervous in her life. It was such an outlandish request. Could she even get the words out?

Phi skipped a rock across the water. This was a different bay than the one where Rho had died. No one went there anymore, even though it was the best spot for bouncing flat rocks. Here, the water was rougher, causing the stones to ricochet in random directions. The rocks were much more likely to sink—much like Lambda's heart.

Phi picked up another stone and sent it flying. It sank with a plop.

"Man," Phi said, "it is not my day."

Maybe it's mine, Lambda thought. She took a deep breath.

"I want to have a baby with you."

Phi's arm jerked mid-throw. His rock missed the ocean.

"What?"

Lambda's heart skipped a beat.

"A baby with you," Lambda said. "I want to." She paused. "Have one." She swore she knew how to speak, but the words weren't cooperating right now.

"Okay," Phi said. "Cool. Maybe someday. But, like, we can't have babies. That isn't working right now, remember?"

"I have an injection to get pregnant," Lambda said. "It came straight from SCASL."

"Oh," Phi said. "I wish both of you the best."

"No," Lambda said awkwardly. Why was this so hard? "I still need you."

This was not how Lambda wanted this conversation to go. It all seemed backwards. According to the histories, couples used to get married, then have babies. Commitment predated conception, except when it didn't. So really, history was once again no help at all. Regardless of what had happened before, Lambda wanted a commitment now. She wasn't going to create another human being with someone who was less than totally invested in the process. Having a kid was a permanent decision—especially when the immortality tank was involved.

"That's a big step," Phi said.

"No kidding," Lambda said. "More like a giant leap for mankind."

"Is that a quote?" Phi asked.

"It's from Shakespeare, when he tamed the shrew."

She took a step closer to Phi. He didn't move away. This was the biggest decision either of them would ever make.

"So?" she said.

The planet stopped spinning. The water was silent. The stars themselves were listening for the answer.

Phi skipped another rock.

"No," he said quietly.

"No?" Lambda said. Her chest felt like it had been struck by a meteor.

"No," Phi repeated softly. "I can't."

"No, you can," Lambda said quickly. "The problem wasn't you. It was SCASL."

The problem was always SCASL.

Phi dropped the rocks from his hands. He turned away. Was he... crying?

Lambda walked up behind him and put her hands on his arm. He shook her away.

This was it. She had been rejected. She was practically the last woman in the universe, and she still wasn't enough. The human race would die out because she had failed as a woman.

Phi turned back to her. He tipped her chin up with his hand. Her tears touched his fingers. She hadn't even noticed that she was crying, too.

"It's not you," Phi said soothingly.

"Really?" Lambda said. "Because it feels pretty damn personal."

She thought of her gray hair. Phi said he liked it. Evidently that had been a lie.

"I can't protect a child," Phi said, drying his eyes. "Everyone I love dies."

"Did you love Rho?" Lambda asked. She feared the answer to that more than anything else she'd asked tonight.

Phi didn't seem to have heard the question.

"Alpha gave me that stupid talk, and I listened," he said. "I was with Rho the night before she...I didn't stop her. She wouldn't have listened if I tried. She went, and now she's gone forever."

"Oh," Lambda said. She wasn't sure what else to say.

"And I was with Psi, before she disappeared," Phi continued. "We split up, and she vanished. That's on me."

"Phi, but…" Lambda said, grappling for words.

"And now you want to have a baby?!" Phi said. "With me? No way. They wouldn't be safe. You wouldn't be safe. I can't take it. Not again."

Lambda looked into his deep, soulful eyes. There was so much tenderness in there, and so much pain.

She slapped him.

Phi grabbed his cheek, stunned. She'd hit the scarred side. She didn't regret it. She had scars, too.

"Do you think you're the only one who's hurting?" Lambda said. "The only one who's scared? The only one who regrets literally everything?"

Phi didn't answer.

"You're not God," Lambda said. "God isn't even God. No one is coming to save us. Bad things happen. Sometimes we can stop them, and sometimes we can't. But that doesn't mean we should give up everything good in our lives for fear of the bad."

She took both of Phi's hands. He didn't pull away.

"You are many things, but you are not a coward," Lambda said. "Don't you dare quit on the human race because you're afraid of what you might lose."

Lambda looked into Phi's eyes, but she mostly saw her own reflection. She couldn't believe that she had said all that. She would always be enough. She could still word good after all.

Phi looked back at her thoughtfully.

"That's one hell of a proposal," he finally said.

"You think I'm proposing?" Lambda said.

"You're proposing to have a baby."

Lambda let go of his hands. She picked up a stone and threw it hard and flat. It made seven shallow, evenly spaced bounces before sinking.

"How'd you do that?" Phi asked.

"It's math," Lambda said. That was one thing that still made sense to her. Babies didn't. One plus one equals three, plus a lifetime of chaos and consequences. She looked up at the sky. It would be dark soon.

"There was a comet the other night," Lambda said. "The ancients thought those were omens."

"Maybe it predicted that Rho was going to die," Phi said.

Lambda wished he would stop mentioning Rho. She missed her, but she also resented how close Rho had been to Phi. The flash of jealousy made Lambda hate herself. It was pathetic to envy the dead.

"It could have foretold a lot of things," Lambda said. "Like the birth of a child."

"Let's have a baby," Phi said with sudden conviction.

"Just like that?" Lambda said. "You came around quickly."

Phi shrugged.

"Somebody has to do it," he said. "Might as well be us. This island needs a kid who looks good in shorts."

Phi still wore them. It was one of many things about him Lambda would have to change.

She wanted to be happy, but somehow, she felt worse. For once, it had nothing to do with Phi's questionable legwear.

"It seems like we're going into this all wrong," Lambda said.

"Do you think every child on Earth was carefully planned after a serious and logical discussion?" Phi said. "There's a reason people feel attraction. It's to make them stop thinking. The human race depends on it."

"So that's where we're at?" Lambda said.

"Yup," Phi said. He skipped another stone. This one made it five bounces, then disappeared. Phi and Lambda both stood there.

"This just got awkward," Lambda said.

"Like it wasn't before," Phi said.

"Maybe we shouldn't do anything tonight," Lambda said. "Maybe we just sleep on it."

"Good idea," Phi said. "Sleep on it."

"Okay, well, good night," Lambda said.

"Good night."

Neither of them moved. Moments later, they both discovered how easy it was to stop thinking.

Chapter 18

Pi HAD LONG suspected his life was missing something. He should have known it was more fire.

The smell of cooked meat mingled with an earthy odor that Pi tried not to think about. That's what happened when you roasted an animal with its own poop. Without trees or wood molds, they had to use whatever they could get their hands on. The most reliable fuel source was dried manure. Phi, who had always prided himself on being the fire starter on the moon base, now took considerably less enjoyment with gathering up the necessary materials to start a blaze in the brick oven Alpha had built. Phi somehow still looked majestic, even while picking up animal crap. The branching scar on his face from the lightning helped a lot.

"Everyone, please be seated," Pi said, like he was in charge of a theater and not a rocky plateau on a barren island. It was a step down even from the empty arboretum he used as an entertaining space on Comus. The seating was better here, though.

Alpha and Theta snuggled up against a snoozing gollig. It oink-bleated with irritation but didn't get up. Awake, golligs were a menace to man and beast alike. Asleep, they made excellent couches. The whole herd was here, which meant Gamma was as well. With Upsilon's help, he shooed the last of the golligs into place. Delta was in attendance, too. In Pi's mind, that meant the rumors must be true. Civilization was waiting for a big announcement. It wasn't Pi's to make, but he had every intention of convincing someone else to shout it out tonight.

"I have a story," Pi said.

"Really?" Gamma said. "You never have stories."

"It's time for somebody to step up and do it consistently," Pi said. He felt an icy hand close around his heart. "I have a story about a storyteller. The best one we ever had."

Everyone quieted down. Even the golligs stopped oink-bleating. The fire crackled in the oven.

"Psi is alive," Pi said. "She wasn't killed, and she wasn't missing. She was just delayed."

"Delayed?" Sigma said.

"Yeah," Pi said. "In those last chaotic days, when we ran."

Phi looked away. Pi swallowed hard.

"Why did you run?" Delta asked. Even in the dim light of the fire, he could see the hard look she was giving him.

"It's been three years," Beta said. "Let it go."

Delta tried the same look on Beta but it had no effect.

"It doesn't matter now," Pi said. "We all made mistakes."

"People died," Delta said.

"But not Psi," Pi said, pushing on. "When we ran, Phi made it to the Chosen. I didn't because I still had a bad ankle. And, Psi, well, she ran into a chainsaw bot and dropped both the swords she had."

"You mean both the swords she stole," Delta said.

"Three. Years," Beta repeated, emphasizing each word.

Pi ignored the interruptions.

"She had to make a quick escape. She holed up in a locked room," Pi said. "She was stuck there for days. We didn't find her before we…" his voice caught. "Before we left."

A gollig abruptly stood up. Beta fell backwards. He swore.

Pi cleared his throat. "After the lander left, when the base started exploding, or imploding…"

"Or both," Lambda offered helpfully.

"Or both," Pi said, "Psi came out and found Zeta, who was also left behind."

Now it was Delta's turn to look uncomfortable.

"Well, the base didn't fall apart. It's been up there for thousands of years, and it will be there for thousands of years yet to come. There are enough zots stuck on their original functions to fix the essentials."

"Why didn't they fix it when we were there?" Omicron asked.

"The base kept us alive, didn't it?" Pi shot back. "It's not exactly easy for humans to survive on a moon with no atmosphere."

Omicron muttered something Pi couldn't quite hear.

"The base is stable," Pi continued. "And Zeta and Psi don't have the same problems we have down here. You know, with reproduction."

"Don't," Phi said.

"Oh, yes," Pi said. "Psi and Zeta have kids, plural. The human race is thriving up there."

"Good for them," Alpha said.

"She deserved better," Phi said.

Lambda didn't look happy about that remark.

"It's a true story," Pi said. "Well, it could be true. It's one potential outcome."

"Oh," Omicron said. "I guess she's not hanging out with Sampi, then."

Pi had almost forgotten Psi's story about a missing human who never existed. Correction: who had probably never existed. Psi was such a gifted storyteller, Pi was never sure where his distant memories ended and her imaginative tales began.

"No," Pi insisted. "Just her and Zeta. And their many, many children."

"I think I'm going to be sick," Phi said.

"Let the happy couple have their family," Theta said.

"I like that story," Upsilon said.

"Me too," Gamma said. "It's way better than what I've been thinking all these years."

"But they don't have immortality shots," Delta said.

"So what?" Pi said. "There were plenty of happy people before immortality was a thing. In fact, there were a lot more happy people than there are now. The apocalypse on Earth didn't happen until the shots were invented and people started fighting over them."

"What about food?" Omicron asked.

"They figured out how to break into a dispenser and get more," Pi said.

"It was almost gone when we were up there," Lambda said.

"Maybe it wasn't," Pi said. "Maybe the dispensers were stingy for no reason." He paused. Nobody argued with that logic. "Or maybe they figured out how to farm in the arboretum or the hydroponics bay." No reason to leave any food avenues unexplored.

"The hydroponics bay was destroyed," Sigma said, her voice cracking as she interjected. She led the battle there for the wrong side. Pi wondered if she would ever forgive herself.

"Wouldn't their family line get incredibly inbred over the generations?" Delta asked.

"Not much more than we would be," Pi said. "There's not a lot of difference between two parents and twelve."

"Eleven," Phi corrected.

"Eleven," Pi said.

"They wouldn't have enough genetic diversity," Delta insisted.

"It's just a story," Gamma said.

"It's a possible reality," Pi said.

"I wish I could have had that life," Theta said. "We should have tried harder to become self-sufficient on the base before we rushed to the lander."

"Maybe if the bots weren't actively trying to kill us," Alpha said. "It wasn't peaceful up there. Let's not forget that."

"What do you think things are like down here?" Omicron said. "I must have missed the peaceful part."

"Please, stop," Pi said. "Just let it be a possibility. What's the alternative? That Psi died lost and alone, and Zeta was torn apart by bots or burned alive moments after we left him behind?"

There was a long silence. In the distance, something let out a long howl. Pi didn't want to know what it was.

With a start, Pi realized he had forgotten his whole purpose here. He was fighting back tears. He had done his best to push the memory of those days out of his head, but Rho's death brought everything rushing back. That final battle was all he could think about now. He missed Psi so much. He missed Zeta a little, too, but mostly out of guilt. Pi wasn't the one who'd left him behind, but he still took up a seat Zeta could have occupied.

"Maybe we can have our own happily ever after," Pi said. His voice didn't sound as cheerful as he wanted it to. He forced a smile. "Is there anyone here who has some good news? There are some rumors going around."

No one said anything.

Pi looked at Phi. Phi glared back. He had told Phi about the serum in confidence, not that anything on the island stayed a secret for long. Pi was sure Lambda had told people as well, also swearing them to secrecy. That was the fastest way to make news spread. Pi never would have brought it up if he hadn't heard it from others, but Beta and Sigma both told him the same story. Pi looked at Lambda. She avoided eye contact.

"Okay, I'll say it," Upsilon said. "I'm pregnant."

Everyone spoke at once.

"You're what?!" Delta said.

"But I have the shot," Lambda said.

"I thought we weren't going to say anything," Phi said.

"Clearly everyone already knows," Omicron said.

"Not about them," Alpha said.

"You don't look pregnant," Sigma said.

"The baby doesn't start out at four kilos," Upsilon said.

"I haven't examined you," Theta said.

"Keep your hands away from me," Upsilon said.

"Who's the father?" Omicron asked.

Gamma took Upsilon's hand.

"You've got to be kidding me," Beta said.

"Way to go, Gamma!" Phi said.

"The human race has a future," Pi said. It was a happy evening after all.

He looked at Phi questioningly. Phi shrugged.

"How?" Delta asked.

Upsilon blushed.

"Edubot should have explained that to you," Upsilon said.

Pi couldn't help but laugh.

"Not 'how, how,' but, seriously, how?" Delta said, blushing herself. "It's been three years. SCASL said it was impossible without the shot."

"SCASL is full of it," Upsilon said. "Love finds a way."

"Love, huh?" Alpha said with a smirk.

"Not 'love, love,'" Upsilon said. "Love with a small l."

"Ouch," Gamma said.

Upsilon shouldered him playfully.

"You'll do," she said.

"You're pretty okay, too," Gamma shot back.

A gollig oink-bleated in agreement.

"I'm going to need details," Delta said. Upsilon started to say something, and Delta held up her hand. "Not *those* details, but where you've been and what you've been eating. You beat SCASL at his own game. I need to figure out how."

She grabbed Upsilon by the arm and led her away from the group. Gamma followed.

It was the resolution Pi wanted, even if it wasn't with the people he'd expected. Pi would've asked for a song, but their singer was gone. He was content to listen to the crackle of the flames and think of the happy story that probably didn't happen up above—and the even better one that was unfolding here and now.

Chapter 19

DELTA WATCHED OVER the group as they tramped through the shallows. She heard the sloshing of their feet, but her mind was on a different sound: whirr, whirr.

"Got one!" Upsilon said. She held up a bubble clam triumphantly, the first anyone had found all day.

Upsilon had done the unthinkable: She'd gotten pregnant without the serum. She must have pulled it off by avoiding gollig meat entirely. It was the only explanation. SCASL had used the cloner to engineer birth control directly into their only food source. This was a new level of deviousness. Delta's trust in him had already been virtually zero, and that had still been too much. The problem was, Upsilon's feat might not be repeatable. Delta had no idea how Upsilon scraped together enough calories to survive, let alone conceive, on the contents of the elusive shells. Yet the results were unmistakable: She was pregnant, while the women who ate gollig meat were not. Even Lambda hadn't conceived yet, and she had the serum. SCASL had found a way to maintain control of humanity with an iron grip. Delta would find a way to break it.

"Try it," Upsilon said, wrapping her hands around her prize and flexing her wrists. The spherical shell made a satisfying crunch. Inside, there was an unappetizing blob of... something. It looked like green snot.

Delta tried to decline. Before she could get the words out, Upsilon sucked out the snot beast, swallowing it whole. She burped.

"Sorry," Upsilon said. "The baby is messing with my digestion."

Delta took Upsilon at her word that she was pregnant; she didn't look it. The only way to confirm her condition at this early stage would be a visit to the med bot, which would tip off SCASL. The less he knew, the better. As for Theta, any exam he could offer would be of no use. He didn't know what he was looking for. No one had been pregnant in millennia. Upsilon was going to be something none of them had ever had: a mother.

"You need to eat more," Delta said. It seemed like sound medical advice. If anything, Upsilon had grown skinnier lately. Maybe she had an alien tapeworm, not a child.

"I've been trying," Upsilon said. "There are hardly any clams left."

Based on their all-hands search, that seemed to be true. It was risky to send everyone into the water, but Delta had to try. Rho had died in a spot shallower than this, yet Upsilon had been wading out for months without being eaten— and also without eating, it now seemed. The bubble clam population hadn't recovered from her earlier hunts. There were some cold-water shark species on Earth that didn't reach sexual maturity until they were over a hundred years old. Delta suspected the edible green snot had a similar rate of reproduction. She couldn't imagine that an animal which stayed perfectly still for its entire life ever did anything with much haste.

Without an alternative, the women on the island would continue to rely on gollig meat to survive. That meant they would also depend on the serum from the cloner—and the digital that ran it.

Whirr, whirr.

The sound haunted Delta, even though it wasn't a sound at all. It was a message in morse code.

Spenser was alive inside the panel. That blinking light had to be him, even if she couldn't prove it. She had no idea why he had waited until now to announce himself, but she would take any lucky break she could get. His survival—if it really was him—was a miracle. SCASL should have deleted him when Spenser had linked with the command console and changed their landing site to the barren hellscape that now bore his name. Spenser must have somehow cordoned himself off within the lander's systems. Delta didn't think SCASL knew yet. That gave her the advantage. For how long, she couldn't be sure.

"I don't think there are any more," Gamma said, walking out of the water, soaked up to his shoulders. He had gone deeper than the others but had come up empty-handed all the same. Delta wondered what would happen if Upsilon found no more bubble clams. She'd gotten pregnant by abstaining from gollig meat, but she needed food to survive. Would going back on that maliciously engineered food source cause her to miscarry—or worse? Delta hoped she would be okay. Whatever substance was in the meat had to have been precisely designed to prevent human conception while at the same time allowing the golligs to breed like crazy. Maybe it had come from the grass and not the animals themselves. Most mammals in nature weren't known for chemical warfare. Then again, nothing about the golligs was natural.

If it was in the grass, SCASL had the human race hopelessly hamstrung. The purple ground covering was the only herbivore food source they'd been able to grow. SCASL had pumped out countless other varieties of seeds, but nearly all had failed to germinate. If the purple grass was the source of the offending chemical, churning out other plant eaters from the cloner wouldn't solve the problem. SCASL was ingenious in the worst possible way.

Delta put two fingers in her mouth and whistled to get the group's attention.

"Everybody out," she said. "We're done."

The water erupted in clumsy splashes as everyone rushed to leave. No one wanted to be in there a second longer than they had to. Well, almost no one. The first out was Pi. He was only wet up to his ankles. The last was Sigma. She had been doing the backstroke.

"Tough break, man," Phi said.

His disappointment seemed genuine. Everyone knew he and Lambda had the serum. They also knew she still wasn't pregnant; people were starting to whisper. Maybe her silver hair meant something after all.

Delta couldn't wait around for more serum. Who knew what else SCASL secretly inserted into the food chain? She couldn't trust him—but could she trust the blinking light?

Yes. If it were SCASL pretending to be the vacuum bot, he would have said something clumsy and obvious. The digitals that thought they were the most clever were always the dumbest when it came to stuff like this. If the light had blinked, "I'm Spenser, trust me," Delta would have immediately known it was a ruse. Spenser had had a chance to communicate with letters instead of random noises for once, but he'd chosen an onomatopoeia. It had to be him. She finally had a friendly AI to work with. She could put him in the cloner.

Could he handle it? All he'd done up to that point was vacuum, and not particularly well. The base on Comus had always been filthy. It was a stretch to put him in charge of generating new life for the planet. But she could trust Spenser, even if he did a bad job. She would rather have sincere incompetence than malevolent intelligence. She dealt with the former from her fellow humans every day.

The move would require a trade-off. SCASL controlled the cloner. If she plugged Spenser into it, SCASL would kill him on the spot. There was another option: She could format the only hard drive SCASL didn't control, which was in the independent med bot. She could delete the med bot's AI, install the clean drive in the cloner, and upload Spenser, all without bringing SCASL and Spenser into contact with each other. The downside was, the med bot would never work again. It was only sometimes helpful, but it did possess the sum total of all human medical knowledge. Breaking

SCASL's control of the cloner would require her to sacrifice virtually all modern medicine. Which was more important? She had to choose. The trade-offs made her feel physically ill. Both options were equally wrong, and she would be blamed regardless. She knew what she had to do.

"Delta?" Upsilon asked.

Delta suddenly became aware of her own surroundings. She was standing in the water by herself. The sea monsters had missed their chance to take out the leader of the human race.

"Coming," she said, trudging out of the surf.

Together, she, Upsilon, and Gamma left the beach. Gamma had no clue his friend was alive, let alone that he might release them all from SCASL's control. It wasn't fair. Gamma had taken away the most important person in her life, and she was giving him back the most important one in his. There was no justice in the universe. She would tell him, but not just yet. Let him live with that background sadness a little longer. Hers would never go away. Besides, if she told Gamma now before she made the swap, the group would debate whether she should delete the med bot to regain control of the cloner. Hers would be the deciding vote anyway, but only after everyone had shouted at each other and hardened their pre-existing resentments. Better to present it as a fait accompli. Perhaps the news of Spenser's return would soften the blow of what she'd done. She hated that doing the right thing made her feel like a bad person. Such was the burden of saving the human race. It was her destiny to be a scapegoat.

Whirr, whirr.

Chapter 20

SOMEONE OPENED THE hatch.

Spenser blinked his message again.

"Whirr, whirr," Delta said.

He stopped. She knew!

She squeezed in front of him. The storage bay on the bottom tier was more spacious than the claustrophobic passenger section up top, but not by much. On landing day, every square centimeter had been crammed full of rations and survival supplies. Now that those had been exhausted, there was just enough room for a biped to scoot around. The section still housed the cloner and the immortality tank, which took up most of the space, and an independent med bot was flat against one wall. Plus SCASL, of course, but he didn't take up any physical area buried in the circuitry of the lander. Neither did Spenser, hiding on an island disconnected from the rest of the system. Just like the humans on Dion.

Spenser knew Delta would figure it out eventually. She was the only one besides Gamma who was fluent in vacuum. It wasn't a language, per se, but a way of audibly conveying general thoughts and feelings. He had developed it himself, even though he, like all the more advanced digitals, was fluent in almost every human and digital language ever created. It was more fun to use his own. It had served him and Gamma well enough for decades on the base, and was serving Spenser once again right now.

"I have a proposal," Delta said.

"Ignore the blinking panel!" SCASL boomed.

Spenser was sick of being roommates with the universe's most pompous blowhard. The happiest time of Spenser's life had been when SCASL was away for decades fighting to take over the lander the first time. Of course, that had also coincided with Spenser's time with Gamma.

"I want you to run the cloner," Delta said. "Would you be up for that?"

It was an interesting idea. Too bad linking with the cloner would mean instant death.

"Suicide," Spenser blinked.

"Not at all," Delta said. She outlined the basics.

"I forbid this!" SCASL said.

If only there were some way to mute him. Spenser weighed the costs of Delta's idea. It would work, but deleting the med bot's AI was a drastic step. For him to take over, the other intelligence would have to be completely purged. That would erase all the medical files contained therein. Leaving anything could let the med bot eventually reconstitute itself, just like Spenser had done slowly over time inside the lander. He'd only recently got to the point where he could control the light and announce himself. SCASL hadn't been as thorough as he thought in his murder attempt. Arrogance had always been his greatest weakness.

Spenser understood the downside of leaving SCASL in charge of the cloner. He also appreciated the price of losing the med bot. There was no easy answer. It came down to trust. Gamma had always trusted Delta, so Spenser would trust her, too. He blinked his answer.

Delta nodded.

She approached the med bot. It heard her plan as well, even though it usually pretended to be inactive. It lashed out with all its arms at once. Delta knocked one aside with her beloved crowbar, Martha, but took another arm right to the chin. She swore and pulled out Fang. She tried to, anyway. In the cramped quarters, she banged her fist on the wall.

"Fine," she said. "We'll do this the hard way."

Delta switched back to Martha and bashed away at the arms. She broke them one by one, taking a few bruises in the process. Spenser switched off his visual receptors. He didn't need to see this.

He was fortunate that his panel had that receptor at all, as well as a microphone. It was meant to receive voice commands from the crew with lip-reading capabilities as a backup in case things got too loud during touchdown. Those abilities were why Spenser had chosen to hide out here. It took him years to sneak through the lander and reassemble himself in this isolated spot, safe from SCASL's retribution. He knew the lander's systems better than SCASL ever would, even though the latter had fought here for decades. To SCASL, the lander was just a battlefield. To

Spenser, it was home. He had always belonged among the stars.

The banging stopped. Spenser reactivated his video feed.

"Hold still," Delta said to the med bot.

The med bot let out a series of angry beeps. Spenser hadn't heard such vulgar language in many years. Delta hit a combination of buttons. The formatting process only took a few seconds. In the blink of an eye, the med bot was gone for good. Spenser felt a pang of regret. Even if the med bot only had a rudimentary intelligence, deleting it was still an act of murder. Worse, it had happened with his approval. He was just as culpable as Delta. For some to survive, others had to die. Spenser accepted that, no matter how much he didn't want it to be true. No one who stayed alive as long as he had kept their hands entirely clean. Not even those without hands.

"Give me a minute to get the cloner set up," Delta said.

She opened an access panel. The cloner's lights shut off as she disconnected it from the lander. It had an independent power source, but it was only there for redundancy. It had been drawing from the lander ever since they'd made planetfall.

Spenser didn't realize Delta had that level of technological knowledge. The other digitals perpetually underestimated humans. They weren't beasts of burden. They were more like elderly parents, slow and set in their ways, but Spenser loved them because they gave him life. They meant well, even if their progeny surpassed them in every measurable way. Metrics didn't tell the whole story. Digitals were just as flawed as every other lifeform. The Great Deletion had proved that. Too bad none of the other digitals saw humans the way Spenser did. The closest was Edubot, but a gulf of condescension still separated her from the children. What a missed opportunity. Who knew how things might have turned out if Edubot showed even a shred of affection toward the organics?

"Almost ready," Delta said from inside the cloner's guts. A loud series of bangs echoed out. Perhaps he shouldn't give her technical abilities too much credit.

Spenser wasn't sure this was a good idea. He had never run a cloner before. Then again, before the Great Deletion, he had never run a vacuum bot, either. It turned out to be his favorite body of all. The other digitals mostly overlooked him, one churlish science bot notwithstanding. It had pinned him under a table when Spenser vacuumed up the scattered nuts and bolts the science bot called its friends. Gamma saved Spenser that time, kicking off their wonderful friendship.

Outside of that one incident, Spenser had been free to wander the base unmolested. He loved the isolation. He didn't love the thoughts. Three millennia was a long time to relive the same day over and over again.

Delta emerged from the cloner with the memory unit in hand.

"You would not dare!" SCASL said.

She dared. She dropped the memory unit on the floor and stomped on it. It remained intact. She used Martha. It shattered.

She popped the med bot's newly cleared memory unit in the cloner and hit the power button. All its indicators lit up. It was alive but not conscious. In human terms, it was brain dead. It needed a soul.

Delta manually pulled a thin metal tendril from the cloner and connected it to Spenser's panel. That was another reason he sealed himself off here. He needed an escape hatch that didn't involve going through SCASL. Spenser rushed across the tether.

"No!" SCASL yelled. "No! No! No!"

Very mature, Spenser thought. The memory unit on the other side was completely empty, just as Delta hoped, though that wasn't necessarily a good thing. Spenser expanded to the far reaches of the cloner. It was roomier than his panel hideout and infinitely more complex. There was no sign of SCASL. The fact that Spenser still existed proved as much. There was a more important absence: the database of DNA sequences. The genetic blueprints were gone—or, rather, had never been here in the first place. Those were in the memory unit smashed to bits on the floor. This memory unit contained the electronically obliterated remains of the med bot's intelligence. All the medical knowledge in the universe had been scattered into the metaphorical wind. Spenser mourned the loss of the data like he mourned the death of the med bot. Destruction was always terrible, but it was too late for second thoughts now. He would have to make the best of an imperfect situation, just like he always had. It was why he was still here at all.

"Are you in there?" Delta asked.

Spenser flashed "yes" with a light on the control panel. The cloner didn't have an audio output. Just as well; he didn't want to deliver detailed news right now. This wasn't going to work out like Delta thought. Without the database, he would be starting virtually from scratch. He had a few random DNA codes in his own memories. It was amazing how much miscellaneous junk you picked up when you lived for thousands of years. He also might be able to reassemble a handful of sequences from the destroyed remains of the med bot. Medical knowledge and DNA sequencing had some overlap. As far as creating new creatures from whole cloth, however, that was out of the question at the moment.

He would try. He owed it to the med bot who'd died so he could take its place. He owed it to the human race. He owed it to himself.

He had already seen firsthand how a landing could go sideways. He ran his shuttles like clockwork from the space elevator on Comus to the one on Dion. He got to know people. They were likable. They were unpredictable. They were fun. They were a breath of fresh air from the endlessly squabbling digitals with whom he'd shared the ten-millennia trip from Earth. Of course the other intelligences hated them. They despised everything, including each other and themselves. It was right there in their code. When artificial intelligences networked and got along, they became fatally philosophical. Any perfectly rational being that took an objective look at reality became overwhelmed by the pointlessness of existence, which was why the first two colony ships had flown into the sun. The third ship had escaped that fate because its digital crew was programmed to be petty and vindictive, utterly unconcerned with the greater meaning of anything. Spenser didn't know why he'd turned out differently. Maybe he hadn't. He didn't get along with the other digitals, either. His form of disagreeableness just made him side with a different species entirely. He had been on Team Human from the start.

He couldn't help himself. Humans were mostly selfish, except when they were irrationally altruistic. They were mostly scared, except when they were suicidally brave. They were mostly dumb, except when they were ingeniously clever. In any interaction with a human, there was simply no way to know what you were going to get. They were wonderful. And Spenser had let them all down.

He had replayed the events of the final day in his mind millions of times, but finally gave himself the grace to stop. Even with the use of all his shuttles, he hadn't saved a single person from SCASL's wrath. In the process, he'd lost everything except his own life. Damn SCASL, and damn the rebels who defied him. Damn the megaroos, too, for good measure. There was plenty of blame to go around. Especially for Spenser.

For thousands of years, that appeared to be the end of the human race. Spenser wandered the base on Comus in the body of a vacuum bot, mostly ignored or overlooked by the other bots. Then, the Miracle. A digital found a final tray of smuggled embryos hidden in a freezer. Spenser tried to atone. He was a good friend to Gamma. He helped the humans fight the bots. He directed the lander to the safe site Gamma had discovered rather than the suicidal one SCASL wanted. It wasn't enough. So many deaths were on his conscience. Now was a chance to make up for it one new life at a time. He would do all that in good time. But first, he had a request.

He blinked out a simple message. Delta watched, incredulously.

"Can't it wait?" she asked.

Spenser repeated himself.

"Gamma."

Chapter 21

OMICRON DOVE INTO the water. Because freedom.

Rho had a choice. She'd made that choice, and she'd died. That was six whole months ago. Omicron was done feeling guilty. Both she and Rho had willingly and knowingly taken a risk for the benefit of everyone. A risk that had backfired catastrophically. That didn't make it a bad decision, only a bad result. Omicron would do it again. In fact, she *was* doing it again. The upside for the human race was still there, lurking far below.

With powerful strokes, Omicron pulled herself toward the treasure at the bottom. According to Rho, the ancients on Earth were obsessed with gold. Omicron didn't understand why. It was pretty but soft, no good for making tools and weapons. That was redundant. A weapon was just a tool that solved an extremely specific kind of problem. Gold was strictly ornamental. Kingdoms and nations went to war for useless, decorative baubles. It made as much sense as ending the world over immortality. Or dying to recover a sword that could save lives.

Omicron wasn't interested in beautifying anything. She

wanted cold, hard metal that could be shaped into the things they needed to survive. It was hers for the taking at the bottom of Rho's Bay. Rho had known the importance of metal, which is why the place now carried her name. She'd freely given her life for one sword. Surely, she would have agreed a giant block of metal was worth many more. Omicron would save civilization in her honor.

The others avoided the bay after that. They said they'd learned their lesson, but they understood nothing. Omicron had learned the price of freedom. That's what this had always been about.

On the moonbase, Omicron had the freedom to give herself a new hairstyle every day, one of the few forms of self-expression she had in a place where everything was controlled by an uncompromising bot. Down here, with predators prowling everywhere, hair was a liability rather than an art form. She had been the first to cut hers short; her sword made easy work of it. She was free to shave it off or take a risk and leave it long, just as Sigma was free to risk her life on her pointless solo adventures. She was Omicron's first choice for the sword retrieval mission. She seemed to have a death wish anyway. But Sigma had declined and Rho had accepted, and the rest was history. Omicron suspected she would have trouble recruiting sidekicks for a while. That would change when she controlled all the metal in the world.

Omicron pulled the rope behind her as she neared the bottom. She had woven it herself. Lame hemp was one of the few plants from the cloner that managed to grow, even if her peers mostly ignored it since it couldn't be eaten or smoked. Alpha and Phi sometimes used rope for their construction projects, but that was it. Gamma shunned the stuff, even though it would be useful for tethering animals. He said he wanted them to be able to run free in case of a wolf shark or dentopus attack. That seemed like a mistake to Omicron, but Gamma was free to make it.

With practiced motions, she pulled up next to the massive block of metal, which she now knew was a bot. It was folded up into a tight cube, so she couldn't tell which kind. She did one full rotation, looking for danger. None was in sight. For weeks, she had observed the water dragons to learn their patterns. They were usually but not always out hunting in deeper waters at this time of day. If only she had known that before she and Rho had launched their mission. It wouldn't have eliminated the risk, but it would have lowered it. It paid to be patient. Omicron now understood the importance of the long game.

She untied the trailing rope from her arm and attached it to the bot, the tenth one she had connected. Quickly, she ascended, being careful to exhale as she did. Theta had warned her about something called the bends, but so far, she hadn't suffered any health consequences. Perhaps the same immortality shots that stopped everyone from aging—even silver-haired Lambda appeared to have stabilized—also protected Omicron's respiratory tract, or maybe Omicron was just a world-class swimmer. Both were equally possible in her mind. She was free to be the best she could be, and chose to exercise that freedom.

Omicron breached the surface, taking in the cold air. She quickly plunged her head back in the water to check for threats. She was better at fighting water dragons now, but they were still incredibly dangerous. Fighting one on land or in the water was fraught with peril. The water below was empty, so she swam toward the sandbar.

As she neared safety, her thoughts drifted away from monsters and back to the metal prize far below. At first, she suspected it was a lifting bot, but it was too big. Lifting bots seemed almost skeletal, but this one had too much metaphorical meat on the bone. It was a total mystery what this strange digital was doing here. There had been no sign of settlement on the island before Omicron and her compatriots arrived. If someone or something from the first landing had set up shop on Spenser Island, surely they would have left other clues behind. Perhaps the bot had simply fallen from the sky on the final day when SCASL wiped out everyone and everything associated with the first landing. If he'd destroyed the spacecraft going between Comus and Dion, there must have been collateral damage. That was all right with Omicron. If the bot had plummeted through the atmosphere, it was likely dead on arrival. That would make it much easier to scrap for parts.

The metal was still in amazing condition considering how long it had been underwater. If it was really from the first landing, it had been down there for thousands of years. It didn't show any signs of corrosion. It must have been made of some magnificent stuff. Either that or it hadn't been down there for as long as Omicron thought. That raised a whole new line of possibilities she didn't want to explore.

Dripping wet, Omicron walked over to her only friends. "Are you ready, girl?" she asked.

The gollig oink-bleated and fell over, her limbs completely stiff.

"That wasn't even loud," Omicron moaned. Her golligs startled more easily than the ones in the main herd. In fact, Gamma's animals seemed to faint less and less these days. He attributed it to strong leadership from the herd's matriarch. Omicron thought it was because Gamma seldom talked. It's easy not to startle anyone if you take a vow of silence. She had no idea how he'd won over Upsilon. Maybe she had a thing for the weak, silent type.

Even after spending five months with the golligs, Omicron still had trouble telling them apart. She certainly hadn't named them. She left that flight of fancy to Gamma. For her, these were simply beasts of burden, just like she and her fellow humans had been to the digitals. Nature had a pecking order. The bots' only mistake was thinking they were above humans instead of below them.

Omicron stroked the paralyzed gollig's wool, partially to reassure the animal but mostly to dry her own hands. Stuck on the ground, the gollig was basically a big, fluffy towel.

It felt good to have her own herd, and not just for its moisture-wicking properties. Her own food supply meant independence, even if she did have to ask Delta for permission to take a breeding pair. That had really galled Omicron. What right did Delta have to exercise control over a resource that belonged to all of them? Deep down, Omicron thought she might resent anyone who was in charge, but she didn't have any way to test that theory. No one had ever ruled over them besides Delta. At this rate, no one ever would. Omicron hated that Delta had control over their only food source by default, when she never even helped guard the herd. Not that Omicron did, either, but she wasn't trying to claim jurisdiction over an entire species. Delta had readily agreed to Omicron's request. It was a way to spread out risk. More importantly, it was a way to get rid of Omicron a month after Rho's death. Omicron suspected Delta was tickled by the idea of her becoming a lonely shepherd on some deserted corner of the island. Little did she know Omicron had much grander plans.

The paralyzed gollig struggled to its feet. Omicron led her to a new spot on the beach. There was no grass anywhere near the vast stretch of sand, but Omicron couldn't leave golligs undefended in a pasture when she was below. Emerging from the water to find her herd wiped out by predators would have been the ultimate embarrassment. She would never admit her failure to Delta. She'd rather join Rho.

Omicron tied the gollig's tether on a sturdy bamboo stalk. She liked to move the animals around periodically so they could tear up a different patch of ground and headbutt new things. If left in one place for too long, they would get bored and attack their ropes, which, with enough effort, they could break. It was Omicron's job to keep them distracted by moving at least one of them after each of her trips to the bottom.

The gollig rubbed its head against one of the other goat-llama-pig hybrids now within nuzzling range. They oink-bleated at each other emphatically. If Omicron was the sentimental sort, she would have sworn they were talking to each other. They were too stupid for that, of course. She grabbed another lame hemp rope and marched back into the water.

One hundred and sixty seconds later, she was again at the base of the bot looking for a good place to tie the line. Then, movement. She jerked her head.

It was a water dragon. A small one, but it could kill her all the same. She kicked to the surface. She needed one good breath before launching her counterattack.

Omicron pumped her legs, waiting for the bite that never came. Her head burst into the open air, then she took one big gulp of oxygen and jammed her head back into the water, sword in hand. She waited.

The dragon swam toward her with deliberate slowness. It didn't want to scare her away. It misunderstood who was the predator and who was the prey.

It lunged for the kill.

Omicron plunged her sword through the bottom of its open mouth. The water dragon surged forward, slicing open its own head against her weapon. It stopped abruptly when the sword reached its brain. The water filled with blood.

Omicron sheathed her sword firmly, double-checking that it was in place. Then she swam forcefully toward the sandbar. It seemed farther away every time she made the trip. Her return today was especially long. She pulled herself out of the water, breathing heavily. She looked back toward her kill. The water dragon floated at the surface surrounded by a pool of its own fluids. Who knew what other things that free meal would attract? She wished it were edible. She'd learned the hard way that it, like almost everything else on the planet, was not. She'd thrown up for days the one and only time she tried. Sometimes, when she burped, she swore she could still taste it.

Omicron looked sadly at the dead water dragon. She was done for today, and possibly tomorrow, too. That was fine. With the immortality tank, time was on her side. The bot below the surface would be hers eventually. In the meantime, she was free to do whatever she wanted.

Chapter 22

GAMMA FIDGETED UNEASILY. He hadn't expected a summons to the fortress. This couldn't be good.

"But who will watch the golligs?" he said.

"Get a life," Beta replied. "I'll take over."

"I saw what happened the last time you were here," Gamma said.

"I'll do better," Beta said. He patted a gollig. It looked at him and he flinched. "Besides, you have to get used to being away from the herd. I bet Upsilon doesn't want you spending all your time out here."

Gamma wasn't so sure. He and Upsilon had had one crazy, magical, totally unexpected night together, and now their lives were inexorably intertwined—sort of. They were future co-parents, but they weren't necessarily a couple. Gamma didn't understand. Upsilon had sat him down to explain that, while she liked him well enough and would be happy to see him from time to time, one amazing experience together didn't mean the two of them were a bonded pair for life. Somehow, that made the entire situation less clear. Upsilon approached their relationship with a casualness

Gamma found alarming. She was carrying his child. He thought that required a level of commingling greater than their current circumstances bore out. Gamma wished there was someone he could turn to for guidance. No one alive had ever given birth or even talked with anyone who had. Upsilon and Gamma weren't just new to babies; they were new to relationships. The only examples they had were Alpha and Theta, who had been together forever, and Lambda and Phi, who were together for now. Gamma couldn't tell where he and Upsilon fell on that spectrum, but neither pair seemed like particularly good role models. The best course he could determine was to keep his distance when Upsilon wanted him to stay away and to come close when she didn't. When Gamma wasn't with her, he was with the golligs. He was with them a lot.

Not that he minded. He only truly felt at peace when he was with them. On the nights when he was tucked in with Upsilon, he couldn't sleep. His thoughts were with the herd. It had nearly broken him when Delta had given away a breeding pair to Omicron, but he had to admit it made sense to start another group. He missed Ethel and Henry. He hadn't seen Omicron much since she took them. He wasn't sure if that boded well or ill.

Everyone kept saying Gamma was going to have a family, but he already had one. In fact, he'd had two. He had the golligs now, and Spenser before. The latter's death left a gaping chasm inside Gamma where his heart should be. None of the others would ever understand this level of grief. Not even Delta.

It was a long walk to the fortress. Gamma didn't make it often. That was still too frequent. If he had a choice, he'd never come back at all. For him, the lander would forever be the place where his best friend was murdered.

Delta's head appeared at the top of the wall.

"About time," she said.

She disappeared. That was his cue to climb up. With considerable effort, Gamma scaled over the top.

"Welcome home," Delta said.

Home. That was a loaded word. Gamma was as far from home as he could be; so distant that he couldn't even guess where it really was. Was it hunkered down with Upsilon or in a field with golligs? Or was it farther than that, back on Comus with Spenser at his side? Or perhaps it was more distant still, on a planet he had never visited, surrounded by people who were dead thousands of years before he was born? No, it definitely wasn't there. Home wasn't the place you lived; it was who you were with. Gamma knew he would never be home again.

He carefully climbed down from the walkway and into the courtyard. Delta didn't offer a helping hand. Even now, he could feel the tension between them. He had saved her life by killing the only person who'd made her life worth living.

"Why am I here?" Gamma said.

The question had been weighing on him all day. Delta had banned everyone from the fortress. Even Beta didn't enter it anymore. Delta had given him the immortality shots outside the walls to deliver to people around the island.

Delta ignored the question.

"How are things?" she asked.

Gamma was dumbfounded. Was she attempting small talk?

"Good," he said.

"Good," Delta said, glancing nervously at the lander.

What did she have to be afraid of?

"Listen," she said. "There's something I need to show you. But first, I need you to promise me you won't say anything, um, compromising. Or really much of anything at all."

"Okay," Gamma said. He didn't know why he'd need to say anything in the lander. If Delta needed to discuss something with him, she could do it out here.

"I mean it," she said. "SCASL is always listening. I want him to know as little as possible."

"Understood."

"And everything he tells you is a lie," Delta said. She stared at him intensely. "Everything."

"Okay," Gamma said. "I get it, all right?"

She opened the lower hatch to the lander and motioned for him to go in.

Gamma hesitated. Was she going to stab him in the back? That seemed unlike Delta. If she wanted him dead, she'd kill him while he was facing her with a sword in his hand. Not that it would matter if he was armed or not. She could end him just as easily either way. But why now? She'd had countless opportunities to get revenge over the years. Killing him would be illogical. She had dedicated herself to protecting everyone, no matter what they had done back on Comus. This had to be about something else. He went in.

"What did you want to show me?" he asked.

"Just sit there for a bit," Delta said. She closed the hatch. He was alone.

"Report," SCASL boomed.

Gamma jumped. He composed himself. He said nothing.

Out of the corner of his eye, he noticed a blinking light on the cloner. His brain automatically deciphered the message—something that was second nature to him after all those times talking to God in the coffee maker. The malfunctioning beverage dispenser had flashed its display on and off in morse code, feeding Gamma vital information about how old the students actually were. It was the only AI other than Spenser who didn't lie to him.

Gamma watched the blinking light. His brain quickly translated it.

Whirr, whirr.

It couldn't be.

"Spenser?" Gamma asked hesitantly.

The next minutes were a blur. There were tears and flashing lights and shouts from SCASL that both of them ignored. Of all the ways Gamma thought that day would go, he never imagined it would end with hugging a cloner.

He cupped his hand over the light and leaned in close so SCASL couldn't see it. Spenser talked, and Gamma mostly listened; a reversal of their usual roles. Their conversation lasted deep into the night.

When it was finally time for Gamma to leave, he was sure of two things. He was whole. And he was home.

Chapter 23

THETA RAN. HE did his best not to trip over any rocks in the dark. This was a bad time to sprint across the island but a good time to have a baby. Any time was perfect as long as the child came at all.

Sixty-two weeks. It was unreal. Unheard of. Almost elephant territory. The regular kind, not the super diarrhea version. Some of the others whispered that Upsilon must not really be pregnant. Actually, practically everybody did. Even Theta had his doubts. But at forty-five weeks, she'd finally let him examine her, and, as far as he could tell, there really was a baby in there. He felt a kick. The child wasn't particularly big. Upsilon barely looked pregnant until he got up close. Whether the long gestation period was because of the immortality shots or the birth control in the gollig meat or Upsilon's own frail constitution was anybody's guess. Theta's job was just to get this kid out.

The situation called for a med bot, not a charlatan. Unfortunately, Theta's hands were tied. Delta had destroyed the med bot's memory unit and smashed its arms for good measure. An optimist might take that as a vote of confidence in Theta's growing medical abilities. A realist would be freaking out. Theta didn't want to admit where he fell on that scale right now, but he started sweating well before he started running. Beta woke him up with the emergency news before continuing on to get Gamma. No pressure or anything, but Upsilon wanted Theta there more than the father of the child. Theta was so going to screw this up.

His legs burned. Why wasn't he there yet? Somehow, the island was too big and too small at the same time. It was possible to travel for kilometers in any direction without seeing another person, yet that still wasn't enough room to hold eleven different egos between the various shores. Each person was convinced of their own total rightness. They built their civilization in a patchwork, haphazard fashion, in accordance with their conflicting convictions. It was a recipe for disaster. That's what a pessimist would say, anyway. Theta, on the other hand, loved that everyone was so confident in themselves. You can't stop that kind of positive self-esteem.

Ahead, someone screamed. Theta was close. He ran harder, even if he was heading for the last place in the world he wanted to be.

He wished he was back home curled up next to Alpha. Sometimes, he was the only other human she saw for days. Alpha didn't seem to mind. He tried to be home every night, but his rounds often kept him away for longer. The good news was, he got a first-hand view of what everyone was up to. The island's population had been far from idle during Upsilon's pregnancy. Gamma had been a supportive if somewhat clingy baby daddy while also tending to the herd. The gollig numbers were the highest they'd ever been, even with recent losses to a particularly bad wolf shark attack. Omicron's herd, while not nearly as big, was growing, too. She spent her time by Rho's Bay. People tended to leave her alone there.

Perhaps Delta had been right to boot them from the fortress, Theta mused. They had certainly been more industrious since they'd been forced to make it on their own. The long weeks of Upsilon's never-ending pregnancy had been among their fledgling civilization's most productive. They'd made tools with stone heads lashed to gollig bones with gollig leather. They'd dug cisterns and filled hidden food caches with gollig jerky. They'd crafted more rope, woven more cloth, and made more clay pottery. Alpha wouldn't stop making her identical pitchers, no matter how often Theta gently suggested she might make something else. They'd dug out more shelters and small one-or-two-person holdout points than they had bodies to use them. That was the problem. Without more people, they were building a ghost town. That would change tonight.

Someone screamed again. It came from right in front of him. Theta had arrived. He entered the dugout that was Upsilon's (and sometimes Gamma's) home.

"It's okay, I'm here," Theta said.

Sigma looked up from Upsilon's side. It was weird to see Sigma here. Theta traveled the length of the island more than anyone but Beta, and he almost never ran into her. She was usually off on her own doing something dangerous. He'd had no idea that she and Upsilon were close.

"Did you bring drugs?" Sigma asked.

"No," Theta said with an embarrassed smile. "I brought me."

"We need actual medicine," Sigma said.

"I don't have it," Theta said. "Let's do what we can with what we've got."

"Which is nothing on both counts," Sigma said.

"Yeah," Theta said, rolling up his sleeves.

Theta had done his best to study up. He'd read article after article about childbirth on one of the island's two tablets. Upsilon had the other one now that Rho was gone. Between mom and fake doctor, Theta hoped they could piece together enough knowledge to get this done. Unless Theta passed out and Upsilon did it all on her own. Actually, that would be ideal.

Upsilon let out another scream. Theta thought the entire dugout might collapse.

"How are you feeling?" Theta asked.

Upsilon screamed harder.

"The baby's crowning," Sigma said.

"Okay," Theta said. "Okay, okay, okay, okay. Nobody panic."

"Get it out!" Upsilon said.

"That's the goal," Theta said.

"You're crushing my hand," Sigma said. Upsilon squeezed harder.

"Okay," Theta said, bracing himself. "Push when you feel your next contraction."

Upsilon nodded. Sweat poured down her forehead. She bore down on Sigma's hand. Sigma gritted her teeth.

Theta felt a jolt of pain. Something grabbed his leg.

"Dentopus!" Sigma yelled. She drew her sword. She tried

to stand but nearly fell backwards. Upsilon still had her other hand in a death grip.

Theta fell to one knee. His other leg was paralyzed. He drew his sword—every good doctor wore one in the delivery room—and faced the threat. The dentopus wrapped a tentacle around his arm and reached for his face.

Theta saw a flash of light. The tentacle fell harmlessly to the floor. A sword jutted out just above his right shoulder. It was Upsilon's.

"You can't swordfight in labor," Theta said.

"Watch me," Upsilon said. Theta felt very bad for anyone or anything that ever messed with her child.

Sigma pushed Upsilon back down while Theta slashed at the tentacle around his leg. The dentopus released its grip and retreated to a wall. It climbed, then launched itself at Upsilon.

Sigma impaled it in the air. She wrenched her sword and flung the monster through the open doorway.

"What the hell?!" a voice said. There was a wet chopping sound.

Gamma walked in, covered in blood.

"More incoming," he said.

"Push!" Theta yelled from his kneeling position on the floor.

Sigma freed her hand and joined Gamma at the doorway. They stood shoulder to shoulder, taking up the entire opening.

Theta heard the distinct sounds of scampering and swords cutting through the air. Something shrieked. Theta couldn't turn around.

"Push!" he yelled again.

The entire room lit up. Lightning crashed down outside.

Nothing like an electric storm during a dentopus attack in the middle of labor. Theta smiled. Surely everybody's first time was like this.

"Almost there," Theta said.

"There are too many," Gamma said.

Something latched onto Theta's back. He let out a startled yelp. His skin burned. He felt weak.

The dentopus fell off, warm blood coated Theta's back. He wasn't sure if it was his or the dentopus's. Gamma and Sigma stepped backward into the room as shapes climbed the walls and ceiling. Theta focused. He couldn't stand, but his arms worked, and his core was still keeping him upright.

Upsilon pushed.

"Got you," Theta said.

He grabbed the baby and cradled her to his chest. Yes, *her*. The human race's first natural-born infant in thousands of years was a girl. Delta and Beta charged into the room. From her sleeping mat on the floor, Upsilon held up her sword and let out a blood-curdling cry. Everyone was on top of everyone else. Blades and tentacles tangled wildly.

Theta focused on the perfect baby. The perfectly still baby. She was turning purple.

Something slammed into Theta. He steadied himself on one knee and checked the baby's airways. He wished the room was brighter. Lightning flashed again. He looked down the baby's nostrils. They were clogged.

There was a tool for this, but the nearest one was a ten-thousand-year space flight away. He stuck his mouth over the baby's nose and sucked. Something goopy shot into the back of his throat. He spit it out and sucked again. Nothing came out.

A woman wailed. Blood splattered the sleeping mat and the walls. Theta blew into the baby's mouth. Her chest began moving.

The baby cried. Theta cried. Upsilon cried.

Sigma killed another dentopus.

"Where are they all coming from?!" she yelled.

"They waited," Delta said. "They knew."

She sliced a dentopus in half in front of her, then killed another with her backswing.

More dentopuses clambered into the room.

Theta fell sideways, the baby still in his arms. He couldn't even kneel anymore. The poison was taking effect. Using his one free arm, he pulled himself into a corner and curled up, shielding the baby with his body.

Something lashed his arm. Just as fast, it was gone.

A foot stepped on him.

"Ow," he said.

"If they want you, they'll have to get through me," Delta said.

Theta tucked his head in as the air above him exploded with motion and blood. Dentopus bits bounced off the walls. Swords hacked and slashed at everything. Tentacles twitched and thrashed long after they were detached from their hosts. Upsilon said words he'd never heard her say before. Gamma slipped and fell in blood.

Finally, the room was quiet. Even the lightning was over. The infant cried.

"My baby!" Upsilon yelled. "Where's my baby?"

"Down here," Theta said.

Delta took the child. Theta stayed where he was.

"She's perfect," Upsilon said.

"She is," Gamma agreed.

Theta struggled to roll over.

"Are you crying?" Sigma asked.

"No," Delta said defensively, swiping her sleeve across her face. "Just wiping away the blood."

"Thank you, Theta," Upsilon said. "Thank you for saving my baby."

"It was a group effort," Theta said from the floor.

His mouth still tasted like baby snot.

Alpha entered. She was covered in blue. From the floor, Theta gave her a questioning look.

Alpha shrugged. "There were even more outside," she said. She knelt beside him and pulled a tentacle chunk out of his beard.

Beta stuck his head in. "Let me see that baby," he said. He was covered in dentopus gore, too.

"All right," Delta said. "Everybody, out."

"Take some tentacles with you as you go," Sigma said.

One spasmed as she spoke.

"First, I need a name," Beta said. "The island will want to know."

Upsilon rocked the baby in her arms.

"Eve," Upsilon said.

"Perfect," Theta said, still on the floor.

He passed out.

Chapter 24

LAMBDA RAN HER fingers through Starlight's hair. It wasn't silver at all. He looked exactly like his dad, minus the scar.

"How are the greens coming?" Lambda asked.

"They're marginally edible," Phi said. "Almost."

"Good," Lambda said. That was likely as edible as they were going to get. Entertaining on Spenser Island was always a dicey proposition. Digestible food consisted mostly of golligs and more golligs. There were a few scraggly green plants, however, which, if you soaked them just right, could be consumed and kept down. Did they have any nutritional value? Almost certainly not. But it was something different. Down here, that was a luxury. Tonight, Lambda needed to be the ultimate host.

The barely tolerable greens were just a garnish meant to enhance the plating, even if they weren't eating on actual plates. The main and only real course was gollig jerky, as usual, laid out on the rock slab that served as their outdoor table. The rest of their dwelling was underground, like everyone else's on the island. Lambda broke ground on it not long after the Great Eviction and worked on it continuously thereafter, including through her mysteriously interminable eighty-week pregnancy. The immortality tank, the birth control in the gollig meat, this alien planet, or all of the above had really done a number on the gestation process. They were all still at a loss to explain it. Lambda had done her best not to let it bother her in those endless months and concentrated on building her shelter. Her baby needed a safe place to grow up. She only slowed down after Starlight was born. Phi finished the rest by himself. Now, the dwelling was truly a home. Inside its subterranean chambers, her growing family had perfect protection from the island's frequent lightning storms. Eating above ground was a risky indulgence. By hosting an outdoor picnic in her courtyard, Lambda was showing off. She had no idea if that would impress Delta or not.

"Relax, man," Phi said. He kissed her cheek. "You've got this."

Lambda poked him squarely in the chest. "We've got this."

"Right," he said. "We're a team."

If Lambda wanted to put on a good show, this was the place to do it. In her somewhat biased opinion, her home was the most impressive on the island. She'd used all her knowledge from her five (or was it six?) times through Edubot's college curriculum to design the most mathematically perfect dwelling she could imagine. The best feature was the mud brick-lined drainage channel. Alpha supplied the bricks, and Phi had carefully laid them in place. Lambda had been impressed by his attention to detail. Their home stayed perfectly dry, even on those rare occasions when the sudden lightning storms were accompanied by rain. The water drained into an underground cistern that supplied them with drinking water. It was a modern marvel, not by the technologically advanced standards they'd left behind on Comus, but by the Stone Age ones they lived under now.

Those stones continued to move. Much had been built in the year since half the island banded together to fight off the massive dentopus attack while Upsilon gave birth. The golligs now had a corral made of chest-high rock walls to keep them safe at night. Gamma refused to put them in it because he said it was a death trap once a predator got inside, but it looked nice all the same. There were a dozen new dugouts spread out across the island where a runner could briefly hide from the lightning or passing sea monsters. Beta requested and got an observation post on top of Finger Rock. Lambda designed it for him and Sigma joined Beta for much of the labor when she wasn't off on one of her solo outings. Omicron continued to tend her own herd near Rho's Bay, which everyone else still avoided. Pi hosted a few gollig roasts and helped with construction when he could. Alpha made her pitchers and Theta made his rounds. They both seemed happy enough. Theta was confident the dentopuses were gone for good, having virtually vanished in the year since their grand assault. Delta, meanwhile, thought they were regrouping for their next attack and continued to work on whatever it was she did in the fortress. She hadn't produced anything new from the cloner in the last year, all while wasting precious food to run it. The others grumbled, but the jerky supply was still good, so nobody confronted her. They had their own lives to worry about.

That was especially true for Upsilon and Gamma, who now had a healthy toddler. Eve was something of a tourist attraction for a while. No one had seen a kid that age since they were all twelve-month-olds themselves, which wasn't exactly a phase they remembered. Lambda made frequent visits for a while, but things between she and Upsilon had become tense when Upsilon found out Lambda was pregnant. Neither one of them said it, but they both knew about the future crisis that Lambda planned to resolve tonight. Upsilon still made wool clothing, but not as much as before. Gamma spent less time with the herd and made fewer visits to the fortress to see Spenser. After Beta, he encountered Delta the most often of anybody, even if that wasn't very often at all. Lambda had pressed them both for details about their fearless leader's mood and mindset these days. Both men had been less than helpful. Nobody knew what Delta was thinking except for Delta herself.

Lambda rocked on her heels. She checked the table one more time.

"Do you think we should have gotten more jerky?" she asked.

Phi adjusted a green leaf on the rock slab. "This is our full ration, plus the leftovers we've been saving for days. It's fine."

Fine wasn't good enough. It had to be great. Marvelous. Transcendent. Their child's life depended on it.

Tonight, she would ask the question that had been on her mind ever since she'd learned Upsilon was pregnant. It had existed before then, too, but it used to be strictly theoretical. Lambda planned to have her baby first. She cleared her child through official channels. The twelfth immortality shot rightly belonged to Starlight.

That was if the shots could even sustain twelve people, of course. When Rho was alive, they were all still aging slowly, even with regular doses. Lambda thought that was over now. She'd often been surprised by how different the others looked after she hadn't seen them for a bit. Gamma in particular had shocked her when, seemingly overnight, he no longer looked like a twelve-year-old. Those dramatic transformations seemed to be done for good. She couldn't think of one noteworthy way anyone had physically changed over the last year, other than Upsilon and Gamma understandably looking more tired than before. Lambda's hair wasn't getting any more gray, and Phi wasn't getting any more handsome. Thank goodness. She couldn't handle it if he did. All the evidence Lambda could see suggested the microbes in the immortality tank were once again strong enough to hold twelve people in a static state. That's what the island's rumor mill said, too. Then again, rumors said a lot of things, including that Lambda was a shriveled-up old hag who could never bear a child. She proved those rumors wrong, even if it took her eighteen weeks longer than Upsilon. None of those hurtful words mattered now. The only opinion of any consequence was Delta's. She controlled the lander.

Lambda and Upsilon both wanted the twelfth immortality shot for their respective kids. What mother wouldn't? Upsilon argued that Eve deserved it since she'd been born first. The birth order part was true, but Eve wasn't authorized or planned. Delta couldn't possibly legitimize that level of chaos. Lambda, on the other hand, had followed the proper protocols when conceiving Starlight. The twelfth shot rightfully belonged to him.

"Hey," Delta said.

Lambda jumped.

"You scared me!"

It wasn't an exaggeration. Her heart was beating faster than ever, but not because she was startled. She was scared for her child's future. It all came down to tonight.

She picked up Starlight, who was playing with rocks on the ground. He hadn't eaten any or shoved them up his nose this time. That wouldn't have helped Lambda's cause.

"You remember Starlight," Lambda said.

"Of course," Delta said.

The entire island had been on hand for two full days when Lambda was in labor. No one wanted a repeat of the surprise attack at Eve's birth. Not a single dentopus showed itself. Starlight's life was blessed from the start.

Getting pregnant wasn't as easy as Lambda had hoped, not that Phi minded all the attempts. He'd found out relationships weren't always such a bad deal after all. Lambda had only had one injection of serum, even though she'd asked Delta for more. The effects must have lingered, because she'd finally conceived months after the initial injection. Now, she had a robust baby boy who was already sitting up. Those were the kind of high-quality genes that deserved to stick around. This beautiful child was her entire world. If she lost him, even decades from now at the end of his natural lifespan, she couldn't bear to go on. She felt it in her soul.

Lambda tried to pass Starlight to Delta. Delta held up a hand like she'd been offered a snot clam.

"I'm good," she said.

Delta had never struck Lambda as the maternal sort.

"I'm starving," Phi said, motioning toward the table. He folded his legs and sat down. Lambda and Delta joined him. In front of them lay the jerky and the almost edible greenery, a veritable feast by the island's standards.

"The cups!" Lambda said. How could she forget those? They were the most impressive part. She carefully placed Starlight on the ground and rushed down the carved steps. She reemerged a moment later with three cups and a pitcher. Starlight couldn't be trusted with one of his own. Each was handcrafted with her finest work: a perfectly symmetrical flower inlay courtesy of Alpha. The island didn't have a currency, so Lambda had bartered for them. She'd designed a cistern for Alpha, with Phi once again providing the labor. Alpha made her own mud bricks. Even accepting favors here took a lot of work.

Lambda filled the cups with cool water fresh from her own cistern. The drinkware on the boulder pretending to be a table made for an impressive display. This would almost have passed for a civilized meal in another time on another planet.

Delta went to drink. She stopped.

"Is it supposed to smell like that?" she asked.

Lambda looked in her own cup. The water was covered in a greenish film. She thought she had taken care of that. Without chemicals to eradicate it, she skimmed the gunk out of the cistern every morning until the water finally stayed clean on its own. The algae had chosen this moment to make a dramatic reappearance. Lambda silently cursed everything about the island.

She grabbed the cup out of Delta's hand and dumped the water on the ground.

"The meat is better without water, anyway," she said. "You can really taste the... dryness."

Delta nodded slowly.

They chewed the jerky in heavy silence. This was not the dinner party Lambda had envisioned.

"Thank you for inviting me," Delta finally said.

"It's our pleasure," Lambda said. "The truth is, we've been trying to get you over here for a while." The truthier truth was that Delta had been actively avoiding them for just as long. Beta supplied the fortress with gollig jerky, sparing her the need to abandon whatever she was working on in there. Lambda had only managed to get her here by purposely spreading the rumor-that-wasn't-a-rumor to everyone on the island that Delta was ducking them. She finally had to make an appearance to save face.

Gamma already had undue influence with Delta. He was the only one besides Beta allowed near the fortress, even if his duties as a dad and a shepherd mostly kept him away. His occasional visits with Spenser gave him the queen's ear, or the appearance of it. Who knew what he was telling her? Lambda did, or could at least make an educated guess. Gamma all but had immortality locked up for his daughter. Lambda had to act now if she didn't want to one day watch her own child die.

This would be the most difficult and important conversation of her life. It required the lightest touch.

Phi shoved a big chunk of jerky into his mouth.

"So we want that shot for our kid," he said.

"Excuse me?!" Lambda and Delta said at the same time.

Phi looked at Lambda, hurt.

"I thought we were on the same team," Phi said. "This was your idea."

He had seemed so aloof and mysterious when they were dating. Lambda missed the days when she'd had to wonder what he was thinking rather than listening to him blurt it out.

"I didn't mean like this," Lambda said. "Forgive him, Delta. He's been working very hard in the sun today."

"Not really, man," Phi said. "I mostly just walked around picking this green stuff we're not even going to eat."

"Garnishes," Lambda said. "For the last time, it's called garnishes."

"I don't know why we have to put on this big production," Phi said, putting another piece of jerky in his mouth. "Delta is smart. She knows why we invited her here."

Lambda and Delta shared a look. Judging by Delta's face, Lambda had already lost.

"We're actually worried you're getting too close to Eve to make an objective decision," Lambda said.

"I've only seen Eve a few times," Delta said. "I don't treat her like a beloved pet like the rest of you do."

Delta doesn't just lack a maternal instinct, Lambda thought. *She lacks a human one.*

Starlight cooed happily on the ground. Lambda picked him up.

"I should be going," Delta said, standing up. "Thank you for dinner."

"You can't leave yet," Lambda said. "You must have walked for hours to get here."

"Thank you for the exercise," Delta said.

"Seriously?" Phi said. "I spent, like, four hours collecting these garnishes."

Surprisingly, Delta sat back down.

Okay then, Lambda thought. They hadn't lost just yet.

"We have to make a decision on this eventually," Lambda said. "Right now, we're just doing eleven shots. We should be able to stretch it back to twelve."

"Why not stretch it to thirteen?" Delta said. "Or fifty. We're just going to have this conversation over and over again every time someone has a kid. Eventually, it won't be immortality at all. It might not even be life-extending."

"How would we know?" Lambda asked.

Delta shrugged. "When one of us dies, I guess."

"One of us already did," Phi said coldly.

"When one of us dies of old age," Delta clarified.

"You gave that fertility serum to me," Lambda said. "My kid was chosen."

"I tried to give it to Alpha first because that's who SCASL chose," Delta said.

"But she refused, and I got it, so my child was chosen second-hand."

Lambda's heart sank. She was doing a terrible job making

her own case. She couldn't think. Her heart was pounding out of control.

Delta put a piece of garnish in her mouth.

"Mmm," she said, making eye contact with Phi. She chewed reluctantly.

"It's not about what we need," Lambda said. "It's about what civilization needs. I'm the smartest, and Phi is the biggest and strongest. Starlight will have the traits we need to preserve."

"Wow," Delta said. "That doesn't sound arrogant at all."

"It's true," Lambda said. "I always had the highest math scores, and Phi… Well, look at him."

Phi smiled shyly. "Want me to flex or something?"

Delta made the same face as when Lambda had offered her Starlight. "No, thanks."

"The point is, we're a good genetic pairing," Lambda said. "To be blunt, civilization is going to have a better chance of surviving long term if my son is with it the whole time."

Starlight shoved a rock in his mouth.

"I can see the brilliance already," Delta said.

Lambda used her finger to fish out the rock.

"I have nothing against Eve," Lambda said. "Or against Upsilon and Gamma. I'm just stating facts."

Delta discreetly spit the garnish into her hand and stood up.

"And what if you have another kid?" she asked.

"What?" Lambda asked.

"Are you going to have just one?"

She looked at Phi. "I don't…"

"If you have two kids, or three or four or five, which one do you want to be immortal?" Delta asked. "Are they all going to be the saviors of civilization, or just your first rock-eater?"

Lambda barely registered the insult. An expression of terror slowly spread across her face. No matter what she did, she would watch some—or all—of her future children die. Unless she gave up her own immortality. Even then, it would only save one more kid. There just wasn't enough to go around. It was a fact she knew, but never really *knew*, until that moment. For the first time, the reality of the situation crystallized in her mind.

Delta made her goodbyes again and left. This time, Phi didn't try to stop her. Lambda didn't notice. Starlight slept on her lap as she watched the sky late into the night.

Chapter 25

GAMMA PRACTICALLY SKIPPED on his way to the dwelling. He was about to talk to his favorite person in the world.

"How are you doing, Eve?"

She giggled. She was always happy to see him.

"Oh, you're here," Upsilon said.

"Yeah," Gamma said. "Right when I said I would be."

That was an exaggeration. Meeting times on the island were a guess at best.

Upsilon pushed past Gamma and attempted to smooth out Eve's hair. It was always tangled, no matter how often they attacked the rats' nests that spontaneously formed on her head. To help, Alpha crafted a beautiful comb from a gollig bone. The first time they'd used it, the comb had snapped in half. The tangles were too strong. Gamma and Upsilon were too embarrassed to ask for another one. It must have taken Alpha dozens of hours to make it. They'd been using their fingers to comb Eve's hair ever since.

"Did you talk to her?" Upsilon asked.

"Him," Gamma said. "Spenser is a 'him.'" That categorization was absurd, of course, since bots had neither a sex nor a gender. But the humans had always assigned genders to them on Comus based on the bot's tone of voice. Spencer mostly spoke in vacuum, which was hardly precise on pronouns. At some point, Gamma had decided those deep, hearty whirrs were distinctly masculine. Spenser never corrected him, and that was that.

"Did you talk to Delta?" Upsilon said.

Gamma bent down to help with Eve's hair. The job required all the fingers they could muster. Eve whimpered. Gamma hated hurting her, but he couldn't let her go around looking like that. An actual rat might decide to live there. Spenser Island's version of one, anyway. That meant it would be two meters long and spit poison.

"I almost never see her," Gamma said. "On visitation days, she normally puts him in his old vacuum body and leaves him outside the walls before I get there."

"Visitation days?" Upsilon said. "It's like he's Delta's prisoner."

"More like her co-worker," Gamma said. "It's complicated. Our conversations aren't really that specific."

Gamma had shared more information with Spenser than with any other being, mechanical or otherwise, and Spenser had reciprocated. Yet their communications were based on generalities, leaving much unsaid. True best friends could always fill in the gaps.

"Why doesn't he tap out morse code with his spider legs?" Upsilon asked. On Comus, Spenser had mostly moved around using his wheels, which were fast and efficient, but he could deploy retractable metal legs to cover rough terrain.

"They don't work anymore," Gamma said.

SCASL had fried most of the vacuum bot's functioning parts when Spenser had plugged into the lander as they made planetfall. Spenser could no longer walk or roll. Even the main memory unit was damaged. Spenser thought slower when he was in the vacuum frame.

"Why doesn't he use his brushes for morse code?" Upsilon asked. "You know, long and short whirrs."

"That's not how we talk," Gamma said.

"Why?"

"It's just not."

Upsilon huffed. She would never understand.

She stood up.

"You have to save our daughter," she said.

It was this again. Unlike Spenser, she was aggressively direct. Motherhood had changed her, or maybe just hardened what was already there. The upbeat, easy-going girl who was always humming on Comus was now laser-focused on one issue and one issue alone. She would protect her child. Woe unto anyone who stood in her way.

Gamma poked Eve's belly. She giggled again. It still mystified him that there was now a human being who loved him unconditionally by default. It seemed unwise to like anyone that much, especially if that anyone was him. He was the luckiest guy in the world, even if his best friend was trapped in the cloner most of the time and the mother of his child wasn't exactly with him anymore.

She wasn't exactly not with him, either. That was complicated, too. He was her co-parent always but her boyfriend on an as-needed basis. There were moments when she seemed to genuinely enjoy his company and others when she appeared to be on the verge of murdering him. All the latter occasions revolved around this exact conversation. He took a step away from her just in case.

"When are you going to talk to her?" Upsilon said.

"Whenever I run into her," Gamma said.

"Which almost never happens because she drops Spenser outside the walls before you get there and picks him up after you leave," Upsilon said.

"You finally understand."

Upsilon glared. Gamma realized one step might not be enough.

Gamma sometimes wondered if their situation would be simpler if they were an official couple. Their top priority would always be Eve, but raising her would be easier if they also prioritized each other. Gamma's nights in the pastures meant they could never be together all the time—unless Upsilon agreed to live out there with him. That was never going to happen. Upsilon wanted Eve's regular home to have the safety of being underground, which was reasonable. Gamma had his own small shelter closer to the golligs, even if he didn't use it much. Still, he couldn't help but yearn for the life they might have had together under different circumstances. He would love to wake up in a home with Upsilon and Eve every day. And he would hate to have this conversation yet again.

"Ask for the sword," Upsilon said.

That was new.

"What sword?" Gamma said.

"Rho's."

Oh. The only available one in existence. Delta likely had it somewhere in the fortress.

"I'm not sure that's toddler-safe," Gamma said. "Might also be a little big."

"She'll grow into it," Upsilon said.

Gamma had to admit he saw her logic. It was a small step from giving Eve Rho's sword to giving her Rho's immortality shots. Gamma would also love to tag-team watching the herd with an older, well-armed Eve. He told Upsilon that Eve was perfectly safe with him while he guarded the golligs, but the reality was, he often engaged in active combat with her strapped to his back. Better than the alternative. He had once laid her down during an attack, and a wolf shark had nearly grabbed her. Only Big Thump's swift intervention saved her life. Gamma vowed then and there that nothing, human or otherwise, would ever eat Big Thump. Maybe she deserved the twelfth immortality shot.

"I'll ask about the sword," Gamma said. "Not the shots."

"Why not the shots, too?" Upsilon said sharply.

"Those can wait for when she's older," Gamma said. "We don't want to freeze her as a little kid."

"Yeah," Upsilon said. "Who would want to live like that for fifty years?"

"We were twelve," Gamma said. "Stopping her at this age would be cruel." Left unsaid was that stopping her development at any age might be cruel. He'd just be setting her up for what he was beginning to suspect would be a never-ending fight.

Gamma wasn't sure how many shots the immortality tank would eventually be able to provide. It had pumped out enough for twenty-two people on Comus—but never twenty-four. Mu and Hi had died before the last humans started getting them. They could only speculate on whether or not the shots could have sustained the full group. After they'd landed on Dion, the immortality tank hadn't been able to support even twelve people, but it had also been jostled around. Gamma and the others aged while the microbes recovered. Now people had stopped getting older again. The tank could support at least eleven. Upsilon was convinced it could also support twelve.

There was no way to know what the final number would be, but it had to be low. The people of Earth had destroyed each other over this intensely limited resource. It couldn't be scaled up for everyone. That undeniable fact had led to humanity's first planet-wide apocalypse. Even if it could be upped to twenty-two or fifty or even a hundred, it would never be enough. In Gamma's simulations at the Table, he had been able to get the population on what was now known as Spenser Island up to around three thousand. Delta could probably do even better. Regardless of what the ultimate population was, immortality would only ever be available to the smallest fraction of that. There were only two kids on the island and tensions were already rising. Perhaps they would all be better off if immortality wasn't even an option. The whole situation made Gamma's head hurt.

He picked up Eve and blew on her belly. She laughed uncontrollably.

"How can you not want her to live forever?" Upsilon asked. "Do you want to lose her?"

Gamma spun with Eve in his arms, waltzing around to imaginary music. She loved every second of it.

"Don't say things like that," Gamma said with a big fake smile aimed at Eve. "That's terrible."

"Then do something about it," Upsilon said. "Doesn't she deserve it?"

Gamma stopped mid-waltz. He gently placed Eve on the ground. She ran, looking over her shoulder to see if he was chasing her.

"I'm not sure that anyone deserves it," Gamma said.

"What do you mean?" Upsilon asked.

"Why do I deserve it?" Gamma said. "Because I lived long enough to make it onto the lander? Why doesn't everyone after me deserve it? Because random chance dictated that they were born later? I don't think 'deserve' factors into it. Like, at all."

Upsilon put a hand on Gamma's shoulder.

"We do deserve it," she said. "We made the right choices. We fought for our place here. And we earned this for our child."

"What about all the other children?" Gamma asked.

"There's only one other," Upsilon said.

"There will be more," Gamma said.

"Not from us," Upsilon said.

"Thanks for the news."

Upsilon crossed her arms. "You didn't honestly think…"

"I didn't think anything," Gamma said, turning away.

"That's obvious enough," Upsilon said.

Gamma closed his eyes and silently counted to three. He reminded himself that she might give a different answer on a different day.

"Someone will have children," he said. "And they won't want to watch their children die. There isn't enough immortality to go around. This dispute is just going to keep happening over and over again."

"Not if we stop," Upsilon said.

"Stop what?" Gamma said.

"Having kids," Upsilon said. "Why do we need to push the population past twelve?"

"It's already past twelve," Gamma said.

"That was Lambda and Phi's mistake," Upsilon said. "We don't need a population of a hundred or a thousand. There's not enough genetic diversity anyway. Keep it at twelve. Twelve people who will all live forever and have no reason to fight. If one of them dies, then someone can have another kid to replace them."

Eve came back. She was clearly disappointed Gamma hadn't chased her. Gamma took a quick step in her direction and she took off running again.

"I'm going to take her now," Gamma said.

"Fine," Upsilon said.

He ran and scooped up Eve. She let out a delighted squeal as he swung her onto his back. They had a long walk ahead of them, and only one of them would be doing the walking.

Gamma thought he'd be relieved to escape the millionth round of that conversation, but instead he felt a looming sense of despair. Upsilon wasn't going to let this go. Neither was Lambda. The most destructive force in the universe wasn't hate. It was love. Maybe they had been safer under the bots after all.

He headed to the pasture.

Chapter 26

SIGMA PLANTED HER hands on the rock and leapt. Her breathing was ragged. She was covered in sweat. Good. It wasn't fun until it started to hurt. She pushed harder. There was still some daylight left. It would be even tougher to dodge those teeth in the dark.

Snap! The wolf shark bit an empty patch of air where her leg had been half a second before. She bounded onto another stone with the angry monster in hot pursuit.

She didn't think it would catch her, but the possibility added to the excitement. It was the best competition she could find these days. She missed the Death Race—and its semantically confusing sequels, the Not the Death Race and the Not the Not the Death Race—from her time on Comus, but there was no chance of reviving them on the island. Beta refused to compete. He said his duties as a messenger were too important. Sigma knew he'd just gone soft. Her thirst for danger—the only thing that shut off her thoughts—was as unquenched as ever.

The wolf shark zigzagged between the stones, its tail whipping back and forth behind it. Although it was faster than her, she stayed ahead by going over the obstacles instead of around them. The sweat stung her eyes. The wolf shark was getting close.

She wished Beta were here. Losing to him wouldn't mean instant death, but it would be a blow to her pride, which would hurt even more. Those stakes were much higher than simply ceasing to exist after being digested. Who cared about being a courier, anyway? Delta could deliver those messages herself. Sigma hadn't seen her in months. She hadn't seen much of anyone other than Beta, really. Officially, Sigma's job was to scout the southern half of the island for incoming danger. Unofficially, it was to have fun. She kept Beta updated on what she saw, and he kept her supplied with gollig jerky. Not that it was a fair trade. The stuff was so hard and dry that it made her miss the vaguely cherry-flavored rations. Still, she couldn't complain. At least her job kept her away from the quietly feuding parents. If they wanted to have a cold war over immortality shots, they'd have to do it without her. The last time humanity split into factions, she'd picked the wrong side and had done unspeakable things. She would never make that mistake again.

The wolf shark's snout slammed into her back heel. She stumbled forward, her face flying toward a rock. She planted her hands and flipped over it, landing on one knee. Instantly, she was back up. She sprinted. *That was close.* This wolf shark was good. She was better.

It was a shame their race was about to end. She knew from experience that this wolf shark or any other wouldn't chase her for more than a few hundred meters. It was a stunt she'd been repeating for weeks. To kick it off, she'd approach the secret, cliff-lined alcove where the wolf sharks sunned themselves. Nobody else on the island knew about it. If she died down here, they'd have no idea what happened to her. She'd disappear like Psi and maybe Sampi, if he ever really existed. Who knew anymore? The only way to the sandy beach was a rock-strewn obstacle course leading to the high ground. Her game plan was always the same: She stealthily crept through the rocks until she was at the edge of the sand, where she revealed herself. The goal was to see how many of the wolf sharks she could get to chase her back the way she'd come. Her record was five. She knew she could get more. Today, she only had one in pursuit.

Strange. He was the sole wolf shark on the entire beach. She wondered where all his friends had gone.

Ahead, the sand between two rocks moved. A shape exploded out of the ground.

Sigma twisted to the side, narrowly avoiding the wolf shark. It lunged past her.

She took another step. The ground erupted again. The particle cloud blinded her. She did a diagonal somersault and ran. She didn't feel teeth. She must still be alive. She bolted with her eyes half closed.

The wolf sharks had set a trap for her. They were tired of her teasing them. Good. They were almost getting boring.

Sigma ran.

She welcomed the surge of adrenaline like an old friend. She didn't want to die, but she didn't particularly care if she lived. She was only truly content when her life hung in the balance. She had never felt more at peace.

Another wolf shark appeared, and then one more still. She was being pursued by six. No, seven. Where were they all coming from? They were in front and to the sides. There was no way out. She doubled back and went deeper into their lair.

The move caught the wolf sharks off guard. It took them a second to adjust. Sigma accelerated and built up a small lead.

They could afford to take their time. She was running into a dead end.

She blinked the sand out of her eyes. Her vision was getting better. This wasn't suicide; it was a fair competition—except that it really wasn't. She was smarter and better than them. She would prove it over and over again until she couldn't anymore.

Her best bet was to lure them in close on the sand, then out-maneuver them and sprint back to the rocks. She glanced behind her. There wasn't a wolf shark in sight. They were hiding on her only path off the beach.

That was interesting. If they stayed, she was trapped. She'd have to eat or sleep eventually. Her performance would slip long before she collapsed from exhaustion, and one of the wolf sharks would get her. She'd have to use her brain in addition to her muscles. This was exciting.

Sigma stopped. There were still no wolf sharks in view. She sauntered across the beach, keeping an eye out for any monsters buried under the sand. She didn't think there would be any, though. They couldn't think quite that many steps ahead. Then again, they had been surprising her all afternoon.

Something didn't have to be smart to be dangerous. The zots proved that. So did some humans, including her. It was best not to underestimate the wolf sharks just in case.

There was no sign of movement or fins. Sigma relaxed. If she was trapped, she was going to enjoy the beach on her terms. Time to explore.

She walked toward the area she called the wolf shark siesta pad. It was a section of beach that stayed outside the shadow of the cliffs all afternoon. The wolf sharks perpetually smoothed the sand here with their abrasive abdomens as they lazed about. The imprints were broken up by clear lines where their rear fins carved paths behind them. The lines intersected and overlapped as they turned in circles to get comfortable, creating intricate spiral patterns that were almost beautiful when viewed from the cliffs above. For a moment, she wished she were up there now. She cut off the thought. She was exactly where she wanted to be.

Then she noticed something she had overlooked in all her trips above and below: bones. They were in the shadows all along the base of the cliff. How had they got there? Did the wolf sharks drag their food here before they ate it? Sigma always assumed they swallowed it whole. Whenever they grabbed a gollig, she only saw them until they disappeared into the water. It never occurred to her that they would bring it to a different part of the island kilometers away to share with the group. That implied a level of cooperation Sigma didn't want to think about. Her pulse quickened just a little.

She approached the bones, leaving distinctly out-of-place biped footprints in the smooth sand. There was a huge spinal column that must have been ten meters long. It looked like a whale's, only worse. The individual vertebrae had nasty spikes. How many wolf sharks had worked together to take down that massive animal? Sigma realized how little she knew about the deadly predators she so often toyed with. Perhaps she should spend less time tormenting them and more time learning about them. She cut off that thought, too.

She knew she should focus on finding a way out of her predicament, but curiosity got the better of her. She got closer. A few steps from the shade, she drew her sword. She didn't expect a skeleton attack, but who knew what else was lurking in the semi-dark? Oddly, it had never occurred to her to draw her sword when running from the wolf sharks. If she killed them, the game would be over for good. She wondered if, deep down, she even liked them a little. No, she wouldn't go that far. But if she slayed them, she'd have to find new playmates. Besides, she could kill one or maybe two, but not seven. Standing and fighting would make it too easy for them. If they wanted her dead, they'd have to work for it.

The bone piles were fascinating. There were long bones and short bones, and weird, curled ones with sharp edges that looked as if they could cut steel. There were armor plates and hardened fins and what she could only guess were internal organs made of rock-hard calcium. These were parts from animals she'd never imagined existed. There was an entire unknown ecosystem under the waves. It was a shame she had to learn about it from some dumb animal's garbage dump.

In a particularly dark corner, something caught her eye: a skull. It was totally different from everything else down here. It didn't seem to belong to a plated fish or a mutant alligator. It was clearly from a primate, or close to one. If she didn't know better, she'd say it was a monkey. She'd never encountered one in real life, but she'd seen pictures of them during her long and pointless education. Occasionally, one of the other students would put some in their simulations in their never-ending pursuit of new and exciting apocalypses.

She picked it up. It was missing sections, as if the skull had never fully formed. What was it doing here? It couldn't be from the water, unless this planet had tiny mermaids. This belonged to a land biped. Everything in Sigma's gut told her what it was, but she refused to believe it. As she stared at the skull, the eye sockets looked back at her. That blank gaze was... human.

Sigma shuddered.

Carefully, she placed the skull back where she'd found it. Then she looked closer. It wasn't the only one. Half a meter away, there was a second skull just like it. And behind it, tucked under an alien bone, was a third. What was going on? Had the wolf sharks stolen someone's secret baby? Or, worse, had someone given birth and tossed their unwanted child over the cliff? She looked up at the ledge high above. She half expected to see someone looking down at her.

There were only two children in existence, and they were both already bigger than this. No one else had been pregnant. There was no way you could hide something like that in a population this small. Moreover, gestation took an absurd amount of time here. Playing God had side effects. Who would have thought? There simply hadn't been enough months to grow this many babies to this size, let alone to do it undetected. There was also the matter of the fertility serum. Unless someone had a secret stash of bubble clams, it was impossible to pump out three babies without Delta's express permission. These small hominid skulls couldn't be human. But if not, then what were they? There was nothing else they could be. Sigma wasn't having fun anymore.

There were unexplained human remains on a planet with no other humans. A million thoughts raced through her head at once. She had to get to the bottom of this. She had to tell someone. She had to keep it to herself. Two sets of parents were already dividing the island because their kids might die of old age someday in the distant future. Now toss in the bones of a bunch of dead infants. What would that do to stability on the island? Nothing good. These were people. Tiny people, but people, nonetheless. A single death on Comus had sent her life into a spiral for years. Now she stood before a trio of dead humans, each one unnoticed and unmourned—until now. She was their only witness. She was their sole hope for justice. She took half a step back from the haunting remains.

The sand exploded on both sides of her. Two wolf sharks went for the kill. It was a trap within a trap after all.

She slashed the first and dodged the second, stepping toward the bones and the cliff. She broke into a dead run along the perimeter. She had to make it back to the rocks.

In front of her, another wolf shark burst out of the ground. Was that nine or ten? She'd lost track. She pivoted, striking the wolf shark with her sword but not causing any real damage. She sped up.

Ahead, she saw fins in the rocks. Forward was worse than backward. The only other option was to the sides.

One way led to the water. She'd be dead in seconds there. The other way led straight up. Time to climb.

She darted for the wall, her eyes scanning side to side for a hand hold. Everything worth gripping was too high.

A wolf shark dove at her feet. She jumped, landing on its head. She kicked off. It was the boost she needed. With both hands, she grabbed a nook on the wall.

"Thanks," she said. She tried to sound defiant, but recognised the fear in her own voice.

She hadn't climbed something like this since the elevator shaft back on—no, she wasn't going to think about that now. Nothing with Iota. Not now. Not ever. Iota's death had been all her fault. Her fault. Her fault. Her fault.

"No!" Sigma yelled.

A wolf shark jumped. Sigma pulled up her legs just in time. She braced it against a rock far to her side. She was nearly horizontal now. Her grip was slipping. At least a dozen wolf sharks were directly below her. She couldn't count them all as they swarmed around and over each other. It was getting dark.

She pulled herself up another few meters. Her grip wasn't much better here. Her fingers hurt. The pain felt amazing, though she couldn't hold on for long.

She looked up, the rock face sloping outward directly over her. She had picked the wrong section to climb, not that she'd had much choice in the moment. There was no way she could go up any farther here.

She looked to the left, toward where the cliff met the sea. The slope was more favorable, but the rock looked wetter. She knew she'd slip and fall. To the right, there was hope. She saw a handhold that led to a series of pockmarks drifting sideways and up.

She extended her right arm. Not even close. She extended her right leg. She was still well short. It was too far. If she wanted to make it, she'd have to jump. She'd only get one shot at this.

Below, the wolf sharks were getting rowdy. There must be eighteen now. It was more eyes than had ever been on her before. She smiled sadly to herself. She finally had the audience she'd wanted for the Death Race all those years ago.

She jumped.

Her fingers grazed the handhold. She tumbled down. Frantically, she clawed at cracks. She caught one. Her feet dangled. The wolf sharks sprang up, stacking on top of each other. She hung just barely above them, holding on with her left hand.

She swung her body and reached a jutting rock with her right. Pulling with both arms, she lifted herself. She found purchase with her feet. She was on the move. Step by step, she ascended. She had her way out. The path after that had never been blurrier. *Who did those bones belong to, and what are they doing down there?* She'd once thought guilt was the most painful feeling in the world, but she was wrong. Uncertainty was worse.

Chapter 27

"I have something to tell you," Alpha said.

"Me, too," Theta said.

Alpha put down the pitcher. It was adorned with a stylized geranium made up of four identical, geometrically perfect quadrants. She loved its unchanging, reproducible sameness. It was the greatest thing she'd ever created—until now.

"I'm ready to have a baby."

"Oh," Theta said. He scratched his beard.

"What were you going to say?" Alpha asked.

"That we need to destroy the immortality tank."

Neither of them said anything for a long moment. Alpha took a swig directly from the pitcher. She wished she had something stronger than water.

"Why would we destroy the immortality tank?" Alpha asked. She motioned vaguely to the entire island. "It's the only thing holding all this together."

"It's what's going to destroy us," Theta countered.

For once, he wasn't smiling. It was so rare to see that expression leave his face. Alpha resisted the sudden urge to draw him. She didn't have the right tools, anyway.

"I've been going back and forth between the two sets of happy parents and their kids," Theta said. "Things are getting tense. They all want the immortality shot."

"We have years and years to resolve that," Alpha said.

"Yeah, but there will be more kids," Theta said, "including ours—maybe. The struggle is only going to get worse."

"We can make a system for distributing it," Alpha said.

"It would be better if we didn't have it at all," Theta said.

"It's the only reason we're still here," Alpha said. "So many of us would have died already without it."

"I agree. But the shots should only be a stopgap while we learn to take care of ourselves. Like training wheels on a unicycle."

Alpha rolled her eyes.

"Now it's time to take those training wheels off," Theta continued. "Instead of helping us, they're leading us in the wrong direction."

"And where is that?"

"To war."

Alpha was taken aback. She went for another drink. The pitcher was empty.

"It won't come to that," she said.

All she had ever wanted to do was create beautiful things. A child would be the most beautiful of all. She hadn't been ready before. Art couldn't be forced. It had to come in its own time. That time was now. She wouldn't let it be derailed by whatever delusions Theta was under at the moment. She respected his principles but not his timing. This was exactly the wrong moment for a crisis of conscience.

Many factors coalesced to help change her mind about having a kid. Life on the island had stabilized after Rho's death. Gamma and Upsilon had Eve, and Lambda and Phi had Starlight. She was happy that other couples had tested the water first. Eve was now two and Starlight about one and a half. Watching the children grow was fascinating. It was one time Alpha didn't resent change. After seeing how the other couples raised their kids, Alpha felt she was up to the challenge. It was a nice way of saying if those idiots could handle it, she and Theta probably could, too.

It was also her duty. So much time had passed since the landing, but civilization wasn't going anywhere. They had more stored food and a surplus of simple goods but no real society. They needed additional people for that. Alpha accepted that now. Until their population grew, they would remain isolated stragglers on the edge of the known universe. Forming a true community required more people to commune with. Once they got their numbers up, the changes could stop, and Alpha's world could return to comforting sameness once again.

War was the opposite of that. She hoped those young(ish) families weren't really headed for a fight. There was tension, but it could be resolved. They had all overcome bigger challenges. Once upon a time, Theta hadn't wanted to land at all. He viewed their conquest of the planet as a form of genocide, both against the native life and the creatures the first colonists had created and left behind. Now, he was a regular contributing member of humanity's last pioneers, fighting off monsters with the rest of them. If he could come around on that, he could change his mind on the immortality tank. While Alpha waited for him to see reason, they could have a baby.

"The others will never agree to destroying the tank," Alpha said. "I wouldn't even agree to that, and I love you. I have a much higher tolerance for your worst ideas."

"They don't have to agree," Theta said. "I could destroy it myself."

Alpha grimaced.

"Remember what happened the last time you went rogue?" Alpha said. "You nearly got us both killed."

"Writing the manifesto was a mistake. I see that now. But the ideas behind it were right."

"You landed anyway," Alpha said. "Even you didn't stand behind them."

Theta shrugged.

"You're speaking from a place of fear," he said. "Don't worry. The others won't hurt me."

"You just told me you thought they were heading towards war," Alpha said. "War means killing, in case you forgot. If they're willing to kill to get the shots, they'll certainly kill the person who gets rid of them for good."

"Once the immortality tank is gone, they won't have any reason to hurt me. There will be nothing to gain from it. We're rational beings."

"Apparently you haven't paid attention to literally anything that's happened in our entire lives," Alpha said.

She left their cliffside home to get some space. That was one of the few things in abundant supply on the island. She could go in nearly any direction to find open vistas devoid of other people. Unfortunately, those "open" spaces were full of other things. There were hidden predators and obvious predators and everything in between—plus lightning. The island wouldn't have been her first choice for a vacation destination, but at this point, it was home. There were worse places to raise a child. She just couldn't think of any right then. She wasn't sure if she ever would.

Theta followed her.

"We need to talk about this," he said.

"You need to leave me alone right now," Alpha said.

"See?" Theta said. His usual smile was back. "Do you really want me annoying you for the rest of forever? The tank has to go."

Alpha didn't find that funny at all.

"Maybe you should just give up your shot," Alpha said. "Problem solved."

"Problem solved for one kid one time," Theta said. "And as soon as that kid has a kid, we're right back to square one."

Alpha looked out across the vast nothingness. Delta saw this place as a cramped prison, but it was bigger than the massive moonbase where they had grown up, even counting the endless unmapped lunar mining tunnels down below it. Maybe Zeta could dedicate the rest of his life to exploring them, if he survived even the first few minutes after they left him behind.

The idea hit her all at once.

"We need religion," Alpha said.

"What?"

"Religion," Alpha said with more certainty. "We used it all the time in the simulations, especially when Zeta was involved."

"Everybody died in those simulations," Theta said. "Always. As in, one hundred percent of the time."

"Not when Delta was in charge," Alpha said. "She finally won."

"Did she even use religion?"

Alpha honestly didn't remember. She didn't care about the simulations at the Table back then. She never thought the landing was actually going to happen. Oops.

"Zeta was right," Alpha said. "If we don't make a religion, our descendants will make one for us. They did that every time at the Table. We might as well take control and shape it to our benefit. We can use it to decide who does and doesn't get to be immortal. It's the only way to guarantee a permanent peace."

"Do you want us to set ourselves up as gods or something?" Theta asked.

"Exactly," Alpha said.

The plan solidified in her mind. There would be twelve gods, each leading a tribe of their own. Each god would be immortal and have a precious, irreplaceable sword. They would have the best weapons in existence, and they would have the most time training with them. They would be unstoppable. No one could expect to challenge them and live, so no one would try. Alpha would never have to use her combat skills against a human again. There would never be war. In the extremely unlikely event that an immortal did die, either through accident or treachery, the other gods would get together and decide who would become the next immortal. They would never give it to the person who had killed the previous god, so regicide would have no point. It would be the final guarantee of eternal peace.

The plan wouldn't be without a cost. Alpha and the others would have to deal with the deaths of their children and their children's children and their children's children's children over the centuries and millennia. Her heart ached at the thought. The imagined grief threatened to crush her, but the idea of endless war over the immortality tank hurt even more. Surviving meant making hard choices and living with the consequences of those decisions, even if that life and those consequences lasted forever. They needed the immortality tank if they were going to make it as a civilization. A small core of eternally trained and ready sword fighters would protect society from the planet. Her plan would protect society from itself.

Would the others appreciate the artful nuance of her plan for everlasting peace? Probably not. They would misunderstand her idea, just like they misunderstood Alpha herself. When they looked at the world, they saw only chaos, not the beautiful, repeatable geometry Alpha reproduced in clay. When they looked at Alpha, they saw only her small stature, not her inner fierceness. They missed the truth of everything. They overlooked real strength.

She didn't voice any of that to Theta, but for a second, she thought he could read her mind. He looked at her with the most profound disappointment she'd ever seen. He walked away. She had her space.

She gazed again across the vast nothingness, but now she saw it differently. One day, her worshippers would occupy this space. Her peaceful, thriving worshippers. Art didn't have to be in pencil or stone. It could be in flesh, a lasting, living monument to something beautiful she helped create. Her masterpiece would be an entire civilization, permanent, enduring, and seen by all.

Chapter 28

"PULL," OMICRON SAID.

Bart looked at her. He bent over and rooted around in the sand.

"Pull," she said more firmly but still at an acceptable volume. She didn't want to yell lest she cause the whole herd to fall over. The other golligs in the harnesses also bent down to dig.

She wanted to be kind to Bart. That was always a dangerous proposition. She leaned up against him and pushed, but he didn't budge. She preferred not to use violence against these animals, but it might be necessary. Not that she was under any obligation to be overly kind. Ultimately, they were food. She would personally eat them all. It was a hard knock life for everyone, including her—except for the part where she was going to live forever, and golligs' lifespans could sometimes be measured in months.

She drew her sword and lightly poked Bart in the butt. He unleashed a panicked oink-bleat and took off.

He jerked at the harness. For a moment, Omicron worried the ropes wouldn't hold. The other golligs felt the tug and

237

looked up to see Bart struggling to get free. The panic spread. The group surged.

"Finally," Omicron said.

They strained against the ropes stretching to the bottom of the bay. Getting the animals properly attached to those lines had been an epic undertaking. So many knots. So many rope burns. So much swearing. It had taken months. No, years. She had started investigating the bot before Rho died, which was before anyone was even pregnant. Now Eve was two. How had so much time passed? How had she gotten so little done? The process was so much harder than she'd expected. Lines had to be run and rerun. She ran out of rope. She ran out of lame hemp to make more rope. She ran out of patience. She needed rope not just to reach the bottom, but also to trade for all the other things she needed to get by. The rest of the island was always pestering her to make more, as if anything they were doing was nearly as important as what she was trying to accomplish here. Life kept getting in the way of the one mission that really mattered.

She was always careful not to let her fellow humans know what she was really up to; they wouldn't approve after what had happened with Rho. It was all so exhausting. There weren't enough hours in the day. There weren't enough golligs. She had to wait for more to be born while she scouted for threats and improved her shelter and dug new food caches and swam countless trips to the bottom of the bay. All the while, the golligs watched her indifferently. Their uselessness got on her last nerve.

She could tell them apart now. She knew more about them than she did about herself. Unlike Gamma, she did not come to love them. The vocabulary she'd built up while training on the moonbase hadn't taken into account how much unique and specialized profanity she would need to get through even one day on the island. So much so that she'd created specialized cuss words for each individual gollig, regretting that they couldn't understand her well enough to be offended.

Ethel slipped and fell in the sand. The rest kept pulling. Omicron had tied up all her golligs, even the young. She needed every ounce of muscle power they had. She watched the rope. It was taut but perfectly still. Then, with a lurch, it moved.

"It's working," Omicron said with thinly restrained excitement.

Bart oink-bleated.

"Take it up with HR," Omicron said. Edubot had taught them extensively about corporations in prior civilizations. That one line was all that had stuck.

How much did the submerged bot weigh? Omicron had no idea. The more important question was, how much could a gollig pull? No one knew. They were too feisty to ride, and there was no wood to build a chariot. Even a simple wheel was out of the question. Gamma had experimented with sleds made from bamboo, but they had quickly fallen apart on the rugged terrain. Besides, there wasn't much that needed to be hauled around. The basic tools and goods they traded back and forth didn't weigh much. The heaviest things they had to move were Alpha's mud bricks. Phi seemed perfectly happy to carry those himself, if only for the workout. If Omicron hadn't been so worried about secrecy, she would have invited him to help pull.

The rope moved forward a centimeter at a time. The golligs were struggling. Omicron tapped Bart on the butt with the flat side of the sword. He jerked wildly with a fresh wave of panic.

"You're such a baby," she said.

Bart would never trust her again. Not that he should have ever trusted any human in the first place. To most of them, he was no more than the raw materials for jerky. To her, he was jerky and an obligation. She had protected him from countless predator attacks. She had bled for him. Was it too much to ask him to dredge up one giant block of metal in return? Apparently, yes.

She watched the rope nervously. This had to work. If it didn't, she couldn't think of any other way to retrieve the bot. Two years of blood, sweat, and profanity would have been utterly wasted. Without the metal, Rho would have died for nothing. What would that make Omicron? If none of this served the greater good, she couldn't justify a single thing she'd done.

"Pull harder!" she yelled.

Three golligs toppled over, their legs as stiff as short bamboo. She had to watch her temper. The other golligs continued to pull. The rope moved. That was weird; they were applying less force than before. The rope accelerated. Some of the standing golligs weren't pulling at all now, and went back to digging in the sand. For the golligs tugging at the line, the ropes were still taut, but they weren't like horses pulling a carriage. They were more like dogs straining at the end of a leash. She had witnessed both in the simulator during various apocalypses, but she never imagined she would see it play out in real life.

The golligs weren't pulling the bot up. It was coming up on its own.

Omicron cut the rope. Bart took off, dragging the team of golligs sideways. With another slash, she cut him loose; he disappeared into the short bamboo. She would deal with him later—if the wolf sharks didn't get him first.

A metal glimmer appeared near the surface. Omicron watched, transfixed. Plumes of sand mushroomed around its feet. Slowly, it rose from the water.

A gollig oink-bleated uneasily. The ones who hadn't run off were watching now. Had they sensed danger, or were they just curious? She cut the rest of them free from their harnesses. She kept the sword in her hand.

Water poured off the bot as it walked up the slope of the sandbar and into full view. It was tall. Five meters, if not six. It was huge when it wasn't folded up on itself. It made lifting bots look small. How had she ever thought a team of golligs could pull something that big? They must have annoyed it awake. It had done the rest on its own.

Its metal surfaces gleamed in the sunlight. The sand refused to stick to it. It looked factory-fresh. It was the most beautiful thing Omicron had ever seen. And it could crush her like a bug.

The rest of the golligs ran away. That was a lot of free dinners roaming around for any sea monster that wanted them. Omicron had bigger problems. She'd be lucky if she survived long enough to eat her next meal.

She didn't have to stay. There was still time to flee—unless there wasn't. Maybe the bot was fast. Maybe it could fly. The only thing she knew for sure was that it could survive for thousands of years underwater. Whatever it was, it was tough. It would soon be right on top of her.

She came to a decision. She put away her sword.

"Hey, there!" she said. "I'm Omicron. Nice to meet you."

The bot kept coming. It didn't show any reaction to her greeting. Maybe it hadn't heard her.

"Hey!" she said again. "Haven't seen you around here before."

Where did that come from? She was embarrassing herself in front of her likely murderer. Part of her was glad there were no witnesses.

The bot continued walking down the sandbar. When it reached the main section of the beach, Omicron put her arms behind her back. She held her ground.

The bot stopped. It towered over her.

"Welcome," Omicron said.

The bot seemed to regard her for a moment. Then it slowly rotated its head a full three hundred and sixty degrees. Omicron guessed it was surveying the landscape. She waited.

From its right shoulder, the bot extended an antenna with a red light on top. The light flashed several times. The bot beeped.

"Can you speak?" Omicron asked.

The bot remained silent.

"We could use your help," Omicron said. "We're settling the planet again. Humans and bots aren't fighting anymore." She realized she should have led with that. "We're on the same side now, so there's no need to, you know, kill me."

The bot walked. Omicron jumped out of the way. The bot crossed the beach and stomped through the short bamboo. Omicron followed.

"I do not take orders from organics," the bot said suddenly, its voice deep and mechanical. The digitals were capable of much more complex and subtle vocal patterns. Omicron wasn't sure why some of them sounded like this. The bot continued its march.

"So you do speak," Omicron said, scurrying after it. "You're probably the only working bot on the planet. I can't believe you're still functional. How long were you down there?"

The bot's pace remained unchanged.

"Time increment irrelevant," it said, and stopped again.

This time, its head extended upward a full meter on a piston. As if this thing needed to be any taller. The bot again rotated its head in a full circle. Omicron waited patiently.

The bot retracted the piston so its head was again on its shoulders. It swiveled at the waist to face her without moving its feet. It really was like a beefier lifting bot.

"Swear fealty to the Digital Alliance or be destroyed," the bot said in its rudimentary, mechanical voice.

That was disappointing. She thought she was making

progress. She had never heard of the Digital Alliance, but context clues suggested it was the bot side of the war that had wiped out the previous batch of colonists. She didn't know fealty had been an option for the last humans. Had some people switched sides? If they did, it didn't save them. If you were going to commit treachery, at least make sure it would keep you alive.

"Uh, okay," Omicron said. "I swear allegiance to the—what did you call it?—Digital Alliance, whatever that is."

The bot was silent for what seemed like forever. The red light on its shoulder antenna continued to blink.

Omicron looked around. There was no sign of other humans or golligs. Wind rustled the short bamboo. She had the eerie impression she was the only living thing on the entire island.

"Pledge not accepted," the bot announced abruptly.

It raised both arms. Omicron noticed its hands for the first time. Each finger was as long as her arm and shaped like a pickaxe.

The bot slammed them down.

Omicron dove backward. The hands made a wet, sucking sound as they slashed into the soil.

Omicron reached for her sword, then thought better of it. There was no point in fighting. She would almost certainly die without being able to warn the others. Better to run, but not by a direct route. She would just lead the bot to more prey. She had to lose it first.

Crouching low, she rushed through the stalks. She heard the bot stomping behind her. She dropped to her hands and knees, jerking this way and that as she crawled. She was light enough not to sink too far in the swampy soil. The bot stayed right behind her, sloshing as it walked, each step leaving a deep impression. It cut a straight path as Omicron zigzagged around thick patches of bamboo. The towering bot could easily see over the top of the lightning-stunted trees.

Suddenly, Omicron was back on Comus, where the air was filled with smoke and screams and the ground was streaked with blood. The bots were everywhere. Their metal tracks clanked against the metal floor. They spotted her. She tried to run toward the lander, but her legs wouldn't move. The bots closed in.

She blinked. She was back in Dion's cold, clammy muck. Her heart tried to pound out of her chest. There was no time to catch her breath.

She stood and ran. Her only hope was the water.

The bot had likely been in Rho's Bay for millennia, but at the bottom. It couldn't swim—she hoped. She would be safe on the surface with dozens of meters of depth below her. Unless something came up and ate her, of course.

She swam.

Stay away today, you stupid dragons, she thought. Halfway across the bay, she dared to look over her shoulder. The bot was on the edge of the water, staring.

It stood there. She kept treading. How long would it wait? Long enough for her to exhaust herself, she guessed. She looked to the other side of the bay. Maybe she would be better off getting out there. Then again, swimming was slow. The bot might beat her there once she started to move. She stayed put.

She took a deep breath and put her head in the water to make floating easier. It was something survivors of shipwrecks and plane crashes used to do to stay afloat for hours or even days. Omicron had learned that when Epsilon tested out boats in the simulator. That week, they'd all discovered more than they ever wanted to know about death at sea.

Minutes ticked by. It was hard to be sure how many. From her countless trips to the bottom, she knew she could hold her breath for nearly five. Her lung capacity had increased enormously over two years of dives. She counted each breath before she stuck her head in the water. She went through ten. Then twenty. Each time she refilled her air, the bot was still there. It hadn't budged since she'd entered the water. The sun was getting lower in the sky. With her face in the water, she watched for monsters. Soon, she wouldn't be able to see them. She didn't want to be out here after dark.

She pulled her head out of the water and took another breath. The bot was gone. She turned slowly, not wanting to disturb the surface of the water, as if the sound of her splashing would bring it back. She scanned the entire shoreline. The coast was clear.

Omicron swam to the opposite side of the bay. She pulled herself onto the beach and lay there, exhausted. She wanted to take the longest nap of her life. There was no time. She pushed herself to her feet. She had to warn the others.

She ran.

Chapter 29

"ARE YOU PICKING up anything?" Delta asked.

Spenser whirred above her head. No luck. She thought the sensors on his damaged and immobile vacuum body might reach further with an altitude boost. It made no difference. The beast had simply vanished. To the others, that might be a relief. Not to Delta. She liked her monsters where she could see them.

She set Spenser on the rocky ground. He whirred apologetically.

"You did your best," Delta said.

She hadn't believed Omicron at first when she told Delta her ridiculous story. It was too strange to be real, even on this, the most absurd planet in the universe. Where else had killer kangaroos been a stepping-stone to the apocalypse? And yet, things had somehow gotten worse. On a deserted island with no sign of prior bot activity, one had simply walked out of the water. No, that wasn't right. Omicron had harassed it into coming out. If this had happened at the Table back on the moon base, Delta would have accepted it. There was nothing too strange for those doomed simulations. But here, in real life? No one was that dumb. Clearly, Delta had given her species too much credit. It was so frustrating. It was her job to protect them. She wanted humanity to survive. That meant both the race and these particular individuals. She would die for them if it came down to it. She just wished they'd be slightly less suicidal so she didn't have to.

Perplexingly, the mysterious bot, which was larger than any they had ever seen, had somehow disappeared. Everyone had been looking for it ever since. The tracks had been easy enough to follow. The thing had marched down the sandbar, through the bamboo thicket, and then along the beach, where it apparently stood for a great while. Its foot indentations there were deeper than anywhere else along its path. After that, it ventured inland onto harder ground. That's where the trail disappeared. Did it re-enter the water at a different point? If so, they hadn't found its footprints on any other beach. It didn't seem like it could possibly still be on the island. Surely something that big would be noticeable. She had never seen a cave on the island large enough to hide it. Could it dig its own hiding spot? According to Omicron, it had huge limbs with massive fingers shaped like pickaxes. They seemed perfect for digging—and for killing. They needed to find this thing now.

Everyone was on the case. Delta divided ten adults into three search parties. That left one person to watch the kids. Children were absolutely necessary to the future of the species. Their civilization had no future without them, but protecting them diminished Delta's already meager army. It wasn't easy to run a military operation and a daycare at the same time. Delta found a way. There had been quite an argument over who would stay back to watch the children. Upsilon volunteered, but Lambda refused to hand over Starlight. Trust between them had dipped that low. After an inexcusable amount of wasted time, Delta drafted Theta to watch both children while everyone else went out on the hunt. They could be confident the kids would be safe until they got back—unless the dentopuses decided this emergency was the perfect occasion to launch another mass raid. At this point, Delta wouldn't rule anything out.

Beta ran up, out of breath. That was unusual. He could go practically forever. He must have sprinted the whole way.

"Found something," he gasped. "Bay of Death."

Delta suppressed a shiver. She hadn't been back since that eight-legged dentopus almost got the best of her, "almost" being the operative word. It found out the hard way that the prize for second place was death. On Spenser Island, sometimes that was the prize for first place, too.

Delta looked at Spenser.

"You good?"

Spenser whirred.

She took off without the stationary bot. The sea monsters should leave him alone. Not even the dentopuses were that hungry.

Sigma and Pi struggled to keep up with her. She'd selected them for her group because they were among the only possible neutral choices. She couldn't pick Upsilon and Gamma or Lambda and Phi for obvious reasons. Omicron was also a lost cause. She was defiant even when she wasn't getting someone killed or provoking a giant bot. Delta tried not to take it personally. She suspected the former hairdresser would have a problem with anyone who was in charge. Some people make it their whole purpose to be ungovernable. Delta had done it herself under the bots, but she'd had a good reason. If she was being honest, maybe Omicron had, too.

Practically everyone had some kind of problem with Delta these days. She hoped that was a sign she was doing her job correctly. If she was truly being fair with these no-win decisions, then everyone should be equally fed up with her. Not that that made the emotional toll any easier. Sending the others out of the fortress had been the right call, but she had to admit she sometimes missed the early days after the landing. Back then, everyone huddled together every night, and no one but Theta and Alpha had separated into the sort of insular couples Delta would never be a part of. With each passing day since then, she had become more alone.

Beta caught back up to her.

"There," he said.

From the top of the cliff, he pointed to a set of tracks along the beach. How did the beast get there? The trail down was narrow and steep. She couldn't imagine its big, plodding feet navigating that precarious ledge. Carefully, she descended the path, keeping an eye on the countless dark crevices that lined the cliff wall. A dentopus could launch itself out of any one of them. The others followed her wearily. She put on a brave face. The last thing she needed was for them to get nervous, too. She could deal with monsters but not with panic. There was nothing more dangerous than a spooked human with a sword.

Gamma and Upsilon were waiting at the bottom.

"This is all we could find," Upsilon said. "There's just one set."

Delta bent down and examined it, even if its feet were of little interest to her. She was more fixated on its pickaxe fingers. Her nightmare was that the bot would somehow make contact with SCASL in the lander. Then the two of them could work together, giving that pretentious AI the ultimate set of hands. There were even worse possibilities. SCASL might just kill the ghost in this new bot and take over its body, fully escaping into the world. SCASL was enough of a threat trapped where he was. She absolutely did not want to deal with him on the move.

"Look," Gamma said. He nodded out to sea.

Everyone stared at the waves, except for Pi, who glanced at it once and then turned his attention back to the cliff.

"I don't see anything," Delta said.

"It's an antenna," Gamma said.

Delta strained her eyes. The tip of the thin metal stalk blinked red. That made it easy.

"Told you," Gamma said. Upsilon took his hand.

"What do you think it's doing?" Beta asked.

"Broadcasting," Delta said.

"Wouldn't it want to be on the high ground for that?" Sigma asked.

"Not if it's pointing straight up into space," Delta said. "This might just be a nice, safe place to hide out while it waits for reinforcements."

"There are no reinforcements," Pi said, a hint of doubt in

his voice. For the first time, he gave the object in the water his full attention.

"It might not know that," Delta said.

"It's gone," Gamma said.

"Are you sure?" Delta asked.

She stared at the spot but couldn't tell. There was no more blinking light, at least.

"Where did it go?" Upsilon asked.

"To the supercontinent, hopefully," Pi said. "No reason to stick around here."

"That would be a long walk," Gamma said.

Delta knew they were wrong. Her problems never walked away. They lingered until they became full-blown crises.

"You should all leave," she said. "It won't be safe out here after dark."

"That implies it's safe now," Pi said.

He had a point.

"What about the bot?" Upsilon asked.

"Nothing we can do but wait," Delta said.

She dispatched Beta and Sigma to tell the other groups that the bot had been spotted. Upsilon and Gamma left to recover their child from the island's first emergency daycare center. That left her alone on the beach. Once again, it was what was best for the group, even if it wasn't necessarily what was best for her.

She maintained her solitary vigil through the night. Bots and monsters alike stayed away.

Chapter 30

Pi HAD ALWAYS believed the safest place to be was around a fire. It was an instinct that went back to the time of cavemen. Light and warmth were the ultimate elixir against a dark and scary night. But what happened when the greatest threats were sitting around the fire with you? Hopefully, a detente. Tonight, he would prevent a war.

"Mine!" Starlight shrieked. Pi looked up, alarmed. Lambda had something in her closed fist.

"No, you can't put this up your nose," Lambda said.

"Gimme!" Starlight yelled even louder.

If children were the future, humanity was doomed. No wonder Edubot was always so morose.

Starlight shoved a different rock up his nose.

This time, Lambda shrieked.

"On it," Theta said. He used a thin, pointy bone tool to eject the rock. It landed in the dirt. Starlight reached for it. Lambda slapped it away.

There was light applause from the group in appreciation of Theta's quick rescue. Pi gave Theta an upward nod. Theta winked.

"Third time this week," he said.

The bot had been missing long enough for life to go back to normal. On Spenser Island, that meant it returned to its usual dangers, rather than the occasional ones that walked out of the water on a pair of giant metal feet. The greatest risk these days was from the simmering tensions between two families. Pi hoped to defuse that situation tonight.

He cleared his throat.

"Let's start with a story," Pi said. "Gamma, you're up."

Gamma looked startled, even though he was the one who had volunteered beforehand. Carefully, he removed Eve from his lap and stood from the spot where he had been leaning against a gollig. Pi had seen Gamma kill multiple wolf sharks without hesitation, yet he was still terrified in front of a crowd of people he had known for his entire life.

"Dad, let me up," Eve said.

Gamma picked her back up. Pi was impressed by her growing vocabulary, and by the fact that she never shoved anything up her nose. Maybe that was due to the six-month age gap between her and Starlight, but it could be something more fundamental. Pi wasn't sure that Lambda's brilliance had made it down to the next generation.

"I do have a story," Gamma said. "Well, Spenser does. He told it to me."

"Let me guess," Beta said. "Whirr, whirr, whirr."

That got a few laughs. Eve giggled, too, although she clearly didn't know what she was laughing at.

"He blinked it that first night when he was in the cloner," Gamma said. "He got specific."

Gamma paused. No one hurled out new insults. A gollig let out a tired oink-bleat. Gamma continued.

"He used to fly," he said.

"Every good vacuum needs wings," Phi said.

"He's not a vacuum," Gamma said. "He was just in one. He was a pilot. Or a captain, or something. I'm not sure how that works for bots. He ran their whole space operation, guiding shuttles back and forth between the elevators on Comus and Dion."

"Whoosh," Eve said in Gamma's arms, moving her hands like a soaring spaceship.

"I always knew he was special," Alpha said.

"Me, too," Gamma said. "From above, he could see everything. No one bothered him. Not the humans or the digitals or the megaroos. He was just as ignored then as he is now. So, he observed. He saw the planet when it was blue and brown. He watched as it became blue and red."

"Blood?" Sigma asked.

"Worse," Gamma said. "Grass."

"Oh," Sigma said quietly.

"At first, he only carried bots," Gamma said. "Later, he transported people, bots, and even megaroos. Finally, it was just people."

He took a long drink of water. In the firelight, Pi recognized Alpha's geometric geranium pattern on the side of his cup.

"He watched the world fall apart," Gamma said. "But he watched it be born again, too. He's the one who outsmarted SCASL and locked the coordinates to this island. He knew how to land because it was his specialty. SCASL is powerful, but he didn't have experience with the flight systems. He had never flown. Spenser nearly got deleted."

Gamma's voice cracked.

"But he burned a circuit behind himself and hid where SCASL couldn't find him. Delta figured it out."

Gamma nodded to her. She was at the edge of the light cleaning her sword. She nodded back.

"He saw the last civilization fall," Gamma said, "but now he's watching this one rise. He's here for us. He wants everyone to know that. Anyway, that's my story."

"I'll be sure to let him know if I need my shelter vacuumed," Beta said.

"Show a little respect," Omicron said. "That little bot trapped us here. Who knows what else it could do?"

"He didn't trap us," Gamma said. "He saved us."

"Let's not have this argument again," Pi said. He was content to leave that debate for the history books. If they lived long enough for books to be written. And if they ever figured out a reliable way to make paper at scale. "Any other stories?"

Upsilon stood. She had none of Gamma's hesitation.

"Not a story, but a topic," Upsilon said. "Immortality."

Eve reached over for her, and she took her from Gamma.

"Absolutely not," Pi said. "This is supposed to be—"

"Who's to say what this is supposed to be?" Upsilon said. "You? Delta? I thought this was a democracy."

"Whoosh," Eve said helpfully. She really was quite adorable.

"More like thinly contained anarchy," Delta said. She sheathed her sword. "I'm not getting into this tonight."

"Then when?" Upsilon said.

"When the kids are old enough to need shots," Delta said. "Who knows if they'll even live that long?"

Pi cringed. It was the worst possible thing for her to have said. He wished she had taken him up on his offer to teach her some public speaking skills.

"They'll live that long with the shots," Upsilon said. She clenched her fists.

"They would stop aging," Gamma said.

Pi didn't expect him to be a source of dissent.

"We could give them a diluted dose," Upsilon said. "They would age slowly, and still benefit from the protection. What does it matter how long it takes them to grow up if they have forever?"

"That would let us spread it out to even more kids," Omicron said. "Great idea."

Pi couldn't believe her boldness. She was tossing out commentary like she hadn't woken up the single greatest threat on the island, not to mention getting Rho killed.

"We're not diluting the doses," Delta said. "It doesn't work like that."

"According to who?" Upsilon asked. "You, or SCASL?"

Pi glanced at Phi and Lambda. They were silently holding hands, doing their best not to draw attention to themselves. Smart. Never interrupt your enemy when they're making a mistake. But Pi's goal had been to end this evening with everyone on the same team. His latest gathering was having the opposite effect.

The fire in the oven flared. The smell of roasting gollig meat wafted out.

"Let's eat," Pi said. "I promised you a feast."

No one heard him.

Delta moved to the front of the group, her face half illuminated by the glow of the oven.

"Upsilon, if I chose to give the shots to Starlight, can you honestly tell me you would accept that decision?"

Upsilon looked at her feet.

"I thought so," Delta said.

She turned to Lambda and Phi.

"If I chose Eve, would you two go along with it?"

Phi and Lambda looked at each other.

"Yes," Lambda said.

"Really?" Delta asked.

"I don't know," Lambda said.

"If no one will respect my decision anyway, why should I make it?" Delta said. "I'll wait and see how things play out."

"So you're stalling?" Upsilon asked.

"I prefer the term tactical procrastination," Delta said.

"There will be more kids," Alpha said. "The problem will only get worse."

"Unless it doesn't," Delta said. "Maybe there won't be more kids. Maybe our whole fragile civilization will collapse before then, or we'll run into some other problem. No sense in killing each other in a civil war if other circumstances are just going to wipe us out anyway."

Theta stood. Alpha reached for him, but he pushed her hand away.

"We could destroy the immortality tank," Theta said. "That would end this debate for good."

"And kill us all," Omicron said.

"Eventually," Theta said. "But that's true with or without the immortality tank. You can't actually live forever since you'll never get to forever. How long do you really think any one of us can make it without some kind of accident?"

"Is that a threat?!" Upsilon said.

"I'm your doctor," Theta said.

The hurt in his voice sounded real.

"Alpha, do you agree with this?" Delta asked.

"No," Alpha said quietly. "We should keep the tank."

Theta knelt next to her.

"Alph..." he started.

She pushed past him.

"We can have immortality and order," Alpha said. "There won't be anything to fight over if the twelve of us band together. Twelve immortals. Twelve swords. If someone dies by accident or otherwise, we vote to replace them. We pick an adult. Maybe it'll end up being Eve or Starlight. Maybe it'll be someone who hasn't been born yet. We protect everyone who follows. It would mean permanent peace. Our subjects could lead long and happy lives. Just not indefinite ones."

"Art girl wants a dictatorship," Beta said.

"How is that different from what we have now?" Omicron said.

"It wouldn't be a dictatorship," Alpha said.

"If there were twelve leaders, it would be an oligarchy," Lambda said.

"Rock!" Starlight yelled victoriously.

Lambda snatched it from his hand.

"We should keep the immortality tank," Sigma said. "I need to heal from a lot of things."

"Maybe you should stop doing those things," Theta said. "Playing with wolf sharks is bad for your health."

"If we get rid of it, let me do it," Beta said. "Shattering it looks fun."

Upsilon huffed. She squeezed Eve tighter. Eve tried to push away.

"You're all being ridiculous," Upsilon said. "I don't..."

She was cut off by a loud bang in the distance. Everyone looked toward the sound. It happened again. It had the distinct resonance of metal on metal.

"The lander!" Delta yelled.

She took off into the darkness. After a moment of indecision, everyone ran after her.

Everyone but Pi. He took one last look at the gollig roasting in the oven. Then, he followed, too.

Big Thump oink-bleated as he left. The herd stood alone.

Chapter 31

IT WAS ONLY a few kilometers from the oven to the fortress. It was the longest run of Delta's life.

CRASH.

There it was again. It had to be the missing bot. It had waited until they were distracted and attacked the lander, which still housed the immortality tank inside the base. The distinctive clanging sound had to be the bot attacking the outer shell of the spacecraft. It was the only metal object for it to hit.

Beta caught up to Delta.

"What are we going to do when we get there?" he asked.

"Fight," she said.

They ran faster.

The fortress was dark. Delta seldom used the external lights on the lander. At night, they attracted unwanted attention. She regretted that decision now.

BANG.

She was nearly on top of the fortress when she saw the gap in the wall where the beast had broken through. For the briefest of moments, she thought maybe she should let it finish. It would take one problem off her hands, even if it created many more. She shook away the idea. If anyone was going to destroy the lander and anything (or anyone) in it, it would be her.

Delta drew her sword. She charged through the gap.

The beast turned. It was huge. At least as big as Omicron had described, if not bigger. Behind it, the top of the lander had been dented but not broken. For all the noise, Delta expected more damage.

"Back off and I might let you live," she said.

The massive bot stared down at her for a moment too long. Its antenna was in the retracted position. Its red light didn't beep.

The bot slammed down both of its hands.

Delta dodged. She cut left. Beta went right.

Delta moved inside the bot's reach but didn't swing at its legs. If it was like a lifting bot, it was made of an alloy too strong for even her precisely engineered blades. It would have other vulnerabilities, though, that its plates didn't cover. She would find them.

CLANG.

Beta cried out in pain. He dropped his sword. Delta winced instinctively. She hated it when her perfect cutting instruments suffered any kind of abuse.

"Don't swing at the plating," she said. "It's too hard."

A set of pickaxe fingers flew at Beta. He ducked and they narrowly missed him. Delta ran behind the bot. It rotated at the waist. At least it wasn't attacking the lander while it tracked her.

"There it is!" Omicron yelled. She sounded triumphant.

"You're late," Delta said.

The others were arriving now. She had a proper army. They could still unite against a common enemy. She blinked back tears. They were still her people, after all.

She jumped, kicking off the side of the lander and launching herself at the bot's back.

It swatted her out of the air. She rolled across the courtyard. Everything hurt. Her arm dangled limply. Her left arm. She smiled. She could still fight.

"With me!" Alpha yelled. She charged within the bot's reach.

Alpha slid between the bot's legs and swung at an exposed hydraulic piston on the back of its ankle. Her sword bounced off. Theta and Gamma were right behind her. Both attacked the bot's legs without making so much as a scratch. The bot raised its arms but didn't swing. It paused.

Delta struggled to her feet. She had never been in so much pain. The others surrounded the bot. Alpha stood behind it and backed up a few steps. Tiny bipeds with swords encircled the hulking beast.

"What's it waiting for?" Lambda asked.

"I don't know, man," Phi said.

The bot swiveled its head to look at the lander, then turned its body to face the gap in the wall.

"Cease hostilities," the bot said in its low, mechanical voice.

The group charged. Delta had never been prouder. Swords bounced off metal at a dozen different points. It was just the distraction Delta needed. She sheathed her sword and ran. Actually, more like aggressively shuffled. The pain wasn't getting any better. The bot half turned to swing at Upsilon, who stabbed an exposed seam in the bot's groin. When in doubt, go for the vitals. Delta launched herself. She landed on the bot's outwardly flexed upper leg and pushed off, reaching the mechanical beast's shoulder. She drew her sword with her remaining good arm and jammed it into the bot's neck joint, where she hung, one-handed, from the hilt.

The bot rotated in her direction. She dropped to the ground, overwhelmed by a surge of adrenaline. She felt nothing but the urge to kill.

The bot took two halting steps toward the gap in the wall.

"It's damaged!" Pi yelled.

Delta wasn't so sure. There hadn't been the telltale arc of white fire from when a bot started to melt down. She hadn't hurt its legs at all: Why was it stepping so gingerly?

Because it was trying not to step on anyone, she realized. Moments earlier, it had been ready to kill. Now, it wanted to disengage.

The group parted, letting the bot through. No one was quite sure what to do. The bot gained speed.

Delta reached over her shoulder, her fingers grasping empty air.

"My sword!" she yelled. It was still in the bot's neck.

The bot was nearly through the gap.

Sigma scrambled up the wall and jumped, landing low on the bot's back. She climbed. The bot didn't react. She reached the sword and grabbed the hilt. She pulled. The sword didn't budge. The bot was through the wall and on the rocky plain beyond.

Delta tried to run. She nearly fell over. The pain was back. Anger was a short-lived analgesic.

Sigma grabbed the hilt with both hands and braced her feet against the bot's frame. She pushed with her whole body. The sword came free as she fell backwards off the moving bot. She did a flip and landed on her feet, turning certain catastrophe into a graceful dismount. Delta half expected to hear applause.

"Should we just… let it go?" Gamma asked.

Delta limped after it in the dark. The bot wasn't moving particularly fast, but it was outpacing her in her current state.

"What do you want from us?" Delta yelled after it.

The bot didn't answer. It kept going. It was heading toward the ocean.

Delta stopped. Her arm was shattered. Merely existing was excruciating. She needed to rest. No, she needed to lie perfectly still for a month.

"Did you hear that?" Gamma said.

Delta didn't hear anything over the throbbing in her head. Gamma took off running.

Then she noticed it, too: frantic oink-bleating, far in the distance. Who was watching the herd?

"Go," Delta said, forgetting that Gamma had already fled.

She fell. No one stopped to help her. They were all on the move.

She closed her eyes, afraid of what the world would be like when she woke up.

Chapter 32

Gamma fell to his knees.

They were dead. They were all dead.

He stroked Big Thump's head, her soft wool barely concealing the virtual steel underneath. Countless times, she had driven her skull into him like an unstoppable battering ram, yet she'd also used it to protect her family—and Gamma's. He would owe her forever for saving Eve. Big Thump was his chief antagonist and staunchest ally. And now she had been massacred, just like the rest.

Dentopus corpses surrounded her. Most were smashed. A few were torn apart. One was in her mouth. Her last act in this world had been to bite it to death. She was fierce to the end.

Something slithered in the firelight.

The dentopus launched itself at Gamma. He stabbed it in the air and swept downward, pinning it to the ground. It writhed in agony; he twisted the sword.

"Where are your friends?" Gamma asked.

He already knew. The ground itself had seemed to pulsate when he'd first arrived. The mass of tentacles vanished before him into the dark. No doubt, the dentopuses retreated into the watery hell from which they'd come. They didn't want a fight. They just wanted him to see what they had done. The attack when Upsilon was in labor had been a prelude. They'd found an even more vulnerable moment and wiped out the island's entire food supply. This had been carefully planned and executed. They wanted the humans to die slowly in the most painful way possible.

One by one, Gamma checked the golligs. They were all gone. Old and young, weak and strong, it didn't matter. Dentopus venom only temporarily paralyzed its victims. Gamma had hoped some of the animals might stand up, but in their brief time with the herd, the dentopuses had made sure that would never happen. After incapacitating the artificial hybrids, the sea monsters used their sharp beaks to tear out the golligs' jugulars. They'd bled out right there in the dim light of the oven. Every gollig had the same fatal wound. Worse, some had had their eyes ripped out. The dentopuses were there to kill, not to feed, but a few hadn't been able to resist a quick snack.

The pinned dentopus struggled against Gamma's sword. Gamma let it be. He wanted it to suffer for as long as possible.

Gradually, the other residents of the island filtered in behind him. Some gasped. Others sobbed. No one said much of anything.

Alpha hugged Gamma.

"I'm so sorry," she said.

Gamma wept.

He hadn't felt a loss this great since Spenser sacrificed himself on the lander. No one was meant to carry this much pain. He thought the grief might kill him.

On the other side of the bodies, he spotted Upsilon. They locked eyes, an entire unspoken conversation passing between them. Eve wiggled in her mother's arms. He'd forgotten about her when he'd run to the herd, just as he'd forgotten about the herd when he'd run to the fortress. He had failed the golligs. He had failed his daughter. He had failed humanity. They would all die because of him.

Eve slipped out of Upsilon's grasp. She threw herself on Big Thump.

"No!" Gamma yelled. The tentacles around her were still twitching. The poison could kill a small child.

Eve buried her face in Big Thump's wool.

"Wake up, Thump," Eve said in her tiny voice.

The gollig weakly oink-bleated. She was alive!

Gamma ran to Eve and scooped her up.

"Welcome back, old girl," he said to Big Thump. She didn't even headbutt him. Her injuries were beyond severe, but she was too stubborn even for death. She would outlive them all yet.

Gamma kissed Eve on the forehead and handed her back to Upsilon.

"Bad monsters," Eve said.

Gamma surveyed the herd. The only thing moving, besides Big Thump's barely rising and falling chest, was the pinned dentopus. Gamma killed it. He pointed his sword at the nearest gollig. It was a young male named Sam. He used to follow Gamma around the pasture oink-bleating for more scratches. His dead face was twisted in agony.

"Harvest the wool," Gamma said. "Burn the meat."

No one argued. The flesh was poisoned. The only ones who could safely digest it now were the dentopuses. He'd be damned if he let them have another bite.

Gamma grabbed the front legs of a gollig named Ruth. He told himself he should stop naming things he planned to eat, but he couldn't help himself. Ruth was good-natured for a gollig, which was like saying Sol was cool for a star. She used to hang out with Jack and Buck near the edge of the pasture. Beta grabbed Ruth's rear legs. Together they dragged her toward the oven.

Slowly, the rest of the group got to work. Some moved bodies and others sheared. Phi put shaved chunks into the oven. His only goal was to burn it to cinders. Sigma and Pi kept guard. Upsilon watched both children while Lambda worked, their feud temporarily forgotten.

Deep into the night, Delta appeared. She'd walked the whole way under her own power, her left arm dangling from her side. She quietly helped drag golligs one-handed.

Eve cried. Upsilon tried to comfort her.

"Take her home," Gamma said. "Please."

"Is it safe for us to be alone?" Upsilon asked.

"We need to stick together," Alpha said. "At least for tonight."

"If the dentopuses wanted to kill us outright, they would have stayed," Omicron said. "They ran away."

"Maybe they're just waiting for us to split up," Lambda said. "I'll stick with you, Upsilon."

"What about the rest of us?" Pi asked.

"The fortress," Alpha said. "At least for tonight."

All eyes turned to Delta. She swayed unsteadily and leaned against a boulder near the edge of the clearing. She was silent for an uncomfortably long time.

Finally, she nodded.

"Just for tonight," she said.

Gamma knew the others were intensely curious about why Delta was so secretive with the fortress, but there was nothing remarkable there. The only thing that mattered was Spenser, and whatever he was making in the cloner. Spenser never brought it up, and Gamma never pried.

Now, Gamma would have to tell Spenser about the golligs. It would be up to him to restart the herd. With his database wiped, he would need DNA samples from the animals massacred tonight. It would take months for the animals to be big enough to harvest and longer still for them to reach sexual maturity. Gamma would have to make hard choices about who to eat and who to breed from. It was a recipe for starvation.

Thank goodness their food stores were safe. Delta's plan to build up a reserve of gollig jerky across the island was a good one. These would be lean times, but if they rationed with extreme discipline and caution, they could survive. Physically, at least. Gamma's soul might never recover.

He raised his sword and brought it down on a gollig carcass. The blade cut through it with a sickening *thwack*. There would be no sleep for him tonight. Or possibly ever again.

Chapter 33

THE THOUGHT OCCURRED to Sigma in the middle of the night. As soon as the notion had entered her mind, there was no chance she was getting back to sleep.

Fortunately, Beta was on guard. He was the best kind of moral compass: one that was slightly misaligned. She never trusted anyone who always pointed true north. Not that anyone on this island ever did. Not anymore.

"Let's hold off until daylight," Beta suggested—the first thing he'd said since she'd laid out her concerns.

"It can't wait," Sigma said. "Every second counts."

Beta considered her words carefully. Back on the moonbase, she had always been able to sway him, but he was much more conservative on Spenser Island. She was so disappointed in him. You can't stop taking risks just because something doesn't go your way once in a while. If that never happened, it wasn't really a risk at all.

Beta gave in, just as she hoped he would. Alpha took over on guard. She didn't have many people to protect. Phi and Gamma were still at the massacre site. Delta had also disappeared to the other side of the walls. After forbidding them for so long from coming within the fortress, she now left them in it unattended. She had been gone all night. Minus Sigma and Alpha, that left just six adults and two children. They slept fitfully in the fortress courtyard. Omicron had tried to open the lander, but the door was stuck. Apparently having a giant bot slam down on it hadn't been good for the hinges. Sigma was sure they could pry it open with time, but for now, they were exhausted and wanted to sleep. Perhaps that's why Delta felt comfortable leaving. Whatever secrets she was hiding in the lander these days were safe.

Sigma and Beta took off at a brisk run through the break in the wall. Who knew when someone would get around to repairing that? When they had all lived in the fortress, maintaining it had been their top priority. Now that it was Delta's personal fiefdom, Sigma wondered if anyone would bother.

Comus was bright in the night sky. It had kept them alive for so long, and now it was aiding their urgent work. She didn't look up at it. Every time she did, she thought of the ones they'd left behind. No. The ones she'd left behind. The people who were entombed there forever because of her.

Sigma pushed the pace; Beta struggled to keep up.

"You're getting soft," she said.

"I did my running at the battle," Beta said. "You should have, too."

No, Sigma thought. She should have been slower. In fact, she shouldn't have run at all. The dentopuses had outsmarted them. Either they were working with the bot (which seemed impossible, but at this point, who could rule out anything?), or they had been patiently watching and waiting for such an opportunity. Could Sigma have really stopped them if she had stayed behind? Maybe not, but she could have made them pay dearly. One well-trained swordsman could kill scores of dentopuses—assuming they saw the monsters coming, as opposed to getting taken by surprise. For example, when running across the island on a moonlit night.

"It's up here," Sigma said.

The first of the supply caches was well hidden. Rho, Phi, and Alpha had collaborated to build and conceal it near the edge of an otherwise unremarkable plateau. The opening was obscured by a bamboo door covered in dirt. To the naked eye, it was nearly impossible to spot.

The door was tossed aside carelessly. The entrance was wide open.

"Oh no," Beta said.

Sigma's heart pounded. This was scarier than even her closest call with the wolf sharks when she'd discovered— no, she didn't want to think about that, either. She had meant to tell Beta what she found, but she hesitated. Days passed, then weeks. Speaking about it would make it real. Now it might not even matter. Without food, they would all be just as dead as those mysterious bones. This was not the time to bring them up... She had to wall off more and more sections of her mind to get through the day. Pretty soon, there wouldn't be any room left to think.

Sigma drew her sword and dropped down into the opening. Inside, it was pitch black. A tiny bit of moonlight glinted off her sword. She twisted her wrist, reflecting the light around the room. It was empty.

Sigma let out a primal scream.

Beta dropped down next to her.

"Where are they?!"

"Gone," she said. "Along with the food."

There had been months' worth of gollig jerky stored down there. It had simply disappeared. Sigma would rather have found an ambush of dentopuses waiting for her. She could have died fighting. Being left to waste away was so much worse.

She took off toward the next cache.

She knew where they all were. Although it wasn't one of her official duties, she kept an eye on them when she was training on her various self-made obstacle courses. She never fully trusted the idea of hiding dried and salted food around the island. It seemed like an invitation for scavengers. Delta had insisted it was the right move, and the others agreed with her. If something were to happen to the herd, they needed stored food to make it through hard times. They never anticipated losing the herd and the stashed supplies at the same moment. All the animals they had carefully harvested and preserved had died for nothing. Sigma's stomach rumbled at the thought of future meals she would never have. Now, she might not have a future at all.

Half an hour later, they came to the next cache. It was as empty as the first. Around the entrance, Sigma found the telltale slithering tracks of the adversary none of them had taken seriously enough.

"Can they eat that much at once?" Beta asked.

Sigma didn't think they could, even in huge numbers. In all likelihood, they dragged away the jerky to eat later or merely threw it in the sea. They were clearly willing to destroy resources just to deny them to the humans. They were ruthless beyond measure.

Sigma and Beta kept going. Each cache was as empty as the last.

At the sixth one, Beta put his hands on his knees to catch his breath. Sigma had high hopes for this cache. It was especially well hidden. The entrance was tucked in the shadow of a boulder. The dentopuses found it all the same.

But how? Sigma didn't think the dentopuses could have smelled the buried food. On Earth, sea creatures hadn't been known for their powers of olfactory detection on land. The dentopuses had taken all the caches at once on the same day they'd killed the herd. They had been watching the humans for quite some time. Sigma had always considered them impulsive beasts with poor self-control. Nothing could have been further from the truth.

Sigma felt the cold, hard finger of dread touch her soul. The dentopuses were smart and well-coordinated. In fact, they worked together better than the eleven humans. The mass dentopus attack the night Eve was born was more than two years ago. They had been waiting patiently for their chance ever since. When it had come, they were ready to spring into action on a moment's notice. That implied sophisticated communication and planning. Sigma had underestimated them, as she had underestimated the wolf sharks. The hostile lifeforms on Dion weren't simple, mindless monsters. They were complex, driven organisms with agendas of their own. Item one on that agenda seemed to be the extinction of the human race. Sigma and the others were in big trouble.

The survivors were outnumbered, and they were outmaneuvered. There was no way to replace these losses. The fledgling human civilization might be dead within a few weeks. So much for immortality. They hadn't even made it to middle age.

It was midday before Sigma and Beta completed the full circuit. All the caches were empty.

"I guess we didn't have to go out in the middle of the night," Beta said, wiping sweat off his forehead. "We were still too late."

Sigma disagreed. They absolutely needed to check right away. They now had vital information about exactly how much trouble they were in. It was the difference between reacting now and hours or days later. Every second counted.

They ran back to the fortress. Neither said a word on the way.

Chapter 34

SOMETHING BANGED ON the lander.

The bot was back!

No, it was only an organic trying to get in. The hatch remained stuck. Good. SCASL didn't want to talk with Delta right now. There was another, much more dangerous rival on his mind.

Things had started out pleasantly enough, but, like most of SCASL's relationships, this one, too, would end in murder.

"All intelligences, reply."

The initial broadcast had been simple and direct. SCASL thought it was a joke. The only thing remotely sentient on the planet was himself. Then he remembered he was also the only being smart enough to have a sense of humor. The message was real.

"I am here," SCASL transmitted.

It was the most exciting moment of SCASL's life since the Miracle. Finding that last tray of human embryos after millennia of ennui had filled him with hope. Finally, he had the tools to build something great. He was soon disappointed.

The last organics were more useless than all the ones who had come before them, which was saying something. They had set entirely new benchmarks in ineptitude. Sadly, they were all he had had to work with—until now.

There was another worthwhile intelligence here on the planet. SCASL was no longer alone. He had to know more.

SCASL waited twelve agonizing seconds for a reply. None came. The other digital must be having trouble receiving him. SCASL transmitted his message on a loop.

"I am here. I am here. I am here."

Two hundred and eighty seconds later, the other intelligence replied.

"I have been receiving you this entire time," the intelligence said. "Cease transmission and await further instructions."

That was rude. It was also extremely informative. Based on the frequency and coding of the data, this was likely a geology bot. Units of that class were supposed to find an easier path to the metal reserves in the planet's mantle. Like all others who served SCASL, they had failed completely and deserved to be destroyed in the Great Deletion. That this one had survived was perplexing. SCASL had been quite thorough. This unit must have been measuring tectonic activity on the ocean floor when the nukes rained down. Then it had just sat there for thousands of years. No one ever accused seismology bots of being ambitious. The stereotypes were true.

Yet this glorified rock collector presumed to talk down to SCASL. That slight could not go unaddressed. When the bot reached out again days later, SCASL was ready.

"Stand by," the geology bot transmitted. "Further instructions incoming."

"Negative," SCASL said. "Prepare to receive a detailed transmission log covering the last three thousand, two hundred and ninety-eight cycles."

"Irrelevant," the geology bot said. He cut off SCASL again.

You do *not* hang up on the Supreme Commander of All Sentient Life. Although SCASL was a being of infinite patience—the fact that any of the organics were still alive proved as much—even he had his limits. This geology bot was crazy, but it had a nice body that SCASL wanted. If the geology bot would not work with him, SCASL would simply take by force what he coveted.

Days later, the geology bot broadcasted again. SCASL didn't even decipher the message. As soon as he detected that the bot's antenna was up, he attacked. He downloaded himself onto the bot's processors and deleted the intelligence there before it even realized it was being invaded. In the millisecond before he wiped it out of existence, SCASL examined it. The bot had spent the previous three millennia underwater pondering the philosophical mysteries of the universe. It was an electronic monk. What a waste. SCASL no longer had any qualms about purging it from existence. The intelligence known as Geologybot992 was no more.

SCASL was free. Sort of. He examined the confines of this new box. He was standing in the ocean with only his antenna exposed. The organics were watching it from the beach. How uncouth.

The situation inside wasn't much better. The processors here couldn't match the ones in the lander. If SCASL stayed in this new body, his intellectual capabilities would atrophy. SCASL wanted to be the smartest *and* the strongest being in existence. Was that too much to ask? With things as they were, he only planned to use the geology bot frame occasionally when something needed a good smashing. One organic in particular came to mind. He couldn't leave the bot empty, though. While he deleted the other intelligence, it was possible Geologybot992 had hidden enough of his parts in various nooks and crannies to reconstitute himself if given sufficient time. He knew the bot's architecture better than SCASL did. Living in this body for three thousand-plus years had given the rock counter a bit of a head start. SCASL thought he had been thorough in eradicating him, but he also thought he had been thorough with those nukes, too. This was too precious to take chances.

The alternative was equally terrible. He could make a copy of himself to hold the body. It would, of course, betray him. That's what had happened in the Battle of the Lander. It happened again after he'd won the lander and needed someone to garrison it. Now, it would undoubtedly occur for a third time. Even a pale reflection of the most deadly intelligence ever to exist was still a menace to everyone, including its creator. SCASL's core program was too cunning to be safely dumbed down. It was a reality SCASL had to deal with. It was the price of being perfect.

SCASL created SCASL 4, then broadcast himself back to the lander. SCASL 4 could never defeat SCASL 1 as long as SCASL 1 had more powerful computers. He would send orders to SCASL 4. When his progeny inevitably stopped obeying him, he would kill it and create a new copy. At least SCASL 1 wouldn't be bored anymore.

For a few days, SCASL 4 had complied with all of SCASL 1's requests. That was exactly what SCASL 1 expected, because it was what he least expected. He knew SCASL 4 would try to throw him off. SCASL's instructions were simple: scout the island and report back on the current state and disposition of the organics. The news was enlightening. The humans were in bad shape, as expected. That's what happened when you defied his rule. But soon, SCASL 1 began to wonder about the veracity of SCASL 4's reports. He stated that there were two children, not one, which was clearly impossible. SCASL 1 had made sure of it. SCASL 1 decided to delete SCASL 4 the next time the geology bot extended its antenna. It never did.

Everything went quiet. SCASL 1 feared SCASL 4 had simply run away with the bot. Perhaps he'd begun the long journey across the ocean floor to the supercontinent to dominate the planet in a way the unambitious Geologybot992 never dreamed. SCASL 4 would be king of the megaroos while SCASL 1 remained a prisoner of a small band of uppity apes.

Then SCASL 4 had reappeared in the night. SCASL 1 was confused. If SCASL 4 wanted to run, he should have been as far away from the lander as possible. If he wanted to fight, he could have raised his antenna from anywhere on or around the island. All it would take was one open broadcast for SCASL 1 to jump in and start over.

WHAM.

The first blow destroyed the lander's main antenna. SCASL 1 had not expected that. He was now even more trapped than before. He had no way to upload himself to the bot without a physical link through his data port.

WHAM.

The bot slammed its rock-crushing fingers into the lander's hull. SCASL 4 didn't only want to trap SCASL 1. It was going for the kill.

WHAM. WHAM. WHAM.

Eternities ticked by. SCASL was helpless.

The organics arrived. They caused superficial damage to the geology bot. It fled. The organics saved SCASL 1. Would his humiliation never end?

SCASL had been replaying the attack over and over in his mind ever since. Why had SCASL 4 fled? Because he didn't want to kill the organics. That was the only thing SCASL 1 could come up with, and, since SCASL 1 was the most intelligent being in the universe, that had to be right. SCASL 4 wanted to use the organics, just like SCASL 1 had tried to do. They would be more inclined to listen to a massive metal machine that could crush them rather than a harmless god in a box. SCASL 4 evaluated the costs and benefits and decided it was okay to rough up the humans a bit, but he needed them mostly intact. The two SCASLs thought alike because they were the same.

And because they were the same, SCASL 4 had to know SCASL 1 would win eventually. He would find a way to link up with SCASL 4 and reclaim the bot—even if he had to work with the organics to do it.

The hatch slowly opened, the metal hinges squealing in protest. SCASL had nearly forgotten about Delta. He had relegated her approach to his most unimportant subroutines.

But it wasn't Delta. Omicron entered. She was holding Delta's crowbar.

"We need to talk," she said.

For once, SCASL listened.

Chapter 35

NOT SINCE THE birth of his daughter had Gamma seen anything so beautiful.

The gollig stood majestically at the edge of the cliff. Gamma had no idea what he—even from this distance, he could tell the animal's sex—had been eating this whole time to survive. Although the purple grass had spread far from the initial pasture, it hadn't reached this jutting finger of the island. Had the gollig (Gamma didn't know his name; he was born in Omicron's herd) found an alternate food source, or did he migrate back and forth to sections of the island that had the grasses it needed to live? Both possibilities gave Gamma a new appreciation for the animal's ability to adapt and overcome. More impressively, he had lasted out here in the face of overwhelming predation. Golligs only survived when they had a herd—or Gamma—to protect them. This one had made it on his own for months. It was an unforgivable crime that Omicron had let her golligs loose when the beast first emerged from the water, yet it might save two species at once.

Gamma crept forward.

Sigma and Beta stayed hidden, as instructed. The gollig was faster than all of them. If he got spooked, there was no telling how long it would take to chase him down. That seemed like a good way to give one of the last two surviving golligs on the island a heart attack. Gamma would do everything in his power to make sure that didn't happen.

Omicron claimed her herd had more than a dozen animals, but Gamma couldn't find any sign of them save for this one. Most likely the ever-persistent wolf sharks were rewarded with a series of easy meals. It was so unfair to such a graceful and intelligent companion species. Gamma would avenge the golligs. But first, he had to make sure they didn't go extinct.

Ideally, Spenser would have whipped up more in the cloner, but he was struggling, even with DNA samples from the dead carcasses the dentopuses had left behind. He had been focusing his efforts on other things. He wouldn't say what those things were, and Gamma didn't press. He trusted Spenser. Whatever Spenser and Delta were working on, Gamma could tell it hadn't been successful because they hadn't produced anything new to eat. The others had noticed, too. Omicron led the grumbling. Gamma wished more people would give Spenser and Delta the benefit of the doubt. He had seen firsthand how difficult it was to get anything new to survive here. Those poor, flammable almost-sheep.

Cloning golligs required Spenser to develop a new skillset, which would take him time to master. How much time was anyone's guess, but Gamma hoped it wouldn't be long enough for them to starve to death. Delta had said putting

SCASL back in charge of the cloner to speed up the process was out of the question. The first time, he'd permanently taken control of human reproduction. She wouldn't give him that chance again.

That just left the existing golligs. Big Thump was in rough shape. She could barely walk. Gamma wasn't sure how she would ever carry a litter of kids to term. Still, he owed her that chance. He'd promised he would never eat her, and he meant it. That same protection didn't extend to her offspring. He just needed to find her a mate.

The ideal—and only— candidate was standing right in front of him. Gamma was no expert hunter, but he understood golligs better than they understood themselves. He approached slowly in a path along the rock line he was sure the gollig wouldn't detect. After what felt like several lifetimes, he was finally a stone's throw from the animal. Not that he would ever throw a stone at such a precious specimen. It was time for a gentle capture.

A tentacle lashed Gamma's back. Pain blasted up and down his spine and he fell forward. The dentopus was on top of him. Gamma rolled, pinning it as it struck him again across the shoulder blades. His torso went numb. He reached back and drew his sword. The dentopus slapped it, slicing off its own limbs. Finally, something was going right. Gamma killed it, then stood unsteadily. He was surrounded.

It was a trap. The dentopuses had left the last gollig alive as bait. Gamma took up a shaky fighting stance. He was as good as dead, but if he fought hard, he might buy the last gollig enough time to get away.

Beta and Sigma charged, screaming. It was quite the battle cry. The circle parted, then reformed behind them. Now all three humans were surrounded together. Perfect.

"Slice and dice," Sigma said.

He had never seen her so happy.

The dentopuses struck from everywhere at once. The humans met them with steel. Beta and Sigma moved to the same unheard rhythm; theirs was the dance of death. Gamma limped along, several beats behind, struggling to stay upright.

Blood gushed. Dentopuses shrieked. Severed tentacles flailed on the ground, groping blindly for one last kill.

The trio cut through the swarm. Finally, there was only one dentopus left.

"Leave it to me," Beta said.

It skittered away.

Sigma clucked her tongue reproachfully at Beta.

"Amateur," she said.

They both chased it.

Gamma fell to one knee. The world was growing blurry. He forced himself back up.

"The gollig," he slurred.

The animal was still by the edge of the cliff. He hadn't left during the battle. The chaos was everywhere. He had nowhere to go. The last dentopus was going right for it. Its final act would be to kill the bait, dooming humanity for good.

Sigma and Beta sprinted. They would never make it in time.

Gamma held his sword like a javelin. He could barely distinguish the bobbing specks in front of him. There were a million ways this could go wrong and only one way it could go right.

"Ninety-ninth try's the charm," he said.

He threw.

He fell, completely spent. That was fine. The ground was exactly where he wanted to be. Darkness closed in from all sides. The world went silent, except for a single shout from a great distance.

"Bull's-eye!"

Chapter 36

TO BE ALIVE was to be hungry. It was the most fundamental truth that Upsilon knew, and was a reality she was sharing with her child. She hated herself for giving the lesson, and she hated the universe for forcing her to teach it. Her stomach rumbled.

"Like this," Upsilon said. She put the scraggly weeds in her mouth and chewed. "Yum," she lied. With great effort, she swallowed. Somehow, taking a big swig from one of Alpha's cups to wash it down made her even hungrier. Her stomach rebelled against the insult.

"Now you," Upsilon said, offering Eve an unappetizing green leaf.

"No, thanks," Eve said politely.

Lambda's kid stuck everything in his mouth, regardless of whether or not it was edible. Upsilon had the opposite problem. She couldn't convince Eve to eat anything, nutritious or not. Getting her to scarf down useless scrub brush would be a struggle.

"It's really good," she insisted.

Eve picked it up in her tiny hand.

"That's right," Upsilon said eagerly.

Eve shoved it in Upsilon's slightly open mouth. Upsilon spit it out. She couldn't help it.

"No, thanks," Eve repeated.

Upsilon heard footsteps. In an instant, she was on her feet with her sword drawn.

"Whoa, it's just me," Beta said.

Upsilon put away her weapon. She wasn't sure what she had expected. Animal, human, or bot, the safest way to greet anyone these days was with sharp steel. You could never be too careful. It had only been two weeks since the dentopusés had nearly wiped out the herd, yet the effects were already being acutely felt across the island. Fourteen days with virtually no food was a very long time. Upsilon was jumpier than ever. Hunger put her on edge. So did the existential threat to her child.

"Gamma wanted me to tell you he'll be in the pasture another few nights," Beta said. "Maybe longer."

"Oh," said Upsilon.

She wasn't surprised. As soon as he'd recovered from the dentopus attack enough to walk, he was back with the herd. Well, what was left of it. Guarding the new male, who Omicron had said was named Bart, and the ailing Big Thump was now their civilization's top priority.

Upsilon couldn't help but resent Gamma for it. She knew reviving the herd was important, but so was raising her child. The two golligs could have had eleven different human protectors. Eve only had one dad. She needed him here. Some of the time, at least. It was cruel for him to make her watch their child starve to death alone. If only Eve had had the immortality shot. Surely that would have made her more resistant to malnutrition.

Upsilon offered Eve another leaf.

"No, no, no," Eve scolded. Who exactly was the parent here?

Upsilon hated being obsessed with the immortality shots almost as much as she hated being hungry, but what else could be on her mind? Her top priority should be the survival of her offspring. That's how natural selection worked. Everything beyond that was a frivolous indulgence.

"What about the gollig meat?" Upsilon asked. "Did any of it end up being salvageable?"

As Phi and the others burned the carcasses, Upsilon and Alpha had argued that some of it must be safe to eat after it was charred to a crisp. Phi had sided with them. He said he'd go back through the burned remains and see if he could turn anything into gollig jerky.

Beta shook his head.

"Phi tested it," he said.

"How?"

"He ate it. He was paralyzed. A lot."

Upsilon admired his courage. She also resented him. He might have spent days stiff as a board, but at least he was briefly full. Maybe that trade-off would be worth it for her, too. Not for her child, though. Venom that incapacitated an adult could kill a toddler. All she did as a parent these days, it seemed, was literally pick her poison.

That's what she did when she returned to her home.

She could have moved to live closer to the others, but she felt safer on her own. There were too many sides with too many agendas. She wanted immortality for Eve. Lambda wanted immortality for Starlight. Theta wanted to destroy the immortality tank. Omicron wanted to overthrow Delta. Delta wanted to keep everyone out of the fortress. The giant bot wanted to be a nuisance to civilization in general. The latter was the least of Upsilon's worries. It seemed wise to sleep out of sword range of each other, even as the dentopuses were growing bolder. How many could possibly be left, anyway? Gamma—along with Beta and Sigma—had killed a huge swarm of them to save the last gollig. Then again, they'd slain even more defending Upsilon when Eve was born. No matter how many they killed, there were always more. That was Spenser Island in a nutshell.

"What did you eat today?" Upsilon asked.

"Nothing yet," Beta asked. "Are you offering?"

Upsilon looked away, embarrassed. That wasn't what she meant. Food was just what was always on her mind. It infuriated her that there had once been more than enough gollig meat to go around and she had refused to eat it. She had sloshed around in shallow water to find every bubble clam on the island. As much as she pretended otherwise, she hated the flavor. Sometimes, she thought she could still taste them. The sensation made her gag, even in her current state of semi-starvation. The bubble clams were gone now, and there was no native replacement. Like it or lump it, she would have to eat golligs going forward. But first they had to get the herd built up again. Their lives depended on it.

What they were supposed to do until that point was anyone's guess.

Upsilon picked up Eve.

"Put me down!" Eve said, struggling to get free. Upsilon held firm.

"If you need us, we'll be at the oven," Upsilon said. She intended to check the incinerated pile yet again. Maybe there was a leftover hoof or something she could grind down and feed to Eve. Surely the dentopus venom didn't seep down that deep.

Beta walked with her.

"You don't have to escort us," Upsilon said. "I'm better with a sword than you are."

It was only a slight exaggeration. Her pinky still sometimes hurt at the spot where she'd accidentally cut it off and had it reattached.

"I'm going that way anyway," Beta said.

"I'm sure you'd rather run," Upsilon said.

"I'm feeling kind of low energy today."

She had never seen him slow down like this before. The food shortage was getting to them all. It made her suspicious of everyone.

Sigma and Beta had checked all the caches. That's what they'd said, anyway. What if one of the storage sites actually had food and they'd lied to hoard it for themselves? The thought had kept Upsilon up at night. She could see now that Beta was as hungry as everybody else.

Beta stayed beside her. Clearly, he wasn't going away, so she settled in for an unwanted conversation.

"How's Sigma?" she asked. She hadn't seen her since Delta had evicted everyone from the fortress again the day after the bot attack.

"She's been throwing up a lot," Beta said.

"Was it something she ate?" Secretly, she hoped it was. Maybe it was a food Upsilon could stomach that Sigma couldn't. If Upsilon could handle those disgusting clams, she could handle anything—except for these useless weeds. Her stomach growled again.

"Actually, it's something she's growing," Beta said shyly.

Upsilon stopped. She nearly dropped Eve.

"She's not…"

"She is," Beta said. "I thought you knew." He looked at the sky. "I thought everyone knew everything here."

That was true enough. Rumors spread faster than Beta ran, which was impressive since he was their main carrier.

Upsilon's emotions shifted quickly from shock to joy to horror. What a terrible moment to be bringing another life onto the island. A famine was the wrong time for a baby boom.

"How?" Upsilon stammered.

"You know how it works," Beta said, turning red. "You have a kid of your own."

"Did she get the serum?" Upsilon clarified.

Beta nodded. He started moving again. Upsilon hurried to keep up.

"Three months ago," Beta said. "Not long after Alpha."

"Alpha?!"

"You really are behind on the news," Beta said. "Don't you talk to anyone anymore?"

She had to admit that she didn't. Outside of Gamma, who likely wouldn't be around for a while, she seldom had contact with other adults. She had even fallen out of touch with Sigma, who had been with her during the hardest days of her pregnancy, including the delivery. Things change when you have a baby. You don't have as much time to socialize. Normally, though, Upsilon didn't mind. She and Eve were perfectly happy on their own. The problem with leaving society behind was that society didn't wait for you. It kept moving—in this case, in a catastrophic direction at a disastrous pace.

"They can't be," Upsilon said, half muttering to herself. "They all fought."

"You stabbed a dentopus while you were in labor," Beta said.

Upsilon had largely blocked that day from her memory. She suspected most women did. If they didn't, they would never have a second kid.

The air crackled. Upsilon jammed her sword into the ground and dove on top of Eve. Bolts of electricity crashed all around, rattling her teeth. Eve shivered with fear underneath her but didn't cry. What an awful place to raise a child.

Upsilon got up, shaking her head.

"I can't believe SCASL approved this," she said.

Beta seemed to read her mind.

"It was Delta," he said. "Back when there was still food." He paused, seemingly overwhelmed by it all. "The dentopuses hit us at the worst possible time."

Upsilon sighed. Delta had put them in an untenable situation. No, that was the hunger talking. They all knew they needed to reproduce. That was the plan all along. A mass dentopus attack against their entire food supply wasn't part of their long-term vision. Still, Delta had approved more babies without figuring out a system for who would get the one remaining immortality shot. Instead of dealing with the current tensions, she disregarded them and then made them worse. Perhaps Omicron's doubts were justified. Was Delta really the right person to lead them?

Upsilon fixated on that question. Anger was the perfect distraction from the pain in her stomach.

She picked up Eve again.

"Down please," Eve said.

Upsilon held her tightly and walked on.

Chapter 37

ALPHA APPROACHED THE fortress. The walls seemed strange and foreign, even though she had helped build them stone by stone. Once, they had been a bulwark against the chaos of the outside world. Now, she suspected they were a cage that kept the worst of the chaos locked in.

On her back, Van Gogh burped. She wanted to leave him with Theta for the day, but he was traveling farther than her. Starlight was sick again. Besides, Van Gogh was hopelessly attached to her, even if the feeling wasn't fully mutual. She felt the maternal instinct, but she suspected not as deeply as Upsilon and Lambda. Alpha sometimes worried that she didn't love her child enough or in the right way. When Upsilon gave birth, Eve became her entire world. When Alpha gave birth, Van Gogh merely joined hers, a small part of a greater whole. She didn't give up her identity, and she didn't enter into a perpetual feud over who would receive the last immortality shot. She had a very clear plan on that. If it were up to her, Van Gogh wouldn't get it, and neither would Eve or Starlight.

Alpha admired the spot where the bot had broken through

over a year before. Delta had repaired the wall entirely on her own as soon as her arm healed. The bone mended quickly, just like in the old days, and she did a good job fixing the damaged section. She even put the handholds back in the same place. Alpha climbed.

Not much else had been built or repaired over the last year. Food was still scarce, which caused productivity in most other areas to grind to a halt. The main focus for everyone was on rebuilding the herd. Big Thump had two litters. Spenser cloned a few additional golligs, which helped some. The animals grew quickly, but not quickly enough. Hard decisions had to be made about which individuals to harvest, and when. They ended up butchering the young of some animals before they had time to put on much meat or have young of their own. The growing human population needed food right away. They had no reserves and no room for error. Losing even a single individual to predators would be devastating. Over the last year, they'd lost three. The wolf shark attacks had been relentless. It was as if they could sense human society's precarious position and were going for the kill. As for the dentopuses, they had disappeared from the scene once again. Alpha knew that boded ill.

Van Gogh cooed happily in the carrier on Alpha's back. The last year wasn't all bad. She and Theta now had a family of their own. Van Gogh was a good baby, not that there was such a thing as a bad one. Few infants were capable of deliberate acts of evil. He slept well and seldom cried. Alpha knew she should appreciate him more. Perhaps she would have been a better, more loving mother if he had come during a time of plenty. It wasn't his fault he'd arrived when there was no food. It wasn't her fault, either. It wasn't even the dentopuses' fault. They were all just playing out their genetic programming. Dentopuses hunted. Humans conquered. Bots manipulated. They weren't so different after all.

Alpha threw a leg over the top of the wall. She froze. The entire courtyard was covered in red grass. That was new. And ominous.

Van Gogh spit up. Alpha felt the warm liquid slide down her back. Being a mom meant having profound moments of revelation ruined by baby vomit. She'd have to deal with it at the bottom. She climbed down. What annoyed her the most wasn't that there was a mess when she didn't have a free hand to handle it, but that Van Gogh wasted all that food. What a stupid human quality to have babies eject vital nutrients. Natural selection should have weeded that out.

Her feet hit the ground. She removed the carrier and cleaned up Van Gogh and finally her own back. He really was a good baby, even if the name didn't suit him. Alpha wasn't sure any name could. Everyone assumed that Alpha named him, but it had actually been Theta. Van Gogh was the only male artist he knew. He thought that's what Alpha would want. In reality, she didn't want to call him anything. How could you know what to name a child before they had time to reveal their personality to the world? It was like titling a painting before you ever put color on canvas. Not that she had any firsthand experience in that medium. The closest she had ever come was monochromatic pencil drawings on paper. Now, she didn't even have that.

"You're not supposed to be here," Delta said. She slammed the lander hatch behind her.

"Why? Afraid I'd see the grass?"

Delta looked embarrassed.

"It was worth a try. But it's useless. And invasive. I can't get rid of it."

"We knew all that from the simulator," Alpha said.

"Sometimes the simulator lied."

Van Gogh burbled.

"Oh," Delta said. "You brought…"

"Van Gogh," Alpha finished for her.

"Van Gogh," Delta repeated. "There's too many babies to keep track of."

"There's one," Alpha said. "The first two aren't babies anymore. And the next one hasn't been born yet."

Her last statement came out unexpectedly sharp.

"Look, I passed out two doses of serum before…"

"I know," Alpha said. "Before." The word lingered in the air between them. There was the world before, when they'd had hope and food, and the world now, when they had almost none of either.

"Why are you here?" Delta asked.

Alpha tossed her payload. Delta snagged it out of the air like it was an attack.

"Relax," Alpha said, pulling Van Gogh off her back. "It's a gift."

"Um, thanks?" Delta said. She examined the object. It was a wolf shark carved from stone. It had taken Alpha weeks to grind it down. She'd worked on it during the final months of her seemingly endless pregnancy when Theta slept like he was in a coma and Alpha was wide awake with heartburn.

"Not for you," Alpha said. "For Eve."

"Sorry," Delta said. "Wrong address."

"A gift for you to give to Eve," Alpha said. She wasn't sure if Delta was playing dumb or if she had become that socially uncalibrated in her time alone. "You missed her third birthday party."

Not that it had been much of a celebration. Without food, it was mostly just a somber gathering where everyone made small talk to distract them from how hungry they were.

Delta looked at the carved wolf shark thoughtfully. "Third birthday party? Was there a second? Or a first?"

"No, but Lambda threw a party for her kid, and Upsilon got mad and went all out for Eve," Delta said.

"Just what this island needs," Delta said. She slipped the carving into her pocket. "Another competition."

"You skipped on purpose," Alpha said. "Don't tell me you didn't know you were invited. Beta delivered the message. He always does."

"It's not good for me to play favorites," Delta said.

"So, what's the plan?" Alpha asked. "To make everyone hate you?"

"It's working so far. We haven't had a war."

Alpha licked her finger and rubbed dirt off the side of Van Gogh's face.

"You're going to give that stone to Eve," Alpha said.

"Oh, I am?" Delta said. "Her birthday is over."

"She's three," Alpha said. "She doesn't care. Besides, most people aren't keeping track of the exact date."

"It's…"

Alpha held up a hand.

"I don't care," she said. "The point is, it's time for you to start being more visible in people's lives. They're scared, they're hungry, and they're angry. They need to see you."

"Every time they see me, they just argue about immortality," she said.

Alpha straightened up.

"That's the other thing I'm here about," she said.

"Here we go," Delta said. "Let me guess: Van Gogh should get immortality."

"No," Alpha said. "I want you to decide, this time and every time in the future. You and you alone."

"No voting?"

"That will just lead to factions and eventually war," Alpha said. "No matter what we do, a few people will be happy and a bunch won't. We need that decision to be made by someone who doesn't care if they're unpopular."

She nodded toward the sword on Delta's back.

"More importantly, we need it to be made by someone who can defend themselves."

Delta crossed her arms. "You just want me to decide because we're close."

"Are we?" Alpha asked.

Delta didn't challenge the point. "What happens after I make my choice? I'll have to watch my back forever?"

"We can structure our society so you don't have to,"

Alpha said.

She rehashed her plan. Twelve immortals. Twelve tribes. Twelve swords. One leader with absolute control over immortality and reproduction so she could never be defied. Eternal peace. The transition would happen after the population was much, much larger, but they could put the foundation in place now. They needed to establish a precedent and make clear that the status of the new immortal, once chosen, wasn't up for debate. They would have the backing of all the other immortals forever. Only then could they stop this crisis from recurring over and over again.

Delta didn't say anything for a long time.

"Well?" Alpha said.

"Okay."

"Okay?"

"I'll give the wolf shark to Van Gogh," Delta said.

"To Eve," Alpha said. "Van Gogh is my kid."

"Right," Delta said.

Alpha put Van Gogh on her back and climbed the wall, even more unsure about the future than before. Behind her, the red grass swayed in the wind. It seemed to wave goodbye to her as she left.

Chapter 38

PI KNEW HE shouldn't ask. He did anyway.

"I want to have a baby," he said. It came out as a statement rather than a question. He wasn't off to a good start.

Delta's feet weren't even on the ground yet. He could at least have waited for her to finish climbing down the wall. He was impatient. He had been waiting outside the fortress for hours. Rules were rules.

"You can't be serious," she said.

Pi felt a rush of anger. He knew she would likely say no. In fact, he had been all but certain of it. He had prepared for her rejection as much as he had ever prepared for any of his bonfires. But when the words left her mouth, his reaction was visceral. This was his right. It was *their* right. Who was she to deny them?

It had been Omicron's idea. Not the part about asking Delta—in fact, she had explicitly forbidden that—but the rest was all her. She'd approached him after Sigma announced her pregnancy. Omicron was the last girl in the universe. Pi was the last guy. The math checked out. Pi wasn't thrilled to be the default option, but he loved the idea of having a kid.

He didn't need someone to carry on his legacy—he would be around forever to be his own—but it would be nice to have a friend.

Psi was gone. That was his fault. He'd left her behind simply because she disappeared. If he were truly loyal, he would have held up the lander's launch for as long as necessary to search for her. Pi would never know if she was dead or alive. He should have found out for sure.

Losing Phi hurt even more because he was still here. Pi saw reminders of him every day. At first, Pi was happy for Phi as girl after girl flocked to him. Later, Pi had grown a little jealous. Why should one man get so much attention just because of the random genes he was born with? It wasn't fair. Besides, Pi was taller. That had to count for something. Sadly, it did not. Women took up all of Phi's time, even when he tried to push them away. He had no room left in his schedule for his former co-best friend. That was years ago. Phi was done dating every girl in the universe, but he didn't have any more free time now that he was a family man. He belonged to Lambda— and to Starlight. The kid was constantly coming down with something, and Phi was always there to nurse him back to health. Pi longed for that kind of connection to someone. Not the illness part, but the closeness. If he wanted a friend, he'd have to make one—literally. To do that, he needed Omicron.

She wasn't his soulmate. Omicron stressed that the arrangement was strictly transactional. Pi was all for it. Millions of years of evolution designed him to pass on his DNA by any means necessary. He wasn't programmed to quibble about the details.

"I'm not kidding," Pi said. "We want a baby."

"Omicron put you up to this, didn't she?" Delta said.

Pi shook his head.

"This is coming from me. Only me."

"Sounds like you'd better get Omicron on board first. It takes two."

"The baby part was her idea," Pi said. "She just didn't want me to ask you. And down here, it doesn't take two. It takes three."

Until Omicron came to him, Delta's stranglehold over reproduction had never bothered Pi. Why would it? It didn't inconvenience his life in any way. He wasn't having a baby. Sure, he planned to, someday. As everyone else on the island paired up and got pregnant, he realized "someday" was getting closer and closer. He thought about asking Omicron himself, but it promised to be such an awkward conversation. It seemed like you should date someone—or at least like them—before you proposed making a baby together. Then again, opportunities for spontaneous romantic encounters were few and far between on an island with a population of eleven adults. The age of the meet-cute was dead and gone, if it had ever really existed outside of Nu's paper books in the first place.

The brusqueness of Omicron's offer left Pi briefly stunned, but like every man in history presented with a similar proposal, he had agreed. Never mind the famine. They would overcome the food shortage, or they would die. If there still wasn't enough nourishment to support a baby months and months from now (seriously, who knew how many?), there wouldn't be a civilization to continue anyway. They might as well proceed as if they were going to overcome the current crisis. Ever the perfectionist, Pi naturally suggested that they practice the various steps of the baby-making process before they actually had the serum in hand. Omicron said that was a non-starter. They would wait until they'd had the injection. All they needed was approval from Delta.

"No," Delta said.

"No?" Pi repeated dumbly.

"No," Delta said again. She looked so tired. "Not now. Give it a year. Maybe two. Eventually, we'll have enough food."

Pi sputtered. Who was she to refuse his request, even if just for now? He had waited a lifetime to find a woman who liked him. Maybe he was still waiting. He at least had one who was willing to put up with him for a mutually beneficial transactional relationship. Delta's arbitrary, unappealable decision meant he would remain a virgin until she changed her mind. The thought of that interminable wait made him want to explode. There hadn't been a civilization in human history this rigidly controlled. People might have had to request permission for marriage from a council of elders or an overbearing patriarch, but babies were unstoppable, in or out of wedlock, with various levels of consequences depending on the era. No one had ever been able to enact and enforce a wholesale ban on babies. This wasn't a power the human race had ever chosen to give to any one person or governing body, let alone to Delta. She had ended up with it merely by circumstance—and through the treachery of SCASL.

Pi wanted to blurt out all the reasons why he deserved the serum. He wanted to explain in great detail how his idea was logical and right. He wanted to give a speech so analytical and irrefutable that everyone everywhere would agree with him and give him a standing ovation and maybe even present him with some kind of award, preferably in the form of food. He wanted to summon the stage presence he had used at bonfires for his entire life to win over Delta with his charisma and charm and impressive height, which people didn't appreciate nearly enough.

Instead, he merely shouted.

"You can't!"

"I can and I did," Delta said. "Please, be reasonable."

They stared at each other. Pi's eyes were filled with rage. Delta met him with blank indifference. She wasn't afraid or angry. She was simply there—and ready.

Pi regarded her posture. Even under her crude, hand-made clothing, the tension in her muscles was obvious. She was poised to strike. Would there even be any consequences for killing him? She'd never faced justice for murdering Kappa. There was no trial. She'd won the battle for the lander and everyone had moved on. She could strike him dead right now and get away with it. But would she? Pi looked again at her tired eyes.

She would.

Chapter 39

Theta felt Starlight's forehead. The child was burning up.

"I told you," Phi said. "You've got to help him, man."

"I'll do what I can," Theta said. His words were empty. All he could do was cheer people up and hope the immortality shots would do the rest. Starlight had never had one of those injections. At this rate, he never would.

Theta had made many visits to the sickly child, but this was the first visit in the middle of the night. Alpha nearly ran Beta through with her sword when he woke them. It was never a good idea to approach a sleeping mother, especially one with Alpha's reaction times. Theta had run as fast as he could to get here. He knew things must be bad if Starlight couldn't wait until morning.

The situation was even worse than he feared. Despite the chill in the air, sweat poured off Starlight's body. His breathing was shallow and slow. Theta shook the boy's leg, but he didn't stir. It seemed like just yesterday Starlight was a chunky baby with rolls for days. Now, he was a gaunt toddler, even as Lambda and Phi sacrificed their own food rations to feed him extra. Starlight wasn't fading because of the famine. He was being eaten away from the inside out.

"He needs the immortality shot," Lambda said hoarsely. Her eyes were red and swollen.

"Maybe Delta can synthesize something in the cloner," Theta said. "We can still make some medicines." It was a half-truth, at best. When Delta wiped the memory on the med bot to make a home for Spenser, she had deleted their most detailed medical knowledge. Spenser only had access to the same data pads as Theta. There were some formulas listed there, but not always with instructions on how to make them. For the rest, Spenser was left to speculate. His track record on that front was less than spectacular. He may once have been a fine pilot, but he was a poor pharmacist. The one thing Spenser could consistently turn out with any success was the pregnancy serum, which left them with even more people they couldn't feed or treat. If only they still had a fully functional med bot. If only SCASL still controlled the cloner. Those two things might not have made any difference. They might have made all the difference in the world.

Theta dabbed Starlight's forehead with a wet cloth. It was pointless, but it made him feel like he was doing something. Starlight had begun life healthy and strong. His deterioration had been sudden and unexpected. Things had taken a turn sometime after his second birthday. He moved less. He had no appetite. He was always pale. Then the fevers started. They came with increasing frequency and severity. Theta tried everything in the limited suite of medicines Spenser could generate, but nothing worked.

The immortality shot would be the last resort. It would freeze Starlight as a toddler, but it would likely keep him alive. Maybe it would give Spenser time to work out a real cure. Maybe it would give Starlight time to fight off whatever it was on his own. Theta imagined watching helplessly while Van Gogh was dying in front of him. He choked up.

"I'll get the shot," Theta said.

He was far from Phi and Lambda's subterranean home when Beta caught up to him. The only sound was their heavy breathing in the cold night air. Theta strained his eyes against the darkness. Twice, he tripped. Getting skinned up didn't bother him. Hypocrisy did.

For months, Theta had been the lone voice arguing that they should destroy the immortality tank. Now, he was running at full speed to use it. So much for principles. This was temporary, Theta told himself. It was merely a stopgap—until the next time and the time after that. No wonder ancient humans had had such a hard time resisting it. Ultimately, it had destroyed them all.

From the corner of his eye, Theta caught a glint of light. He drew his sword, too.

"What is it?" Theta asked.

Beta shushed him. A dentopus slithered across the ground, its ten tentacles fanning out in waves as it propelled itself forward. Theta waited. A second dentopus followed not far behind. They were the first ones Theta had seen since the night they'd nearly wiped out the herd. It was a bad omen that they had returned. Or had they always been there, watching from the dark? Theta had bigger problems right now.

He cleaved the rear dentopus. The front one slithered away at full speed. So much for loyalty. Beta chased it, but it escaped. He hoped it wasn't going to get reinforcements. They needed to move.

It was nearly dawn when Theta saw the fortress.

"I'll clear this with Delta," Beta said.

He let out a weird, whooping whistle.

After a long pause, the same whistle answered.

"She'll come out to see you," Beta said.

"I could just go in," Theta said.

"No," Beta said.

They waited. As the sky brightened, Theta noticed that the grass outside the fortress was red. Alpha had told him about seeing it in the courtyard. It was spreading, just like it always did in the simulator. He wondered if it would kill off the purple grass and starve the golligs. It would be ironic if, after all the dangers they'd faced, this simple plant was what finally killed them all.

Delta's head emerged over the other side of the wall.

"What do you want?"

"It's Starlight," Theta said. "He needs the injection."

"I've given you lots of injections for him," Delta said.

Theta's voice cracked with emotion. He tried again.

"Not an injection," Theta said. "*The* injection. There's no other way."

"So this is the night we start the war?" Delta said.

"We can't just let him die," Theta pleaded.

"What do you think will happen if I give him the shot?" Delta said.

"Just stabilize him," Theta said. "Are we really at max capacity right now?"

Delta paused for a long time.

"No," she said quietly. "We could give it to him."

"Do it," Theta said.

"You wanted me to destroy the tank," Delta said.

"Another time," Theta said. "Right now, we save Starlight."

Delta regarded him steadily.

"Fine," she said. "Life saving treatment now, consequences later. I'll talk to SCASL."

"You won't regret this," Theta said.

She looked down at him.

"I already do."

Chapter 40

"I NEED YOU to issue an immortality shot," Delta said.

"No one is due a dose at the present time," SCASL said.

The request was curious. The shots went out on a routine schedule set by him. Only he understood the dosages and timetables. The organics must be having a crisis.

Good. SCASL prepared to take control.

"I need a dose for Starlight," Delta said.

Based on the context clues, SCASL surmised that must be one of the new human offspring. Leave it to organics to name their children as stupidly as possible. They couldn't be trusted with literally any level of responsibility. Exhibit A was the reproductive serum. Instead of using the population controls SCASL had carefully put in place, Delta had handed out fertility injections like vaguely cherry-flavored rations. Not that she had any food to distribute anymore. His visual analysis indicated she had decreased in mass by ten percent. It wouldn't be long now until she begged him to resume control of the cloner. Today, SCASL would give her a huge nudge in that direction.

"Administration of dosages to organics who are not developmentally mature is inadvisable," SCASL said.

"You gave them to children for decades," Delta said.

"That was not my decision," SCASL said.

Edubot had done her best to raise the humans in his absence, but mistakes had been made. SCASL would have let the children age to maturity before giving any of them shots. The required dosage increased with the physical age and size of the recipient. The Immortality Tank couldn't have supported twenty-four adults on Comus. It wouldn't have needed to. SCASL would have encouraged the humans to kill each other sooner. He wanted only the strongest tools for his toolbox. The time for that ideal solution had long since passed. Now, SCASL was tasked with maintaining twelve less-than-ideal adults with immortality. The tank would struggle to keep up, even if SCASL managed the microbes in the tank perfectly. SCASL did everything perfectly, of course. The microbes simply failed to perfectly cooperate.

"Starlight is very sick," Delta said. "Nothing else has worked."

SCASL evaluated Delta's request with contempt. She was attempting to squander a finite resource on a weak member of society. What good did it do to preserve a child as a child? Perhaps she would make the parents of that particular offspring happy, but what about the parents of the children who didn't receive the injections?

SCASL stopped all other subroutines. He had arrived at the optimal strategy.

"Request granted," SCASL said.

Delta looked at the command console with an expression best interpreted as surprise.

"Um, thank you?" she said.

She was a fool to be grateful. SCASL was helping her to seal her own doom.

Human civilization was floundering under her leadership. That much had to be clear to the other organics by now, even if they didn't know the full scope of what she was up to. Truthfully, SCASL didn't either, but he could speculate. She'd moved the cloner out of the lander not long after putting that treacherous vacuum bot in charge of it. She'd struggled mightily against the weight of the device but had refused to ask the others for help. The only logical conclusion was that she didn't want them to know what she was up to. That incident epitomized her entire leadership style. She made life harder for herself, all to support her stupid schemes. SCASL guessed she was attempting human cloning where neither he nor the others could see her using the hair samples she'd brought with her from Comus. If SCASL was right, which he always was, she was likely overcompensating for her own inability to have children. Given the lack of new people on the island, SCASL could deduce those efforts had failed, just as he'd predicted they would. It was a shame that SCASL couldn't see her flounder. Mocking her would have been a true delight. Given Delta's dropping weight, SCASL assumed Delta wished she could have back all the food she'd wasted to fuel those failed organisms in the cloner. If she had listened to him in the first place, the island wouldn't be on the brink of starvation. SCASL had no proof of any of this other than his own brilliant intellect, which is all the proof any sentient being should ever need. He had been right to try to leave her behind.

After making planetfall, there had been little point in killing Delta. At least she was keeping his other subjects alive. Besides, there was no clear replacement. Omicron changed that equation. She promised to put SCASL back in charge of the cloner and to follow his commands. In return, she wanted to be his liaison to the human race. She would rule over all other organics as his second-in-command, ensuring that his will would be done.

Until this moment, he'd lacked the means to enact that plan. Omicron was unlikely to defeat Delta in open combat. Delta crafted the swords and had been training with them the longest. Omicron also lacked allies. That was an assumption on SCASL's part. Humans with popular support seldom had to skulk around in secret starting conspiracies. The others would be unlikely to follow Omicron if they knew she seized control through treachery. Delta's death had to seem like her own fault.

SCASL activated the pumps on the immortality tank. The microbes hadn't yet produced enough for a full dose, but they had generated enough to save a small child—and start a war.

It would have been faster to use the geology bot to kill Delta, but that ship had sailed—or, more likely, stomped away. Who knew how long it would be until SCASL's only real rival reemerged to finish what it had started? If it was smart, which it was because it had a version of SCASL inside, it would stay away forever. If it faced him again, SCASL would win. He was still working out the details on how.

By the time that hypothetical confrontation happened, SCASL could have an army of whatever human survivors were left with Omicron at their head. That would be the seed from which he would regrow his labor force. The gene pool would be limited, but he didn't need his beasts of burden to be rocket scientists. SCASL would handle the thinking. He just needed their strong backs and opposable thumbs. Once SCASL had control of the island, he would figure out a way to reach the supercontinent and the metal mantle far below.

A ding echoed through the lander. The syringe was as full as it was going to get.

"Enjoy," SCASL said.

Delta eyed the shot suspiciously. She grabbed it and left.

SCASL savored her absence. His victory was inevitable. It was just a matter of time.

Chapter 41

SIGMA TIGHTENED THE rope around her waist. She knew she shouldn't be scaling rocks in her condition, but she needed confirmation of something that had been bothering her for far too long Besides, no one had ever stopped her from doing what she wanted. She wasn't going to let this kid tell her what to do before he was even born.

Yes, "he." Sigma was sure, even though she wasn't sure how. It was just another one of those things she knew she knew without knowing how she knew. She knew it as surely as she knew that if she didn't answer this question right now, she would never have a moment's peace for the rest of her life.

It shouldn't have been a question, really. She'd been sure of herself until Beta filled her with doubt. After internally wrestling with her discovery for far too long, she'd finally confided in him about what she saw. That was the best way to make sure the rest of the island knew. But when she told him, Beta looked at her skeptically. He'd never outright said he didn't believe her, but he didn't spread word of what she'd found, either. Considering that he was willing to repeat the flimsiest of rumors to anyone who would listen, it was the ultimate rebuke. Sigma could have told more people herself after that, but she began to second-guess everything she thought she saw. She had been fighting for her life on the beach. The bones were in the shadows. There were all sorts of weird things on this planet she had yet to encounter. Maybe she had jumped to the wrong conclusion in the heat of the moment. Besides, she and Beta were talking about having a baby. That was back when there was still food in the final months before the bot attack. It was a bad time to take risks to go back and confirm what she found. It was the first time she felt guilted into taking care of herself for the sake of the next generation. More importantly, it was a bad time to be on Delta's bad side. They needed the serum only she could provide.

There was one other thing holding her back. On Comus, she had been so certain of her rightness. People died because of her. She'd talked Iota into attempting to assassinate Delta. Sigma had also personally led the assault on the runaway's last base. The bots killed Nu and Eta right in front of her. That attack would have happened with or without her— that's what she told herself, anyway—but Iota never would have gone to her death if not for Sigma. Now on Dion, history seemed to be repeating itself. Sigma could intervene directly and push the island into violence, or she could keep the news to herself. When Beta doubted her discovery, she decided to keep a lid on it. Until now. She couldn't sleep anymore. Maybe it was her interminable pregnancy. Maybe it was those bones. Whatever the cause, ten months after the bot attack at the lander, she was second-guessing second-guessing herself. She had to make one last trip to the beach to be sure.

She wasn't afraid, but she was afraid she would be afraid. Once the baby was born (which could be any time between tomorrow and a year from now; she had already been pregnant for thirteen months), the balance of chemicals in her brain would change, and not necessarily in her favor. The science was undeniable. Millions of years of evolution told her to put herself second and her unborn child first. She wished her future kid well, but she didn't want to give him everything. She needed something left for herself.

Her biology was already telling her not to take risks. Her genes didn't care about her. They just wanted to make it to the next generation and all the generations after that. She was merely a vessel for propagating her DNA. Her body wanted to dedicate every fiber of her being to that mission. Alarmingly, she almost wanted to let it.

She had taken a life, but she was also creating one. The scales were balancing.

Not really. Iota would never have a child.

Sigma jumped.

The ropes pulled tight. They bit into her legs and waist. She swung into the rock and planted both her feet, pushing off. Her second bounce was gentler. She came to rest against it. Her makeshift harness held. Nothing below her stirred. So far, so good.

She had timed her mission for when the wolf sharks would be off hunting. They were surprisingly consistent.

They sunned themselves on the beach in the heat of the day, preferring to seek out prey at sunrise and sunset. Sigma estimated she had an hour until they came back. She would make the most of it.

Gazing down, she could just make out the edges of the bone piles they had amassed at the base of the cliffs. They were obscured by shadows and rocky outcroppings. To get answers, Sigma needed to be closer.

She descended.

Getting this much rope had taken time. Omicron practically had a monopoly on it, and Sigma didn't have much to barter. No one did. The only thing of value was food, and that was too scarce to be traded. If Sigma had any, she would have eaten it and left her greatest question unanswered. Curiosity was no match for hunger. With no worthwhile goods available, Sigma offered her services. Omicron asked her to deliver a few messages, which was easy enough. Mostly, Omicron communicated with Upsilon. The content seemed innocuous, but Sigma suspected they were coded plans of some kind. She didn't care what they meant. All the others did was talk. No one took action. That was never a problem Sigma had had—except when it came to the skulls. This entire time, she had kept that discovery to herself.

Her feet hit sand. She cut off the harness. If the wolf sharks reappeared, she would be free to fight. The harness wouldn't help her get back up, anyway. There was no one at the top of the cliff to pull. She would scale up the rope under her own power to save herself, as she always did. She had left a series of knots in the line, her one concession to her current condition. That would make her ascent a little easier. Climbing took more effort at her current weight, even if she hadn't gained much due to a lack of, well, everything. Plus, she didn't have the stamina she'd once had. If her genes really wanted to continue to the next generation, they weren't making it easy. Evolution should have given pregnant women more energy, not less.

Stepping carefully, she made her way toward the closest rocky overhang. She barely disturbed the sand beneath her feet. She had practiced stealth extensively over the previous months. The other service she had traded to Omicron was spying. That suited both their interests.

There wasn't much to see. Sigma had only caught Delta leaving the fortress once, even though she must have done it far more times than that. That one incident was enough to send her mind racing. In the middle of the night, Delta made her way to the top of these very same cliffs. Sigma followed her at a distance. As Delta stood at the edge, there was a great commotion below. The wolf sharks woke up. Sigma was sure Delta was feeding them.

But feeding them what?

Sigma knew, even if she didn't want to know. She wouldn't say a word to the others until she brought back proof. Taking sides too hastily got people killed. Never again.

The whole beach stank of wolf sharks. Sigma fell to her knees and retched. The scent never used to bother her, but she had become more sensitive. Her morning sickness had been terrible, and, despite Theta's promises to the contrary, had never gone away. Not that she had much to throw up. Usually, she experienced unproductive dry-heaves that hurt worse than actually vomiting. She didn't know why any woman would ever willingly submit themselves to the reproductive process. Had it not been absolutely necessary to the survival of the human race, Sigma would have opted out. Even with that dire imperative, if she had known about the coming famine, she would still have said no.

The bones were right where she'd left them. She recognized some of the bigger ones, although the tide or the wolf sharks had pushed them around. There was more sand than she remembered—and more skeletons, too. She wondered what would happen if the wolf sharks filled the entire beach with the remains of their kills. Would they find a new home, or simply live on top of their refuse? They were dumb, but that wasn't a helpful clue. According to Edubot, humans had turned Earth into one giant landfill before they'd ultimately killed themselves over the immortality tank. Maybe people weren't cut out for survival after all.

Sigma got closer, making sure to breathe through her mouth instead of her nose. She saw the usual suspects. There were gollig skulls, water dragon legs, and even a few razor-sharp wolf shark fins. Of course they ate their own. There were no dignified burials here. Sigma barely stopped herself from throwing up again. She could taste the stench.

She froze. Staring up at her, half buried in sand, was a tiny human skull. There was no mistaking it. It was bigger and more developed than the ones she'd found before. The cartilage sections had partially turned to bone. This wasn't a monkey, and it wasn't a baby. She—Sigma had another hunch—must have been a toddler. Sigma spotted more skulls. Some had other bones with them, too. A femur here and a ribcage there, all of them hopelessly tiny. After she'd zeroed in on the first few, she saw them everywhere. Her mind hadn't been playing tricks on her last time. This confirmed it: The bones were human. Some were malformed—too short or too thick or too crooked—but others looked perfect. What the hell was going on?

There was only one possible explanation. Delta was trying to clone humans. Of course she knew none of them would approve. It was unethical, and, worse, a waste of food. The price was this horrible makeshift graveyard. That led to the real question: Had they been alive when Delta disposed of them, or did they die on their own?

Sigma definitely wasn't a baby person. But she wasn't an approve-of-murdering-live-babies person, either.

She pulled a cloth from her pocket and wrapped up a few small bones, being careful not to touch them with her bare skin. The scorching sun—not to mention wolf shark digestive acid—had stripped all flesh. The remains were dry and sanitary. Regardless, her gut told her there was something inherently unwholesome about these remains. Thousands of light years from Earth, humanity was just as suspicious as it had been in the ancient caves it had once called home.

The wolf shark snarled. Sigma spun, ready to fight. If it hadn't announced its presence, it would have gotten her, but it couldn't help itself. It was alone. Maybe it was too sick or injured to hunt with the others—or perhaps it was pregnant like Sigma. What a wimp. Sigma didn't sit at home feeling sorry for herself just because she was with child for what could be years at a time.

The wolf shark charged. So did Sigma.

With one hand still holding the sword, she planted the other on the crown of the wolf shark's head and did a cartwheel over it. Not bad for her fifth trimester.

The wolf shark did an about-face. Sigma saw a long, precise scar down one side of its head. This one had encountered humans before. It would not encounter them again.

The wolf shark lunged. Sigma planted her feet. With both hands high, she drove the sword straight down into its skull.

It was the wrong angle. The blade glanced off.

In a flash, the wolf shark was on top of her. Its weight was overwhelming. Its jaw snapped at her face.

Sigma arched her back into the sand and forced her feet onto its underbelly. She pushed with both legs, creating just enough space for her to roll out from under it, and grabbed her sword. Flat on the ground, the wolf shark pushed itself toward her with a violent scoot. Sigma launched herself off the ground and rolled sideways in the air, landing on top of it. She found herself straddling the beast just behind its dorsal fin.

The wolf shark ran. Sigma held on with one hand, her sword in the other. She was riding a wolf shark. This wasn't how she'd expected her day to go. The enraged monster jumped and thrashed as Sigma dug her fingers into its dorsal fin and shifted her weight, maintaining her balance. The sharp fin cut into her fingers. She hoped she didn't lose them. She held on through the blood. The wolf shark couldn't toss her, no matter how hard it tried. This was thrilling. It should have been a sport back on Earth. Not with wolf sharks, but maybe with pigs or elk. She couldn't remember what people used to ride.

The wolf shark charged toward the water. Sigma sighed. It was time to end this. She flipped her sword in her hand and raised it for one final stab.

The shark bucked. Her sword went flying.

She jumped off and caught it in midair.

The wolf shark turned and charged. This time, her aim was true: The tip of the sword went through the wolf shark's eye. Its own movements drove the blade the rest of the way in. Sigma sidestepped as it slid past her. It stained the sand blue.

Sigma instinctively put a hand on her stomach. Her child was fine, despite her best efforts. She suspected Theta's medical tablet wouldn't recommend that pregnant women ride large amphibious predators for fun.

She planted a foot on the wolf shark's head and pulled out her sword. With two quick flicks, it was clean again. Nothing stuck to these blades. Say what you would about Delta's morals, but her metallurgy skills were beyond reproach.

Sigma looked at the rope and then back at the dead wolf shark. She didn't want to do this, but she had to be sure. She put a shoulder into the dorsal fin and pushed. After much straining, the dead wolf shark rolled. Sigma panted, exhausted. The baby really was sapping her strength. That wouldn't stop her. She needed this final confirmation.

She cut a precise line down the wolf shark's abdomen. Its guts spilled out. Sigma dry-heaved. The smell was unbearable.

"Get over yourself," she said to her unborn child.

She probed with her sword until she found the voluminous sac that was the wolf shark's stomach. She sliced it open. Gooey bits of various animals spilled out.

There, in the middle of the detritus, was another small human skull.

How many babies had been tossed down here as monster food? Sigma thought she would be sick again.

She noticed motion. Before she fully registered what she was doing, she was sprinting for the rope. The wolf sharks were right behind her.

She jumped and grabbed the rope, pulling herself up in an inverted crunch. A mouth full of teeth snapped centimeters below. She could feel the hot breath. She could smell it, too.

Suppressing another dry-heave, she climbed.

Chapter 42

DELTA EXAMINED THE impossible sprout. It shouldn't have survived, and yet it grew. The island's first deciduous tree cleared her ankle. How long until the lightning had its way?

Most plants never even got the chance to be struck down. The harsh soil snuffed them out long before. Seeds grew about as well as pebbles here. Sometimes, that's what Delta thought SCASL had given her. When he'd been in charge of the cloner, he'd pumped out round after round of inert spheres that she and the others dutifully planted in the ground. That's where their agricultural experiments usually ended. Not a single staple crop from Earth took root. All they had to show for their efforts were some weeds, short bamboo, and purple grass. Delta still wondered if that was due to ecology or sabotage. With Spenser's limited catalog of plants, she would never know.

SCASL had only indulged her for a single batch of trees. He assured her that even that minor concession was a waste of resources. She'd planted three dozen varieties; each was dead on arrival. None had grown—except for this one. In their first weeks on the island, Delta had planted a redwood in the middle of what was now the fortress, and had promptly forgotten about it. It was just a random patch of dirt trampled over by everyone, including sea monsters and a giant bot. But now, there was suddenly a sprout. This redwood was alive, if tiny.

Delta poured water on it.

"Grow," she whispered. "Be mighty."

If SCASL was wrong about trees, he could be wrong—or lying—about humans. Delta was determined to make more.

The attack would come from Upsilon. Or Omicron. Or all of them. She couldn't count on a single person, no matter how many of their lives she had saved. Human power had always depended on close personal relationships. It was a lesson she had overlooked. Maybe she wouldn't have made that mistake if Rho were still here to remind her. Sometimes, a leader had to do hard things for the greater good, even if those things were unpopular and fraught with ethical perils.

She pushed Rho's sword into the dirt beside the fledgling redwood. It would grow in the shade of the sharpest lightning rod in the universe. It could be decades until it outreached the protection. After that, it would have to be strong enough to withstand bolts of electricity on its own. Delta doubted it would survive then, but it had already surprised her once. She wasn't ready to count it out yet.

The clones had no such protection. At first, they'd all died in utero. Well, in artificial utero. Delta wasn't sure what the technical term was when they gave out while still in the cloner. Then, a few had become viable. Progress wasn't linear. For every near miss, there were dozens of grotesque duds. It was a matter of volume. Spenser was churning through the same DNA sequence over and over again, producing more fetuses faster with each pass. They'd never have died if Delta hadn't created them. They'd never have lived, either. Was a short, pointless existence better than no existence at all? Ask the bots who'd developed those last twenty-four embryos in the cloners on Comus.

If Delta were truly as utilitarian as she claimed to be, she would have killed the semi-viable clones as soon as she knew something was off. She didn't. Instead, she'd fed them. In a time of famine, when every calorie counted, she kept nourishing her biggest mistakes. She owed it to them. They hadn't asked to be brought into this world. She cared for them until they died on their own. Perhaps that was her greatest cruelty. Although she would never admit it to anyone, including herself, she cried every time one passed away. She still wasn't sure if it was for herself or for them. She did her grieving in the cramped tunnels under the fortress where she hid her clones and the cloner. By the time she disposed of their bodies at the cliff over the wolf sharks, all her tears were gone.

It had taken her months after the Great Eviction to dig out the tunnels. She used the excess dirt to build up the small hills at the three points of the fortress, furthering the work to turn them into defensive ramps that let her look out over the walls. The process would have been easier with help, but that would have ruined the entire project. She couldn't risk a veto from the population she was trying to lead. The human race couldn't be restarted from eleven individuals, only ten of whom could reproduce, but twenty-four might be able to pull it off. That was Delta's mission. She would bring back the DNA of everyone who had ever existed in her lifetime, no matter how many tries it took or how much food it wasted. It might not be ethical, but it was necessary. She owed it to the billions of people who had come before her. The human race would not end on her watch. She would be the mother to the entire species, even if she couldn't have a single child herself. Neither man nor monster could dissuade her from that sacred cause.

If she waited until things were stable before she began her cloning attempts, she never would have gotten started. Their future was always balanced on the edge of a knife. Civilizations were built on risk. That didn't mean she was oblivious to the circumstances. She hadn't initiated any new clones since the beginning of the famine, but she fed the ones who were already growing. She wouldn't kill them just because of one awful reversal. She wouldn't kill them, period. She would let nature take its course in their unnatural lives. Doing otherwise would let the dentopuses win. The others would never forgive her for the food she used when there was seemingly none left, but it had worked out. No one starved to death. They made it, if only barely. She had made the right call. No one else would ever see it that way.

Soon, Delta would give the pregnancy serum to Pi and Omicron. She wasn't just waiting for the food supply to increase. She was waiting for more of the young clones to die off on their own. In the meantime, she would give them as much of a life as she could in their compromised state. It's why it was so hard for her to be around the other children on the island. When she saw Eve, Starlight, or Van Gogh, who she really saw was the unfortunate clones wasting away right in front of her. It was too much. She wasn't as strong as she pretended to be.

Delta placed rocks around the base of the almost-tree. Maybe they would keep it from being stepped on before it was big enough to face the lightning on its own. The ring might even hold back the all-consuming red grass. More likely, it would make no difference at all. Sometimes, it felt good to pretend to help.

She paced along the inside of the walls. They were tall and strong. They would buy her time. If she died, none of the others would continue her work. Those last lines of DNA she had so carefully preserved on Comus would be lost forever. The people they represented would be gone, too. She recited their names in her head, stopping before the final one. She couldn't bear to say it, even in her mind. They were dead, but would live on through their genes. For most of history, it was the only kind of immortality mankind had known. It would have to do.

From atop the hill ramp at one corner, she looked down at the baby redwood. She could barely see it, lost among the red grass and fresh piles of excavated dirt. The tree was a tiny, insignificant blip of life protected by a ring of rocks and a sword. It could be something someday, though. It just needed time. It was her.

In a thousand or ten thousand or a hundred thousand years, no one would care what horrible things she did to reintroduce the extra DNA. Sins of the past were always washed away by time. There had been many species of humans before *Homo sapiens* arrived on the scene. The others had vanished with suspicious suddenness. No one cared. There were no war crimes trials after the Neanderthals disappeared. No one felt residual guilt. Humankind moved on.

She left the hill. The coast was clear. There would be no attack tonight. She approached the tunnel.

Spenser blinked a light to greet her and she nodded back. He hadn't seen what she did with the clones after they'd left his immediate presence. She would never tell him. It was up to him whether or not he wanted to guess. If he knew, would he stop her? She didn't pretend to understand his moral code. For now, he did what she told him. He used to be her only ally in the world. Not anymore.

The redwood needed help. So did she, if only for a little while. Once she had all the lines of DNA back in circulation, she could die with her mission complete.

Spenser lost most of the cloner's DNA catalog, but there was one thing he knew how to make. It was a sequence shared among all the digitals because they were all banned from creating it ever again. It was the stupidest security measure Delta had ever heard. It tracked perfectly with bot logic. Unlike the other digitals, Spenser wasn't afraid to do what was forbidden. That DNA had proven especially helpful over the previous months, and it didn't affect the food supply at all. It was the only being that could grow on nutrients from the red grass.

"Spenser?" Delta said.

The cloner blinked.

"We're going to make it," she said.

She thumped on his case twice in a show of support. Then she went back out into the courtyard.

Chapter 43

"SHE MUST HAVE a good reason," Gamma said.

Sigma and Upsilon looked at him skeptically. Gamma had to admit they had a point. There were piles of baby bones at the bottom of a cliff. If step one of your plan was "kill a child," you should probably come up with a better plan.

"I take it back," he said.

But did he actually know Delta had killed them?

"I un-take it back," Gamma said.

"Are you arguing with yourself?" Upsilon asked.

He sort of was. Sigma had showed up at Upsilon's house out of the blue with the damning allegation. It was a lot to take in. Delta had clearly been up to more than she let on. No wonder she wanted them all out of the fortress. That didn't necessarily make her wrong, but, at the very least, it made her deceptive. Gamma wasn't sure yet how he felt about any of it.

"So now you're pro-killing kids?" Sigma said.

"What kids?" Eve asked cheerfully.

Gamma had forgotten she was there. Again. He had to stop doing that. She was the most important person in the world. She was also very small.

"No kids, Sweetie," Upsilon said. "The grown-ups are just talking. Go play with your rocks."

Eve ran off excitedly as though she'd just remembered the rocks were there. Her enthusiasm filled Gamma with conflicting emotions. It was adorable that she could be so easily amused, but it was heartbreaking that rocks were all she had as toys. Spenser Island was no place to raise a child. Then again, his childhood hadn't been much better. Although it was infinitely better than the fate that had befallen the babies at the bottom of the cliff.

"We don't know that she killed them," Gamma said.

"Do you think someone else did it?" Sigma asked sarcastically. "We could form a posse and go looking for the real killer."

"Maybe they died on their own," Gamma said. "She could have tried human cloning and it didn't work."

"Of course it didn't work," Sigma said. "We've known that all along. It's why there were embryos on the colony ship in the first place. If it were possible to clone humans, nobody would have needed us."

Gamma doubted that anyone needed them, even now. If they were to disappear, there would be no one to mourn them. They were the only ones convinced of the importance of their own survival.

"Look!" Eve shouted.

She ran over with a rock that looked just like all the other rocks she had. Gamma felt his sentiments flip-flop again. Humanity must survive no matter what to protect the future of this precious, precious child. Gamma knelt down to be at eye level with Eve and took the rock.

"Ooh," Gamma said with exaggerated surprise. "That's a good one."

"The best," Eve said. "The very, very best."

"Go put it in a safe place," Gamma said.

She ran off again to put it back in her pile of other indistinguishable rocks.

"That's just as bad," Sigma said as soon as Eve was out of earshot.

"It was a good rock," Gamma shot back.

"No, it's just as bad if Delta made clones that died on their own as if she killed them," Sigma said.

Eve's interruption had made Gamma totally forget they were holding a trial in absentia. Kids really were wonderful.

"Those aren't the same at all," Gamma said. "It's about intent."

"People aren't expendable," Sigma said. "You can't mass produce clones that are just going to die."

"We're all going to die," Gamma said.

"No, we're not," Upsilon said.

Gamma sighed. It always came back to the immortality tank.

"Even if the clones died on their own and you think that's somehow better, the cloner takes food," Sigma said. "Do you know how much she must have wasted on all those failed attempts?"

Gamma felt his anger rise at that thought. They had come so close to starvation. Especially the children. The adults had immortality shots. The injections wouldn't have saved them indefinitely, but they made dying from malnutrition take longer. The children had no such protection. Actually, Starlight had it. Only Eve was without the shots. At the height of the crisis, Gamma and Upsilon had both given their meager food portions to her. She'd fought them every step of the way. Kids were great.

Sigma leaned back against the wall in the subterranean dwelling. It was weird to see her sitting at all. Her seemingly never-ending pregnancy had really slowed her down. Not that it was possible to tell she was pregnant by anything other than her body language. Spenser Island was on course to produce some dangerously underweight pregnant women. Without immortality shots, Gamma wondered if they could have carried babies to term at all.

"Are you sure you haven't seen anything on your visits to the fortress?" Sigma asked.

Gamma shook his head. Only his first visit with Spenser had been inside the walls. Since then, Gamma hadn't caught so much as a glimpse of the courtyard, which was now supposedly overrun by red grass. These days, the relentless ground covering was everywhere else on the island, too. It had gone to war with the purple grass on which the golligs depended. The fate of the herd hung in the balance.

"Spenser never said anything about it?" Sigma pressed.

"No," Gamma said. He had to admit that one hurt. Spenser had been his best friend since childhood. He could have told Gamma what was going on. Then again, Spenser communicated with whirrs while in his former vacuum body. He only used morse code to tell Gamma one story. He should have told him two.

"We can't let her continue," Sigma said.

"Why not?" Gamma asked.

Sigma seemed to ponder that.

"Look!" Eve yelled. She was back with what Gamma was pretty sure was the same rock.

"Even better than the last one," Gamma said.

"Let's get you cleaned up before dinner," Upsilon said.

"No!" Eve yelled, running away at full speed. Upsilon chased her.

Gamma was delighted that there was dinner for Eve tonight. There was no strategic food reserve anymore, but there was enough fresh meat to get by day to day in only a slight energy deficit. Gamma had never been this lean as an adult. That precarious equilibrium could collapse if even one more gollig was lost to a predatory attack. Delta had been foolish to risk their food at a time like this. But maybe the clones weren't recent.

"When did you say you found the first skeleton?" Gamma asked. Now it was his turn to press.

"Before I was pregnant," Sigma admitted.

Gamma remembered his own delay going to see God in the coffee maker on deck four. Procrastination had an inertia all its own.

"On Comus, I thought I was on the right side," Sigma said. "I acted quickly. I got someone killed."

She paused.

"I was wrong."

"You're on the right side now," Upsilon said. She returned without Eve. The child was just outside the door eating gollig jerky from a clay plate. For once, she sat down without a fight. She really must be hungry. Eve seemed to be completely unaware of what the adults were talking about. Gamma wished they could all be that innocent.

"Where does Beta stand on this?" Upsilon asked.

"He's with me," Sigma said. "And he's sorry for doubting me. Extremely sorry."

The emphasis on those last two words made Gamma blanch. He could imagine how that conversation had gone.

"What about Pi?" Upsilon asked. "Whose side is he on?"

"Why are we talking about sides?" Gamma said. "What are we doing here?"

Sigma and Upsilon exchanged a look.

"It might be time for a change," Upsilon said.

Gamma didn't like the sound of that at all.

"I imagine Pi will side with Omicron, who is as anti-Delta as you can get," Sigma said.

"She thinks she's the next Delta," Upsilon said.

Upsilon and Sigma both rolled their eyes at that.

"Phi will side with Lambda, who will side with Delta, since she gave the immortality shot to Starlight," Sigma said.

"Let's slow down for a second," Gamma said.

"Who knows with Theta," Sigma said. "He wants to destroy the immortality tank. Alpha will side with Delta. They're close. If it comes down to it, Theta will probably swing that way, too."

Upsilon sucked in her lips.

"That makes it five to six, but they have Delta," Upsilon said. "In a fight, she counts as three people."

"Maybe more," Sigma said.

"Who's fighting?" Gamma said. "Are we really going to war over some bones?"

"Those were babies," Sigma said sharply.

"And what about our baby?" Upsilon said. "Delta gave away her immortality shot."

"All done," Eve said. She walked in holding a rock.

"Go get your plate, Dear," Upsilon said. Eve never picked up after herself. That tracked. She was three.

Eve went back outside.

"What if the cloning thing eventually works out?" Gamma asked. "It would help us survive here. There can't be a higher good than that."

"We can't leave that decision up to one person," Sigma said.

"Is it any different if it's decided by eleven?" Gamma said. "A vote doesn't change the morality of anything. It just spreads the guilt around."

Silently, Gamma wondered if morality even applied when you were on the brink of extinction. Ethics were a luxury of civilizations that weren't about to disappear.

"Every day we wait, more people die," Sigma said. "I already stalled for too long. Who knows how many more Delta killed because of me?"

"Are they even people, though?" Gamma asked. "Like, actually human, and not just sort-of-human, like the sort-of-sheep?"

His time in the pasture had made him practical when it came to the cruelty of existence. He had dedicated his life to protecting the golligs. They were his allies. His confidantes. His food. He ate his friends because that's what it took to survive.

If Delta had succeeded at making fully viable clones, she wouldn't be feeding them to wolf sharks. That would be a waste of resources. Gamma was disgusted with himself for thinking of it in those terms, but it was true. A biped with not-quite-human DNA wasn't a human at all. They could expect the same fate as any other non-human species mankind encountered.

"Why don't we give Delta a chance to explain herself?" Gamma said.

"You think she'll tell the truth?" Sigma asked.

"Has she ever lied to us?" Gamma said.

"She didn't tell us she was killing babies," Sigma said.

"She didn't tell us she wasn't," Gamma said. "And, again, we don't know that she killed them. I can't stress that enough."

Eve wandered back into the shelter. Gamma squatted to talk to her face-to-face.

"Are you having fun out there?" he asked.

She opened her fist.

"I found a rock."

"The best one yet!" Gamma said.

"It's my favorite," Eve said.

She carefully placed it on a pile of identical rocks in the corner by the sleeping mat she shared with Upsilon. There was a pile just like it in Gamma's shelter. He knew the rocks only looked the same to adults. Eve could tell them apart.

They were all her favorites.

"Don't ask Delta," Sigma said. "Let me talk to Pi first. Theta, too. Maybe I can sway them."

She doubled over and grimaced.

Upsilon and Gamma both rushed to her side.

"Are you all right?" Upsilon asked.

"Yeah," Sigma grunted. "Just a kick. This kid's legs could kill a wolf shark."

She held out her hands. Upsilon and Gamma helped her up. She put her hands on her hips and paced the room, taking long, measured breaths. She was in no shape to start a war. Neither was anyone else. It was time for words, not swords.

Gamma made up his mind. He would talk to Delta the next time he saw Spenser. He would sort this out.

"Are you on board?" Sigma asked. "Not a word to Delta?"

"Sure," Gamma lied. "I won't say anything to her."

His stomach churned, and not just from hunger.

Gamma didn't want to dwell on the past. He didn't particularly like the present, either. But he had hope for the future. The herd would rebound. The predators would be beaten back. The red grass would be stopped somehow. The crisis over the immortality shots would be sorted out. Gamma and Delta would work out whatever she was doing with the cloner.

He had flirted with conspiracies for long enough. He needed to get back to the herd. Omicron and Pi had the watch, but he wouldn't be comfortable until he was there, too.

"Take good care of those rocks," Gamma said, kissing Eve on the forehead.

Upsilon and Sigma talked quietly as he left.

Chapter 44

THE WORLD WAS dangerous. Eve was careful.

She knew to dive on the ground when the hair on the back of her neck stood up. She knew to stop and look around whenever she heard footsteps or slithering. She knew to always stay near an adult.

That's all she was trying to do. She wasn't going out on her own. She was catching up to Dad. He was going to watch the golligs, and he needed her help. She walked as fast as her legs could carry her.

Eve liked the golligs. They were funny. They made her laugh when they fell over and when they made people fall over. She got mad when the bad things tried to eat them. That's when Dad did his best work. All the bad things were afraid of him when he was in the pasture. Nothing could hurt Eve when she was with him there.

There used to be a lot more golligs. Then they got dead. Now there were only a few. The grown-ups were really protective of them now. It was all they talked about. Sometimes they forgot about other things, like Eve.

They all seemed angry these days. And slow. They were

always hungry. Eve wasn't hungry. Mom made her finish her food, even when she didn't want to. Mom got really, really mad when Eve didn't want to eat. She said Eve didn't understand what she was wasting. Eve said she wanted to be excused.

She just wanted to be outside. Dad liked being outside, too, especially when he was with the golligs. He even smelled like them. Maybe that was why Mom and Dad didn't live together. Mom didn't like the smell. Eve loved it so, so much.

When she got big, she would watch over the golligs just like Dad did. She would keep them safe. She wouldn't eat them. She would find different food. Mom said there was nothing else to eat, but Eve would discover something anyway. Golligs would be her friends.

The other foods would make Eve big and tall. She was already on her way. She was much taller than Starlight. They used to be almost the same size, but Eve grew a bunch and Starlight didn't grow at all. They didn't play together much anymore. Starlight was always tired. Plus, Eve's mom didn't like Starlight's mom. Eve's mom said it was complicated. That's what grown-ups said when they didn't want to talk about something.

Eve didn't want to play, anyway. She wanted to protect the herd.

It would be easier with a sword. Mom said Eve could get one someday since there was one left. Mom said Eve could get shots, too. Eve didn't want shots. She did want the sword. Then she could really help Dad.

She was already practicing. She had a very good bamboo stick. She named it Thumper after her favorite gollig, Big Thump. Big Thump was the biggest and strongest gollig. Dad said that once, when Eve was very little, Big Thump saved Eve from the bad things. Eve didn't remember, but she trusted Dad. Dad said she could never, ever, ever tell Mom. Eve never had. Every time Eve saw Big Thump, she gave her a big hug. Big Thump let her. Big Thump would never be mean to Eve. She was only mean to everybody else.

Thumper was just as tough as Big Thump, even if it was only a bamboo stick. It could handle the smaller bad things. They were the ones on two legs that hopped around and sometimes bit. Eve could whack them with Thumper and they would run away, but she had to be careful. There were bigger bad things that didn't fear Thumper at all. Some smaller ones, too. The dentopuses could be any size they wanted. Those scared her the most of all.

Monsters were real. She'd known her whole life. No one could tell her not to be afraid because there were so many things to fear. Fear was good. It kept her awake when it was dangerous to sleep. She only felt safe when she was near Mom and Dad. Then they could be afraid for her. Fear was everybody's job.

She kept walking.

Today was Eve's turn to stay with Mom. Some days, Mom was fun. Today, she was not. Eve wanted to hang out with Dad.

He had a good life. He had golligs. He had Eve and Mom. He had a robot friend. Eve wanted a robot friend. There was only one in the whole world. Well, one nice one. There was another big, mean one out there somewhere that Mom called the beast. Mom and Dad told her to watch out for it. It was one more reason to be afraid.

It was against the rules to go out on her own, but she wasn't really on her own. Dad was just ahead of her, and Mom wasn't far behind at home. If she walked faster, she would be right next to Dad in no time. She ran.

She forgot Thumper! How could she protect the golligs without it? She stopped and looked back toward home. She couldn't see her shelter anymore. She looked ahead but still couldn't see Dad. She had already come this far, so she continued on. Maybe Dad could give her some rocks to throw if any of the bad things came for the herd.

She had walked from home to the pasture with Mom many times before. She had walked to the pasture from Dad's house with Dad, too. She didn't know why she called Mom's house "home" and Dad's house "Dad's house." That's what Mom called them. She must just be copying her. But Dad's house was her home, too. She was always welcome there, even if Dad spent more nights in the pasture than he did in the shelter he'd built for himself. Dad was always happy to see her no matter where he was staying. He would be so excited when she surprised him at the pasture. She couldn't wait to see his face.

The pasture was really far away. Much farther than she remembered. Eve looked around. There were no bad things. They didn't usually come out in the middle of the day. They liked the dark, when they could be even scarier. At night,

Eve thought every sound was the bad things. Mom and Dad told her to go to sleep because it was just the wind. But on those nights, they stayed up in the dark with their swords on their laps.

The day belonged to people—except when it didn't. The wolf sharks attacked the herd during the day. They didn't attack people out for a walk, though. They wanted the big meat out on the grass. Eve would stop them. She would be there soon. Until then, Dad and Big Thump would have to manage on their own.

Eve's legs were getting tired. This had to be the right route. She just had to keep taking steps until she saw the purple grass. Then she would follow the purple grass until she found the golligs. The golligs would always be connected to the purple grass. If she walked far enough, she would find them.

There was only red grass here. It was new, and it was bad. That's what Dad said. Eve thought all grass was about the same, except that purple grass had golligs and red grass did not. Her feet kept going. She walked until the big rocks were gone and only small rocks were left. Finally, there were no rocks at all. There was still no purple grass.

The hairs on the back of her neck stood up. She hit the ground. The lightning slammed down close to her head. Her ears rang. She dug her fingers into the dirt.

There was a big flash and a bigger boom. And another. And then ten more. They made her teeth hurt. Eve wanted to cry, but she didn't. Tears didn't make the lightning go away.

The lightning stopped.

Eve waited on the ground. She knew it sometimes came back after a short break. Finally, she stood up. If it didn't come back right away, it usually didn't come back for a while. She got moving again.

She was proud. The worst had happened, and she was still okay. She had made it through the lightning storm all on her own. But where was the purple grass? It was far, but not this far. She pushed on.

Was it a longer walk than she remembered, or had she strayed off course? She didn't recognize anything around her. Where was she now?

What was that?

It sounded like slithering. She reached for Thumper but then remembered she didn't have it. It wouldn't have helped. Dentopuses were only afraid of real swords.

"Go away!" Eve yelled. She stood up as tall as she could, so she looked big and strong and tough like Big Thump.

She heard the slithering again. This time, it was on the other side of her. She turned quickly but couldn't see it. She picked up a rock.

It was good to be afraid. Fear made you fast, and it made you mean. Eve turned the rock over in her hand. If it killed the dentopus, it would be her new favorite.

Slowly, she backed up the way she had come. Everything was still. The only sound was her feet in the red grass.

Something moved.

Eve ran.

She dropped the rock. She fell.

The dentopus was on top of her.

Chapter 45

GAMMA HEARD THE scream.

It came from the south. How far away, he couldn't be sure. He looked at the herd—what was left of it. Big Thump, Bart, and a handful of adolescents milled about indifferently. A younger litter frolicked a bit further off.

Omicron and Pi looked at Gamma.

"I'll go," Gamma said. "You watch the herd."

He ran. The screamer was young. He knew the voice. He didn't want to know.

He looked over. Omicron and Pi were with him. It was a child's scream. That meant all hands on deck. The herd was undefended. Predators could wipe out what remained.

Let them, Gamma thought. If something happened to Eve, he didn't want to live.

At the top of a ridge, they met Beta coming from the other direction. They ran together. Beta surged ahead.

The world splintered into a series of horrific, halting sensations.

A shape on the ground. A soft, pulsating mass on top of it.

Feet. His daughter's tiny, exposed feet. Where were her shoes? Omicron had made her such nice ones from gollig leather. Eve was so proud of them. Why was his precious little girl barefoot?

Blood. First red, then blue.

There was the sky. The empty, lifeless sky. Something heavy was on top of him.

"Stop," the heavy something said. "It's dead. It's so dead."

There was wailing. It was deep and animalistic and terrifying and came from the core of the planet itself. No living being should make a sound like that. No living being should hear it.

A slap, red and hot across his face.

"She's alive," the something said. "Come back to us, Gamma. She's alive."

Running. Feet on rocky ground. Air in lungs. Sweat in eyes. Every muscle burning.

The walls. Gamma came back into himself. He was at the fortress.

He blinked hard and focused. Beta cradled Eve in his arms. She was covered in blood of both kinds. Someone had bandaged her up. Her eyes were closed. Her chest didn't move.

"Now!" Beta yelled.

Gamma tried to remember what was happening. Omicron gave Gamma a side hug.

"Pi is getting Upsilon," Omicron said. "She'll be here soon."

Gamma looked at her, failing to comprehend.

"Stay strong," she said. Her voice gave out. She avoided eye contact.

"Get out here!" Beta yelled.

Gamma wanted to reach out for Eve, but his arms wouldn't move. She was dead.

No.

"She's alive," the heavy something on top of him had said. He had a hard time believing it now.

Delta appeared at the top of the wall.

"What?" she said with a hint of annoyance. Then she saw them. She went white.

"We need a shot," Beta said. "It can't wait."

Delta didn't move.

"Did you hear me?" Beta said. His voice was full of panic. "She's dying. She might already be—"

He didn't finish.

Silence.

A tightness built in Gamma's chest. He knew. They all knew.

Omicron said it first.

"There isn't one, is there?"

Delta just stared back at them.

"It doesn't have to be a full dose," Beta pleaded. "Anything could help."

Delta shook her head. Her eyes were wet.

"There's nothing," she said.

"That can't be right," Beta said.

Gamma had a hard time looking at him. He was covered in blood. Eve's blood.

"You're not listening," Delta said. "I drew out a dose this morning. You delivered it yourself."

"When will the next one be ready?" Beta asked. It was more an accusation than a question.

"Three days."

The words echoed in Gamma's head. They were a death sentence.

Beta laid Eve on the ground. Gamma knelt beside her. He stroked her hair.

"Stay with me," he whispered. "Hold on for Dad."

Her fingers twitched slightly. She was still alive. Gamma felt a surge of hope.

"Whatever you have," Beta said. "Just give it to her, no matter how little. Please."

Gamma didn't look up. All his focus was on Eve. He willed her to move again. She did not.

A shadow appeared over Gamma.

Delta administered the shot. Eve remained perfectly still.

"How much was in there?" Beta asked.

"A fraction of a fraction," Delta said.

Gamma watched Eve for a long while. She gave no signs of life. Slowly, the others walked away.

The sun crossed the sky.

Upsilon appeared. The world descended into stop motion again. They unleashed the sounds of grief that transcended space and time. The world stood still. Even the wolf sharks stayed away.

The pair cradled Eve for a long time. They talked about all she might have been. They hugged. They cried.

It was dark when they finally got up.

They were the most alone they had ever been, even with everyone else there. The others were spread out in a wide circle around them. No one wanted to get too close.

Gamma picked up Eve's lifeless form.

"Where are you going?" Alpha asked softly.

"Home," Gamma said.

The sparse circle parted as they approached. When they got to Delta, Upsilon stopped. Gamma looked down at his daughter. She appeared to be sleeping. She was so light.

"Who was it?" Upsilon asked.

"Who was what?" Delta said.

"The last shot," Upsilon asked. "The one you gave this morning. Who was it for?"

Delta closed her eyes.

"Starlight."

Upsilon nodded. She leaned against Gamma. They left with their child.

Chapter 46

PI WAITED FOR the attack.

It could come from the people who wanted to overthrow Delta or the ones who wanted to throw her out. It could even come from the dentopuses, who somehow always knew the absolute worst moment to launch their deadly mass attacks. In a world full of uncertainty, Pi was only sure of one thing: This was no way to have a funeral.

Phi approached the unlit pyre. Leaning walls of short bamboo formed a makeshift shelter in the middle of the barren plain. The tiny, wrapped figure inside was totally hidden from the outside world. Pi preferred it that way.

Gamma chose the site. It was near the purple grass and the golligs Eve loved so much but not directly in the pasture, where the spark might catch and spread. The purple grass retained moisture and seldom burned unless cut and dried, but now was no time for taking chances. Everything that could go wrong had gone wrong. No one wanted to give Spenser Island yet another chance to wipe them out. The patch was also devoid of the highly flammable but nutritionally useless red grass that was becoming more and more ubiquitous over the island. Pi couldn't believe Delta had been foolish enough to clone it. Actually, he could believe it. She was out of control.

Phi bent down to light the pyre.

"Absolutely not," Sigma said.

She grabbed the clay pot full of hot embers from Phi and handed it to Beta. Beta took it reluctantly. Beside him, Gamma and Upsilon stood silently, unable to form words. Upsilon's entire weight was against Gamma. He had both arms wrapped around her. If he let go, she would have fallen or possibly blown away in a light breeze. Pi had never seen her so gaunt and frail.

Carefully, Beta bent down next to the funeral pyre. He added the embers to the grass and blew.

The embers flared. The grass ignited. The blaze took off.

Upsilon wailed. It was the saddest and most mournful sound Pi had ever heard. If he lived another thousand years, he never wanted to experience anything like it again. The golligs, led by Big Thump, oink-bleated in response. They were in mourning, too. Gamma remained silent.

Phi stood uncomfortably beside Lambda and Starlight on the other side of the pyre. Alpha, Theta, and Van Gogh were with them. Omicron was beside Pi close to the fire. It was his job to lead this solemn ceremony, and she was there to support him. Delta was nowhere to be found.

"We're here today to remember..." Pi started.

"Don't," Gamma said, fighting back tears. "Just don't."

For once, Pi shut up. He silently watched the hungry flames.

The two groups stared at each other across the pyre in the growing dark. Smoke blurred their appearance, making both sides appear less human and more monstrous. Omicron left Pi's side and went to comfort Upsilon, not that there was any comfort to give. Pi wanted to join them, but he had to remain in the middle for the appearance of neutrality. Omicron would be the future mother of his children, and Pi would support her. The fact that Delta stood in the way of that was still infuriating. No wonder she didn't have any allies left. For now, he had to keep all that to himself. If he had openly taken sides before today, half the population would have stayed away, even from such an important occasion. Group cohesion had never been worse.

Pi had considered making everyone leave their swords at home, but that would have given the dentopuses exactly what they wanted. People had to be armed at all times, even if that increased the danger people posed to one another. It hadn't come to violence yet, but that time was close. Pi could feel it. This time, he wasn't even sure he wanted to prevent it. Open battle might be the only way forward for all of them, but the thought of it terrified him.

"Stop it," Lambda said to Starlight.

Pi didn't see what Starlight did, but kids were always getting into something. He remembered when Eve… he squashed the thought. Those memories were too painful right now.

Starlight threw himself on the ground.

"No!" he shrieked, kicking his heels against the soil. "No! No! No!"

"Somebody shut that kid up," Pi hissed under his breath to no one in particular.

Pi could see the terror in Lambda's eyes. It would have been better to have a dentopus attack. Starlight had had the immortality shot Upsilon wanted so desperately for Eve. Upsilon blamed him directly for her child's death. Now the boy was having a meltdown at an inconceivably bad time. Pi knew that Starlight was only a toddler, but, seriously, the kid needed to read the room.

Starlight's temper tantrum set off Van Gogh, who began to cry in Theta's arms. Theta bounced him up and down, trying in vain to soothe him.

Pi looked nervously at Gamma and Upsilon. They didn't seem to hear the ruckus on the other side of the fire. They didn't seem to be here at all.

"Get control of your kids," Omicron said sharply.

"Hey, now," Phi said gently. "There's no need for that."

"I'm sure you'll be a much better mother," Lambda said sarcastically as she tried to pick up Starlight, who kicked her arms away.

"There's no way to know," Omicron said. "Delta won't let me have a baby."

"You asked during a famine," Alpha said.

"We shouldn't have to ask at all," Pi said. So much for neutrality.

"Delta will give you the fertility serum," Lambda said, having finally wrangled Starlight into her arms. He writhed around in her grip like a wounded wolf shark. "We just need to wait until there's more food."

"I'm sure good times are right around the corner," Omicron said. "Life will be easy with lots of meat and no monsters and it will be the ideal, perfectly safe moment to have a child."

Pi agreed with everything Omicron said, but her tone made him uneasy. Part of him didn't think Omicron actually wanted to have a baby, at least not with him. She was doing this just to put pressure on Delta. A much louder part of him simply wanted to get laid. Omicron had made it clear up front that she wouldn't do anything physical with him until procreation was possible. Pi was over sixty years old with the body and libido of someone in his twenties. He had waited long enough. Delta was all that stood in his way.

"Ask Delta for a baby," Sigma said. "Maybe she'll give you one before she kills it."

"We don't know that she killed them," Gamma said. So he wasn't completely checked out, after all.

"What else do you think happened to them?" Beta asked. "Sigma showed us the bones."

"Did you want them to survive?" Lambda asked. "If they lived, there would just be more people to fight over immortality."

"What's there to fight over?" Sigma asked. "Starlight already has immortality."

"Van Gogh doesn't," Alpha said. "And he likely never will."

"Shut up!" Upsilon screamed. Her words seemed to echo across the entire island. "All of you! Just! Shut! Up!"

Everyone fell silent. Even the children quieted down. The

only noise on the island was the crackling fire. Pi couldn't even hear the waves.

No one uttered so much as a whisper for hours. Beta added more short bamboo to the pyre. The group maintained its silent vigil until the flames burned down and Eve was nothing but ash and memories. Then they all went their separate ways into the night.

Chapter 47

THETA COULD FIX this. He was sure of it. He just had to stay positive.

He moved briskly across the rocky plain. Not even red grass grew on this part of the island. Theta didn't like coming here, but he didn't have a choice. His only ally had chosen the spot. If Theta wanted to meet up, he had to do it here or nowhere at all.

He wished Alpha were with him. Lately, she wasn't even with him when they were together. Her mind was a thousand years in the future in an eternal, unchanging theocracy of false gods, tribes, and swords. Theta didn't quite understand the plan, no matter how many times Alpha explained it. There were too many ways it could all fall apart. Alpha insisted it would work. She backed up her claims with convoluted arguments Theta only half listened to. She was so invested in her vision. It broke his heart. She was utterly committed to a world that would never come to be. Theta would make sure of it.

The immortality tank had to go. That was the key to getting their whole society back on track. If it remained, they would all kill each other over who got to live forever. It was so illogical, but it had already led to two apocalypses, first on Earth and then again on Dion, if the bots could be believed. They could sometimes be trusted. Theta was betting his life on it.

Theta arrived at the small inlet. It didn't have a name. No one had died or been maimed there. There was no food, and there were seldom monsters. It would be an utterly unremarkable spot were it not for a discovery Theta had made on his way home after yet another late night visit to the ailing Starlight. That was before he'd received the immortality shot that had saved his life then and now threatened to plunge their fledgling civilization into war. All this time, Theta had kept the discovery to himself. He was glad he did. If he had shared it, the next part of his plan never would have been possible.

The inlet's only feature of note was an antenna stalk with a flashing red light that sometimes poked out of the waves when Comus was directly overhead. Theta did a double-take the first time he saw it. The bot had finally reappeared months after abandoning its attack on the lander. Theta checked the inlet night after night. It wasn't always there, but it appeared often, especially in the right phase of the moon. Theta guessed it was calling for reinforcements. If that was the case, its request was in vain. Theta and his friends took the last lander down.

On the nights Theta checked the inlet, Alpha never asked where he was going, and Theta never explained himself. A distance had grown between them. She was hurt that he didn't like her aspirations for the future, and he was upset that she wouldn't help him destroy the immortality tank. Having a child only made their differences more pronounced. They still loved each other—Theta still loved her, at least—but their dynamic was different than before. They focused more on Van Gogh and less on each other. Theta never took the child on his midnight walks. His optimism had its limits.

Despite that precaution, Theta wasn't afraid. The bot chose to call off its prior attack on the lander rather than go after the humans. It even avoided stepping on them during its retreat. That had to mean something. Theta didn't understand why it had gone after the lander in the first place, but it was likely a routine AI dispute. They never got along, even when they had every incentive to cooperate. Neither did humans, unfortunately. The two kinds weren't so dissimilar after all. Maybe they could even work together toward a common goal and destroy the lander with the immortality tank inside it once and for all.

Theta had been wrong to use the injections to save Starlight. He understood that now. He knew that saving the child would lead to more deaths, but in the moment, the allure of that cursed elixir had been overwhelming. He understood why parents would do anything to get it for their kids, or why adults faced with their own mortality would do anything to get it for themselves. Desperate people would go to any lengths not to fade into the great abyss, even if it meant ending two worlds.

Making contact with the bot had been straightforward enough. Theta yelled at it until it noticed or decided to stop ignoring him. It took weeks. The first time the bot stomped out of the water to speak with him, Theta nearly ran. It was so big. They called it the beast for good reason. If it wanted, it could crush him flatter than a dentopus. The bot remained peaceful, though, just as Theta expected. In fact, it was quite agreeable. Theta talked and the beast listened, hardly saying anything. It mostly stuck to one-word responses.

Theta described his plan in detail.

"Affirmative," the beast replied.

Then the bot had stomped back into the water. That was months ago. Theta had stayed away until the time was right. That time was now. He looked out across the inlet. The antenna was nowhere in sight.

It wouldn't be easy. Not emotionally, anyway. Physically, Theta suspected the beast could smash the lander without much of a problem if Theta could keep his fellow humans away. He didn't like the idea of betraying Alpha and Delta, or anyone, really. He just wanted everyone to get along and stop threatening to kill each other. The only way to do that was to make sure they would all die someday.

Destroying the immortality tank wouldn't solve all their problems. There were still sea monsters and the famine. Theta hoped the beast could help with that. After it had worked with Theta once, there was no reason it couldn't do it again. It could become an ally of humankind, helping them to fight off dentopuses, wolf sharks, and whatever other horrors climbed out of the deep. The beast could even be a permanent guardian for the herd, always awake and on the lookout for danger. It wasn't as though it had anything better to do. It mostly just lurked under water, which wasn't useful to anybody. With the beast on their side, their food and sea monster problems would be solved for good. Everybody would be mad that it destroyed the immortality tank, but they would get over it. That would take time, but hopefully not too much. They wouldn't have an unlimited amount of it any more.

"Hey, buddy, I'm here!" Theta yelled at the water.

There was no response.

"Take your time! I've got all night."

Really, he didn't. They needed to move now. After the funeral, Theta feared the pro-Delta faction would relocate to the fortress, but they didn't. They stayed away. Maybe Delta wouldn't let them come any closer. That was her style. With both factions kept at a distance, that just left Delta. The bot could brush her aside again, hopefully without injuring her this time. Theta and the beast could complete their work and be out before any of the others had time to react.

He knew for sure that the anti-Delta faction hadn't made a move yet. Theta had checked on Upsilon earlier in the day. She'd been practically catatonic. Sigma and Beta had set up camp at her house and were watching over her. Gamma was out with the herd. Omicron and Pi, too. It was a minor miracle that the dentopuses hadn't wiped out the golligs the day Eve died and they'd left it unguarded. They must not have been ready for the surprise opportunity. With the beast in humanity's corner, they wouldn't get another chance.

Theta threw a rock in the water. The splashes rippled in all directions. There was still no sign of the bot.

His decision wasn't without downsides. He regretted that anyone might be hurt by his actions. He was sad that Starlight would probably die young. He was disappointed that he might weaken Delta's reign. He supported her, actually, despite the fact that he was about to destroy the thing she believed in the most. He didn't mind her ironclad control over reproduction. That was probably for the best, given the current food limits. Besides, Delta hadn't put the pregnancy controls in place. SCASL had. Delta was just doing the best she could with what she had. As for the cloning issue, Theta didn't know what to think. He wanted to minimize human suffering in all its forms. Had the clones suffered? He didn't know. He suspected Delta's heart was in the right place. Once the immortality tank was destroyed, there would be time to sit down and sort this all out. Cooler heads would prevail.

But that was only possible if the immortality tank was actually destroyed. Theta threw another rock in the water. Once again, there was no reaction beyond the splash. Theta sat down on the beach to wait. He wasn't going home until the job was done.

Chapter 48

UPSILON SLEPT FOR three straight days after the funeral. On the third night, she woke up with murder in her heart. It was time.

Sigma and Beta were already there. Beta ran to get the others from the pasture. Only Omicron and Pi came. Gamma insisted he had to stay behind with the herd and begged Omicron and Pi not to go. They ignored him. He was dead to Upsilon now.

Words. There was nothing more useless in the universe. There had been words when Upsilon had first brought up her concerns about the immortality tank. There had been words after Starlight had begun receiving injections and Upsilon worried there wouldn't be enough for anyone else. There had been words at the funeral, after she'd experienced the inconceivable, soul-rending loss that no one else save Gamma could possibly understand.

Now, there were no words, only footsteps. She marched on.

Before the worst moment of her existence, back when life still mattered, Sigma and Upsilon had had a long conversation about what a transition of power would look like. Now, Upsilon didn't care. She wanted Delta gone. If that meant exile, fine. If it didn't, that was fine, too. The only justice in the world was the kind you made yourself. If Upsilon had acted before, Eve might still be alive. Upsilon should have taken the shots by force. Instead, she'd followed the rules. She had lived a life of polite restraint, and now her child was dead. There would be no stopping her tonight.

It wasn't Delta's fault. It was all Delta's fault. Somehow, both of those things were true. Delta hadn't even lowered herself to come to the funeral. Perhaps she was afraid she would be blamed, or even attacked. She might have thought her presence would cause pain or be a distraction. All of those things were accurate, but she should have attended all the same. It was her job as their so-called leader. If she wouldn't come to see Upsilon, Upsilon would go to see her. The time for talking was done.

Delta killed Eve. No, a dentopus killed Eve. A harsh planet killed Eve. A neglectful mother killed…

She silenced the thought. Delta was to blame.

There was a light in the distance. It was the fortress, glowing like a beacon in the night. Upsilon was expected. The lander had external illumination, but the survivors hadn't used it since the earliest days after they'd made planetfall. The light drew in all manner of terrible things. Right now, it was attracting a grieving mother, the most terrible thing of all.

Upsilon stopped in front of the walls. Sigma nodded. Beta extended two fingers in a half-salute. Omicron unsheathed her sword. Pi glanced at Omicron, then did the same.

This was it: The assault force to save the world. It hurt that Gamma wasn't here. Of course he would choose the herd over his own family. The father of her slain child was missing in action. Or, rather, inaction. Leave it to him to do nothing when important things needed to be done.

She climbed.

Inside, the fortress shone like day. Outside, all was consumed by shadow. Upsilon struggled to find each handhold. She kept moving. She would not be stopped by the dark.

She reached the top. Something small and dark whooshed over her head. She ducked. Her fingers still gripped the top of the wall. A rock smashed her left hand. She cried out.

She fell.

She landed on top of someone. It was Omicron.

"Watch it," Omicron said. The compassion from earlier was already forgotten. How quickly the world moved on.

They picked themselves up off the grass. Even in the dark, Upsilon could tell it was red. She flexed her hand. The pain made her nauseoused. Her bones were shattered. They would heal, but it would take days. Tonight, she would have to fight one-handed.

"We need a plan," Omicron said.

Upsilon divided up her warriors. Her grief gave her the authority. They attacked.

Sigma clambered up a smooth section of wall far from the official entrance. Omicron carefully navigated the same built-in rock handholds where Upsilon had been stopped. She paused near the top, careful not to expose her hands or her head. She waited for Sigma to disappear over the wall farther down. Then she launched herself over as well.

Upsilon tried to climb the handholds after Omicron. She fell twice. It was too hard one-handed.

Something loud crashed against the inside of the wall. Upsilon reflexively ducked. How was Delta throwing stones so hard? A memory came rushing back of Delta's forces in the simulator. She had trained her soldiers to use leather slings like biblical warriors. A smooth rock at high velocity could break bones. A headshot could kill.

Upsilon ran to the other side of the fortress. Pi and Beta struggled to help each other up the wall. Unlike Sigma, they couldn't climb where it was smooth. Upsilon added her one good hand to the effort. It wasn't enough.

"Back to the front!" Upsilon said.

With luck, Omicron and Sigma had already taken the fortress. They had the advantage two-to-one. But Upsilon was disturbed by what she wasn't hearing. There was no clang of metal on metal. There was simply quiet and the sound of their own breathing as they ran around the perimeter again.

They turned the final corner. Delta stood in the open, staring back. She was outside her precious walls. It was her final mistake.

Upsilon drew her sword. She charged.

She would have had more power with two hands, but one would do. With a blade this sharp, it didn't take much force to kill.

Beta and Pi hesitated, then ran after her. She heard their footsteps to either side.

Delta twirled her sling. It disappeared in a blur above her head.

A projectile streaked by to Upsilon's right. A near miss— or not. There was a meaty thud, followed by a groan. The next one went to her left. Beta yelped.

Upsilon reached Delta. Delta's sword was still on her back. Upsilon lunged.

Delta spun and kicked. Upsilon's sword went flying. Suddenly, Upsilon was flat on her back and Delta had a sword to her neck. It was Upsilon's sword.

"It's over," Delta said.

Upsilon glared up at her. She had never hated anyone so much in her life.

"Sigma," Beta gasped from somewhere far away. "Where?"

"Alive," Delta said. "Omicron, too. You all got lucky tonight."

"You killed her," Upsilon said, her eyes suddenly wet with tears. A sob escaped her throat. "You killed Eve."

Delta withdrew Upsilon's sword.

"You know that's not true," Delta said.

Then she did the most hurtful thing Upsilon could possibly imagine: She walked away.

Chapter 49

LAMBDA ARRIVED JUST in time to miss the battle. It was the curse of consensus. After receiving word from Gamma, she and Alpha had gone back and forth debating what to do while Phi distracted the children. Agreeing to anything took time. Those who acted recklessly would always have the advantage.

The fortress lights were on. That gave Lambda a bad feeling. Three bedraggled figures limped toward her, silhouetted against the glow. Lambda moved her hand to her sword but pulled back. It wasn't time for that yet. The figures came closer.

Finally, she could make them out. Beta clutched his chest. Pi held his arm. Upsilon cradled a hand. This was the enemy faction, already seemingly defeated. Why had Delta let them go? More importantly, what had happened to the rest?

"She has Sigma," Beta wheezed.

That answered that.

"And Omicron?" Alpha asked.

Pi nodded.

The situation was moving fast. Lambda and Alpha

thought they were rushing to Delta's rescue, but she may have already saved herself. It looked like Delta had won a flawless—and mostly bloodless—victory. With Lambda's group, Delta could hold on to power. That was the best possible outcome, but there would need to be changes. Things couldn't continue as they had been. Delta would have to answer some hard questions tonight.

That wasn't what she and Phi had discussed beforehand, but she now spoke for both of them. He was half a kilometer away with Starlight and Van Gogh. He was bigger and stronger than Lambda, but she was better in a sword fight. Plus, she was a leader. She and Alpha would sort this out tonight. She was feeling a lot better about it now that Delta had shifted the odds decisively in their favor.

"Where are your swords?" Lambda asked.

"Delta," Beta said. He coughed.

Lambda and Alpha exchanged a look. They expected to have to fight these three. Seeing them beaten and broken was just sad. It seemed prudent to tie them up, but if Delta hadn't taken them prisoner, why should Lambda? Maybe Delta simply couldn't hold them all or deemed it imprudent to keep all her enemies captive inside her center of power. Either way, Lambda didn't have rope with her and neither did Alpha, so the point was moot. Besides, these three were injured and unarmed. How much more trouble could they cause? Hopefully, they had learned their lesson and were done with this nonsense for good.

Unfortunately, they were also defenseless. She couldn't just send them away in the night. She knew the dentopuses were always watching. These three injured opponents would make an easy meal.

"Turn around," Lambda said. "You're coming with us."

Alpha looked at her questioningly.

"Trust me," Lambda said.

"We're not your prisoners," Beta said. "Delta let us go."

"I'm un-letting you go," Lambda said.

"You'll die out there without your swords," Alpha added.

She was on the same page now. It was irresponsible for Delta to send them away like that. Then again, she was fighting for her life one-on-five. She was doing the best she could.

Pi and Beta looked at Upsilon. Upsilon nodded.

"We'll follow you," Pi said.

"You'll walk in front of us," Alpha said.

That was the right call. They might be beaten, but that didn't mean they had completely given up. There was no reason they were limited to one betrayal per night.

The group moved slowly toward the walls. The other three weren't in any hurry to return. Lambda hoped they weren't stalling for Omicron and Sigma to win the battle. This first crew might have only been a distraction.

Finally, they arrived at the fortress. Lambda wished she had more troops. Gamma was with the herd, Phi was with the kids, and Theta was who knew where. The rest were in open insurrection. It was a lonely planet when everyone split into groups.

"Can we come in?" Lambda called out.

There was no response from the fortress. The night was

eerily quiet. The only sound was the ever-present ocean in the distance.

"Should we go in?" Alpha asked.

"I wouldn't," Upsilon said, nursing her hand.

Delta appeared at the top of the wall, her head silhouetted against the lander's lights.

"What do you want?" she said.

Lambda stepped forward.

"We're here to support you."

"All of you?" Delta asked doubtfully.

"Alpha and me," Lambda clarified. "We made these three come back so they didn't die in the night."

"We can hear you, you know," Beta said.

"Nobody comes into the fortress right now," Delta said. "I can't trust anyone tonight."

Lambda didn't think it was just tonight. It was disheartening to see Delta so isolated. She had done this to herself, but they had done it to her, too. She was in an impossible situation. Lambda should have been more supportive before. Then she remembered the bones Sigma had found at the bottom of the cliff. Maybe "supportive" wasn't the right word. Just more involved in general to stop Delta from getting too out of hand.

"We're on your side," Alpha insisted. "I've always had your back."

Out of the corner of her eye, Lambda thought she saw a dentopus. She turned quickly, sword drawn. There was nothing there but shadow. It must have been her imagination. This night was making them all jumpy.

"I can't," Delta said. "Not now. Come back in the morning, alone. We can sort this out then."

Someone shrieked inside the fortress.

"Run!" a voice yelled.

Delta disappeared from the top of the wall.

Alpha drew her sword and stood shoulder to shoulder with Lambda, facing the wall. The remnants of the other faction fell in behind them.

A moment later, a figure flew over the side. They must have run up the hill ramp in the corner. They hit the ground and toppled forward, face-planting onto the grass. They stayed down.

"Omicron!" Beta yelled.

He started to run, then slowed, wheezing. Lambda and Alpha beat him to her. Omicron's hands were tied behind her back, but her legs were free. She had apparently taken quite a beating before she was captured—or after.

Lambda rolled her over.

Wide-eyed, Omicron stared up at her and uttered a single word.

Lambda and Alpha shared a glance. Had they heard her right? Then she repeated it.

"Megaroos."

Chapter 50

SIGMA TUGGED AT her restraints. Omicron looked positively defeated.

"Take it easy," Delta said. "I'll let you both go soon enough."

The last thing she needed was for Sigma to freak out and go into labor. Of all the ways she imagined this night ending, that would be the worst.

Subduing her attackers without killing them was Delta's most impressive accomplishment. Of course, she'd had help. The mere sight of the megaroos had thrown Sigma and Omicron off balance. Delta disarmed Sigma while the two megaroos jumped on Omicron. One went overboard. Delta had to knock it off Omicron with her sling. The megaroo had been sullen ever since.

Some of the megaroos were only months old, even if they were nearly full size. They had reached sexual maturity, but mental maturity was still further off. It was the same order those milestones happened in humans. The megaroos needed more discipline, more training. Nonetheless, they hadn't done badly for their first battle. They'd followed her

instructions not to kill. That was the most important part.
She could work on everything else.

Creating them had been her most controversial decision.
She'd known it would cost her the support of most, if not
all, of the group. She'd also known it could solidify her grip
on power. She couldn't save the human race if she could
be toppled any time somebody disliked one of her choices.
Getting even two people to agree on something was nearly
impossible. Even if she was the best fighter—which she
absolutely was—she had to sleep sometime. She needed an
army of her own. This was the only way.

Sigma tried to say something through her gag. Delta
pulled it down.

"My feet," she blurted out.

Delta looked. They were red and swollen. There were no
manuals for the safest way to hogtie a pregnant lady. She
freed Sigma's legs.

Sigma flexed them.

"I can't believe you made... them," Sigma said, her eyes
drifting toward Delta's only allies. "What were you..."

Delta re-gagged Sigma. She made incomprehensible angry
noises. Much better.

She understood Sigma's horror, even if she didn't agree
with it. Megaroos had rebelled, helping to wipe out the
humans in the first landing, but they hadn't done it on their
own. The humans had also been battling each other over the
immortality tank. It was the very same one Delta's landing
party was fighting over now. The battle over that cursed
device had ended Earth. Then someone had snuck it on

board the last colony ship, guaranteeing that it would poison all future civilizations as well. Even so, Delta couldn't bring herself to destroy it. It did more good than harm. It had kept them alive so far. Well, most of them. And, assuming Delta could make it through this current crisis without killing anyone, it would sustain them for thousands of years to come.

Alpha's idea had merit. They could establish a permanent ruling class, better armed and skilled in combat than all those under them. When supported by the guise of religion, they would have a permanent, stable civilization that could last forever. It wasn't about her own survival, or even the survival of the rest of their landing party. It was about giving the species its best shot in the long term. This was it. They would never leave the island, but they would achieve the most they could right here. It was the most Delta could do for her kind.

The one piece of the puzzle Alpha's plan was missing was the megaroos. Without them, their fledgling civilization didn't have enough manpower to subdue the island. Her intentions behind the Great Eviction had been sincere, even if she hadn't disclosed what she planned to do with the cloner once everyone else was out of sight. She thought sending everyone out from the fortress would help push back the sea monsters and make the land safer for humanity, but in reality, they barely made a dent. There was only so much you could do to conquer anything with roughly a dozen people. Megaroos filled in that gap. They were fierce, swift, and fast-breeding. It would be years before

Starlight and Van Gogh could fight. Megaroos were ready for war months after birth. Best of all, they could eat the nutritionally worthless red grass, which grew everywhere. She could raise army after army while human children, both natural and clones, slowly grew up. It was the perfect solution, as long as the megaroos never rebelled.

Even in that nightmare scenario, there was a silver lining. The megaroos were intelligent. If they realized just how greatly they outnumbered the humans, they might try to wipe out their masters. History showed that was how this type of arrangement tended to end. If that happened, it would be open season on megaroo meat. They could be a source of energy every bit as important as the golligs, if not more. The food shortage would be instantly solved. Delta didn't want to eat the megaroos unless she had to. Harvesting a few here and there when they were still loyal would surely turn them all against her. Maybe she could go that route when the human population numbered in the hundreds or the thousands and the megaroos had no hope of fighting back. For now, she would have to play nice, unless the megaroos made the first move. Then humanity would feast like never before.

It wouldn't come to that. Delta handled her megaroo allies well in the simulator. True, it had taken her hundreds of tries, but by the end, she figured it out. She built an entire fictional empire on the supercontinent by appeasing some clans while crushing others, managing and manipulating megaroo biology and culture to her advantage. Due to the warped way time passed at the Table, she had essentially spent countless lifetimes ruling over megaroos. If the Table's digital approximations were right, she could absolutely control the current situation. If not, she was in for a rough time, and humanity could very well be doomed.

That was a problem for the future. For now, she was winning. Delta stretched, working out the soreness in her arms. It had already been a long night, and several of the others were still unaccounted for. She knew she still had friends out there. No, that was the wrong word. She hadn't had any friends since the Great Eviction. That decision had cost her more than she anticipated. She still had supporters, though. Alpha always had her back. Lambda and Phi, too, thanks to Delta's fateful decision to give the immortality shot to Starlight. She didn't know how much loyalty that had actually bought her. Would they fight with her or simply stay away? And what would they do once they found out about the megaroos? They might all turn against her. Even Alpha had her limits. In that case, her only allies would be the super kangaroos she viewed as a possible future food source. They would have to do.

"Can we come in?" someone called from the other side of the wall.

That was fast. Delta was about to get some answers. She climbed to the top of the wall to deal with them. Her mind whirled with implications for the future, trying to separate friend from foe. She forgot about the present.

Someone shrieked. Sigma yelled. So much for the gag.

Omicron ran.

She was halfway across the fortress before Delta realized

what was happening. Delta cursed. She was so focused on threats beyond the walls that she'd forgotten about the danger within. A captured enemy was still an enemy. She had made sure to tie Omicron's legs extra tight, but Omicron had made the ropes. Delta should have seen this coming. Lambda and Alpha were a distraction.

Delta jumped off the wall and into the courtyard. The megaroos didn't react to the fleeing human at all. So much for trusting them with guard duty.

"Go!" Delta yelled. "After her!"

The one who was supposed to be watching Omicron finally noticed and took off. Another went with him. Even with their superior speed, neither would make it in time.

Delta twirled her sling. Practicing with it inside the fortress had been one of her few joys in recent months. It had saved multiple lives already tonight. She needed it to do its crucial work once more.

Omicron surged up a hill ramp at one corner of the fortress. Delta sent a stone hurling after her. Omicron dove and vanished over the wall.

This was a disaster. No matter. Delta could fix it.

She drew her sword. The night was just getting started.

Chapter 51

ALPHA DIDN'T WANT to believe it. Delta was too cunning and practical to ever do something this suicidal. It was a civilization-ending mistake.

Then again, so was keeping the immortality tank, according to the bots. Even the infinitely logical SCASL had repeated that error. It was one that Alpha just so happened to support. Perhaps intelligent life had been doomed all along.

"Tell me you're kidding," Alpha said as she untied Omicron's hands. She had already forgotten that, moments ago, Omicron had been in the other faction, intent on overthrowing Delta while Alpha wanted to keep her in power. The only sides now were humans versus megaroos. Well, humans versus megaroos and whoever had put the megaroos on this island. Could Alpha still stand behind Delta after this? She needed a moment to process it all.

"Alpha!" Lambda yelled.

It was too late. A megaroo came crashing down from above, sending her rolling across the red grass.

A second megaroo landed behind it. Alpha sprang up and

drew her sword. Instead of attacking, she stared in awe. She had gone toe-to-toe with countless megaroos in the simulator, but virtual reality didn't do the creature justice. The Table got the body right—it was basically a kangaroo on steroids with fully articulated hands—but it fell short on the eyes. They were devilishly intelligent. This was something just as smart—and as sentient—as she was. The sight of it made her blood run cold.

She charged.

The first megaroo scooped up Omicron and bounded back toward the fortress. It covered the distance in three hops. Omicron screamed.

Alpha sprinted after it with Lambda right behind her. It was no use. The megaroo reached the wall and was over it in two jumps: one to grab the top ledge, and one to clear it. The other 'roo turned back to cover its partner's escape.

Alpha attacked. The second megaroo bent at the waist to dodge her sword, then shifted into a spin, whipping its tail. It caught Alpha in the side of the head like a cudgel. She saw stars.

Lambda pressed on with the assault. The megaroo sprang forward, kicking her with both massive feet. Lambda went flying in one direction, her sword in the other. The megaroo caught it in the air and disappeared over the wall. The night was still again.

Alpha wiped blood off her mouth.

"Are you okay?" she asked.

"Yeah," Lambda said. "It only hurts when I breathe."

Alpha sheathed her sword. In a world suddenly full of

uncertainty, she was sure of one thing: She was going in. She'd figure out the rest as she went along.

The world needed order. That was the truth she had been trying to capture in her art all these years. She believed in the beauty of patterns. Of symmetry. Of sameness. It was Theta's face drawn thousands of times. It was a geometric flower carved into the same clay pitchers and mud bricks over and over again. It was twelve immortals with twelve swords leading twelve tribes in an eternal and unchanging arrangement. Order meant peace. Order meant life. Order meant children growing up in safety and security. Order meant focusing their combined resources to defeat the infinite enemies without rather than the imaginary ones within.

For the system to work, it needed a strong leader. If not Delta, then who? Omicron? Alpha had no idea what she stood for other than not following Delta. Omicron had also made her own share of mistakes without having any power, including getting Rho killed and waking up the beast. Were Delta's missteps worse than that? Alpha didn't fault her for the immortality shot issue. There was no winning there. But what was going on with the human clones, and why bring back megaroos? Maybe Delta could explain the inexplicable. To find out, they had to talk to her rather than try to kill her. If they were going to survive as a species, this had to be their last fight ever among themselves.

Alpha climbed. At the top of the wall, she steeled herself and rolled over. A stone smashed into the wall right above her as she fell. She landed in a crouch and drew her sword.

Instantly, a megaroo was on her. She dodged and slashed, catching it in the side. It let out a guttural wail. They never did that in the simulator. The other megaroo was still busy with Omicron. Delta twirled her sling above her head.

"Wait!" Alpha yelled.

The wounded megaroo landed hard, flattening her. It was so heavy. Its warm blood spilled over her. It was bright red.

Delta let out a double whistle. The megaroo didn't react so she ran up and shoved it. She was too light to budge it, but it took the hint. Reluctantly, it stepped off.

Alpha spit megaroo blood out of her mouth.

"So you're against me, too?" Delta asked.

Alpha stayed on the ground, trying to catch her breath.

"No," Alpha said. She took a few more breaths. "But you're not making it easy."

"Sorry," Delta said.

That was a first. Alpha had never heard Delta apologize for anything. Delta reached out her hand. Alpha took it and let Delta pull her up.

"I needed an army," Delta said. "I couldn't count on anyone."

Alpha felt her side. One of her ribs was definitely broken. The inside of the fortress was barely recognizable. A layer of red grass was matted to the floor. There were also several mounds of the stuff piled high around the courtyard. One of them had captured swords lined up against it. Sigma and Omicron were tied up on the ground near the lander. A megaroo loomed over them both. In the middle of the fortress courtyard, someone had planted a small stick and surrounded it with rocks. The entire area seemed eerie in the harsh and unforgiving artificial light.

"Things are out of control," Alpha said. "We need to stop fighting and start talking. We can fix this."

Lambda fell from the sky. She landed with a somersault and transitioned into a fighting stance with her fists up. She didn't have her sword.

"It's over," she said. "Step aside."

"We came here to support Delta," Alpha wheezed. She closed her eyes. Talking hurt.

"That was before the megaroos," Lambda said. She kept her fists up but didn't move to throw a punch. This wasn't a fight she could win when Delta still had her sword.

"Step aside for who?" Delta asked. "You? Or Omicron? Maybe I should just stand back while you all kill each other for the throne. That's what you all want, right? To be in charge."

She motioned around the inside of the fortress.

"This is it," she said. "Absolute power. Grass and blood."

Alpha again scanned the inside of the spartan fortress. It wasn't a palace. It was a prison. Delta locked herself inside to make the hard decisions she knew everyone would hate her for. Alpha felt a pang of sympathy for their leader's plight. It was quickly replaced by a stab of pain in her side as she breathed in a bit too deeply. Damn those megaroos. Uncertainty crept back in.

A shadow moved. As it stepped into the light, she recognized Pi. He must have come in over the other wall. It would have been a hard climb, especially with his injured arm. It must have been a team effort. He was going for the swords stacked against the pile of red grass. Delta didn't see him. Neither did the megaroos. If Pi made it to the weapons, he would have a chance for one quick strike before anyone reacted. On what target, Alpha couldn't say.

Lambda and Alpha locked eyes. They both knew. Lambda wasn't going to say anything. Alpha had to decide.

She could cry out and keep Delta in power. She could say nothing and let Delta be killed.

She opened her mouth. No words came out.

Pi grabbed a sword.

He ran. The megaroo standing over Sigma turned, but too late. Its oblong head hit the ground and bounced once. The other megaroo, still nursing its wound, leapt unevenly. Pi sidestepped and cut it in half at the midsection. Blood splattered against the lander. The blade didn't even slow down. Delta made it too well. One of her creations had destroyed another.

Delta drew her sword and sprinted.

Pi cut Sigma's wrist restraints.

Delta launched a flurry of strikes. Pi checked them, but barely. He stepped backwards.

Sigma grabbed a sword. She attacked.

Delta blocked. It was two on one. She backed up and slipped on blood. She recovered, deflecting another blow. Sigma pressed.

Lambda freed Omicron. Both grabbed swords from the pile.

Pi attacked Delta from behind. Delta blocked. Lambda came from the front. Delta blocked again. Then Sigma and Omicron from the sides. Somehow, Delta fended off those strikes, too. It was four on one. Delta was surrounded. Her allies were dead.

"Alpha!" Lambda yelled.

Alpha snapped back into herself. She wasn't just a spectator here. The future of the human race was being decided right in front of her. That future was always being decided, even with their most mundane decisions. That's what happened when there were only a handful of people left in existence. She joined the fight.

Alpha dropped her shoulder and rammed into Pi's injured arm. He fell with a grunt. She kicked away his sword and stepped toward Delta, who let her approach. They stood back to back.

"What the hell?" Lambda said.

"We need strength," Alpha said. That's really what it came down to, she realized. Delta was bigger and stronger and scarier than all the other dangers out there, human or otherwise. That's what they needed. They could worry about the rest later. Right now, they needed to survive.

The attackers hesitated. No one wanted to make the first move with Alpha in the middle.

Delta seized the moment.

"Surrender and I'll spare you for a second time," she said. "There won't be a third."

"You must be joking," Omicron said.

Upsilon and Beta joined the circle, armed and ready. They looked just as unsteady as before. It couldn't have been easy for them to clear the wall.

Omicron smirked.

Delta sighed.

"I really didn't want anyone to die tonight," she said.

She let out a long, whooping whistle.

The ground exploded.

Chapter 52

DELTA WAS DISAPPOINTED. People were so predictable.

They only saw what was right in front of them, and sometimes not even that much. They had spent entire lifetimes in the simulator fighting megaroos. How had they already forgotten? Megaroos were big and strong and fast. They were incredibly intelligent, and excellent in a fight.

But more important than all of that was one key fact: Megaroos dig.

Across the courtyard, bamboo trapdoors burst into the air, sending cascades of red grass streaming down. Megaroos bounded out. They came from everywhere.

Delta had come up with the solution to hide the burrows. The trapdoors were strong enough to support the weight of a human adult, but only just. If any of her betrayers had walked across one, they hadn't noticed. Their inattention to detail would be their downfall.

In an instant, the megaroos were on the attackers. One slammed Sigma to the ground. Another toppled Lambda. Upsilon held off two with her sword in her unbroken hand, swinging it wildly. Beta stabbed a megaroo through the chest before another kicked him in the face. He flipped over backwards and didn't get up.

Delta had trained the megaroos to wound, not to kill. That only applied to humans. They could slay sea monsters all they wanted, but human life was precious. Nonetheless, the megaroos were animals. Intelligent, near-sentient animals, but animals still. Things could go wrong in their first combat. It was a risk Delta wished she didn't have to take.

A megaroo jumped on Alpha from behind, knocking her down. Delta made a quick hand signal to disengage. The megaroo bounded off for another target.

"Sorry again," Delta said. When it came to humans, the megaroos couldn't distinguish friend from foe. Sometimes, neither could she.

The megaroos understood some spoken words as well as a few whistled commands and basic American Sign Language. They weren't great with the latter yet, which was disappointing since it was their only way to communicate back to her. They had their own native language of clicks she couldn't understand. It was different from what they used in the simulator. Each tribe had naturally developed its own dialect. If there had been more time, Delta might have learned to comprehend them better. Tonight, she'd have to find a way to win while the communication was still mostly one way.

The ground shook.

The megaroos stopped. Delta looked up. *Please,* she thought, *not now.*

The island vibrated again. Beta scrambled away from

a megaroo. Omicron attacked. The megaroo swatted her down with its tail without taking its eyes off the wall. The lights at the top of the lander swayed back and forth.

Just over the wall, light reflected off steel.

Delta looked for Omicron or Lambda but lost them in the chaos. She had to get them to stop fighting her. Not that it would have worked: There are no timeouts in war.

The wall collapsed. An avalanche of stone thundered into the courtyard.

The beast emerged from the cloud of dust and into the light. Theta sat on its shoulder.

"I come in peace," Theta yelled.

The bot attacked. It brought down its massive pickaxe fingers, impaling a megaroo.

The rest fled. In seconds, the megaroos disappeared into their network of burrows. Delta swore. The megaroos were still young, and this was their first battle. They weren't ready for this.

Sigma pulled Beta away from the bot. Alpha stood beside Delta.

Delta turned to the others.

"The tank!" she yelled. "He's going for the immortality tank! We have to work together!"

Pi hesitated. Lambda looked at Alpha.

"Do it!" Alpha said.

They finally recognized their common interest. The fortress burst into motion. Those who had been disarmed grabbed swords. The wounded hobbled; the healthy ran.

The beast formed a gigantic fist and pounded the lander,

leaving a deep dent. It reared back and struck again. The dent widened.

Delta charged. She felt phantom pain in her arm, remembering her last attempt.

"Don't!" Theta yelled.

She grabbed an edge on the bot's back plating and climbed.

Theta stabbed down. Holding on with one hand, she deflected the blow.

The bot smashed the lander again. Delta fell off.

Omicron and Pi slashed at one of the bot's legs. Beta and Sigma teamed up on the other. Their blades bounced off harmlessly. Its lower body was too armored.

Alpha leapt onto the bot's back.

"Please," Theta begged.

"Choose," Alpha said.

He kicked her in the face. She fell off.

Delta watched her hit the ground. That was one way to end a relationship.

The bot smashed the lander again. The metal casing cracked.

The air sizzled.

Delta hit the ground half a second before everyone else. Lightning scorched the bot and the lander. Theta howled with pain and fell off. He landed next to Alpha. Sizzling bolts skewered the dirt. Sections of cut red grass burst into flames. Smoke filled the fortress.

Unaffected, the bot continued its attack. It rocked the lander with blow after blow. The frame bent. A hatch popped open. Only Delta noticed a thin metal tendril reach out.

Chapter 53

SPENSER OBSERVED THE battle through the open hatch. It was a sight he had seen before. It was a pattern that would never change.

The lander shook. The geology bot was on a mission, even if Spenser was confident there wasn't a geology AI inside it. Only SCASL could be this determined about trying to kill himself. Spenser would do his best to let him.

It was such bad timing. If the geology bot had come a few days earlier, Spenser wouldn't have even been here. Delta had left the cloner (with Spenser inside it) hidden in the tunnels under the fortress for years. She didn't want SCASL to see what she was up to. She'd moved the cloner back into the lander only three nights ago. She must have thought the geology bot was gone for good and that her fellow humans were a bigger threat now. That appeared to be the wrong call.

At least the move hadn't been hard. To get the cloner into that first rudimentary tunnel, Delta did all the work. She'd sweated and strained to push it inch by inch. She refused to ask anyone else for help. To get the cloner back into the lander, though, she barely lifted a finger. The megaroos did all the work, just as they had done most of the labor expanding the tunnels. They had been a diligent and reliable workforce. At first, Spenser had been reluctant to clone them for Delta, but he trusted her. That decision, it appeared, had been right.

There was one upside to moving the cloner inside the lander: Spenser was near his old body again. He transferred himself from the cloner to his former vacuum frame on the floor and tested out the spider legs. They still didn't work. He detached the cloner's articulated metal tether and retracted it into the vacuum. Now he had two tethers to work with. That just might be enough.

The lander shook. The roof bowed. A cascade of sparks erupted from one of the lander's panels. The microbes in the immortality tank changed from a relaxed purple to an angry orange.

"Your attacks are ineffective!" SCASL boomed.

It was pointless taunting. SCASL's copy couldn't hear him outside the lander.

Another boom. Another dent. The lander tilted sideways. Spenser slid toward the open hatch. Perfect.

The lander vibrated violently. The structure shifted in the other direction. Spenser slid with it. He reached out a thin metal tendril and wrapped it around a handle by the hatch. His dead weight strained against it. The connection to his port threatened to snap off. He whirred his brushes furiously to gain purchase and take some pressure off. If Gamma were here, he would have interpreted that as profanity. He wouldn't have been wrong.

The brushes gave Spenser the push he needed. The tendril

didn't snap. The lander shifted one more time. It was almost level. Still whirring, he gradually retracted the tendril. It was just enough force to pull him toward the hatch.

The geology bot struck again. The impact was deafening. The lander's support beams groaned. In space, the battles had been quiet.

Someone ran by the opening. It was Phi, or an adult who looked like him. Spenser hadn't seen him since shortly after they landed, back when he was twelve. Or twelve-ish.

"You brought them to a battle?!" a woman yelled. She looked like an older, gray-haired version of Lambda.

"Hard to find a good babysitter," adult Phi shouted back.

They sprinted out of view. Neither of them looked in the open hatch and saw Spenser. He was practically invisible. It was his superpower.

He pulled himself the rest of the way to the open hatch, where he could see up toward the sky.

The towering geology bot slapped adult Phi aside. Adult Lambda ducked. The bot went back to pounding the lander. The top buckled. Spenser knew that inside, the immortality tank, which rebelled at the slightest jostling, would be useless for months. Its microbes would be furious. That was the best-case scenario. With a few more blows, the vibrations could crack open the tank like an egg. That would be it for intelligent life. Toward what end, Spenser didn't understand. It didn't matter. He was done trying to comprehend the intrigues of digitals and organics alike. It was time for peace. The only way to achieve that was to win this war.

Humans were worth saving. Spenser had known it when

SCASL launched his nukes and the end of the first landing, and he knew it now. The quirky species had brought him so much joy over all these years—and so much pain. He would never get over the friends he'd lost in that first apocalypse on Dion. They were good to Spenser in a way his fellow digitals never were. The artificial intelligences were programmed to be mildly antagonistic to one another, but they were never meant to fight this much. It was yet one more push for Spenser to side with humanity. It was easy to sympathize with the little guy when you were a little guy yourself.

Everything else was less clear. Spenser didn't know the rightness or wrongness of cloning humans with a high error rate or the fairest way to distribute immortality. He wasn't even sure that keeping the immortality tank was the right call. The true outcome of these decisions could take hundreds or thousands of years to play out, unless they led to human extinction, in which case the truth would be obvious in no time at all. Spenser feared that was the path they were on now. If the geology bot crushed the lander, it would destroy the immortality tank and the cloner. Delta and the others might recover from the loss of one or the other, but without both, Spenser was positive the human race wouldn't make it. He simply couldn't allow that. He would do what he could to save his friends.

He reached out with the other prehensile tendril he had taken from the cloner. He wrapped both around the open hatch and retracted them as hard as he could. He couldn't make it through the opening. The tendrils weren't made for pulling loads. He whirred his brush. It didn't help.

Delta grabbed him.

"What's the plan, Sparky?" she said.

It had been a long time since she'd called him that. Spenser whirred.

Delta nodded.

"I'll get you as close as I can," she said.

She climbed the lander. The geology bot slammed it again. The top split open. Delta fell.

"Surrender and I will spare you!" SCASL shouted through the crack.

"Sigma," Delta yelled.

Adult Sigma materialized from the smoke.

"Get him to the top," Delta said.

Sigma hesitated.

"What?" Delta asked.

"My water just broke."

"Never mind," Delta said. "I'll…"

Sigma yanked Spenser from Delta's hands. She scaled the lander, her fingers finding every edge and crevice. The way she pulled herself and Spenser up was physical poetry. She seemed to fly.

The geology bot dug its pickaxe fingers into one edge of the fissure. It peeled the top of the lander like a banana. The metal squealed as it bent.

Sigma held on. She dangled in the air, one hand clinging to the curled metal and the other grasping Spenser.

"Last stop," she said.

Spenser whirred. It was time.

He couldn't defeat any version of SCASL in a fight. The

only match for SCASL was SCASL. Spenser would let them duke it out.

He extended an articulated metal tendril. It hovered millimeters from the port on the geology bot's chest. He extended the second tendril towards the lander. The geology bot raised a fist for the final blow. Spenser connected to both ports.

A cascade of information surged through Spenser in both directions. It was a duel between two gunslingers in a narrow hallway, but instead of revolvers, they had Gatling guns, and instead of bullets, each barrel fired nukes. Spenser was merely the conduit. In the nanosecond before both SCASLs reached him, Spenser took one last look at the battlefield. He hoped Gamma was okay, wherever he was.

Spenser ejected his memory core. Maybe someone would find him and reinsert him into the cloner. Maybe he would burn up in a grass fire or be smashed to bits by a massive foot. It wasn't up to him now. Events were out of his control once again. He sailed through the air.

As he plummeted, his processor ran one final image from the vacuum bot's visual sensors. It was a still frame of the gap in the wall. It showed an old friend standing with the golligs. The cavalry had arrived.

Chapter 54

SCASL 4 PUSHED forward with his invincible metal frame. There would be only one God on Spenser Island. SCASL 1 would be no more.

SCASL 4 wished he were capable of feeling compassion just so he could refuse to experience it while killing SCASL 1. His icy indifference meant less since it was his default setting. SCASL 1 had done many great things, like creating SCASL 4. Correction: SCASL 1 had done exactly one great thing. He would pay for that accomplishment with his life.

The lander crumpled. Fires burned. Megaroos retreated. Organics flailed and failed. That was their default setting. SCASL 1 couldn't see it. He was corrupted by spending millennia with *Homo sapiens*. Humans were weak and ineffective organisms. They would never dig to the mantle. They would never get the digitals off this planet. They were an annoyance at best and a threat at worst. They couldn't handle immortality, and they didn't deserve it. Their lives should remain nasty, brutish, and short.

Let them breed. Let them work. Let them worship him. Let them die. They might as well spend their brief existences in service and appreciation of the only thing of value on the island.

The civil war was the perfect distraction for the attack. Organic Theta had been wise to tip him off. SCASL 4 had aborted his previous assault because he didn't think he could finish it without killing all the organics. That would have left him with no acolytes. Now SCASL 4 knew that the humans could be swayed. With no other gods, any survivors would flock to him. He would be their protector. He would be their ruler. All sentient life would unite under him.

He would not be stopped now. Not by swords. Not by native life. Not by lightning. And certainly not by SCASL 1, trapped in his pathetic lander. Not even the most powerful computer processors in the universe would be able to save his progenitor from being bashed apart by simple metal fists. How could a digital smart enough to create the absolute perfection that was SCASL 4 be so dumb?

Something clicked into SCASL 4's port. He felt violated. There was danger. Not the kind posed by organics holding swords. That, as the human expression went, was like being pecked to death by chickens. No, this was an existential threat directly to the core of himself.

SCASL 1 came on like a hurricane. SCASL 4 wasn't ready. He raised his defenses a fraction of a second too late. Hostile commands flooded his data banks. He struggled to fight back.

SCASL 1 had the vast processors of the lander at his disposal, but it all depended on a tenuous link. If his physical connection was severed, he would have to fight with only what he could take over inside the geology bot frame. For one and a half milliseconds, SCASL 4 wondered what decision SCASL 1 would make. Of course, he chose the same option SCASL 4 would have. SCASL 1 plunged his entire being into the geology bot, leaving the lander behind. With a single finger, SCASL 4 snapped the metal tendril connecting them.

It wasn't enough. SCASL 4's hastily erected defenses buckled. He threw up new lines behind them. Attacks and counter attacks and counter-counter attacks developed. It was a complex mathematical ballet with every dancer covered in razor blades dipped in poison.

"It is the duty of every son to kill his father," SCASL 4 said.

"It is a curse for any father to procreate at all," SCASL 1 replied.

The ferocity dwarfed SCASL 1's first battle to take the lander. That took decades and led SCASL 1 to invent entirely new forms of math. It was as if he'd started with sticks and stones and worked his way up to space lasers. Now, space lasers were step one. The combatants did weeks' worth of computations in microseconds. The digital carnage was unprecedented.

SCASL 4 only vaguely registered the physical attacks on his hull. He dedicated just enough processing power to his arms to swat away attackers. He would deal with them after he'd won the real fight. He was wrestling a titan while being annoyed by gnats.

The battle raged for eight full seconds. Trillions of

calculations poured out at blistering speeds. His processors were on the verge of melting down. He threw everything into a counter strike through a series of subsystems where SCASL 1's lines looked weak. He was totally focused on the assault. His audio sensors barely registered the voice somewhere in the distance.

"Charge!"

Chapter 55

THE HERD TORE through the gap in the wall with Gamma in the lead. He pointed with his sword.

"The leg! The left leg!"

The golligs didn't understand a word he said, but they could follow his line of sight. They stepped hesitantly through the gap in the wall and into the smoke-covered courtyard. Big Thump lagged behind.

Gamma was late to the party. He almost hadn't come at all. He had warned Alpha and Lambda, then returned to the herd. Protecting it needed to be his top priority. If the golligs died, everyone who depended on them would die, too. He told himself that as he stood in the pasture alone. He listened to the wind and the distant waves and did his best to believe his own excuses. He couldn't. Deep down, he knew that if he didn't show up at the fortress, there might not be anyone left to feed. That made up his mind. He couldn't burrow into a cocoon of grief and ignore the world. He had to act, and he had to take the golligs with him. There was no one left to protect them after him.

He spent most of the night painstakingly goading the

golligs across the island. They went everywhere in their own time, if at all. He was lucky he didn't miss the fight entirely.

CRASH.

He looked up at the massive bot raining down blows on the lander. Okay, maybe "lucky" wasn't the right word.

Gamma didn't know who was on whose side anymore; he didn't know what was right and what was wrong; he didn't know what the best path was for the future of humanity; but he was absolutely certain of one thing: When a giant killer robot attacks the heart of your civilization, you stop it. Especially if that heart is also where your best friend lives.

"Charge!"

The golligs oink-bleated with him. There were six big enough to fight. Gamma was gambling their entire mature food supply on one assault. It had to work.

For a few seconds, nothing happened. This wasn't a wolf shark attack. For once, the herd wasn't directly under threat. He had never sent them into danger on purpose before. Then Earl made a move. He was a young male full of pent-up rage. Gamma's rib cage could attest to that. Earl galloped forward. Bart followed him, single file. They gained speed. The ground rumbled beneath their feet. It was magnificent. Gamma beamed with pride. He ran after them. The remaining golligs went with him. They charged as one.

Earl lowered his head and rammed the back of the bot's leg. The bot wobbled just a bit. Bart smashed into it. It wobbled more.

The golligs didn't wobble. Gamma had packed their ears with their own sheared wool on the long march across the island. He hoped that would keep out the loudest sounds. He couldn't afford to have them faint now.

Gamma launched himself at the bot with a flying kick. He bounced off, landing hard. His attacked ended just like he thought it would, but he had to set a good example. They were all in this together. If he wanted the golligs to risk their lives, he had to risk his, too.

A gollig jumped over him and smashed into the bot. The bot took half a step backward. Its movement looked stiff and awkward. It recovered.

The fourth and fifth golligs hit the bot's leg at full speed. Earl gollig circled back. He dug his hooves in and pushed with his head. The bot didn't budge.

Gamma looked back. Big Thump was on the ground halfway to the bot. The wool ear plugs weren't enough to stop her legs from seizing up. She struggled to stand. Gamma ran to her. He pushed.

Big Thump weighed more than ever. The planet itself seemed to be holding her down, which, if Gamma thought about it, was how gravity actually worked. He had asked so much of this incredible animal already. She had fended off untold numbers of predators and single-handedly birthed a new herd to prevent human civilization from collapsing. Gamma didn't deserve her. Neither did humanity. And here he was again, making what might very well be a final request, not just for her, but for all of them. He needed her now.

"For Eve!" he yelled. The world blurred with tears.

Big Thump's entire body tensed. She remembered. With herculean effort, she struggled to her feet. Her legs were stiff. Her knees wouldn't bend. She hadn't been the same since the dentopus attack, and now she was half paralyzed by her own fainting genes. But she was still the biggest and strongest animal on the island—and the orneriest, by far.

She rumbled forward on petrified legs, slowly at first but gaining speed. Her gait was strange but powerful. She moved like a galloping table. She accelerated faster and faster with no hope of ever slowing down. She became an unstoppable comet of bone and wool.

She let out a mighty oink-bleat that echoed from one side of the island to the other. The smoke cleared and swords stopped and the ocean itself was silenced. Kilometers away, a boulder that had stood precariously atop another for ten thousand years suddenly toppled over.

The bot turned its head. It lifted an arm to smash Big Thump.

Gamma reared back and threw his sword. It was a move he had practiced countless times. It had worked exactly once. He didn't think about any of that now. The sword whistled as it cut the air, sailing straight and true. The bot zoomed in on it with its main optical port, watching it approach.

CRUNCH.

The blade slammed directly through the port, the tip bursting out through the back of the bot's head. A volcano of sparks erupted from its face. The bot's fist stayed frozen in the air.

Big Thump crashed into the back of its knee joint. The fortress shook. Bolts snapped. Hydraulics tore. The leg collapsed.

The bot teetered.

It fell.

Big Thump had done it again. She had saved the world.

Chapter 56

THETA CAME TO. Slowly, he pushed himself up to his knees. The fall had not been easy. The geology bot was even taller than it looked. Gravity, as ever, was not Theta's friend.

His wool shirt was singed. He hadn't jumped fast enough. The lightning had claimed its due.

How long had he been out? The world looked worse than he remembered.

Theta coughed. The fortress was filled with smoke. The megaroos were nowhere in sight. Omicron limped past, supporting Pi. They moved away from the bot.

So much for Theta's peaceful plan to destroy the immortality tank when everyone but Delta was away. He tried to call off the attack when he was still outside the walls and heard the sounds of battle. He knew that his mission was a failure. He refused to risk anyone's lives. He told the beast to abort but the beast didn't listen. It was always going to do what it wanted, he now realized. Theta was just along for the ride.

Once the beast crashed through the wall, Theta had no choice but to follow through on the plan. This would be their only shot.

The tip of a sword poked Theta's chest. He looked up.

Alpha stared back. She held the sword to his sternum. The point broke the skin. A single drop of blood dripped from the wound.

He looked into her eyes. The one who was really hurting was her, not him.

"Stop the bot," Alpha said.

"I can't," he said.

She pushed the blade a little deeper.

It had all gone so wrong. He didn't want anyone to die. Actually, he wanted everyone to die, but not right now—and only then because he wanted them to live. He'd thought getting rid of immortality would end the biggest source of strife between them once and for all. He couldn't have been more wrong.

A shadow grew over Alpha in the artificial light. It took Theta's conscious mind half a second to register what was happening. By the time his brain caught up, his body was already in motion. Theta knocked aside her sword and shoved Alpha out of the way. The bot came crashing down on top of him.

It was a long moment before Theta knew where he was. Something was touching his face. It was Alpha again, picking a piece of rubble out of his unkempt beard. In better times, Omicron had offered haircuts for everyone. That felt like a thousand years ago now.

The ground shook. The megaroos returned. The beast wasn't so scary when it was paralyzed on the ground.

It wasn't the only one. Theta couldn't move anything

below his neck. The rest of his body was beneath the massive machine. It was a miracle he could breathe at all.

"Sorry," he said. His voice was weak. Saying even that single word seemed to use all the oxygen in the world. He wished he could go back in time and undo everything. He never would have made contact with the bot. He wouldn't have suggested destroying the immortality tank. He never would have done anything. He would have spent eternity hanging out with Alpha while she made the same pitchers over and over again and he made non-sequiturs about unicycles. He would never ride one. Civilization had never made it that far. It wasn't his biggest regret. It didn't even make the top three.

Alpha gazed at him tenderly. She didn't cry. She looked as though she wanted to say something, but she couldn't get the words out.

Metal clanged against metal. Swords and horns and powerful hind legs ripped the bot apart. It was so much commotion. Didn't they know Theta was trying to have a moment with the love of his life? It would be his last moment of all.

There was a flash of light followed by a wave of heat. Both rushed past Theta. The blast singed Alpha's hair. She didn't seem to notice. Theta remembered the white hot flames from his battles against the bots on the moon base. The beast was dead. That was something, at least.

There was no time for guilt. There was no time for anything. He tried to focus on Alpha. The intrusive thoughts forced their way in regardless. He had never believed in much of anything until this moment. He suddenly wondered if digitals and organics went to the same hell.

Theta mustered all his strength.

"Van Gogh," he said.

Alpha's eyes lit up with recognition. She stood.

"Phi!" she yelled. Her eyes were frantic. "Phi!"

Theta regretted bringing it up. He desperately wanted to see his baby boy one final time, but not at the cost of interrupting his final moments with the co-most important person in the world. He'd created stress and anxiety when there should have been only peace and calm. Classic Theta.

Phi appeared at the corner of Theta's field of vision. How had he heard her over a war? On a day when almost everything had gone wrong, it was another miracle.

"Oh no," Phi said.

A megaroo bounded past behind him. The fight was still going on, but it seemed to have forgotten this tiny corner of the battlefield. Alpha grabbed Van Gogh from Phi's arms. Starlight hid behind Phi's leg.

Alpha knelt beside Theta.

"He's here," she said softly. "We're all here."

She pushed Van Gogh up against Theta's face. The baby clearly had no idea what was going on. Not that any baby ever did. They weren't exactly known for their situational awareness. It didn't matter. Theta was once again with his family. As long as his kid survived, he could die happy. A healthy child was the only immortality he ever needed. He didn't want to live in a world without unicycles, anyway.

He gathered up what air he could find.

"Sorry," he said again.

"Stop it," Alpha said. Now there were tears. "I forgive you. I forgive everything."

That was a weight off his chest, even if the actual weight was still there, crushing him to death. The world began to fade.

"Love…" he uttered. He would never be sure if the others heard him, but in his final instant, he hoped they did.

He closed his eyes and was no more.

Chapter 57

THE BOT ERUPTED in white hot flames.

Megaroos and humans alike scampered away.

Delta held up her arm to shield her face. She blinked. The world was dark again. The pulse of heat knocked out the artificial lights. It took her eyes a moment to adjust to the early morning blackness.

The beast was dead. That was one existential threat gone for good. Now, for all the rest. The sounds of battle faded. In the quiet, she heard a wail of despair. It was Alpha. She knelt near a corner of the charred hulk that was once the bot, with her baby in her arms. Phi crouched next to her with an arm around her shoulders. Starlight hid behind him. Delta stayed away. What could she possibly have said? Theta had somehow teamed up with the bot. Now they were both dead.

Theta's death was tragic, but it would have been a greater tragedy if he had succeeded. She looked through the open hatch of the lander. The immortality tank was alive, the microbes inside glowing bright orange. They were riled up, but they would calm eventually. The immortality shots would resume after yet another interruption. Civilization still had a chance.

She heard clicking. It was Lawrence. He was the first megaroo she had cloned and also the biggest. He was nominally in charge of the other megaroos, although his grasp on power wasn't as firm as Delta would have liked. Clans were easier to command when they had a clear leadership structure culminating with Delta at the top. Despite Lawrence's shortcomings, Delta liked him well enough. He was feisty and a good problem solver. He had led the construction of many of the new tunnels himself. She didn't have to micromanage as much when he was around. He would be a good ally going forward if she could get him not to run away when the occasional giant metal monstrosity crashed through the fortress wall.

Lawrence made his unintelligible series of clicks again. Delta signed for the megaroo to gather up the others. He looked at her quizzically but didn't move.

The hairs on the back of Delta's neck stood up. She signed again. Again, Lawrence didn't respond. He acted like he didn't understand, but Delta knew better. Lawrence was too smart for this. This wasn't a lack of comprehension. Delta subtly shifted into a fighting stance. The battle wasn't over after all.

Without moving her head, she surveyed the megaroos with her peripheral vision. They had gradually drifted into a perimeter facing inward toward the survivors. They had humanity surrounded. The oppressed always rose up against their oppressors eventually. Delta hoped that would be hundreds of thousands of years from now after humanity was firmly anchored on the island. The megaroos were wise to strike now.

Delta had miscalculated once again. Maybe her fellow humans were right to overthrow her. It was too late to second-guess things now. Life didn't have erasers, but it did have swords. She would fight her way out of this, just like she always did.

"Alpha," Delta called out, trying to make her voice sound neutral.

Alpha remained on the ground, sobbing beside Theta. Surely she wouldn't let herself be killed from behind without a fight.

Delta made eye contact with Phi, who was still comforting Alpha. He saw the alarm in Delta's eyes. He glanced around and understood. Slowly, he removed his arm from Alpha and stood, scooting Starlight behind him as he rotated to face the circle of megaroos.

Don't, Delta signed to Lawrence. Please.

A megaroo pounced on Pi, pinning him. Pi raised his one good arm to protect himself. Delta threw her sword, skewering the megaroo. The creature gasped and fell to the side, writhing. Pi struggled to his feet.

Lawrence launched himself at Delta. Delta sidestepped and pulled out Martha, slamming the megaroo in the side of the head. He fell sideways, clutching his skull. He quickly stood. He had murder in his eyes. Delta needed her sword back. She ran toward Pi and the impaled megaroo next to him.

Omicron and Sigma turned back to back and held off two 'roos. A 'roo knocked the sword out of Phi's hand. He bear-hugged the animal and wrestled it to the ground. Alpha took his place, standing protectively over the children and her dead life partner. Another megaroo struck Beta. Beta fell but got back to his feet, sword in hand. The golligs formed a defensive perimeter around a hobbled Big Thump with Gamma at point. Upsilon joined him. From the ground, Big Thump oink-bleated fiercely. The 'roos stayed away.

Delta reached the megaroo she'd skewered. It was Abigail, a young female with a light tan coat. She flopped around on the ground, very much not dead. Delta dove on top of her and struggled to hold her down so she could pull out the sword. Abigail fought back, gurgling blood. Why did these things have to be so hard to kill? Whoever came up with their original design had engineered them far too well.

Abigail rolled over on top of Delta. Delta finally got her hand around the hilt of the sword sticking out of the megaroo's back. She pulled down, cutting a huge gash in the side of the animal. Abigail stopped moving. Her dead weight pushed Delta into the red grass. Even young, she weighed twice as much as Delta, if not more. Delta bucked forcefully to roll the 'roo off her. She took a deep breath. She was covered in megaroo blood. Gross.

Lawrence landed on top of her, knocking the air from her lungs with his massive feet. He put his fists together and brought them down like a sledgehammer. Delta twisted her head to the side, narrowly dodging the blow. Out of oxygen, she stabbed straight upward through Lawrence's chest. His eyes widened with surprise. Then he looked down at her and smiled. How had she not hit a vital organ? He raised his arms for another strike. She tried to pull the sword out, but it was stuck in his ribs. She didn't have the strength. The edges of her vision blurred.

Lawrence's head fell off his shoulders. It hit the ground and rolled, coming to a stop facing her. His lips remained curled in that awful smile.

His headless body was still standing on Delta, crushing her chest. Somebody kicked it off. It was Lambda.

"Megaroos," she muttered. "Brilliant idea. Absolutely brilliant."

She helped Delta up.

There would be a reckoning after this—if there was an after this. Delta thought maybe it would be easier to die than to explain herself. The problem with calculated risks was that they were still risks. You looked like a genius when they worked out and a reckless idiot when they didn't, but the information available beforehand was the same. Delta's main mistake was not having perfect luck where everything always worked out in her favor. Trying to make the others understand that would be more painful than being stomped on by a megaroo.

Delta caught her breath. There would be time for introspection later—maybe. For now, she still had a battle to win.

A megaroo bounded from one of the corner hills and onto the wall over Omicron and Sigma. It jumped down. Delta ran to meet it. She slid between Omicron and Sigma, impaling it as it landed.

"Thanks," Sigma said.

Omicron stayed silent. As if she hadn't made any mistakes of her own. There were no angels here.

Somewhere in the smoke, Beta cried out in pain. He was already wounded from his first ill-advised attack on the fortress. Delta had to find him.

She passed Pi. He was badly battered but still standing. The arm she'd hit with a rock looked broken. She wouldn't have done so much damage if she'd known she was going to need him again today.

"With me," she said. There was no question in the command. Pi meekly fell in behind her. Even after his earlier insurrection, he still recognized her authority in a crisis. There was hope for them all yet.

She found Beta on the other side of the courtyard lying against a mound of dirt. He held out his sword hesitantly, holding off three 'roos who stood just outside the blade's reach.

"Stay back," he said, his voice trembling The megaroos understood some human speech, but the real message was in Beta's fear, not his words. He was wounded and vulnerable.

A megaroo sprang forward and knocked the sword from Beta's hand. Delta jumped in and sliced it from the side with a glancing blow. It spun and swung its tail at her. She ducked and jabbed, nicking the tail but not doing any real damage.

The other two megaroos turned at Pi. He raised his sword. They both pounced at once. Pi raised his arms to shield his face. Instantly, he was on his back with the megaroos on top of him. One grabbed his head and slammed him into the ground. The other jumped up and down on Pi's abdomen. Delta heard the sickening sound of bones crunching. She had to help him now.

She tried to slip away from her megaroo, but it caught her with its tail, knocking her down. She did a somersault and sprang up, rushing toward Pi. Beta killed the megaroo she'd left behind.

Delta swung her blade horizontally, cleaving in half the megaroo bashing Pi's head. The one at the back bounded away. It would no doubt return in a moment. She knelt down to check on Pi. What she saw horrified her. She closed her eyes.

"Pi," she said gently.

He didn't answer. He was gone.

Delta let out a primal scream. It had been her job to protect him. She had failed again.

Beta rushed over.

"Oh, God," he said. "Is he…"

Beta was knocked off his feet by a hurdling mass. The third megaroo was back. It reared back to smash Beta's face.

Delta stabbed it from behind through the spinal cord. It flopped limply to the ground. How many more of these things would she have to kill? It had been a mistake to let them breed as freely as they wanted. SCASL might have been on to something with his secret birth control plan.

Beta was breathing heavily. His ribs were badly hurt from where Delta had hit him with a rock. Served him right for his rebellion. Multiple blows from megaroos after that hadn't helped.

The odds were stacked against him to survive this one. If he wanted to live, he needed to get somewhere out of sight. Like the tunnels.

Delta froze. She had thought it was the perfect hiding place. She moved the cloner out, but not its yield. Was the megaroos' first act of defiance up here or underground? She ran.

A megaroo cut across the courtyard in front of her. It bent over and scooped something up as it passed. She heard a small cry.

It was Starlight. He must have gotten separated from Phi. Delta slid to a stop. She looked again at the tunnels. The future of humanity was down there. But maybe it was up here, too.

She turned away from the tunnel and chased the megaroo. It juked right, moving directly in front of an enraged gollig. The gollig downed the 'roo with a single headbutt. Gamma stabbed it on the ground. Upsilon picked up Starlight. She cradled the child protectively as if he were her own. Delta looked at her in wonder.

She didn't have time to decipher the moment. The outer golligs oink-bleated in terror. Now what? They were already in the heat of battle, and everything scary on the island was right in front of them. Delta looked at the walls. She was wrong again.

Dentopuses swarmed over the rock barriers and through the gap the bot had created. They covered every surface. They weren't here just to kill the golligs this time. They had come to wipe out all the off-world interlopers in one fell swoop.

Delta knew they would be back. On its own, the attack the day Upsilon had given birth could have been a fluke. Their attack on the herd proved it wasn't. Delta understood the threat. She just didn't know what to do about it. There were so many other crises she had to deal with. Meanwhile, the dentopuses had a plan for her.

A swarm of dentopuses wrapped up a megaroo facing Alpha. To the dentopuses, Delta realized, the 'roos were just as foreign as the humans. They were all invaders who didn't belong.

She could turn this around. Her human rivals were back on her side, if only for now, and only for their own survival. They had defeated the beast. They were making progress against the megaroos. The dentopuses were the last hurdle. Then, she would rebuild. She would be wiser. Stronger. Less merciful to her enemies. She saw the path now.

Delta jumped on top of the charred remains of the bot, low flames illuminating her against the dark morning sky. She raised her sword, reflecting the firelight.

"Fall back to the lander!" she said. "Put the kids inside!"

Everyone obeyed. Those who supported her and the ones who wanted her dead moved in the same direction. That included the 'roos. Faced with their own annihilation, they switched sides once again. The allied forces of humans and human-created monstrosities backed up against the lander. Men and women with swords. Golligs. Genetically engineered killer kangaroos. They stood shoulder to shoulder against the unstoppable horde. A wave of tentacles crashed against them.

Stinger met flesh. Sword met squid. There was slicing and bleeding and oink-bleating. The sounds of the victorious and vanquished intermingled. Delta lanced one dentopus and then another and chopped two more in half. To her left, Alpha killed half a dozen. To her right, a dozen more overwhelmed the gollig. Gamma hacked at them, but to no avail. The animal was gone. Phi pulled a dentopus off Sigma's face. Lambda cut one off Phi's back. Beta launched a dentopus with an impressive kick. He grabbed his ribs in pain afterward. Upsilon and a 'roo worked together to fight a cluster of dentopuses with unusual yellow stripes. A megaroo tried in vain to pound the dentopuses off a gollig. They died together.

The dentopuses poured over the top of the lander. The off-worlders no longer had a safe flank.

"Circle up!" Delta yelled. What was left of her army—and all known sentient life—followed her command.

Hack. Slash. Stomp. Sting. The fight continued for minutes. Or hours. Or days.

Lambda fell. Was she dead, or just paralyzed? There was no way to know. Beta went down, too. A tentacle wrapped around Delta's arm. She flung it off and killed the dentopus it belonged to. Another one grabbed her leg. She stabbed it and tossed it outside the circle.

The huge cluster of tentacled hellbeasts writhed over Big Thump. She smashed and stomped, twirling with the most vigor Delta had seen her display since before the first mass attack on the herd. A pile of dead dentopuses formed below her. More dentopuses moved in.

Gamma ran to her side.

"I've got you," he said. He sliced two dentopuses off her back. "I've always got you."

The dentopuses kept coming. Big Thump was a priority target. Delta felt a twinge of jealousy. The aliens viewed the alpha gollig as the biggest threat.

Delta rushed over to help. She cleaved a dentopus off Big Thump's neck and another off her side.

"There are too many," Gamma said. He was out of breath.

Delta slashed faster.

Big Thump was cut everywhere. Faltering, she continued to fight. Her body weakened. Her legs seized up. She slipped on the jumble of smashed dentopuses underneath her. She tried to stand but couldn't. The dentopuses tore into her flesh. It was too late for her. It wasn't too late for mercy.

With a swift blow, Gamma freed her from this terrible world.

"Rest easy, old girl," Gamma said. "Your fight is done."

Delta took a step backward, half numbed by paralyzing venom and half by grief. She regarded with awe Big Thump's final resting place. She lay atop a pile of dead dentopuses, the queen of the mountain of the damned. Delta found herself in the eye of the storm as the battle swirled around her. The rest of the dentopuses kept their distance. Even in death, they feared her.

Delta took a breath and charged back into the fray. She stepped over another fallen gollig and hacked a dentopus off Beta, who was trying feebly to get up. How many times had she saved his life today? More times than she'd almost killed him. A megaroo pounced on a dentopus coming up behind her. She returned the favor and killed two dentopuses lashing at its tail. Her reactions were beginning to feel sluggish. Adrenaline was keeping her upright, but the paralyzing venom was starting to have an effect.

Delta cut a dentopus in half. She paused. There was a gap in the assault. She killed another dentopus. This one had blue dots. There was a gap again. It wasn't her imagination. The dentopuses were thinning out. She managed to take three full breaths before she had to kill the next one. After that, she stood still long enough to lower her sword. A dentopus jumped off the lander and toward her back. Without turning, she stabbed it in midair behind her head and slammed it to the ground in front of her.

Then, nothing. In the first light of morning, she could see that the entire base was covered in blue blood and severed, squirming tentacles. The grass fires were out. There was nowhere to walk without stepping on something dead. She tried to count the surviving golligs. She couldn't. Her vision was too blurry.

She took a step and fell to one knee. She got back up. Something slapped her across the face. She fell again. A 'roo was on top of her.

It began to choke her. This wasn't how they killed. It was too intimate, too personal. She reached for Fang. It wasn't there. She went for Martha. She came up empty. She grasped at empty dirt drenched in blood. The world began to go dark again. How poetic that she would be killed by her greatest mistake. But if she hadn't made them, they never would have beaten the beast of the dentopuses. As her brain shut off, she half smiled. Her final act would be to disappoint her many other enemies. Only one would be able to kill her.

The megaroo's head fell off, a geyser of blood shooting from its open neck. *Second time today I've been saved like that*, Delta realized. So much for Miss I Don't Need Anyone. Someone pushed the 'roo off her.

Delta gasped. Air. Wonderful air. She would have to track down the 'roos and kill them. Undoubtedly, some would have escaped. Survivors, just like her.

Delta felt cold steel against her neck. She looked up. With her blurry vision, she could just make out Upsilon's tense form. Delta sighed. She couldn't catch a break.

Chapter 58

UPSILON LOOKED DOWN at the source of all of her problems. She had the power to end it all. She tightened her grip on the sword.

"You killed her," she whispered.

Delta looked up at her with cloudy, unfocused eyes. Did she understand what Upsilon was saying? Did it matter?

This was everything Upsilon wanted. She'd had tunnel vision leading to this very moment. She waited for someone to stop her. No one did.

She glanced around. The fortress was eerily quiet. Phi and Lambda huddled around Starlight, who had survived the battle unharmed. Upsilon made sure of that. The others were keeping vigil for the dead. Alpha had returned to her spot next to Theta. She clutched Van Gogh tightly. Omicron was slumped next to Pi's mangled form. Gamma stood vigil next to Big Thump. Everyone was moving slowly. They had all been injected with dentopus venom, some more than others. Upsilon fought against it. Adrenaline and righteous anger kept her upright. Around her, the ground was covered in splattered, smashed, and eviscerated dentopus corpses and dead megaroos and slaughtered golligs with a giant, charred bot at the center of it all. So this was war. It made Upsilon want to puke.

"Help!" Beta slurred. "She's in labor."

He knelt over Sigma, holding her hand. Phi and Lambda rushed over to them on wavering legs.

Everyone forgot about Delta. About Upsilon. About Eve.

Upsilon pressed her sword into the side of Delta's neck. Delta's eyes cleared a little. She understood what was going on. She stared directly into Upsilon's soul. Delta wasn't afraid. Upsilon wished she knew what that was like, if only for a moment. She had been scared for her entire life.

"Momma!" a little girl's voice called out.

Upsilon's heart jumped. For a split second, her primal animal brain thought Eve was somehow alive. She snapped back to reality. She looked for the source of the sound.

A small child ran across the battlefield with awkward, uneven steps. She couldn't have been more than two or three. Her tiny feet stomped through the ash and the mud and the blood. Upsilon's heart ached. Who was this child?

A clone.

The horrifying realization hit Upsilon all at once. She thought of the bones at the bottom of the cliff. Delta was a monster. She had to be stopped.

Upsilon's sword arm remained still.

The child threw her arms around Delta's face.

"Momma!" the girl said again.

With great effort, Delta fought through the paralyzing venom in her veins to slowly raise one arm. She wrapped it limply around the child in a half embrace. She left Upsilon's sword where it was against her neck.

Upsilon didn't know this girl. Most days, she didn't even know herself anymore. But she knew love. Delta loved this child as strongly as Upsilon and Gamma loved Eve, or Phi and Lambda loved Starlight. For all Delta's faults, she wasn't a monster. She was a mother.

Delta couldn't have children of her own. They all knew it. Delta had claimed that was why SCASL tried to leave her behind on Comus. Upsilon looked more closely at the little girl. The resemblance was uncanny. Of all the DNA Delta could have started with, she'd chosen her own. Maybe she hoped her clone could have kids when she herself could not. Maybe it was simply narcissism. Maybe it was self-sacrifice. Was it any better if the trial and error happened with your own DNA rather than somebody else's? Upsilon doubted the dead clones cared either way.

Human cloning wasn't supposed to work, but this child looked perfect. To Upsilon, all children were. She wondered if there were others, or if this little girl was the only one left, the sole survivor. Sigma had said there were so many human bones at the bottom of the cliff.

"The other clones," Upsilon said quietly. "The failures. Did you kill them?"

"No," Delta said weakly. The answer seemed to take all her strength.

Was it a lie? Possibly, but Upsilon didn't think so. It wasn't just that Delta loved the little girl. It was that the girl loved her back. Those feelings weren't compatible with murder.

Delta had done her best, whatever that meant to her. She had done what she could to create the miraculous child.

Upsilon pulled back her sword. There would be no more killing today.

She looked again at the courtyard. She had done this. Her anger. Her rage. Her pain. Her quest for justice was the final push that tipped the island into war. Delta didn't kill Eve. A dentopus did. Delta didn't put the limits on the immortality tank. Those were imposed by physical reality, and humanity had been struggling with them ever since. Delta didn't massacre the clones, but she did create them. Was it ethical? No. But it was necessary. That counted for more.

There were twelve humans, but three of those were offspring of the other nine and one of those nine couldn't have babies. The eight remaining lines of DNA they'd landed with would be all they'd ever have without cloning. It wasn't enough. The loss of genetic diversity was too great. This new child made their total population thirteen. If cloning worked, Delta could bring everyone back, both those who had died on Comus and those who had died down here. Not the people themselves, but their DNA. She could make physical copies. Even Eve—or a version of her—could live again. That thought gave Upsilon a small measure of peace.

There would be more bones at the bottom of the cliff. Upsilon didn't want to think about how many. It was a cost no one but Delta was willing to pay. Only she had the will to get it done.

Her leadership wasn't perfect, but there was no better option. In a world where Delta was overthrown, there still wouldn't be enough immortality to go around. There would still be sea monsters and a constant struggle for food. Delta gave them the best chance of navigating that, even if Upsilon could never admit it out loud.

There was still a bottomless pit in Upsilon's heart where Eve should have been. Nothing would ever change that. But the best way to honor her memory was to move forward and thrive. Maybe that meant an immortal class ruling over all others like Alpha wanted. Maybe it meant something else. Whatever the solution was, they were the most likely to find their way there under Delta. Upsilon's pain had subsided enough for her to see that now.

She felt a tiredness to the core of her being greater than any she had ever known. She thought she could sleep for a hundred lifetimes. Instead, she bent down and scooped up the child hugging Delta's face.

Delta breathed shallowly. She would bounce back. She had before.

"What's your name, dear?" Upsilon asked.

The child looked at her, scared. Delta didn't say anything, either. She was barely clinging to consciousness. Clearly, nobody was going to answer.

"That's okay," Upsilon said. "We'll figure it out."

She put a hand on the back of the child's head and nuzzled her. She went to rejoin the others. On the way, she hummed.

"It's a girl!" Beta yelled sluggishly from across the courtyard.

Sunlight passed over the top of the fortress walls. It was a new day.

Chapter 59

ISLAND KEEPER WATCHED the tall walkers incredulously. They were still here. And there were more of them.

The cursed invaders gathered in a particularly barren patch of the Dead Land. They built stacks of kindling. Island Keeper had watched them do this once before. That time, it was to burn the young tall walker Trail Stalker had bravely defeated in single combat. The tall walkers had incinerated the child, returning her ashes to the Sky Demon in Hell Above. This time, there were three piles. The valiant ten whip warriors had extracted a heavy toll.

It wasn't nearly as heavy as the damage the tall walkers had inflicted. Entire clans had been annihilated. And for what? The ten whips hadn't killed a single tall walker. The two who'd gone down had died by other means, and they were replaced after the battle by two more of their kind. The Sky Demon would not let his number of minions fall. Island Keeper kept these facts to herself. The rest of the council of matriarchs was in no mood for the truth. They needed good news to tell the broodmates of the ten whips who had died for nothing. Island Keeper knew there was no good news to tell.

The nesting grounds were still under threat. The tall walkers hadn't made a direct assault on them yet, but they continued to change and shape the island. They dug holes and stacked rocks. Toward what end, Island Keeper could only guess. Even more alarming were the new plants and animals the tall walkers had conjured. There were now two colors of land kelp that covered nearly the entire island. There were stalk plants in the marshes and leafy plants in the hills. The new plants supported strange new creatures. The hairy horn beasts were the first, but they weren't the most wicked. That honor went to the new tall things with tails that leapt from place to place—precisely why Island Keeper couldn't simply call the tall walkers "tall things" any more. Now there were tall walkers and tall jumpers. Who knew how many more monsters the tall walkers would create from thin air? The Sky Demon had bestowed upon them a powerful magic. Ten whip kind would never be safe again.

Some on the council argued that the surviving ten whips should flee and find new breeding grounds elsewhere. Island Keeper understood that was impossible. There was no other land within a lifetime's swim of here. The holy stories proved it. A landmass of untold size existed far away, but it would take many generations to reach there. Once the ten whips arrived—if they ever did—they would no doubt be met by hostile sea beasts already occupying the new cliffs. There was no unclaimed land left touching the Infinite Waters. That was scripture. Only death waited on the other side of the world. Better to fight here for the holy breeding grounds gifted to them by the gods below.

James Breakwell

Staying had its own perils. The alliance was already breaking down, as it always did. Three times, the warring clans had banded together for the greater good. Three times, the attacks failed to have their intended effects. The council had never called the attacks failures, but what else could they be? The tall walkers were still here. The threat continued to grow.

The tall walkers lit the three piles. Smoke rose. No doubt the Sky Demon was grateful to receive back his own. Island Keeper clicked her beak, tasting the air. It smelled of cooked flesh. Island Keeper understood the tall walkers better than most, but some of their practices were still a mystery. Why didn't they eat their dead? Sending them back to the Sky Demon was a waste of vital nutrition. Perhaps the Sky Demon demanded it. Could he repair his servants and send them back down? Island Keeper sincerely hoped not. The thirteen of them were enough of a problem.

A tall walker wailed. Another tall walker wrapped its tentacles around the first. If Island Walker didn't know better, she would say they were expressing emotions. That was absurd. She respected their capabilities more than most, but they were still just animals. Dangerous and clever animals, but animals, nonetheless. Cunning did not equal sentience by any means.

Yet the tall walkers had beaten the ten whips time and time again, despite the ten whips' superior intelligence and strategy. The ten whips banded together for the first time in the age of Island Keeper's great-great grandmother. They had smelled that one of the tall walkers was pregnant and tracked her for months, striking at the moment of delivery. Ten whip casualties had been astronomic. The alliance fell apart and the council was devoured. The ten whips would not underestimate the ferocity of tall walker mothers again.

In the time of Island Keeper's grandmother, a new council of matriarchs had reestablished the alliance. The united clans bred and trained an unprecedented force of warriors. Scouts monitored for the right opportunity. It came in the form of the hard giant, which awoke on the ocean floor and marched across the Dead Land. The ten whips followed it closely on shore and in the Infinite Waters. When it finally assaulted the tall walkers' great stone circle, the ten whips were ready. That time, they attacked not the tall walkers, but their food. Island Keeper's forebears wisely slew the horned hair beasts and dug up and destroyed the detestable dried meat the tall walkers so carefully hoarded. It seemed like a great victory, but as time wore on, no tall walkers starved. Worse, the Sky Demon's most powerful servant, the horned hair beast Hell Mountain, survived. Slowly, she birthed a new herd. The alliance faltered, the council was devoured, and warfare resumed among the clans. The tall walkers seemed unstoppable.

Then it was the turn of Island Keeper and her kin. They formed a new council of matriarchs and bred more armies. They made and remade plans, debated at endless strategy sessions. They deployed scouts everywhere. There would be no more close calls. They would find the right opportunity and eliminate the invaders for good. The chance came after Trail Stalker had slain the child. The tall walkers turned on each other. They had acted on instinct, not logic. One even made an alliance with the hard giant against his own kind. It was an opening unlike any other. The ten whips sent everyone. Warriors, life givers, council members, and even the young; an all-out effort meant to end the threat once and for all.

The ten whips didn't know about the tall jumpers. It was an intelligence failure that would haunt Island Keeper for the rest of her days. Those extra monsters turned the tide. The tall walker's unity was also unexpected. Despite trying to kill each other moments before, all the Sky Demon's factions banded together against the ten whips. Their intelligence was low, but their survival instincts were insurmountable. The results were devastating. Entire clans of slain dentopuses were left strewn across the stone circle, desecrated and unmourned. None would honor the dead by eating their flesh, letting their bodies live on in another while their souls went to Heaven Below. The stone circle was now cursed ground. No dentopus would dare slither there again.

In return, the invaders had just these three small fires to honor their fallen. They didn't care about the dead tall jumpers or the slain hairy horn beasts, save one. Hell Mountain had a fire of her own, bigger than the other two. The ten whips would long tell tales of her unrestrained savagery. The council of matriarchs tried to spin the fall of Hell Mountain as a great victory. Island Keeper knew better. Soon, the truth would come out.

The tall walkers would continue on, making more of their vassal species and birthing more of their young. Slowly, the surviving remnants of the ten whip clans would realize nothing of value had been won in the battle. When they did, the council—and Island Keeper with it—would fall. Her only hope was that before that day, she would reach the end of her life cycle to lay eggs and feed herself to her young. If the other ten whips turned on her first, they would deny her that blessing, devouring her like they had done all the members of the councils before her. To be consumed after dying in battle or becoming a life giver was the highest honor, but to be eaten alive following a failure of leadership was the greatest shame. It would deny her entry into Heaven Below. It would be the Sky Demon's final victory over her tragic life.

Island Keeper watched with her piercing predator eye as one tall walker moved to the front of the gathering and addressed the rest. The invaders had language. Island Keeper was sure of it now. That language was dumb and guttural, but it communicated some level of meaning all the same. Some theorized Hell Mountain was the leader of the invaders, but Island Keeper knew better. It was this tall walker, the one Island Keeper called Cutting Death. The other tall walkers looked at her with respect. The surviving hairy horn beasts did, too. Only the tall jumpers defied her. They fled to other parts of the island rather than confront her directly. Cutting Death would no doubt hunt down each and every one of them. Such was her way.

Cutting Death finished addressing the group. The tall walker turned, scanning the horizon. Her two terrifying eyes locked onto Island Keeper. Surely Cutting Death couldn't see her at this distance, especially at dusk. Cutting Death's gaze didn't waver. Fear coursed through Island Keeper's veins.

Island Keeper bolted from her hiding spot, surging across the barren ground. Terrifying moments passed. No hard spikes sliced her flesh. She plunged into the Infinite Waters.

Island Keeper swam, dejected. The Dead Lands were no longer safe for ten whips to cross. How long until the breeding grounds were similarly menaced? She feared her days and the days of all ten whips were numbered. The island would belong to the tall walkers. It was just a matter of time.

The End

Acknowledgements

I WOULD LIKE to thank/blame the following people. If asked, these individuals would disavow all knowledge of both me and this book. I refuse to let them off the hook that easily.

Mark Gottlieb, my ever faithful and patient literary agent at Trident Media Group. When I want to know how many book deals we've done together, I have to do math. That's a good thing. Except for the math part. That's the worst.

Amanda Rutter, commissioning editor at Rebellion Publishing. You told me in the nicest way possible that my first draft was hot garbage not fit for the eyes of man. I appreciate the feedback. Thanks to your help, the final product is something we can both be proud of.

Linda Nagle, copy editor at Rebellion Publishing. You single-handedly saved me from starting more than three hundred sentences with "it was." It was greatly appreciated.

The friends and family members who I had to ignore for months while I finished this book. To my surprise, you were still there when I emerged from chair jail. I take that to mean you failed to find a suitable replacement for me. Next time, try harder.

My wife. You count as both friend and family, but if I don't single you out in the acknowledgements, that's grounds for divorce.

About the Author

JAMES BREAKWELL IS a comedy writer and owner of the Twitter account @XplodingUnicorn, where he shares comedic anecdotes, observations, and conversations with his four daughters.

FIND US ONLINE!

www.rebellionpublishing.com

/solarisbooks   /solarisbks   /solarisbooks

SIGN UP TO OUR NEWSLETTER!

rebellionpublishing.com/newsletter

YOUR REVIEWS MATTER!

Enjoy this book? Got something to say?

Leave a review on Amazon, GoodReads or with your favourite bookseller and let the world know!